"I'm relieved she's feeling so much better."

Arleta stretched to try to reach a bowl from the cupboard.

"Here, I'll get that for you," Noah offered. She stepped aside so he could retrieve the dish. Even so, as he pulled down a bowl, he was acutely aware that he hadn't stood this close to a single woman since he'd courted Hannah Miller.

Then it dawned on him: *Groossmammi* wasn't really that ill! She wanted Arleta and him to eat together without her. She was giving them privacy so they could get to know each other better. And that was why she'd retreated into the living room now, too. Or was it? Not that it mattered. Even if his grandmother was scheming to match him and Arleta, Noah wasn't going to develop a romantic relationship with her or with anyone else.

But that didn't mean Noah didn't notice what a sweet gap-toothed smile she [illegible] the bowl.

Carrie Lighte lives in Massachusetts next door to a Mennonite farming family, and she frequently spots deer, foxes, fisher cats, coyotes and turkeys in her backyard. Having enjoyed traveling to several Amish communities in the eastern United States, she looks forward to visiting settlements in the western states and in Canada. When she's not reading, writing or researching, Carrie likes to hike, kayak, bake and play word games.

Vannetta Chapman has published over one hundred articles in Christian family magazines and received over two dozen awards from Romance Writers of America chapter groups. She discovered her love for the Amish while researching her grandfather's birthplace of Albion, Pennsylvania. Her first novel, *A Simple Amish Christmas*, quickly became a bestseller. Chapman lives in Texas Hill Country with her husband.

CARRIE LIGHTE

&

USA TODAY Bestselling Author

VANNETTA CHAPMAN

A Path to Forgiveness

2 Uplifting Stories

Hiding Her Amish Secret and *A Widow's Hope*

ISBN-13: 978-1-335-46065-3

A Path to Forgiveness

Hiding Her Amish Secret
First published in 2021. This edition published in 2022.

A Widow's Hope
First published in 2018. This edition published in 2022.

For questions and comments about the quality of this book, please contact us at CustomerService@Harlequin.com.

Harlequin Enterprises ULC
22 Adelaide St. West, 41st Floor
Toronto, Ontario M5H 4E3, Canada
www.LoveInspired.com

Printed in U.S.A.

CONTENTS

HIDING HER AMISH SECRET

Carrie Lighte

In memory of my great-uncle

If we confess our sins, he is faithful
and just to forgive us our sins,
and to cleanse us from all unrighteousness.
—*1 John* 1:9

Chapter One

Amish women typically owned four dresses: one for wash, one for wear, one for dress and one for spare. Anything more than that was considered excessive. But there was no limit on the number of socks they customarily owned, and Arleta Bontrager's filled half of her suitcase.

"I didn't know you had so many pairs," Leanna marveled as she sat on the bed, watching Arleta pack. "Do you really need to take them all?"

"*Jah.* You know how cold my feet always are," Arleta answered, feeling guilty for misleading her fourteen-year-old sister. But she would have felt worse for setting a poor example for her. Besides, her feet *were* often cold—although that's not why she wore socks every day. Actually, the reverse was truer; *because* she wore socks every day, her feet felt cold whenever she went without them.

"I'd hate it if my feet got too cold to go barefoot," Leanna said, holding her legs straight out in front of her and stretching her toes apart. "I love to feel the dew on the grass in the mornings when I'm hanging laundry and the softness of the earth in the garden."

"How about the stones or the heat of the pavement when you're walking down the road to your friend Emma's *haus*? Do you love that, too?" Arleta teased.

Leanna shrugged. "I walk on the shoulder of the road most of the way. When it comes time to cross the pavement, I run so quickly I hardly feel the heat."

Few of the women in their little community of Serenity Ridge, Maine, donned footwear during the warmer months, unless they were going to church or to one of the *Englisch* shops. Going barefoot was cooler, more convenient, and it saved wear and tear on their shoes. And as Leanna pointed out, going barefoot allowed them to appreciate the Lord's creation in a way they couldn't if they were wearing shoes all the time.

Arleta used to love it when the weather warmed enough for her to shed her shoes for the season, too. Not anymore. Now she rarely went without shoes and socks—or sandals and socks—outdoors. And when she was indoors, if she had to remove her shoes she always kept her socks on. She even wore them to bed. She'd gotten so used to wearing them they almost felt like a second skin.

"Maybe you have a low thyroid. Emma's *mamm* has that and it makes her fingers and toes cold," Leanna suggested.

"My fingers aren't cold. Feel." Arleta squeezed Leanna's hand. She didn't want her sister to repeat her comment about her thyroid in front of their mother, especially since Arleta was about to leave town for the next four months. She'd stop Arleta from going until she visited the doctor. And Arleta knew there was nothing wrong with her thyroid.

There wasn't even anything wrong with her feet. Nothing physically wrong, anyway. But beneath her socks, Arleta was hiding a shameful secret: two years ago she'd gotten a tattoo on her left ankle. The red heart with her *Englisch* boyfriend's initials in black ink was tiny, no bigger than her thumbnail. But it was in complete violation with Amish beliefs about modest appearances, especially for a female.

When she'd gotten it, Arleta was on her *rumspringa* and she had already decided she was leaving the Amish. In fact, that was exactly why she'd gotten the tattoo—to prove she intended to "go *Englisch*" and marry Ian Fairfax, the grandson of the people whose lake house she cleaned. She'd met Ian when he'd come to visit his grandparents in between his junior and senior years of college. His parents were going through a contentious divorce and Ian didn't want to stay with either of them, so he spent his summer at the lake house.

Ironically, Arleta was so levelheaded her parents hadn't had any qualms about her "working out," meaning working outside their community, with *Englischers.* And Arleta certainly never intended to engage in a personal relationship with one. But Ian was utterly forlorn, and when he followed her around the house, practically begging her for conversation, she figured there was no harm in chatting with him…

And there wouldn't have been, if all they'd done was talked. But one thing led to another and by the end of the summer, she and Ian were so smitten with each other he asked her to marry him and she agreed. Since she had turned eighteen in August, they could have gotten married right then, but Arleta's father had suffered a heart attack that spring—that's why she had to work in the first place—and she wanted to wait until he was fully recovered before she broke the news to him that she was leaving the Amish. She suggested that Ian finish college first, and they could get married after he graduated.

Ian was crushed Arleta wanted to put off their wedding, which was understandable. After all, he'd just seen his parents break up after twenty-five years of marriage; Arleta had only known him less than four months. So she'd gotten the tattoo to show him there was no going back on her word. It was a symbol of her love for him. Of her intention to have him in her life forever.

But now it had become a symbol of her stupidity. Of how she'd almost given up everything she'd held dear. Her faith. Her family. Her community. And for what? A young man who told her—in a letter, no less—that he decided he was too young to get married. That he'd confused his feelings of dejection over his parents' divorce with love for Arleta. And that he hoped she'd find a good Amish man who would marry her and give her a family like she wanted.

Ha! What gut *Amish man would want to marry a woman with a tattoo of an* Englischer's *initials on her skin?* Arleta thought as she rolled another pair of socks to stuff into her suitcase.

She didn't know of any Amish boys who'd gotten a tattoo during *rumspringa*, much less girls. Girls were less likely to rebel against their customs during their *rumspringa* than boys were. Oh, they might wear their hair down and experiment with makeup, but they wouldn't do something that left a permanent mark, like getting their ears pierced. Or a tattoo. The most scandalous thing any girl in her district had done during *rumspringa* was to put purple streaks in her hair, but they washed out eventually.

Ideally, the Amish weren't supposed to hold what Arleta had done during her *rumspringa* against her now. The running around period was a time to test one's beliefs. To make sure the young person wanted to commit to the Amish faith and lifestyle. It was only after formalizing that commitment by being baptized into the church that the Amish were held accountable to the *Ordnung* as adults.

But in practice, Arleta knew that people would judge her if they found out she had a tattoo. She wouldn't have blamed them; she judged herself, too. Not just because of the tattoo, but because she'd pledged her love to an *Englischer*, which was a violation of her Amish faith, regardless of whether she'd been on *rumspringa* or not.

As much as she regretted the past, she couldn't undo it. She had confessed her sin to God and she'd repented and joined the Amish church, yet she couldn't seem to put her shame behind her. But maybe, just maybe she could get rid of the visual reminder of what she'd done. She'd heard that the *Englisch* had a procedure for erasing tattoos. It was expensive, but with what she earned from her new job—

Leanna's laughter interrupted Arleta's thoughts. "It looks like you're bringing a pair for every day of the month, not for every day of the week."

"I don't want to run out of clean pairs."

"Your socks shouldn't get *that* dirty. It's not as if you're going to work on a potato farm."

"*Jah*, that's true. I'll probably spend most of my time indoors tending to Noah's *groossmammi*'s needs and cleaning and cooking. But I'm sure there's gardening to be done, too. I want to be prepared so I can help Noah however he needs me to help him."

Noah Lehman was a metal roofing installer who lived in New Hope, a tiny Amish community north of Serenity Ridge and Unity. Arleta had only spoken to him briefly on the phone, but she knew that his immediate family had all been killed in a house fire about six years ago. Noah hadn't told her that—she knew because all the *leit* from Serenity Ridge and Unity had helped rebuild the house. Usually barn raisings and house building were joyous occasions, but that one was so solemn it brought tears to Arleta's eyes just to remember it.

Now his groossmammi *is ill, what a pity*, she thought, snapping her suitcase closed.

Ordinarily, Amish families and communities pitched in to tend to those within their church districts who were ill, but the New Hope community was only about ten years old, and it was still so small that there weren't enough people to care for Noah's grandmother. So he had asked the deacons in Serenity Ridge and Unity to put the word out he was hiring a woman for the summer to take care of his grandmother, who had been undergoing cancer treatments and was recovering at home.

"I can't believe you're going all the way to New Hope," Leanna said with a sigh. "Now *Mamm* and I will really be outnumbered by the *buwe*. Are you sure you want to go?"

Although New Hope was only twenty miles away, it was a two-day round trip by buggy, and Arleta understood why her sister was confused by her decision. With the exception of the time when Arleta's father had a heart attack, she'd never worked outside of her home. Her role was to help her mother and Leanna with domestic chores, while Arleta's father and brothers supported the family financially, by working with an *Englisch* lumber company. But Noah's sad situation gave Arleta a worthwhile way to earn the income she required to have her tattoo removed and her family didn't object to her leaving, because they recognized Noah needed her assistance more than their own household did.

Knowing her little sister looked up to her and would be lonely without her around every day, Arleta assured Leanna. "*Jah*, I'm sure I want to go. I'll miss you, but it's only for a few months. May is almost over and I'll be back before September."

"What if you like New Hope so much you decide to stay there?"

"Don't be *lappich*. My *familye* is here," Arleta said. "My favorite little *schweschder* is here."

"But you might find a suitor there and fall in love and then he'll ask you to get married and stay in New Hope with him."

There's absolutely no chance of that happening. Arleta cupped her sister's chin and looked into her eyes. "I'll be back before you know it. And by then, you'll be so used to having an entire bedroom to yourself, you'll want me to leave again."

Leanna was still skeptical. "You promise you won't marry a potato *bauer* from New Hope?"

Arleta chuckled at her sister's fear that she'd meet and marry a potato farmer, as opposed to a man who had a different vocation. "I promise you, I'm not marrying a *bauer* of any kind." *I'm not marrying anyone, period.*

* * *

Noah Lehman stopped pacing in the living room to peer out the window. It was already eight forty-five. What was keeping Arleta Bontrager? He'd specifically asked that she arrange for the van to drop her off before eight o'clock in the morning so he could talk to her alone before his grandmother woke at eight thirty. She was already up, and Noah's *Englisch* coworker was due to pick him up at nine o'clock to take him to the house where they were finishing an installation.

For the past six years, Noah had been working for an Amish family's metal roofing supply and installation business. The owners, Colin and Albert Blank, were brothers who lived in Serenity Ridge. Because of Maine's harsh winters, metal roofs were in high demand and the Blank brothers had such a good reputation for their work that they began getting installation requests from *Englischers* who lived in New Hope, too. Initially, they'd turned down those orders, because the distance would have required them to travel too far and they didn't have enough employees to meet the demand. Although they did employ *Englischers* who transported equipment and metal sheeting to their various worksites, the Blanks preferred the majority of their staff to be Amish.

That's where Noah and two other New Hope district members—David Hilty, a man in his late fifties, and Jacob Auer, a teenager—came in. Together, the men worked with Mike Hall, an *Englischer.* Mike drove a truck with supplies, and sometimes he picked up the other crew members when the site couldn't easily be reached by buggy. Maine had endured a particularly severe winter, so business was booming; no one wanted to be caught without a metal roof next year. Their four-man team was usually hard at work by seven or eight o'clock, but today Noah had asked them to postpone their start time so he could be home when Arleta arrived.

"You're going to make sawdust out of the floorboards, pacing like that," his grandmother, Sovilla, scolded, but her tone was one of concern, not annoyance. "Arleta will get here when she gets here."

Her voice startled Noah and he glanced over at her. Instead of wearing her usual white organdy prayer *kapp* pinned to her hair, she had covered her bald scalp with a white kerchief. His grandmother used to have such dark hair and eyebrows—but even those had fallen out after the chemo treatments, along with her eyelashes. She looked so pale. So faded.

"*Jah.* But I hope she gets here before Mike does so I can let her in."

"I'm not so old I can't get off the sofa to answer the door."

Neh, *but you might be too frail*, Noah thought ruefully. *And she won't just* kumme *in, like our neighbors do.*

For the past two months, whenever Sovilla wasn't in the hospital, the deacon's wife, Almeda Stoll, and their nearest neighbor, Sarah Troyer, had been looking after her while Noah was at work. In exchange, Noah helped their husbands install metal roofing on their workshops and homes. But recently, Almeda had traveled out of state to help her ailing elderly sister. Sarah had just given birth to her first child, a son, so she could no longer tend to Sovilla, either.

Almost all of the other Amish women in New Hope,

old and young alike, either had family or farming commitments that prevented them from staying with Noah's grandmother, too. Oh, they were more than willing to patch together a schedule that would allow for someone to drop in on her several times a day, but the more people who came in and out of the house, the greater her chances of catching an illness. Besides, Noah believed his grandmother needed someone with her around the clock as she recovered from her final round of cancer treatments.

That meant Noah either had to take time off from work for a couple of months until she was stronger and Sarah could return, or he had to hire someone from Serenity Ridge or Unity. While Noah wasn't particularly fond of the idea of a stranger, even an Amish one, living in their home with them, he knew a woman could take far better care of his grandmother and the housekeeping than he could. Plus, this was one of the busiest periods of installation. Even with Arleta's salary to pay, he'd still be making much more than what he'd lose if he took time off work.

Earning as much money now as he could was crucial, in preparation for providing his grandmother further medical care if her most recent course of treatment didn't work. Although the Amish community helped pay each other's major medical bills, Noah was reluctant to tap into New Hope's dwindling mutual aid fund more than he already had. Like most Amish, he'd been conscientious about what kind of medical services he'd agreed to for his grandmother, since American hospitals had a tendency to run all sorts of tests, which were costly and sometimes seemed unnecessary.

It wasn't unusual for the Amish to seek experimental

treatments in Mexico, where medicine was less expensive. Still, there would be train tickets to buy and lodging expenses to pay. Not to mention, the loss of income while Noah was away. But he figured if his crew accepted every project they could between now and the time his grandmother had her next tests in a little over three months, and if he took on a few individual installations after hours himself...

"Did you hear me?" his grandmother asked, pulling him back to the present moment. "You seem a hundred miles away."

More like three thousand miles away, Noah thought, considering the distance between Maine and Mexico. But he didn't want to tell her about his plan because it might discourage her if she knew he was worried the treatment might not work. Worse, she'd reject the trip out of hand, saying it wasn't worth the expense. Better to earn the money first, and wait to see what the doctor said at her next appointment. "Sorry, I guess I was lost in thought."

"Aha," she uttered, and the familiar sparkle momentarily lit her dark brown eyes. "You're wondering what kind of *weibsmensch* Arleta will be and whether or not she already has a suitor, weren't you?"

"Neh!" he protested truthfully. "That's the furthest thing from my mind, *Groossmammi.*"

"Well, it shouldn't be. It's only natural for you to want to court. To get married and start a *familye* of your own."

Noah had heard this all before. Many, many times. He'd given up telling his grandmother he had no desire to court or get married. As for starting a family of his own, Noah just wished he had his old family back... He shuddered, thinking of his parents, two younger brothers and sister who died in a house fire one evening six years ago. Noah would have died, too, but he'd been out late. Too late.

Too late to make his curfew and too late to save his family from the fire he saw raging in the second story of the house when he pulled up the lane in his courting buggy. Even now, Noah had no recollection of getting out of the carriage and running into the house. All that stuck in his mind was the terrible noise of the roaring fire and the popping windowpanes. And the wall of heat that was as impenetrable as a wall of stone, stealing the breath from his lungs and prohibiting him from taking another step up the stairs.

And so he'd turned and run. Because his horse had gotten spooked and taken off with the buggy in tow, Noah had sprinted all the way to the phone shanty to call the *Englischers* for help.

"There was nothing you could have done to save them," the firefighters told him afterward. Even with their equipment and protective gear, they hadn't been able to rescue his family.

"It was *Gott*'s will," was the refrain he heard countless times from the deacon, his grandmother, and his Amish friends and community.

Noah tried hard to accept that, but deep down, he knew he was to blame. If he had returned home even fifteen minutes earlier, as he was supposed to—instead of lingering to kiss Hannah Miller on her porch swing—he *might* have been able to save his family.

Now, with the exception of a few cousins and an aunt in Michigan, his grandmother was the only family he had left and Noah was going to do everything humanly possible to preserve *her* life. God willing, the last treatments she'd had were effective—they'd find out in another ten weeks or so—but if they weren't, he wanted to be prepared. Which meant his sole focus was on praying for her healing and earning money for further treatment.

"Please don't start on me about courting, *Grooss-mammi*," he said affectionately. "You know how I feel—"

"I hear a vehicle. Is that her or is it Mike?" Sovilla interrupted, pointing to the window.

Noah turned to face the window again. A silver passenger van was driving up the dirt lane. "It's her."

"Well, don't just stand there. Go carry her suitcase in for her. Make her feel *wilkom*," his grandmother instructed, sitting up straight and adjusting her kerchief.

Noah shoved his feet into his boots at the door and trotted outside and down the porch steps just as the van was pulling away.

"Hi, Arleta. I'm Noah," he said as the short woman with strawberry-blond hair approached him. "I can take that for you."

Young, full-figured and energetic, Arleta looked perfectly capable of carrying her own suitcase, but she extended it to him anyway. "*Denki.* I'm sorry I'm late. The driver was following GPS and it directed him to the pond on the other side of Pleasant Road. It's a *gut* thing I still remembered where your *haus* was from when I came here for the—"

Arleta stopped walking and cupped her hand over her mouth, obviously embarrassed. Noah realized she must have come there when the nearby Amish communities helped build a new house. As painful as it was for him to acknowledge the past, he was relieved that Arleta apparently already knew what happened to his family. It meant there'd be no troublesome questions later. "For the *haus* building?"

"Jah." Her light green eyes, fringed with pale lashes, were full of remorse. "I'm so sorry."

He didn't know whether she meant she was sorry for bringing it up or sorry about what happened to his family. Either way, that was as far as he wanted the conversation to go, so he gave a brusque nod of acknowledgment and then said, "Let's go inside. I want to introduce you to my *groossmammi* before my coworker arrives to pick me up."

To his surprise, instead of resting on the sofa, his grandmother was putting a coffeepot on the stove. "I'm Sovilla. *Wilkom* to our *haus*, Arleta."

"*Denki.* I'm very glad to be here."

Seeing Arleta wiping her shoes on the round braided rug at the door, Noah interjected, "Since my *groossmammi*'s immune system is compromised, you'll need to remove your shoes at the door so you don't track in germs."

"Oops, I'm sorry." Three wrinkles etched her forehead when she asked, "Is it all right if I leave my socks on? My...my feet get cold."

Noah hesitated. "I suppose that's okay, as long as they're clean."

Arleta's cheeks pinkened. "*Jah*, they're clean."

"Of course she's wearing clean socks," Noah's grandmother asserted, giving him a little scowl. To Arleta, she said, "I'm always cold, too, Arleta. You and I are going to get along like two peas in a pod."

As Arleta bent over to unlace her shoes, Sovilla

shook her head at Noah, no doubt to express her disapproval for embarrassing Arleta when she'd just barely crossed their threshold. Noah didn't care. His grandmother's health was at stake. Her *life* was at stake. He'd say or do whatever he needed in order to protect her. Besides, he asked everyone to remove their shoes at the door, so why should Arleta be any different?

"I'm afraid I need to go sit back down in the other room," Sovilla said apologetically. "Noah, why don't you take Arleta's suitcase to her room for her? She can pour us a cup of *kaffi*."

Stepping out of his boots, Noah dutifully carried Arleta's suitcase down the hall. Noah had cleared his belongings out of his room, which was across from his grandmother's, so Arleta could use it. He would be sleeping upstairs in the unfinished loft. When he returned to the kitchen, Arleta was standing on her tiptoes, pulling mugs from the cupboard.

"Don't worry, I've washed my hands," she informed him, as if reading his mind.

"I hope you understand that even a common cold could turn into pneumonia for my *groossmammi*—"

"I *do* understand. And I'll be careful to keep everything extra clean."

As Arleta turned to him and smiled, exposing a little space between her otherwise perfectly aligned front teeth, something about her seemed pleasantly familiar. She'd said she came to New Hope for the house building, but his memories of that day were foggy at best. Was it possible they'd crossed paths in Serenity Ridge more recently when Noah went there to finalize his partnership with the Blank brothers? She'd told him she didn't have any relatives in New Hope, but maybe she had friends here and Noah had seen her in church when she'd come to visit them.

For all he knew, she could have been visiting a long-distance suitor; she seemed about the same age as some of Noah's slightly younger peers. *If she's not being courted already, I imagine there will be a few men vying to be her suitor once they meet her.* The thought unsettled Noah, primarily because he didn't want anything to distract Arleta from helping his grandmother recover.

He lowered his voice to say, "My *groossmammi* is going to tell you not to fret so much, but her doctors said her immune system is like a newborn *bobbel*'s."

Noah crossed the room to remove a notebook from a drawer by the sink. He had intended to review its contents with Arleta before his grandmother woke up, but since Arleta arrived late, he didn't get the opportunity. He didn't want Sovilla to overhear him, so he put the notebook on the countertop.

"This contains important information, like my *groossmammi*'s medication list and her doctor's phone number. The shanty is about two miles south of us—you probably noticed it on your way here. But if you cut straight through the woods out back, you can reach Moses Schrock's feed and grain store. He has a cell phone for business purposes, so if there's an emergency—"

A horn interrupted him. Mike had just tapped on it gently, but Noah was irked. What if his grandmother had been sleeping? It was vital that she got enough rest.

"Don't worry. I'll read through the entire notebook. And there won't be an emergency," Arleta said. Then, because no one could have made such a promise, she added, "*Gott* willing."

Noah should have been reassured by her confidence that everything would be okay, but as he headed outside to get into his coworker's truck, all he could do was pray that she was right.

Chapter Two

As Arleta watched Noah lope across the lawn, she silently prayed, *Please,* Gott, *give him peace of mind about my taking care of his* groossmammi.

From the first moment he greeted her, Arleta had been struck by Noah's brown eyes, which seemed especially large, no doubt because his rectangular-shaped face was so thin. Anyone looking at it might have thought *he* was the one who was recovering from a long illness. At least his tall, sinewy physique appeared healthy, and his dark mane of hair was even thicker than Arleta remembered it being when she'd met him at the house building.

Well, she hadn't actually *met* him. She'd been serving lemonade, and someone commented that they hadn't seen him around. So, with a full glass in hand, Arleta went off to find him. She'd searched everywhere with no success, and she'd almost given up when she wiggled open the door to the little workshop behind the house. He'd been sitting on the workbench, his head bowed. At first she thought he was praying, but when he glanced up there were tears in his eyes and the expression on his face was one of bewildered anguish. Almost as if he was wondering, *How did I get here?*

"I—I'm sorry," Arleta had stuttered, feeling bad for intruding on his privacy. "I thought you might be thirsty."

She'd extended the glass to him, and although he lifted his hand to accept it, he didn't say anything before dropping his chin to his chest again, his face obscured by his hat. Turning, she'd quietly exited the workshop so he could have his solitude.

His expression when she mentioned the house building today wasn't nearly as distraught as it was when she'd walked in on him in the workshop, but there was an undeniable sadness in his eyes and she wished she hadn't brought it up. Especially because he'd been so quick to change the subject. *I'll have to remember to bridle my tongue.*

When she went into the living room to serve Sovilla a cup of coffee, she found the old woman reclining on the sofa, snoring softly. Since she'd said she was frequently cold, Arleta pulled the folded quilt from the back of the couch and covered her with it. Then she tiptoed into the kitchen and read through the notebook.

As Noah mentioned, it contained a medication list, including the dosages and times his grandmother was supposed to take her pills. There were doctors' names and phone numbers and printouts from the hospital regarding patient nutrition, sleep and exercise during the recovery period. There was also a leaflet about caring for someone with a compromised immune system. Arleta read through all of it twice and paid special attention to the section about preventing additional illness and watching for signs of infection.

Sovilla was still sleeping when Arleta finished, so

she went into the basement to begin washing the laundry. Sarah Troyer must not have been able to get to it for a while because there were several baskets of dirty clothes and bedding sitting by the wringer. By the time Arleta had hung everything out to dry, Sovilla was stirring. Arleta brought her a glass of water and took a seat on the chair opposite her.

"It sure is a beautiful spring day," Arleta said conversationally, allowing Sovilla time to open her eyes and adjust to being awake. "I noticed your daffodils have almost finished blooming, but the tulips are beginning to open now."

"I'd like to get out and see them. Sarah, the *weibsmensch* who was here before you, didn't take me outside very often. She always had some excuse. First it was her allergies. Then she said she was too tired because she was with child. She was a dear *weibsmensch* but a *baremlich* fibber. It wasn't her fault—I'm sure Noah convinced her I'd keel over if I went out into the sunlight."

Sovilla gave a little chuckle, but Arleta's concern must have registered on her face because the older woman quickly added, "I *won't* keel over. Not from the sunshine anyway."

This time, Arleta smiled. Sovilla's outlook was the opposite of Noah's, just as he'd told her it would be. "That's *gut*. But I don't want you to faint from hunger, either. It's almost noon. Is there something in particular you'd like me to make for lunch?"

"What does the notebook say I'm allowed to eat?" Sovilla asked wryly.

"I—I," Arleta stammered, unsure whether Noah would have wanted her to acknowledge that he'd given her an instructional notebook about his grandmother's care.

Sovilla's eyes twinkled. "It's okay, dear. I was pulling your leg. But I am aware Noah keeps a list of my dos and don'ts. I never pay it any mind."

Relieved, Arleta laughed. She appreciated Sovilla's sense of humor and independence. "I'll make some *supp*, then. I saw leftover *hinkel* in the fridge. Will that be all right?"

"You can fix whatever you like for meals, as long as you're not insulted if I don't always eat what you prepare. I don't have a big appetite anymore. The medication altered my sense of taste so I don't relish food like I used to… Although I can't imagine not enjoying a sliver of bumbleberry pie if someone were to make it for me," Sovilla hinted.

"I won't be insulted," Arleta assured her. But as she recalled that the pamphlet said it was important for cancer patients to keep their weight up, she silently made it her mission to come up with a nutritious meal plan that would appeal to Sovilla. Including the occasional treat. "As it happens, pies are my specialty. So if you get a craving for one, just let me know."

Sovilla gave a satisfied smile before closing her eyes and leaning her head back against the cushion again. "Didn't I say we'd get along like two peas in a pod?"

Jah—*but I'm not sure that's going to make Noah as* hallich *as it makes you*, Arleta worried to herself as she rose and went into the kitchen.

At noon, as the men scrambled down off the roof of the house they were working on to take their lunch break, Mike mentioned he had to run to the bank.

"Since you're driving past my place anyway, can you

drop me off and then pick me up on your way back?" Noah asked, and Mike readily agreed.

"Your lunch breaks are so quick you're usually done eating before the rest of us have unwrapped our sandwiches," David remarked. "Why are you going all the way home—is everything okay with your *groossmammi*?"

"I think she's fine but I want to check in on her."

"Is it really your *groossmammi* you're checking on, or is it the *maedel* you hired from Serenity Ridge you want to see?" Mike ribbed him.

"That's right, she arrived this morning, didn't she?" Jacob chimed in. He had recently reached courting age and was more outspoken about his interest in girls than many of his Amish peers. Which wasn't to say they weren't interested, too, only that they kept their thoughts to themselves, especially in front of adults David's age. "What's she like? Is she pretty?"

Noah shrugged. "I didn't notice, either way."

"Did you meet her when you picked Noah up this morning?" Jacob asked Mike.

"Nope, but I'll try to this afternoon," Mike taunted.

"*Neh*, you won't," Noah gruffly interjected. "Your boots are crawling with germs. You're not coming into my *haus* wearing those."

"He can take them off." Sometimes Jacob didn't know when enough was enough and Noah had to remind himself to be patient. The teenager had been orphaned as a toddler and raised by his grandmother and great-aunt, so he hadn't grown up with a man in the house to help him mature. "And then he can tiptoe across the floor in his bare feet."

"His feet probably are dirtier than his boots," David suggested, causing Jacob to crack up.

"They may not be dirtier, but they're definitely smellier," Mike admitted good-naturedly.

As Noah and Mike walked toward the truck, Noah reflected on how grateful he was to have found a Christian *Englischer* like him to join their team. Although he was a little rough around the edges, his generosity, skill and dedication more than made up for it.

A few minutes later when Mike dropped him off, Noah said, "I'll be watching for you to return. No need to honk—you'll wake up my *groossmammi* if she's napping."

"She's already awake." Mike pointed to the side of the house where Arleta and Sovilla were walking arm in arm. "So the hired girl's a redhead, huh?"

Noah bristled at Mike's reference to *the hired girl.* "Arleta," he said.

"Huh?"

"The young woman I hired is named Arleta. And her hair is more blonde than red." The words were out of Noah's mouth before he realized he'd spoken them aloud. He opened the door and hopped out of the truck.

"Not that you noticed, right?" Mike chortled as Noah shoved the door shut.

"What are you doing out here?" he asked when he got close enough that he didn't have to shout. It wasn't that the doctor prohibited his grandmother from going outdoors, but Noah wished she wouldn't. He'd had a raccoon problem that spring, and he didn't want his grandmother to inadvertently come into contact with their droppings, which he'd heard could transmit diseases to people.

"Enjoying the *gut* Lord's creation," Sovilla answered, waving to Mike as he drove away. "What are *you* doing here?"

Noah couldn't tell Sovilla he was checking up on Arleta because it was her first day and he hadn't had time to review his grandmother's care with her. "I came for lunch."

"Oh, *neh*! Did the birds fly away with the sandwich you brought to work with you?" his grandmother needled him. He should have known better than to try to pull one over on her.

Fortunately, Arleta cut in. "I've got *supp* simmering on the stove. It must be ready by now and I'm *hungerich*, too. Let's go eat."

His grandmother linked her other arm through Noah's and the three of them shambled so slowly to the house that Noah was concerned Mike would circle back before the trio even made it inside. Finally, they took their shoes off at the door.

"I'm so spent I doubt I can make it down the hall to wash my hands," Sovilla admitted.

That's another reason why it's a bad idea for you to go outside. You need to conserve your energy, Noah thought. He'd have to talk to Arleta about this once his grandmother was out of earshot.

"That's okay. There's no hurry. You can rest a minute, and then we can wash our hands in the kitchen sink and Noah can use the bathroom to wash his," Arleta said.

When he returned, his grandmother was sitting at the table and her cheeks were pink, probably from overexertion. "Are you okay, *Groossmammi*? Your face is red."

"That's because I got my blood circulating for once," Sovilla said with a laugh.

"You overdid it. I wish you wouldn't—"

Sovilla cut him off. "Every day for the past two weeks, you've told me how pale I look. Now I've finally got a little color and you're concerned about that, too. I'm fine, *suh.* You must stop worrying. Arleta is taking *gut* care of me, aren't you, Arleta?"

Arleta turned from the stove. "As best as I can," she said diplomatically and edged toward the table balancing a full bowl of soup.

By exhausting her with a walk around the yard? Noah wondered as she set the soup down in front of him.

Then she served a smaller bowl for Sovilla and one for herself. For the first few moments after Noah said grace, no one spoke as they sipped spoonsful of the hot, savory liquid. Noah was heartened to see his grandmother trying the broth; lately her diet consisted of crackers and ginger tea. Actually, his diet hadn't been very healthy, either. Sarah routinely fixed something for him to eat for supper, but eating alone in the evening really seemed to put a dent in his appetite.

"It's *gut,*" he mumbled.

"I'm glad you like it, because we'll be eating it for a while," Arleta replied. "I'm so used to cooking for my *familye*, I made way too much."

"How many *brieder* and *schweschdere* do you have?" Noah asked.

"Four *brieder* and one *schweschder.*"

"That's not so many. I thought you were going to say you had nine or ten siblings."

"I might as well have, the way my *brieder* eat. I think

they consume half their body weight in food during each meal," she remarked, causing Noah to chuckle.

"A *gut* appetite is a sign of *gut* health," Sovilla said.

"If that's true, they should live to be as old as Methuselah," Arleta joked. "I don't begrudge them their appetites and I enjoy cooking for them. I just wish sometimes they'd leave a crumb or two for the rest of us. Noah, you're fortunate you don't have *brieder* like mine—"

Arleta must have realized what she'd said because she abruptly stopped talking, which Noah felt was better for everyone. Unfortunately, his grandmother didn't drop the subject.

"Noah had two *brieder* and one *schweschder*, didn't you?" Sovilla prompted.

Noah nodded and ducked his head over his bowl, quickly filling his mouth with food so he wouldn't have to speak.

"His *daed*, Elmo, was my only *suh*. My only *kind*, in fact. That's how I came to be in Maine—I moved here from Michigan with Elmo's *familye*," Sovilla explained.

"That's a big move. Do you ever go back to Michigan to visit?" Arleta asked.

"I used to go once a year, when my *schweschder* was still alive. I was actually visiting her when the fire occurred, otherwise—"

"I think I hear Mike," Noah said, standing. Even though it had been six years since the fire, he didn't understand how his grandmother could speak so matter-of-factly about it—or speak about it at all. What's more, he didn't want Arleta to ask where *he'd* been the night of the fire. As he strode out of the house, he said over his shoulder, more to Arleta than to his grandmother, "Make sure to take it easy this afternoon."

* * *

What is wrong with me, making a joke about my brieder *living to be as old as Methuselah and telling Noah he's fortunate he doesn't have any* brieder *like mine?* Arleta silently chastised herself. *He'd probably give his eyeteeth to have his* familye *back again.* It was abundantly obvious Noah didn't like to talk about his family, yet the harder Arleta tried to censor herself from saying anything about them or the fire, the more she slipped up.

Sovilla, on the other hand, was eager to tell Arleta stories about her son and his family. As she took a stroll down memory lane, Arleta listened intently. She wanted to honor the older woman's desire to reminisce about her loved ones as much as she wanted to respect Noah's desire not to mention them at all. Arleta had only been here a few hours and already she could feel the tension between their two personalities. They weren't unkind toward each other—on the contrary, their mutual affection was obvious—but they were *so* different. It was going to be tricky for Arleta to appease them both.

After she'd entertained Arleta with several family anecdotes, Sovilla peppered her with questions about her own family. Finally, she yawned and asked Arleta to help her down the hall. "I need to take another nap. A real nap this time—in my bed, not on the sofa."

Arleta extended her arm and forced a smile even though she felt like weeping. In addition to upsetting Noah with her remarks, she'd tuckered Sovilla out completely. What a fine help she was! After she assisted Sovilla into bed and arranged her pillows, she turned to leave but the older woman grasped her hand.

"Look at me and tell me what's troubling you."

Arleta hardly knew Sovilla and she was supposed to be here to comfort her, not the other way around. "Nothing's wrong."

"You're as bad of a fibber as Sarah was," Sovilla scolded. "Is it that I didn't finish my *supp*?"

"*Neh*, of course not," Arleta protested before she realized Sovilla was only teasing in order to try to trick her into saying what was really on her mind.

"Then what is it? Hurry and tell me, *kind*, or I won't be able to sleep and I'm so drowsy."

"I feel *baremlich* for…for having such a big *moul* and upsetting Noah and for wearing you out on my first day here."

"Ach! You didn't wear me out. I always rest at this time of day. Wasn't that written down in the notebook?" Sovilla gave her an impish wink. "As for anything you said to Noah, don't worry about it. You didn't intend to upset him, just as he didn't intend to insult you by asking if your socks were clean."

"Oh, that didn't insult me. I know he's only concerned about germs because he doesn't want you to get sick."

"Exactly. Likewise, he knows you were just making a joke about your *brieder*." Sovilla released Arleta's fingers and patted the top of her hand. "He's *hallich* you're here and so am I."

Arleta wasn't quite sure she believed that. In fact, she was beginning to think coming here was a big mistake. She returned to the kitchen and as she cleaned up, she thought about how she and Leanna sometimes used to sing during their chores. Now, she hummed quietly to herself. Arleta hadn't even been here a full day and already she felt homesick. At times like these, she wondered how she ever considered permanently leaving her family and community.

She knew the answer: little by little, she'd crossed the boundaries that separated the Amish from the *Englisch*, and right from wrong. It began with her thoughts and soon, her actions followed until… Arleta glanced down at her feet. She was surprised to notice a ring of dirt around her sock near her ankle. How had she missed seeing that? How had *Noah* missed seeing that?

She went into her room and quietly opened her suitcase. She took out a clean pair of socks. Peeling off her dirty ones, she examined her tattoo. In dimmer light, she could fool herself into believing the heart was fading, but not today when the sunshine was streaming through the windows. *What is it Ephesians says about every sinful thing is made manifest in the light?* Arleta shook her head and quickly pulled a fresh sock over her ankle.

As she put the rest of her clothing away, she silently quoted another Bible verse, 1 John 1:9, which said, *If we confess our sins, he is faithful and just to forgive us our sins, and to cleanse us from all unrighteousness.* Reciting God's promise comforted Arleta, who wholeheartedly believed the Lord had forgiven her for the things she'd done during her *rumspringa*, after she'd confessed them to Him.

However, confessing her wrongdoings to other people and having them forgive her was another matter. Arleta reflected on the time she'd almost told Stephen Yoder about her tattoo. Stephen had come from Canada to visit his relatives in Serenity Ridge the summer after

Arleta's baptism, and he'd asked to walk out with her. She'd tentatively agreed and by the end of August, he wanted to know if she'd be willing to continue a long-distance courtship with the intention of getting married when they were twenty-one.

Aware she couldn't carry on a serious courtship—much less, get married—without being honest about her tattoo, Arleta worked up the courage to ask Stephen if he'd ever done anything he regretted during his *rumspringa*.

"*Jah.* Hasn't everyone?" he'd freely admitted, causing Arleta's heart to soar with hope that maybe he wouldn't judge her after all.

"If I promise not to tell a soul, will you tell me the thing you did that you regret most?"

So Stephen had confessed he'd climbed a water tower and spray-painted a love message to a girl on it. Apparently, the note wasn't from him but from an *Englischer* who was too scared to climb the tower himself. Since Stephen was used to climbing silo ladders, he did it for him.

"That's it? That's the worst thing?" Arleta had understood why he'd feel ashamed for defacing someone else's property, but she didn't think what he'd done was anywhere near as terrible as what she'd done. Especially since he'd gotten caught and had to repay the water company to repaint the tower.

"*Jah.* Why, what was the worst thing you did on *rumspringa*?"

Arleta wished she'd never brought up the subject. "It's much worse than what you did. You might not want to be my suitor once I tell you," she reluctantly admitted.

"I can't imagine anything changing the way I feel about you."

"Well, I..." She'd hemmed and hawed. "I guess you could say I kind of did something along the lines of graffiti, too. But what I wrote can't be painted over."

His eyes had gone wide. "Why not?"

Arleta had taken a deep breath and said, "Because it's on my skin. I—I got a tattoo."

He'd paused, his mouth dropping open before he hooted and slapped his knee. "*Voll schpass!* I almost thought you were serious."

"I *am* serious." She'd been on the brink of taking off her shoe and sock to prove it to him, but his expression suddenly turned hard.

"Arleta Bontrager, you can't be serious. *Meed* don't do such things. At least, not any *maedel* I'd ever court."

Arleta had felt like sobbing, but instead, she began to laugh in order to make Stephen think she'd been joking all along. For two months afterward, she'd kept up a long-distance courtship, too. Not because she had any interest in marrying him after that, but because she was scared if she ended the relationship right after their conversation, he'd realize why. He'd realize she'd been serious about her tattoo and he'd tell everyone. They'd all know the shameful things she'd done. They'd know she'd been planning to leave...

As she stowed her suitcase in the closet, Arleta realized she'd been covering one sin with another. For the past two years, she'd been hiding her tattoo with deception, just as surely as she'd been hiding it with a sock. She couldn't stand being so dishonest. *That's another reason I* have *to get Ian's initials removed*, she told herself. Which meant that no matter how much she doubted whether she was being helpful herc and no matter how homesick she felt, she couldn't leave. No, unless Noah outright fired her, Arleta was there to stay.

The crew completed the roof installation and managed to pick up the debris and collect their tools just before five thirty. On the way home, Noah used Mike's cell phone to call Colin Blank's business phone. They discussed the next project, which was closer to Noah's home than the one they'd just finished. The next day, Mike was going to take the measurements, cut the sheeting and edging, and deliver everything from their local workshop to the site while the other men removed the old roofing and repaired any damaged areas they found.

However, Noah wanted to check if there were any small installations he could work on in the upcoming week, like roofing for a mobile home. He figured even if the other men didn't choose to work extra hours, he'd be able to handle a small project himself. Sure enough, Colin had a backlog of New Hope orders. Noah chose to start with a shed roof for an *Englischer* whose home was located right down the street from where Noah lived.

Approaching his house, he was surprised to see all the windows opened—usually his grandmother complained she was too cold. The smell of onions wafted through the air.

"Hello," he said to Arleta as he removed his boots at the door.

She was stirring something in the frying pan and

she momentarily glanced over her shoulder to reply, "Hi, Noah. Supper will be ready in about ten minutes."

"*Gut.* That will give me time to clean up." Before heading to the bathroom, he peeked into the living room to greet his grandmother. Arleta must have spied him from the corner of her eye because she told him Sovilla wasn't there; she was in her bedroom.

"Please don't open her door."

Noah's heart thudded. Was his grandmother still winded from her walk this afternoon? "Why not? Is she sleeping?"

"*Neh.* She doesn't feel *gut.* She told me I could make anything I wanted to, so I made beef and noodle casserole. The recipe called for half a chopped onion, and the smell of it frying made her nauseated."

As Arleta looked at him, her eyes were watery and Noah wasn't sure whether it was from the onions or if she was on the brink of tears.

Noah certainly didn't want her to cry, but he also wished his grandmother didn't feel sick to her stomach. He didn't know what else to say except, "Oh, I see."

Arleta turned back to the stove and continued stirring, so he went into the bathroom. When he was through washing his hands and face, he returned to find her putting the salt and pepper shakers on the table. Wearing a slight frown, she wordlessly took her seat and Noah did, too. They bowed their heads for grace.

"*Denki, Gott*, for this food. Please strengthen us with it. Strengthen *Groossmammi*, too, Lord. Give her healing from the cancer and relief from the nausea." He ended by saying, "And *denki* for sending Arleta to help us during this time. Amen."

Opening his eyes, Noah noticed a change in Arleta's demeanor. She wasn't smiling, but she wasn't frowning anymore, either. She seemed…*lighter*, somehow, as she went to the stove and scooped a big helping of casserole onto his plate and then half as much on hers.

"Are you sure you have enough?" he asked genially, relieved that she no longer seemed on the verge of tears. "I don't want to be accused of not leaving a crumb for you."

She looked taken aback, but then she must have realized he was making a joke in reference to what she'd said about her brothers and she smiled. "I don't think there's any danger of that, especially since your *groossmammi* isn't joining us for supper. I cut the recipe in half, but we're still going to have leftovers."

"That's okay. I can stick them in my cooler and eat them for lunch tomorrow."

"Cold?"

"Hot, cold or lukewarm, it makes no difference to me—I love beef casserole."

"That's too bad, because this is the last time I can make it for you," Arleta said. "I don't want to make your *groossmammi* ill again."

The sincere concern in her voice mirrored the apprehension in her eyes. Studying her, Noah realized she really was trying her best to keep his grandmother comfortable and well. He found himself saying, "It's okay. You didn't know it would affect her like that. *She* probably didn't even know, because Sarah hasn't made any food with onions in it since *Groossmammi*'s last treatment. I'm the one who bought onions and put them in the pantry, so if anyone is to blame, it's me."

"Blame for what?" Sovilla said from where she

leaned against the doorframe, hugging a shawl to her chest.

"For the *schtinke*," Noah answered.

Arleta jumped up and began shutting the windows. "You must be cold. If you go sit by the stove, I'll bring you a cup of ginger tea."

"I will go sit by the stove, but I don't want any tea. I'm *hungerich.* I'd like to try some of that casserole after all."

Arleta cocked her head to one side. "Are you sure?"

"*Jah.* Just bring it to me in a bowl, please." Sovilla shuffled into the living room.

"I'm relieved she's feeling so much better." Arleta stretched to try to reach a bowl from the cupboard.

"Here, I'll get that for you," Noah offered. She stepped aside so he could retrieve the dish. Even so, as he pulled down a bowl he was acutely aware that he hadn't stood this close to a single woman since he'd courted Hannah Miller. Come to think of it, he hadn't spent this much time conversing with a single woman, either.

Then it dawned on him: *Groossmammi wasn't really that ill! She wanted Arleta and me to have to eat together without her. She was giving us privacy so we could get to know each other better.* And that was why she'd retreated into the living room now, too. Or was it? He couldn't be sure. Not that it mattered. Even if his grandmother was scheming to match him and Arleta, Noah wasn't going to develop a romantic relationship with her or with anyone else. How could the Lord entrust him with a new family when Noah had been so irresponsible toward the family he'd already had? No, his interest in Arlcta was solely as his grandmother's caretaker.

But that didn't mean Noah didn't notice what a sweet, gap-toothed smile she gave him when he handed her the bowl.

Chapter Three

Once Arleta and Noah discussed the guidelines for his grandmother's care and home environment and after a few days had passed, Arleta felt increasingly confident in her ability to keep Sovilla well and the household environment healthy. Noah must have felt more confident in her abilities, too, because on Wednesday, Thursday and Friday evenings, he worked late. Which meant Sovilla was the only person Arleta saw for most of the day, since Noah told Arleta he'd put the word out that his grandmother shouldn't have visitors.

Actually, Arleta didn't see all that much of Sovilla, either, since the elderly woman slept off and on throughout the late morning and again in the afternoon. Arleta spent that time cleaning the house, doing the laundry and making meals, just as she would have done at home. She also transferred seedlings and tended the vegetable garden and flower beds. Noah had insisted on taking care of the animals and cleaning the coop and stable himself. Arleta realized he was probably concerned she'd track something into the house, which was slightly offensive, considering how meticulous she was. But she could just imagine Leanna telling her she was crazy to argue with him if it meant she got out of the unappealing chore, so she didn't. Arleta had plenty of time left over for reading, and she even composed a letter to her sister.

She was grateful that she was being compensated handsomely for work that wasn't nearly as arduous as what she did in her own home. And when Sovilla was awake, Arleta genuinely enjoyed her company. But sometimes, while Sovilla was dozing, Arleta would find herself thinking, *This is how it will be for me at home in another ten years once my* brieder *and* schweschder *have all gotten married and moved away and* mamm *and* daed *are older.* But that wasn't necessarily true; she could count on at least one or two of her siblings and their spouses and children residing in her parents' house at some point. That's what she hoped, anyway, because this kind of quietness didn't seem natural to her and she was getting restless.

So on Friday evening when Noah asked if she'd rather take the buggy and go to town for groceries the next morning or make up a list and have him get the food, she jumped at the chance to go shopping herself.

"She doesn't know the way," Sovilla pointed out. "Why would you send her off alone?"

"Because it will give you and me a chance to visit," Noah replied.

"Pah. You're just afraid to leave me on my own," Sovilla responded, and Arleta knew she was right. Then she added, "But this is one time I don't mind if you treat me like a feeble old lady. I've missed seeing your face. You've been keeping awfully late hours at work."

"I've told you, *Groossmammi*, this is the busiest time

of the year for installations. If we don't keep up with the demand, we'll lose customers."

Sovilla clicked her tongue against her teeth. "Even so, I'm surprised Colin Blank expects his crew to spend evenings apart from their *familye.* He ought to care more about the people under his employees' roofs than putting new roofs on *Englischers'* homes."

Arleta noticed a pained look cross Noah's face, and she wondered if he was keeping something from his grandmother. She couldn't imagine what it would be but she interjected, "I don't mind going alone. Most men I know get impatient in the grocery store. This way, I can take my time without worrying about Noah pacing the aisles."

"Uh, I'd actually appreciate it if you'd *kumme* back as soon as you can. I'll need the buggy because tomorrow I'm starting a new project a few miles from here."

"You're working on *Samschdaag*, after all the extra hours you already put in this week?" Sovilla was incredulous.

"I'm sorry, *Groossmammi*, but the *Englischer* whose roof I'm installing wants to be there while I'm working on it. He's at his own job during the rest of the week, so—"

"*Englischer* this, *Englischer* that. If you keep allowing the *Englisch* to influence you, pretty soon you'll be working on *Sunndaag*, too."

"You know me better than that, *Groossmammi.* I'd never do something like compromise the Sabbath because of any *Englischer*'s influence." Noah's cheeks and ears flushed bright red.

Sovilla was quiet for a moment before she acknowledged, "*Neh*, I know you wouldn't, *suh.* I'm sorry."

Noah rubbed his forehead and released a heavy sigh. "It's okay, *Groossmammi.* You're right. I have been working a lot, and I'm going to have to keep up this pace for a while. But I really *am* looking forward to having a quiet *Sunndaag* together."

Then, since she said she wasn't quite tired yet, Sovilla suggested they play a three-person version of spades. Although the tension between her and her grandson had lifted, their remarks ate at Arleta. Sovilla was right, of course; it was important to guard against the practices and temptations of the *Englisch* world. But it hurt to imagine what she might have thought of Arleta if she knew how much *she'd* once been influenced by an *Englisch* boy.

And Noah's disgust at his grandmother's suggestion that he might violate his faith and work on the Sabbath really struck a nerve. He sounded so appalled it reminded Arleta of Stephen's tone when he said, "*Meed* don't do such things. At least, not any *maedel* I'd ever court."

While Arleta didn't blame Noah for being indignant, his assertion that he'd never compromise his beliefs underscored the secret fact that Arleta *had* compromised hers. *If Noah knew about my tattoo—or about the other things I did—would he ask me to leave?* Beneath the table, she self-consciously pulled her feet closer to her chair. After Sovilla won the game and asked if they wanted to play again, Arleta declined, saying she was tired. Then she retreated to her room.

It was warm enough to sleep with the windows open and a quilt was no longer necessary, either. Since she had the room to herself and she didn't have to worry about Leanna seeing her ankle, it was probably safe for

Arleta to go to bed barefoot. It certainly would have been cooler. *But what if Sovilla needs me in the middle of the night?* she wondered. Arleta had already accepted the fact that her tattoo—as well as planning to leave the Amish—had cost her a future as a wife, but she didn't want it to cost her a job, too. So she reluctantly donned a fresh pair of socks, removed her prayer *kapp* and went to bed.

By the time she set out for the grocery store the next morning, the sting of Sovilla's and Noah's remarks had subsided. For one thing, she felt a sense of adventure, exploring a new town. For another, she was anticipating buying ingredients for a couple of interesting recipes she'd found in Sovilla's recipe box.

New Hope's Amish population was large enough that part of the store's parking lot was reserved for buggies only. Arleta had just loaded her purchases into the back of the carriage when another buggy pulled up alongside her and a young woman got out.

"My name's Faith Smoker," she said, introducing herself. "You must be the *maedel* staying with Sovilla—I recognize Noah's *gaul*."

"*Jah*. I'm Arleta Bontrager."

"How is Sovilla?"

"She seems to be getting stronger each day."

"Is she ready for visitors?" Faith asked. "Or maybe I should ask if Noah is ready to allow her to have visitors?"

Arleta bit back a smile. "I'm not sure."

"*You're* probably ready for visitors, though. You must not get to see many other people."

"That's true, I don't. But I really enjoy Sovilla's company."

"Ach. I didn't mean to imply you didn't. Sometimes I really stick my foot in my *moul*," Faith said, and Arleta could empathize since she had a tendency to misspeak, too. "I was only thinking aloud about your situation because some of us are going on a hike through the woods and then having a picnic tomorrow after *kurrich*. There will be a few *buwe* and a few *meed*, all around our age. You're *wilkom* to join us. It's supposed to be a beautiful day."

"Oh, that sounds like *schpass*! But I'll have to talk it over with Sovilla and Noah, first."

"Tell Noah he should *kumme*, too."

Arleta's initial exuberance quickly faded. If Noah wanted to go, that meant she would have to stay behind with Sovilla. Although she recognized that's what she'd been hired to do and she truly did like spending time with Noah's grandmother, Arleta wasn't used to being indoors with only one other person for such a long stretch of time. *Maybe Noah will decide he'd rather be the one to stay home*, she thought hopefully.

She intended to tell him about the invitation as soon as she arrived home, but he was in such a hurry to get to work she'd barely carried the bags inside when he shot out the door in the opposite direction.

"Did you meet anyone in town?" Sovilla asked, coming into the kitchen to chat while Arleta put the food away. Arleta had reorganized Sovilla's cupboards so she could reach everything—Noah and his grandmother were much taller than she was—but now the lower shelves were so full she barely had enough room for the new items. She stood on tiptoes to put a can of tuna fish on an upper shelf.

"*Jah*. I met Faith Smoker."

"Ah, Faith. Her *familye* was one of the first to move to New Hope. She's lived here since she was in *winsdel*." Even though they were alone in the house, Sovilla lowered her voice to confide, "Her *mamm* always expected the community would have grown more by now. She's worried her *dochder* doesn't have enough choices for a suitor. But I heard from Sarah that Faith has her sights set on Jacob Auer, the young man who works with Noah."

"Oh, maybe that's why—" She caught herself, but Sovilla prodded her to finish her sentence. Arleta hadn't wanted to tell her about the picnic until after she'd spoken to Noah about it, but she didn't have a choice. "Faith invited me to go on a hike after *kurrich*. She invited Noah, too—along with a few other young people. I imagine Jacob will be one of them."

It wasn't acceptable for an Amish woman to initiate a courtship with an Amish man, but some women found ways to let the men know they were interested, including inviting them to group activities. Arleta suspected that was why Faith had arranged the hike with her peers.

"*Wunderbaar!*" Sovilla exclaimed, clasping her hands beneath her chin. "This is exactly what Noah needs. A little *schpass* with people his own age."

Arleta bent down to pull a box from the canvas bag so Sovilla wouldn't see how disappointed she felt that Noah would be going on the picnic and Arleta wouldn't. But Sovilla surprised her by adding, "And it will be *wunderbaar* for you to go out with the youth, too. Maybe you'll even find a suitor among the *buwe* of New Hope."

"I don't think that's a *gut* idea," Arleta argued, knowing Noah wouldn't want Sovilla to be left alone for the afternoon.

"Why not? Are you courting someone at home?"

"*Neh*, but that's not why I don't think it will be a *gut* idea..." It was one thing for Noah to risk insulting his grandmother by saying she shouldn't be left alone, but Arleta didn't dare suggest it herself.

"Noah isn't courting anyone, either," Sovilla babbled on. "Can you believe he hasn't walked out with a *meed* since he was seventeen? I keep telling him there's more to life than working and sitting at home at night with his *groossmammi*."

Noah hadn't courted anyone since he was seventeen? This piece of information surprised Arleta. Not that it was any of her business, but it struck her as strange. Noah might not have been the most cheerful man she'd ever met, but he was hardworking, thoughtful and kind. And devoted to his grandmother, a trait Arleta found especially endearing. Not to mention, he was tall and strong and had pretty eyes. Any of her friends in Serenity Ridge would have lined up to court him. And at one time, Arleta would have lined up with them.

She figured Sovilla must have been right: Noah didn't court anyone because he spent all his time working or with her. While his sense of responsibility was admirable, it seemed a pity he hadn't had the opportunity to court a woman in over six years. Arleta knew from her own experience how lonely it felt not to have the hope of a romantic relationship, and she empathized. *Maybe now that I'm here around the clock, he'll be able to go out during the evenings on occasion.*

"This picnic might be the nudge he needs," Sovilla said. "He'll see what he's been missing for the past six years and he'll enjoy himself so much he'll take time to get out more often."

"*Jah.* But the challenge will be convincing him he should go in the first place." *Especially since he's not going to want to leave you alone for several hours.*

With a glint in her eye, Sovilla replied, "Just leave that to me."

On Sunday morning at breakfast, Sovilla turned to Arleta and said, "Tell Noah about Faith Smoker's invitation for this afternoon."

Arleta swallowed a bite of scrambled eggs and coughed before answering. "She and a few other people are going hiking after *kurrich.* Then we'll have a picnic for supper. I made plenty of potato salad and fried *hinkel* to share."

Noah was a little surprised that Arleta hadn't discussed spending the afternoon away from the house before putting her plans into motion. What if he'd had someone to visit and needed her to stay with Sovilla? Then he realized he'd mentioned that he'd been looking forward to spending a quiet Sabbath with his grandmother. Besides, he could understand why Arleta was eager to hang out with younger people for a change.

He smiled and remarked, "I hope you have *schpass.*"

"Faith invited you, too, Noah," Sovilla told him.

"That's nice, but I don't want to go. You and I are going to have a nice, restful afternoon together, *Groossmammi*, remember?"

"*Suh*, I appreciate it that you want to keep me company, but to tell you the truth, I'd prefer to go to Lovina Bawell's *haus* for the afternoon," his grandmother said.

"It's been two weeks since I got out of the hospital, so I don't have to keep isolated any longer."

"But Lovina has six of her *kinskind* living in her *haus.* You heard what the *dokder* said about avoiding small *kinner* for at least a month."

As it was, because Sovilla's immune system was compromised, she should have been avoiding large gatherings, such as for church, too, but Noah had already lost that battle. Sovilla had told him she didn't care if she had to crawl to church on her knees; nothing was going to stop her from worshipping. But at least she'd agreed to wear a protective mask and she didn't mingle after the services.

Sovilla snapped her fingers. "*Jah*, you're right. I suppose Lovina will have to *kumme* here instead. Maybe her *dochder* will *kumme*, too, and we can all play bridge or put together a jigsaw puzzle. Arleta made plenty of chicken and potato salad for us, too. You *kin* can eat your supper on the porch, so Lovina and I can natter away in private in the *haus*."

Inwardly, Noah moaned, recognizing his grandmother had hoodwinked him. Lovina Bawell's youngest daughter, Honor, was a nice enough person, but he knew what it would look like if she found out that he had the opportunity to go hiking and instead he'd stayed home to play games on the afternoon she was invited to visit. His grandmother knew what it would look like, too, and she was using that to her advantage.

"*Neh.* I'd rather go hiking," he glumly conceded. Noah actually used to enjoy hiking on Sundays, but Faith Smoker was barely seventeen years old, and he supposed most of the people she invited would be teenagers, too. People who were just beginning to court and thought of little else. People who were as immature and irresponsible as he was at that age…

"*Gut!* I was hoping you'd want to *kumme*!" Arleta exclaimed, her eyes sparkling. "I'm sure everyone there will be very *freindlich* toward me, but I'll feel more comfortable having you there, too."

She seemed so genuinely happy that Noah smiled, too. But before he could reply, Sovilla said, "*Jah*, once the *buwe* of New Hope find out Arleta isn't being courted, they're going to swarm around her like bees around a hive. Noah, you can watch out for her."

As Arleta dipped her head and scraped the last bits of scrambled eggs from her plate, Noah noticed her ears and the part in her hair that wasn't covered by her prayer *kapp* were turning bright pink. He winced on her behalf. Most young Amish women and men didn't openly discuss whether they were courting anyone, but he surmised his grandmother had wheedled that information out of Arleta. She must have been mortified that Sovilla had announced her courting status in front of Noah like that.

"I—I'm looking forward to the fried *hinkel*," he said, hoping to alleviate Arleta's embarrassment by changing the subject. "Are you bringing some of the whoopie pies you made last night, too?"

Her cheeks were rosy when she raised her head and met his eyes. Even though he knew it was embarrassment that had colored them, he was startled by how becoming she looked. "How many would you like?"

"How many do you have?"

Arleta's face broke into a smile wide enough to expose the little space between her front teeth. Noah was beginning to recognize this as a sign of her authentic amusement. "Nine or ten," she answered.

"Then bring them all."

"Aren't you going to leave a couple for Lovina and me?" Sovilla piped up.

"Lovina's *dochder* can bring dessert for you," Noah suggested, tongue-in-cheek. When he was a teenager, he'd actually chipped a tooth eating a sugar cookie Honor had made—and judging from what she'd brought to recent barn raisings and potlucks, her cooking hadn't improved much since then.

"I'd rather eat onions," Sovilla retorted. To Arleta she explained, "Honor's a nice *weibsmensch* but a *baremlich* cook."

"I suppose that's better than being a nice cook and a *baremlich weibsmensch*," Arleta said, and all three of them cracked up.

Their shared levity, coupled with Arleta's enthusiasm about the outing, boosted Noah's mood. His grandmother seemed to have a burst of energy, too. *Maybe this will be a* gut *change for all of us*, he thought as they journeyed to church.

New Hope's Amish community, like several of the other Amish settlements in Maine, was unusual in that worship services were held in a church building rather than in a host family's home. They still ate a cold lunch together afterward, so while Arleta was helping clean up, Noah spoke to Lovina's husband, Wayne. The plan was that he would drop the two older women off at Noah's house and Noah would take Lovina home once he returned from the picnic.

"We'll be back as soon as we finish eating supper,"

he promised his grandmother, who was resting on a bench nearby.

"Don't hurry home on my account. Lovina and I have a lot of catching up to do."

"It's too bad my *dochder* is still visiting her *schweschder* in Ohio. She would have liked to *kumme* with you," Lovina remarked.

Noah recognized the polite thing to do would have been to express disappointment that Honor couldn't make it, but that would have been insincere. He hadn't even noticed whether or not she'd been in church lately, so he asked, "How long has she been in Ohio?"

"It's been over a month now. I'm surprised Sovilla hasn't told you. She's probably getting sick of hearing me gripe about how lonely I've been."

Noah lowered his eyebrows at his grandmother, who was fussing with her kerchief. She'd known all along Lovina's daughter was away! Her threat about inviting Honor to spend the afternoon at their house was an empty one, but it had worked on him. The question was, did she truly want him to go for a hike so she'd have the house to herself to host her friend, or was it because she was pushing him to socialize more? Either way, Noah had to give it to his grandmother; she could outsmart a fox.

After saying goodbye, as he went to look for Arleta, he bumped into Faith, who asked if he and Arleta wanted to ride in her buggy. "I'm taking three others but if we squeeze together, we can all fit. We can circle back to the *kurrich* afterward, and you and Arleta can go home from there."

"*Denki*, but I'll take my own buggy." If the others decided to linger at the park after supper, Noah didn't want to be at the mercy of their schedule. "We're going to park at the gorge, *jah*?"

"*Jah.* I'm going to round everyone up and head out now. We'll meet you two by the trailhead to Pleasant Peak. Arleta was just washing the last few platters. She should be right up."

So Noah went to wait for her at the top of the stairs leading to the basement, where the kitchen was. He was startled when someone tapped his elbow from behind.

"Waiting for someone?" Arleta gazed up at him. The dress she was wearing was a deep forest green color, and it made her eyes look as bright as spring grass by comparison. She must have gotten hot from working in the kitchen because her forehead and upper lip were dewy with perspiration.

"Noah?" she prompted and he realized he'd been staring.

"*Jah.* I was waiting for you. Everyone else is going to meet us there. I thought you and I should go alone in my buggy." He pivoted toward the exit and then swung back around so quickly he almost knocked into her. "I meant we should go alone because then we can leave when we need to and we don't have to stay as long as everyone else."

Arleta nonchalantly agreed that was a good idea, but Noah felt like a clodhopper, tripping over his words like that. He decided he'd be better off saying nothing than embarrassing himself again. But on the way to the park, Arleta asked him so many questions about the various landmarks they passed that he didn't have any choice but to engage in conversation. The more he talked, the less self-conscious he felt and pretty soon he was regaling Arleta with stories about his childhood escapades with his brothers. Maybe it was the fragrant spring air or the vibrant blue sky or even Arleta's sunny attitude, but reminiscing about his brothers wasn't making him sad the way it usually did.

"See the long stretch of road up ahead? My *brieder* and I used to go skitching there."

"What's skitching?"

"It's hitching a ride from a moving vehicle while you're skating."

Arleta gasped. "You held on to a car while you were wearing rollerblades?"

"*Neh.* We hitched rides from our friends' buggies, not from cars. But they were going pretty fast."

"You were *narrish*! Isn't that illegal?"

"I don't know, but it sure was *dumm*. My youngest *bruder* lost his grip on an incline once. He fell on his backside, chipped his tailbone and broke his wrist."

"Wow. Your *eldre* must have been really upset."

"Not half as upset as the three of us were when we had to pay for my *bruder*'s trip to the emergency room," Noah said.

"Well, your *eldre* probably wanted to teach you a lesson so you wouldn't pull a stunt like that again."

"There was no chance of it happening again. Not because we learned our lesson—but because we had to sell our skates to help cover the medical expenses," Noah explained, making Arleta laugh. When she stopped, he asked, "What kinds of shenanigans did you and your *brieder* get up to when you were a *kind*?"

"Oh, the usual stuff. Jumping across the hay bales on our *onkel*'s farm. Seeing who could slide farthest down the hill in the mud in the pasture. Nothing that was dangerous, just dirty."

"Really? You never did anything reckless when you were growing up?"

"My *brieder* probably did, when I wasn't around. But I didn't."

"Not even on your *rumspringa*?" Noah queried, curious to hear more about Arleta's youth.

From the corner of his eye, Noah saw Arleta shrug. When she didn't answer, he took a longer sideways look at her profile; her cheeks were pink and she was biting her lower lip.

"I sense you're hiding something. Have you got a really *gut* story to tell?" It was unusual for him to banter like this, but then, everything about this afternoon with Arleta was unusual.

"Neh."

"C'mon, please?" He leaned toward her and nudged her elbow with his. "I told you about—"

"Absatz," she said, an edge to her voice.

Noah pulled back. Why was she so hypersensitive about her *rumspringa*? Whatever the reason, he felt like a dolt for getting carried away with his teasing. They rode for a few minutes in awkward silence as he tried to think of a way to smooth things over between them again.

Finally, he asked, "Did Faith mention who else is coming?"

"*Jah.* Someone named Isaiah Wittmer and your coworker Jacob."

Noah suppressed a groan, imagining all the remarks he'd have to endure at work in the upcoming week once Jacob met Arleta and saw how pretty she was. He'd probably give Noah a hard time for acting as if he hadn't noticed.

"So just the five of us?" he asked.

"*Neh.* She said there would be six…but I can't recall the name of the last person," Arleta said. "Oh, wait, I remember—a *meed* named Hannah."

Noah swallowed. "Hannah Miller?"

When Arleta said yes, it took every ounce of Noah's willpower to keep himself from jumping out of the buggy and sprinting all the way home. Instead, he gritted his teeth and resigned himself to spending the afternoon with the woman he'd been kissing the night his whole world went up in flames.

Chapter Four

Arleta did her best to plaster a smile across her face as she and Noah headed toward the trailhead. Although she realized Noah had only been teasing her about *rumspringa*, his comments underscored how much she regretted her behavior during that period in her life. His innocuous remarks reminded her, once again, that in order to protect her secret she was going to have to be careful to keep her guard up. And not just around him and Sovilla—around other people as well, including the new friends she'd hoped to make.

Suddenly, instead of anticipating the fun she'd have, she just wished she could go back to Sovilla and Noah's house. She would have preferred to spend the afternoon completely alone in her room, writing letters to her mother and Leanna.

"There you are!" Faith called, waving wildly, as if she hadn't seen Arleta and Noah for years.

Although Arleta had glimpsed the others in church, she hadn't had a chance to speak with any of them yet, so Faith made the introductions. On first impression, Arleta figured that Jacob and Faith were the youngest in the group. Hannah appeared closer to her midtwenties and Isaiah seemed around that age, too.

"It's *gut* to finally meet you," Jacob said. "Noah never says a word about you at work. If it weren't that his cooler has been filled with bigger and better lunches, I wouldn't have believed you existed."

Noah never says anything about me? Arleta didn't expect he would have said much about her, but *nothing*? Then, Arleta noticed when Noah greeted Hannah, his face turned red. The tall, thin brunette with bright blue eyes also mumbled a greeting and then quickly glanced away, appearing very self-conscious. Their mutual discomfort was obvious in a way Arleta had recognized between her peers before. While a few Amish youth were open about their romantic interest in each other, far more were discreet. Sometimes, Arleta was actually able to discern whether or not a pair was courting by how *indifferent* they seemed toward each other. So she intuitively gathered that Hannah and Noah might be interested in each other, but didn't want certain other people to know. Which could have explained why Noah had been reluctant to come on the hike in the first place.

It also might have explained why Jacob made a point of announcing that Noah never spoke about Arleta. Maybe Noah had confided his interest in Hannah to the guys at work, so Jacob was emphasizing Noah's disinterest in Arleta for Hannah's benefit. Arleta could certainly understand that—if *she* had been courting or interested in courting a young man and he had a strange young woman living with *his* family, she might feel a bit distrustful, too.

It's not as if Hannah has anything to worry about. Noah would never be interested in someone like me and even if he were, I couldn't reciprocate his affection, she told herself. Or was she jumping to far-fetched conclusions? After all, Sovilla said that Noah hadn't courted since he was seventeen. But it was possible his grandmother didn't *know* he was courting Hannah. Or at least, that he was interested in courting her.

In the event Arleta was right, she decided to give Hannah and Noah as much opportunity as possible to chat with each other alone. Although Arleta couldn't have romance in her life, she certainly didn't want her presence in New Hope to hinder Noah and Hannah from having it in theirs. Especially since Sovilla was so eager to see her grandson develop more of a social life. So, as Jacob and Faith dashed ahead of the group, Arleta struck up a conversation with Isaiah. Because he was over six feet tall, she had to hurry to match his stride, leaving Noah and Hannah to lag behind them.

Arleta commented on the beauty of the gorge, adding that it made her a little nervous to peer over the edge, down to the rocks below. "Even though my town is named after a ridge, I don't think I've ever seen such a steep drop-off," she said.

"What about Paradise Point? That's a really high precipice."

"You've been to Paradise Point? That's one of my favorite places in the world!"

"*Jah.* Last summer I went to Serenity Ridge for the first time for the annual fish fry and canoe race. Some of us hiked to Paradise Point after we ate."

At the end of every summer, the Amish community in Arleta's hometown had a tradition of hosting a big picnic and canoe race on Serenity Lake. They invited all of the Amish people in Serenity Ridge, as well as those in Unity. Lately they'd begun to include the growing community in New Hope, too. The daylong event was so popular that the people who lived too far away to make the round-trip in one day by buggy either hired van drivers to take them to Serenity Ridge or else they stayed overnight with friends and relatives in the community, to give their horses a rest.

"Wait a second!" Arleta exclaimed. "Do you know the *mann* from New Hope who fell out of his canoe?"

"He didn't fall—he *jumped.* His *hut* blew off so he leaped in to get it."

"That's right—I'd forgotten. I didn't see it happen, but everyone thought he was a little *narrish*, since *hiet* are a dime a dozen and he got his clothes all wet. And his canoe was in the lead until then, if I remember correctly."

"*Jah*, but what people don't know is that he had secured the cash he'd brought to pay the van driver beneath the ribbon on his *hut*. That's why he jumped in after it."

"Oh, *neh*! Was the money still there when he fished the *hut* out?"

"*Neh.* Unfortunately, as soon as he hit the water, he remembered he'd been worried he'd lose the money and earlier that morning, he'd stuck it under a rock on shore. So he jumped in for nothing."

Arleta chuckled. That was the kind of harebrained thing one of her brothers would have done. "I never heard that part of the story."

"Nobody has—he only admitted it right now. You see, *I* was the *mann* who jumped overboard."

"That was *you*?" She stopped walking and clutched her sides, laughing.

"*Jah.* It was me." Isaiah grinned, too. "But please don't tell anyone the part about my money… I already feel *lecherich* enough that everyone in New Hope knows I was the one who jumped overboard to save my *hut.*"

"I won't," she promised, glancing over her shoulder to see if Hannah and Noah were following closely enough to overhear their conversation.

They were several yards behind, but if they'd heard, it didn't register on their faces. In the brief glimpse she'd caught of them, Arleta noticed Hannah had her arms folded across her chest as she walked, and she was slightly ahead of Noah. They didn't seem to be enjoying themselves. Was she wrong? Were they interested in each other or weren't they? She couldn't help but wonder if they were and this was the first time Hannah had found out Arleta was staying with Noah and Sovilla. Maybe Hannah was annoyed that he hadn't told her before now.

That's pure conjecture, she told herself. *Just because Faith is obviously using this opportunity to spend time with Jacob doesn't mean that there's anything going on between Noah and Hannah.* Still, she didn't want to risk Hannah getting the impression that there was anything going on between Arleta and Noah, either. So, she stuck close to Isaiah's side, chatting away.

"What's your vocation, Isaiah?" she questioned.

"I'm a *bauer.* My father owns a potato *bauerei,*" he answered, which caused Arleta to burst out laughing. Isaiah stopped walking and stared at her, one eyebrow raised. "What's *voll schpass* about being a potato *bauer*?"

Clearly Arleta had offended him, and she felt so bad that she didn't stop to consider her response, answering honestly, "I wasn't laughing at your vocation, I promise. It's just that my little *schweschder* is convinced I'll meet a young potato *bauer* in New Hope and we'll start courting and I won't want to return to Serenity Ridge."

At first, Isaiah looked even more taken aback than when Arleta had laughed. But amusement danced across his face. "Is that so?" was all he said, but Arleta was mortified.

Me and my big moul! *He probably thinks I'm dropping a hint.* Her embarrassment was compounded when she realized Noah and Hannah had caught up with them and they must have heard what she'd said, too. She briefly considered adding that her sister often allowed her imagination to run away with her and the last thing Arleta wanted was a suitor, but she knew if she opened her mouth again, she'd only make matters worse. So, without another word, she silently started walking again, trying to look on the bright side. *At least if Hannah heard me, she'll think I'm interested in Isaiah, not in Noah...*

As the foursome silently trudged along the path that descended toward the floor of the gorge, Noah almost wished he could have spent the afternoon with Honor. Even chipping a tooth on one of her rock-hard cookies would have been preferable to the uncomfortable silence between him and Hannah. The longer it went on, the more difficult it became to break, so instead of forcing small talk with her, he strained his ears to catch snippets of the conversation between Isaiah and Arleta. Judging from their laughter, the two of them were enjoying each other's company.

But he was surprised to overhear Arleta mention that

her sister thought she'd meet a potato farmer to court. Even if she wasn't aware that anyone except Isaiah could hear her, it was a very forward remark for an Amish woman to make to a man. However, Isaiah didn't appear to be at all fazed or put off by her boldness. On the contrary, there was a spring in his step as he walked side by side with her to the bottom of the gorge, where Jacob and Faith were splashing each other in the narrow and shallow but quick-moving stream.

"You took so long that we were concerned you'd lost your way," Faith said.

"You weren't concerned enough to *kumme* look for us," Hannah pointed out.

It was the first thing she'd said during their entire hike. Clearly she wasn't fooled by Faith's remark—it must have been clear to everyone by now that Faith and Jacob had deliberately rushed ahead so they could be alone. Not that Hannah or Noah were in any position to judge. They had done the same kind of thing when they were courting, even if they were more discreet about it.

"*Neh*, but we did wait for you," Faith replied.

"But we're not going to wait much longer—I'm *hungerich*," Jacob complained. "Everybody needs to take off your shoes and socks so we can cross the stream to pick up the trail on the other side."

"Why do we have to cross here? Isn't there some place drier we can walk?" Arleta asked.

"*Neh*. Usually, this *is* the driest spot to cross, but we've had a lot more rain than usual this spring. It doesn't get very deep. Up to your knees at most."

Arleta scrunched up her face. "I'm the shortest one here. The water might get up to *your* knees, but it will be much deeper on me. I'm going to turn around and walk back the way I came."

"That will take forever," Faith warned her. "This is a shortcut. The parking lot is only about ten minutes from here once we cross the stream."

Arleta insisted, "That's okay. I don't mind walking. I'll meet you back there—you don't have to wait for me to start lunch. I brought fried *hinkel.* Noah can get the cooler from the buggy."

It would take a good hour and a half for Arleta to return, and Noah didn't want to wait that long for her to get back. His hope was that they could gobble down their supper and then he and Arleta could be on their way. Besides, since this was Arleta's first time on the trail, she might get lost if she hiked back alone. Noah didn't want to loop back with her, but she was his employee, which in a way made her his responsibility. So he tried to convince her she'd be perfectly safe crossing the stream.

"There are five of us here. We're not going to let you slip and go under, if that's what you're worried about."

"It isn't," she said. "I—I—I just don't want to get my feet and legs wet. I'll get too cold."

"It's not as if it's the middle of winter," Noah argued. If he wasn't mistaken, her forehead was perspiring, so why was she being so unreasonable?

Isaiah, who had already removed his socks and shoes, offered, "I can carry you across, Arleta."

"Oh, *neh*! I can't let you do that," she protested.

"Sure, you can," he countered. "It will be better than walking all the way back, won't it?"

Arleta bit her lip and glanced at the stream. Noah couldn't tell if she was being coquettish—for all he knew, getting Isaiah to carry her had been her plan all along—or if she earnestly was wary about him picking her up. "Oh…okay," she agreed.

Isaiah leaned down and instructed her, "Take hold of my neck." After she did, he wrapped one arm around her back and supported her lower body with the other arm. By this time, Jacob and Faith had already crossed over to the other side and Hannah was midway there. "Grab my shoes and socks, will you?" he called to Noah.

Get them yourself, Noah thought, but he picked the footwear off the rock where Isaiah had set it. He felt irrationally irritated as he watched the strong, tall farmer gently placing Arleta on the embankment on the opposite side of the stream, and when he heard her thank him profusely in return. It made them seem as if they were enamored with each other.

Am I envious? he asked himself. He didn't think so; it wasn't as if *he* were enamored with Arleta. But if she and Isaiah were going to start up a courtship, Noah wished he didn't have to bear witness to it. Just like he wished he wasn't going to have to listen to Jacob carry on about his budding romance with Faith at work the following week. Watching other young people develop relationships with each other didn't make Noah jealous; it made him *sad.* Because it reminded him of the family he'd lost and the family he'd never have.

But that certainly wasn't Arleta's and Isaiah's or Faith's and Jacob's fault. And Noah couldn't hold it against Hannah, either. The night of the fire, she'd kept telling him it was late and he ought to get back home. He was the one who wanted to stay a little longer. To kiss her a little longer… Now, he could hardly stand to look at her because of the regretful memories he experienced when he did. Not that she ever gave him a second look, either. He had broken off their courtship before his family was even buried. And when he did, she hadn't cried, hadn't protested; she'd just remained silent and averted her eyes—just as she'd done while they were hiking—as if she wished he'd disappear…

Recalling that period in his life always made Noah feel glum. After everyone had put their shoes and socks back on again and hurried toward the parking lot, exuberantly discussing the supper they were about to enjoy, he dallied behind them. They took their coolers from the buggies and found a picnic table beneath the pine trees. Fortunately, he was able to sit at the opposite end of the bench from Hannah.

Noah felt so morose by then that he could hardly taste his food, but Isaiah, who was sitting next to him, remarked, "This is the most *appenditlich* potato salad I've ever eaten. And trust me, I know my potatoes. Who made it?"

"I did," Arleta said. "I'm *hallich* you like it."

"Apparently that's not all he likes," Jacob uttered just loud enough for Noah to hear him. "I told you there would be other *manner* interested in courting her. Looks like you lost your chance."

"Absatz," Noah warned him in an equally low voice. "I mean it. Knock it off."

Jacob just chuckled. "Somebody's a sore loser."

Everyone was so hungry from the long hike that they quickly devoured their meal before diving into Arleta's whoopie pies and the bumbleberry pie Hannah had made for dessert.

"Mmm, this is yummy. I can taste that it has strawberries, raspberries, blueberries and… What's the tart taste?"

"Rhubarb," Hannah answered Arleta. "I'd frozen the rest of the fruit from last year's crop, but the rhubarb is fresh from the garden."

"It's amazingly *gut*. Bumbleberry is Noah's *grooss-mammi*'s favorite kind of pie. I've never made one before but I'd really like to. Did you use a special recipe?"

"*Jah*—it's actually Sovilla's. She's the one who taught me how to make this kind of pie in the first place," Hannah replied.

Noah caught his breath, remembering. Hannah hadn't grown up in New Hope; she had moved there when she was about sixteen. Noah's sister, Mary, became fast friends with her and one day, Sovilla offered to disclose her secret ingredient. Noah had been hanging around the kitchen, threatening to listen in unless they promised to give him the biggest slice when the pie was done baking.

That was when he first developed an interest in Hannah, but as he recalled that afternoon now, he didn't remember as much about her as he remembered about his sister. Specifically, that she had literally swept him out the door with a broom! As the only girl in the family, she'd always struggled to keep the boys from intruding on what she considered to be her territory, which included time with her friends. But even when she became annoyed, Noah always felt her affection toward him and he hoped she'd always known how much he loved her, too, despite his teasing.

"I'll ask her for it, then," Arleta suggested. "Maybe one day when her immune system is stronger and the berries are ripe, you could *kumme* over and we could bake a couple of pies together."

Noah felt his stomach twist; but fortunately, Hannah declined, saying, "I don't know when I'd get the time—my *familye* is preparing to open a restaurant and we expect to be very busy, especially once the vacationers arrive for the summer. But I'm sure Sovilla could talk you through the steps, even if she couldn't show you."

Noah breathed a sigh of relief; Hannah seemed to be as averse to the idea of coming to his house as he was to the idea of having her there.

Arleta noticed the brusqueness in Hannah's tone right away. Everyone else in the group had been friendly, but Hannah had hardly spoken a word to her. Was she just a reserved person or was it possible she really was interested in Noah and the two of them were at odds for some reason? They'd seemed absolutely miserable walking together, as if they'd had a spat. Whatever it was about, Hannah couldn't have possibly thought Arleta was interested in Noah after she'd allowed Isaiah to carry her across the stream, could she?

As embarrassed as she'd been by Isaiah's offer and as much as she feared she might have misled him to believe she was flirting with him, Arleta was deeply grateful he'd saved her from having to remove her shoes and socks. She resented it that even a simple thing like going on a hike could potentially result in her secret being revealed. This wasn't like being home, where she knew everyone and every place and she could anticipate situations that might lead to someone discovering her tattoo. Arleta realized that she'd be better off not going hiking again rather than to risk another close call like the one she'd experienced at the edge of the stream.

"If you're done eating, I think we should leave now, Arleta," Noah suggested.

"Why are you running off so soon?" Jacob groused. "We're planning to go to the pond on the other side of the woods."

"*Jah.* Stay a little longer," Faith pleaded.

Arleta sensed the young woman was concerned that if they left, the others might want to go home, too, which would mean her time with Jacob would come to an end for the day. But Arleta was spent, both emotionally and physically, so she replied, "We told Sovilla we wouldn't be gone very long. But it was a lot of *schpass* to meet everyone. *Denki* for inviting me and showing me the gorge."

"I hope we see you again soon, Arleta," Isaiah said. Then, as almost an afterthought he added, "You, too, Noah. It's nice to spend time with you outside of *kurrich.*"

Noah responded with curt goodbyes, and Arleta followed him to the buggy. He was quiet as they headed home, and she wondered if he was upset about whatever was possibly going on between him and Hannah. Regardless of the reason, Arleta got the distinct feeling he regretted going hiking. Sovilla must have noticed his expression when they arrived home, too. After Lovina left and while Noah was out in the barn doing the second milking, she asked Arleta if something upsetting had happened during the hike.

"*N-neh*, nothing in particular," she hedged, reluctant to confide her observation about Hannah and Noah to Sovilla.

Sovilla pressed. "In general, then?"

"*Neh*, in general, we had a nice time," Arleta answered truthfully. Then she quickly redirected the conversation. "The gorge is beautiful—I've never seen anything like it. And Hannah Miller made the most *appenditlich* bumbleberry pie I've ever tasted. She said she used your special recipe. I'd love to make it for you as soon as the berries are ripe for picking."

"Hannah Miller went on the hike?"

Ach. When will I learn that silence is golden? Arleta reluctantly answered, *"Jah."*

"Ah, that would explain it." Sovilla nodded, as if everything made sense.

Now it was Arleta's turn to dig for information. "Explain what?"

"Noah's mood." Sovilla leaned forward. "I probably shouldn't tell you this, but I can trust you not to let on you know, can't I?"

Arleta's curiosity to know what had happened between Hannah and Noah outweighed her guilt about gossiping about them. She nodded. "I won't say a word to anyone."

"I suspect Noah doesn't even know I'm aware of this, but he used to be Hannah's suitor. She was the only *maedel* he courted, as far as I know—and I'm usually right." She adjusted the kerchief on her head and glanced toward the door. "After the fire, he broke it off with her, though. I think he felt like his primary responsibility was to take care of *me*."

Arleta allowed herself a moment to absorb this information. Although she felt a small measure of satisfaction in knowing that she hadn't just imagined the tension between Hannah and Noah, she realized she hadn't exactly interpreted the situation correctly. "And you think she's still upset about him ending their courtship? Or that *he's* still upset about ending it?"

Sovilla shook her head. "What I think might be more likely is that Noah could feel… Well, I suspect being around her might make him realize he passed up the opportunity to get married and start a *familye*. Most of the time I think he's able to suppress those feelings, but whenever he sees Hannah, he has to face the life he could have had. Even catching a glimpse of her at *kurrich* seems to put him in a sour mood."

"But he's so young. He can *still* have a wife and *kinner*," Arleta said. *It's not as if* he *has a tattoo on his ankle and a regrettable past.*

Sovilla sighed, her eyes brimming. "That's what I tell him, but he won't listen. I'm afraid that until I go home to be with the Lord, he's not going to even consider courting anyone. It troubles me deeply to know I'm the reason he isn't pursuing a romantic relationship…"

"That's nonsense!" Arleta was appalled that Sovilla would say such a thing, which seemed akin to suggesting she'd have to die in order for Noah to be happy. "There's no reason he can't start courting someone right now. In fact, there's no reason he—"

She was going to say, "There's no reason he can't court Hannah Miller again if he wants to, provided she'd be willing to give their relationship another try," but Sovilla lifted a finger to her lips as the kitchen door opened. So Arleta excused herself to go to her room, just as Noah came in. She pulled out her stationery to begin her second letter to her sister that week, but instead of writing, she stared out the window, chewing on the tip of her pen. She thought about how remorseful

Sovilla seemed to be that her grandson was apparently putting his responsibility toward her above seeking a relationship that might eventually lead to marriage.

How can I encourage Noah to resume his courtship with Hannah? she wondered. *I'm sure that once she spends a little time around him again, she'll remember what a considerate, kind and responsible man he is. And with a little encouragement, he'll realize that there's no reason he can't be a suitor* and *a dutiful grandson.*

Arleta considered enlisting Sovilla's help in getting them together, but she instantly realized that plan could easily backfire, as Noah would suspect his grandmother was trying to play matchmaker. Then it occurred to Arleta that she was becoming something of a meddlesome matchmaker herself. So she focused on writing a letter to her sister instead. In it, she described the trip she'd taken to the gorge, briefly mentioning that a potato farmer had carried her across the stream. *But don't worry*, she scrawled, *I have no romantic interest in him whatsoever.*

Then, without registering what she was doing, she added, *If I were to become interested in anyone romantically, it would be Noah, not Isaiah.* When she reread the paragraph, Arleta clapped her hand over her mouth. How had that thought crept into her mind and onto the page? Chagrinned, she scribbled it out as quickly as she could and blotted it from her mind, as well.

"Did you have a nice time hiking with your friends?" Sovilla asked Noah when he sat down in the armchair opposite the sofa.

"It was fine."

"Arleta told me Hannah Miller went."

So that was what the two of them were whispering about when I came in. Aware his grandmother was gauging his reaction, Noah responded nonchalantly, "*Jah*, Hannah was there. As well as Faith, Jacob and Isaiah."

"Isaiah Wittmer? Arleta didn't mention he was there, too."

"I'm not surprised," he muttered.

"Why? Didn't the two of them get along?"

"Oh, they got along all right…he carried her across a stream." As soon as the words were out of Noah's mouth, he realized that in an effort to distract his grandmother from drilling him about Hannah, he'd sacrificed Arleta's privacy. He felt a twinge of guilt, knowing his grandmother would ask her all sorts of nosy questions she'd be too polite not to answer. *That's not really* my *fault*, he tried to assure himself. *If she didn't want anyone commenting on her behavior, she shouldn't have been so finicky about crossing the stream like everyone else.*

"Why would he do something like that?"

Because he likes *her, obviously.* Noah was surprised his grandmother didn't leap to this conclusion herself, but he was too embarrassed to spell it out for her. "She was afraid to cross it and she wanted to turn around and walk all the way back the way we came."

"Then why didn't *you* help her?" Sovilla asked. She was giving him the same look she'd given him when he'd asked Arleta if her socks were clean. "I can understand if you didn't want to carry her across yourself, but you should have at least walked back with her if that's what made her feel more comfortable. You ought to be more responsible, Noah. She's our guest."

Neh, *she's our employee*, he silently argued. "Isaiah seemed eager to carry her and Arleta didn't appear to mind, either."

Sovilla exhaled heavily, her shoulders drooping. "I warned you to keep an eye out for her, didn't I?"

"But, *Groossmammi*, nothing happened. She's fine. She didn't so much as get her toes wet."

"*Jah*, thanks to Isaiah Wittmer."

That's when Noah finally caught on: his grandmother didn't want Isaiah to take an interest in Arleta. *I think it may be too late for that. But why would she care anyway?* Was it because she was harboring a hope that *Noah* would want to court Arleta? *If that's what she's thinking, then* Groossmammi *is bound to be disappointed, because I'm not any more likely to become Arleta's suitor than I am to start courting Hannah Miller again.*

He was about to say something to that effect, but his grandmother looked so crestfallen already that he didn't want to upset her further. So instead, he offered to fix her a cup of tea. Then, the two of them chatted and played a couple of games of checkers, which was how he wished he'd spent the afternoon in the first place.

Chapter Five

In the weeks following the outing to the gorge, Arleta noticed a small but definite improvement in Sovilla's energy level. She was still taking naps a couple of times a day, but they were getting shorter and she was able to stroll to the end of the lane daily, arm in arm with Arleta to pick up the mail. Her appetite was improving, too, which made Arleta happy since she'd checked several cookbooks out of the library to supplement the recipes she'd been using from Sovilla's recipe box in an attempt to prepare a wider variety of healthy meals.

Although Sovilla had two more months to wait before being retested for cancer, she saw her local doctor for a routine visit and the doctor was extremely pleased with the improvements in her overall recovery so far. She cautioned Sovilla to continue avoiding anyone who was ill and to keep wearing a mask while attending large gatherings, like church. But she lifted the restriction on visiting households with small children, which was the majority of Amish families in New Hope.

"Let's stop at the Bawells' *haus*," Sovilla excitedly

suggested on the way home. "Lovina's been praying faithfully for me and I want to tell her the *gut* news."

Arleta hesitated. "It's almost four o'clock. Don't you think we should go straight home so I can prepare supper?"

"There's no rush. We had a late lunch, and Noah hasn't been getting home until almost seven thirty or eight o'clock."

It was true; he had developed a routine of going from working with his crew directly to working on extra individual projects by himself. Arleta usually packed him enough food to last through the day. Depending on what time he came home and whether he was hungry still, in the evenings she'd warm up leftovers of whatever supper she'd made for Sovilla and herself.

But since he'd gotten a ride from Mike today so Arleta could use the buggy to take Sovilla to her appointment, she knew he'd have to be dropped off at home to take the buggy to his second worksite. She figured he'd probably want a quick supper before he left again. But Arleta didn't want to dampen Sovilla's joyfulness, so she redirected the horse toward Lovina's house for a brief visit.

As they turned into the dirt driveway, they spotted Lovina's grandchildren rolling down a small hill on the side of the house. It reminded Arleta of when she was young, and it made her miss her family. Although she enjoyed being with Sovilla and felt she was overpaid to do such light work, Arleta still was having difficulty adjusting to being so isolated. *Maybe now that Sovilla is stronger, Noah will relax a little and we can have company more frequently*, she thought.

"Look at how *schnuck* they are," Sovilla remarked

with a sigh. "I wonder if the Lord will ever bless me with *kinskinner*."

Not if Noah keeps up the same work schedule, Arleta thought, pulling up beside the hitching post by the Bawells' barn. After the hike to the gorge, she'd hoped her presence with Sovilla might free Noah up to do a little more socializing on the weekends—especially with Hannah. But he worked from eight o'clock in the morning until almost eight at night on Saturdays. And he was usually so tired from putting in such long hours during the week that all he wanted to do after worship services on Sunday was take a nap and play an occasional game of spades. *At this rate, Lovina's* kinskinner *will be courting before Noah is*, Arleta mused.

"Sovilla and Arleta, what a *wunderbaar* surprise," Lovina exclaimed a few minutes later when they came up the walkway. She'd been sweeping the porch but she set aside her broom to welcome them as Arleta assisted Sovilla up the steps. After taking a seat in the wooden glider, Sovilla told Lovina what the doctor had said about her health. Lovina tucked her chin to her chest and thanked the Lord aloud before settling onto the bench beside her friend.

Just then, three young women came out of the house. Arleta knew Hannah Miller and she'd met Lovina's daughter-in-law, Ruth, at church. The third woman introduced herself as Ruth's daughter Honor, who had been out of town for several weeks. She poured everyone a glass of meadow tea—a sweetened, chilled drink made from water and brewed mint—with lemon slices.

The young women were gleeful to hear about the improvement in Sovilla's health. In turn, she asked after Hannah's parents—her mother was ill—and Ruth's children before the conversation turned to gardening and canning. Hannah mentioned what a plentiful rhubarb crop her family had that spring, adding, "It's *gut* that we've harvested most of it already, since it doesn't thrive in hot weather."

"*I* don't thrive in hot weather, either." Honor fanned her face with her hand. "I don't know how you can stand to wear stockings and shoes, Arleta."

Arleta quickly scanned the other women's feet, realizing none of them was wearing shoes except for Sovilla, and hers were slide-on sandals. "I'm really used to them, so they don't bother me," she answered honestly. Then she quickly changed the subject, asking Honor about her visit to her sister and brother-in-law's house in Ohio.

Honor explained that her eldest sister, Eve, was almost fifteen years older than she was and she'd just delivered her sixth child, so she needed additional help running her household. "My niece Katie is sixteen now so she's finished with *schul*, but she's working out as a nanny, so she's not able to help my *schweschder* with her littler ones."

Lovina clucked her tongue and abashedly explained to the other women, "I know what you're thinking—it's a shame that Katie is taking care of an *Englischer*'s *kinner* instead of helping her *mamm* by watching her own *brieder* and *schweschdere.* Unfortunately, after last year's setback with the barley crop, money is tight in their *familye.* And there aren't many opportunities for *meed* to earn an income where my *dochder* lives. Still, I told Eve she may regret allowing her *dochder* to be yoked to an *Englisch* employer, especially because she's still on *rumspringa* and hasn't been baptized into the *kurrich* yet. The temptations of the world can be overwhelming to deny, especially when a young person comes into contact with them every day."

"*Gott* willing, the *maedel* will hold fast to her upbringing," Sovilla said, comforting her. "Arleta worked out when she was on her *rumspringa*, and she didn't stray from her faith."

Heat rose in Arleta's face. One day when she'd been cleaning the windows, she offhandedly let it slip to Sovilla that her *Englisch* employer had wanted her to use an expensive "green" cleaning solution on the sliding glass doors, but Arleta thought hot water and vinegar were even more effective. They'd had a brief discussion about Arleta's role as the Fairfaxes' housekeeper, but she wished Sovilla hadn't mentioned it in front of the other women, since most Amish people she knew didn't look favorably on Amish youth working out. And she especially wished Sovilla hadn't used her as an example of someone who had been faithful to her Amish beliefs. *If she only knew what I was really like and what I'd been close to doing, she wouldn't be so quick to soothe Lovina's qualms*, she thought.

"When I was at Eve's *haus*, I heard Katie tell her younger *schweschdere* about a handheld vacuum cleaner she used to clean up after the *Englisch kinner* made a mess with crackers," Honor confided in disgust. "It's a shame how she's filling their minds with images of conveniences that might make them envious of the *Englisch* lifestyle."

As the other women expressed their disapproval, Arleta looked intently at the glass she held on her lap. Whoever had made the tea hadn't strained it properly and the drink was speckled with mint leaves. She focused on the little flecks to keep herself from tearing up. She understood why the women were critical of allowing a sixteen-year-old girl to work full-time in an *Englischer*'s home. And she would certainly do her best to dissuade her parents from ever allowing Leanna to work in an *Englischer*'s house if the possibility arose in the future. But a little part of her wanted to ask, *Even if you haven't been tempted by the* Englisch *lifestyle, haven't any of you ever made choices or done things in violation of your faith? Or am I the only one?*

"Arleta?" Sovilla interrupted her thoughts. All eyes were on her. "Ruth asked if you want more tea."

"*Denki*, but no," she replied. "I'm sorry. I was just thinking of my little *schweschder*, Leanna."

"You must miss her," Honor said. "You ought to *kumme* to our work frolic tomorrow morning. Tell her about it, Hannah."

Hannah hesitated before explaining, "Because my *mamm* has been ill, I need help cleaning the restaurant before my *brieder* can move the new tables and chairs in. The last owners left the place in a mess. Honor said she'd help and Faith Smoker will be there, too."

Hannah's comments weren't exactly an invitation to participate. Not that it mattered, since Arleta couldn't leave Sovilla alone for that long, anyway. But it stung a little that she didn't even ask; she hadn't seemed any friendlier toward Arleta today than she had the day they went hiking. Arleta sipped her tea and then discreetly pinched a piece of mint from her tongue and wiped her fingers on her apron.

"You should *kumme*, Arleta," Honor repeated. "Jacob and Isaiah are going to be there helping Hannah's *breider* repaint the walls. Instead of bringing our lunches, we're ordering pizza and I'm bringing peach *kuchen* for dessert."

Sovilla echoed, "*Jah*, you should go, Arleta."

"I'd like to, but Noah won't be home," she protested, knowing he'd object to his grandmother being left alone for the day. To the others, she explained, "He's trying to catch up with a backlog of customers, so he's been working on *Samschdaag* lately."

"All the more reason to go," Sovilla insisted. "You need to get out and enjoy being with your friends, and I need to stay in and enjoy being by myself."

Even though she knew the older woman hadn't intended to hurt her feelings, Arleta's eyes smarted. "I'd be *hallich* to help," she said feebly to Hannah.

"*Gut.* I'd appreciate it," the young woman replied, although Arleta couldn't help but think her pinched expression told a different story.

It had been a long day, and every muscle in Noah's body ached. The crew had been putting in even longer hours than usual this week because they were coming up on a deadline, and Jacob had been out sick on Monday and Tuesday. Ordinarily, Noah would have been concerned about catching Jacob's illness and bringing it home to his grandmother, but he doubted the teenager was truly sick. Instead, he guessed he was run-down from courting Faith on the weekends. Although Noah's parents had been strict about his curfew, he knew many Amish youth who stayed out until one or two o'clock on Saturday and Sunday evenings when they were courting. It seemed unlikely that Jacob's aunts would have imposed a curfew on him, so as the men were dispersing on Friday afternoon, Noah casually remarked, "I hope you're not going to stay out too late this weekend, Jacob."

"It depends on how much *schpass* I'm having," the teenager replied, grinning. Clearly, he wasn't taking the hint seriously, so Noah tried again.

"You have a responsibility to your crew, and we all have a responsibility to our customers," he reminded him. "It's important we honor *Gott* and demonstrate our beliefs to the *Englisch* by working hard and keeping our commitments."

"It's also important we honor *Gott* and demonstrate our beliefs by not valuing earning money above spending time with our *familye* and community," Jacob countered.

Noah immediately understood what he was implying. *It might look like I'm motivated by greed, but he has no idea why I'm trying to earn money. It's for my* familye, he rationalized as he rode home with Mike in silence. He suspected that Jacob was just trying to distract him from the teenager's own behavior, but the comment still troubled him. Did Noah's district see him the same way Jacob did? Did the *Englisch* community see him that way, too? He was tempted to ask Mike his opinion, but he decided against it. *The Lord knows the intentions of my heart. He's the only one I need to please.*

It was a little after six o'clock when his coworker dropped him off. Hungry for supper and eager to hear what the doctor had said, he briskly strode into the house, but he found it empty. Arleta and Sovilla definitely should have been home by now. His first thought was that the doctor had noticed something alarming in regard to his grandmother's health and she'd been sent to the hospital. He immediately bowed his head and asked the Lord to protect and heal her—but even before he opened his eyes, he heard the clip-clopping of the horse's hooves coming up the lane.

"*Groossmammi*, are you okay?" he asked after he'd rushed outside to the buggy to help her down.

"I'm *gut*. I'll tell you all about it as soon as we're inside." Sovilla took hold of his arm for balance, but Noah had been so concerned something was wrong with her that *his* legs felt shaky as they made their way to the door.

While he was thrilled when his grandmother said the doctor was encouraged by her progress, he was less than happy that Sovilla had celebrated by socializing with several women from different households all at once. He wished Arleta had exercised better judgment than to bring her to a gathering the very afternoon she'd received an encouraging health report. He hoped she wasn't going to abandon all of the guidelines he'd made concerning his grandmother's well-being.

His displeasure must have shown on his face because Sovilla quickly added, "We only intended to stay for a few minutes, but it felt so *normal* to sit out on the porch, visiting with a group of *weibsleit* again that I didn't want to leave. Poor Arleta practically had to drag me away—she wanted to get home to cook your supper."

"That would have been nice, but I don't have time to wait until it's prepared." Noah directed his comment to Arleta, who was rushing around the kitchen, washing vegetables and pulling pots from the cupboard.

"It will only take a few minutes," she blithely assured him. "Besides, where's the fire?"

Although he knew it was only a figure of speech meaning *what's the hurry*, Noah felt his stomach cramp into a knot and his appetite completely left him. He nervously muttered, "I—I have to finish installing a roof for a *familye* over at the Grandview Estates. If you can believe it, it's for their *dochder*'s playhouse."

"Oh, I can believe the *Englisch* would spend that kind of money on a roof for their *dochder*'s *haus*," Sovilla said. "But what I can't believe is that you'd rush off to install it for them instead of enjoying one of Arleta's *appenditlich* meals with us. This is a time for rejoicing together, isn't it?"

"*Jah*, you're right, it is," Noah begrudgingly agreed. Even though he no longer felt like eating, he supposed he could spare a few minutes—and spare himself an argument with his grandmother—to sit down to supper with them.

Fortunately, Arleta fixed a light meal that was comprised almost exclusively of vegetables. After giving thanks for the food, as well as for his grandmother's improved health, Noah stuck his fork into a spear of asparagus and lifted it to his mouth. It was unusually tender; his grandmother's steamed asparagus was always so reedy he felt like a cow chewing its cud whenever he ate it, but Arleta had gotten this just right. He could feel his appetite kicking in again, and he downed his meal quickly before rising to leave.

He was halfway to the Grandview Estates when a loud crack of thunder sounded overhead, followed by a brilliant sequence of lightning. He turned around and managed to get the horse into the stable, unhitch the buggy and make it to the porch before the sky let loose a torrential downpour.

"Sovilla went to bed already. I think she was worn out from all the excitement about what her *dokder* said,"

Arleta told him when he came into the kitchen where she was drying the last of the supper dishes.

"*Jah.* And from all the gallivanting around. Tomorrow it might be better if she's not with so many people," he suggested pointedly as he untied his laces and slid his boots off.

"Don't worry. She wants to stay in alone. And I'll even be at a work frolic in the morning."

"You're leaving her by herself?"

"*Jah.* She said she'll be fine. I'll only be gone a few hours—I don't intend to stay as long as everyone else does. I'll *kumme* home after lunch."

"Where is the frolic?"

"It's at the Millers' new restaurant. We'll be preparing it for opening day." Arleta stood on her tiptoes to put a plate into the cupboard. Over her shoulder, she said, "It's too bad you can't *kumme.* We're getting pizza delivered and Honor's making peach *kuchen*—although considering how you feel about her cooking, that might not be much of an enticement."

Noah wasn't in the mood for kidding around. *Why is Arleta going to a work frolic when she knows how I feel about* Groossmammi *being left alone?*

"I appreciate it that you want to socialize and contribute to the needs of our district, but I'm not paying you to help the Millers with their restaurant. I'm paying you to help my *groossmammi* during her recovery," he said.

Arleta closed the cupboard door and turned to face him. Her voice quavering, she replied, "Your *groossmammi* was the one who insisted I go to the work frolic. I tried to tell her I didn't think that was a *gut* idea, but she said she wanted time alone in the *haus.* If you'd prefer I don't go, that's fine with me. However, I'd appreciate it if you'd tell Sovilla why you want me to stay home, since I don't feel comfortable arguing with her about it." Arleta hung the dish towel on its hook and turned on her heel.

After she disappeared down the hallway, Noah plunked onto a chair with a groan. The only thing that ached more than his muscles was his head, and he rubbed his temples in big, slow circles with his palms. *I'm sorry if I hurt her feelings, but I'm not sorry I made myself clear*, he thought. *Because even if it was at* Groossmammi's *request this time, I don't want Arleta to get any ideas that this can be a common occurrence in the future.*

Yet two hours later, when his conscience kept him from sleeping even though he was physically depleted, Noah had to admit to himself how rude—how *wrong*—he'd been to speak to Arleta like he had. *I know better than anyone how insistent* Groossmammi *can be*, he acknowledged. *It must be difficult for someone as forbearing as Arleta to resist her wishes when she wants to go somewhere—or when she wants* Arleta *to go somewhere.*

Noah was ashamed for acting as if Arleta didn't prioritize caring for Sovilla, when he knew full well how diligent she'd been about keeping the house as germ-free as possible and fixing healthy meals for her. *If it weren't for Arleta,* Groossmammi *may not have received such a* gut *report from her* dokder *today*, he told himself. *I need to apologize to her first thing tomorrow morning.*

But the next day she wasn't in the kitchen when he passed through it on his way to go outside to the barn. And by the time he came in from milking the cow, Sovilla was up, too, which meant he didn't have privacy to speak to Arleta alone.

"Guder mariye," he cheerfully greeted them as he removed his boots. "It looks like it might rain." Then, by way of telling Arleta he'd changed his mind about her going to the work frolic, he said, "I can give you a ride to the Millers' restaurant on my way to work, Arleta."

In the instant when she briefly glanced his way, he noticed her eyes were red-rimmed. Had she been crying? "*Denki*, but we're not meeting until nine o'clock. I know you're probably eager to get going right away since you couldn't work last night."

It was true that he'd suffered a setback because of the thunderstorm, but apologizing to Arleta suddenly seemed a lot more important than finishing the playhouse before noon, which was his self-imposed deadline. "That's okay. I don't mind waiting. We can go whenever you're ready."

"What a treat—to have you linger over breakfast," his grandmother responded earnestly, although Arleta didn't look quite as pleased.

She seemed even more reserved when she got into the buggy and they started out toward the Millers' restaurant. As eager as Noah was to apologize, Arleta's quietness unnerved him, and he struggled to come up with the right words to express how much he regretted saying the things he'd said the previous evening.

However, about a mile down the road, she broke the silence by saying, "I want you to know that I understand why you don't think it's fair to pay me when I'm not spending time with your *groossmammi.* And I hope you'll deduct today's wages from my salary for the week."

"What?" Had Noah really come across as being *that* concerned about money? Then he remembered what he'd said about how he wasn't paying Arleta to help with the Millers' restaurant. He turned to look at her. She had twisted her head to the side, gazing out over the meadow to her right, so that he only could see her ear and a part of her cheek. "I didn't mean what I said last night the way it came out."

"*Neh*, it's okay. It makes sense that you shouldn't pay me if I'm not actually doing what you hired me to do," she said softly. "And it makes sense that the timing is probably right for you to hire a different caregiver, too."

"What?" Noah asked again, even more appalled than when Arleta suggested he reduce her pay for the week. "You want to leave?"

Arleta didn't *want* to leave, for several reasons. First, she'd grown very fond of Sovilla and Noah. But even if she hadn't liked them so much, she had made a commitment and she believed she ought to honor it. Second, she needed the money if she ever hoped to have her tattoo removed. However, she'd tossed and turned all night ruminating over Sovilla's and Noah's remarks. And in the wee hours of the morning she'd come to the decision that—as disappointing as it would be—if they wanted her to leave, she'd make her departure as easy and amicable for them as she could.

"Your *groossmammi* is tiring of me—that's why she wanted me to go to the frolic. She said she wanted to be alone. And if I'm not at the *haus*, I can't be of any help to her, which means you're wasting your money paying me," Arleta explained, to show she'd taken his perspective into consideration. "Besides, her health is improving now and you probably don't need someone here full time."

"Whoa!" Noah commanded the horse to stop on the shoulder of the road. He pushed his hat back and peered intently at Arleta. "I'm sorry that what I said last night didn't reflect the depth of my appreciation for all that you've done. But I consider your presence in our home to be a gift from *Gott.* It's invaluable. Please don't leave because of something *dumm* I said that I didn't mean. I was overly tired and irritated at—at one of my coworkers and...well, there's no excuse. Please just forgive me—and don't leave."

Hearing Noah's compliment made Arleta feel as if she'd just swallowed a cupful of sunshine; it filled her with warmth from her cheeks to her toes. But as much as she treasured his words, she doubted Sovilla felt the same way. "I've enjoyed being at your *haus*, too. But your *groossmammi*—"

"She said something she didn't mean, too. Or she didn't mean it the way you took it. If I know my *groossmammi* as well as I think I do, she felt like you should go out and socialize once in a while instead of staying with her all the time. But she knew you'd resist it if she said that, so she turned the tables and claimed she wanted the *haus* to herself for a while."

That thought *had* occurred to Arleta, too. "*Jah*, perhaps."

"I'm sure of it. I can talk to her about it when—"

"*Neh*, please don't. I don't want to turn a molehill into a mountain." Arleta realized she should have spoken with Noah before jumping to the conclusion that neither he nor Sovilla wanted her to stay. But she'd been so homesick yesterday, and she'd felt even more alone after she'd listened to the other women implying how disgraceful it was for a young woman to work out. Hannah's lukewarm invitation to the frolic contributed to her loneliness, too. So by the time Sovilla and Noah made their remarks, Arleta already felt as if no one truly wanted her around and she jumped to the conclusion they would have preferred to employ someone else. She felt too silly to explain all of that to Noah now, so she simply said, "I shouldn't have been so sensitive."

"*Neh.* My *groossmammi* and I shouldn't have been so *in*sensitive." Noah's chocolate-colored eyes conveyed the sincerity of his words. "It can't be easy trying to please both of us at the same time."

Arleta laughed. Since she couldn't deny it, she said, "It might not always be easy, but it's always interesting."

"Interesting enough to stay for the rest of the summer?"

"*Jah*, of course. I'm *hallich* you haven't changed your mind."

"About you leaving New Hope? *Neh!*" he exclaimed. "But I have changed my mind about you leaving my *groossmammi* alone on occasion. *Not* because I think she's tiring of you, but because I think she's right. You need a little time away from the *haus—and* from the two of us."

"*Neh*, that's not necess—"

"It *is* necessary. It will be *gut* for you. And as long as my *groossmammi* feels okay, it will be *gut* for her, too. She never had anyone stay with her before she was ill, so I think being alone on occasion will help her feel as if things are a little more normal again. Kind of like what she said about visiting with Lovina and the others yesterday. Okay?" He looked expectantly at Arleta.

She nodded. "Okay. *Denki*."

"You're *wilkom*." He clicked his tongue and lifted the reins, urging the horse back onto the road. Although he was directing his gaze forward, his profile creased with a grin as he asked, "So, are you really going to be brave enough to try Honor's *kuchen*?"

"I don't think so," Arleta admitted. "I nearly choked on her meadow tea yesterday."

"Too much sugar?"

"Too many mint leaves! I wasn't sure if I was drinking meadow tea or celery soup." She laughed and Noah did, too. "But her cooking aside, I really do like her. She's been very welcoming to me." *Unlike Hannah*, Arleta thought ruefully.

They pulled into the restaurant's driveway next to a hitched horse and buggy she didn't recognize. When she climbed down, she noticed Isaiah crossing the driveway in their direction. He gave them both a big smile. "I didn't know you two were coming to help today."

"Noah's not staying," Arleta explained. "He's got to go to work."

"Cleaning and painting a restaurant isn't work?"

"*Neh*, I meant he's got to work for money. Not for *schpass*."

"I'm supposed to be working on the farm today, too, but I convinced my *daed* that it's more important that I give my friends a hand this morning," Isaiah said. Then he joked, "After all, the potatoes will still be there this afternoon—but the pizza won't still be *here*."

As Arleta chuckled, Noah unexpectedly volunteered, "I might *kumme* back later to help out, too."

Aware that the frolic might be the perfect opportunity for Noah to renew his romance with Hannah,

Arleta knew she should encourage him to return. But instead she heard herself saying, "Don't trouble yourself, Noah. Everyone knows you've got a lot of customers to serve. The Millers have plenty of people here to help already. We'll be fine."

Noah tried not to feel affronted by Arleta's comment, but as he headed toward Grandview Estates, he brooded over what she meant by, "Everyone knows you've got a lot of customers to serve." *Is she implying that everyone thinks I've been serving the* Englisch *instead of serving* Gott *and my* kurrich*?* he wondered. But that didn't seem like something she'd say; *Jacob* might, but Arleta wouldn't. Maybe she just didn't want him to feel guilty if he couldn't return later to help because he got too caught up in whatever project he was working on.

Then another thought occurred to him: maybe she didn't *want* him to return later to help. If that was the case, he had a pretty good idea of what the reason was—she wanted to spend time with Isaiah without Noah noticing they were romantically interested in each other. Which would have been hard to miss since Isaiah had practically tripped over his own feet crossing the parking lot to greet her. But even if that wasn't the reason—even if she just wanted to be on her own with her peer group for a while—Noah knew it wasn't any of his business.

All that matters is that Arleta and I are on gut *terms with each other again and that she has no intention of leaving,* he told himself. *I encouraged her to take time away from* Groossmammi *and me and now I need to let her do just that.*

But the harder he tried to put the matter out of his

mind, the more he thought about it. When he'd told Arleta she should feel free to get away to socialize on occasion, he'd envisioned her participating in a work frolic with her female friends. Or a quilting bee. A sister day. He hadn't imagined she'd be hanging out and eating pizza with Isaiah.

For the first time since…well, the first time in years, Noah wished *he* could be hanging out and eating pizza with other single people around his age, too, instead of working alone. In fact, his desire to be with his peer group—with Arleta in particular—even outweighed his awkwardness at seeing Hannah again. So when another thunderstorm broke out shortly after noon, forcing him to postpone completing the installation a second time, he decided he'd go lend a hand at the Millers' restaurant.

When he entered the building some twenty minutes later, Noah spotted Faith, Honor and Hannah mopping up the floor while Hannah's brothers were both standing on chairs by the window, apparently trying to manage a leak in the roof. Unsurprisingly to Noah, Jacob was sitting on a tabletop, swinging his legs and eating a slice of pizza. "What are you doing here?" he asked after Noah greeted everyone.

"I came to help. I can't stay too long because I don't want to leave my *groossmammi* alone all day, but I can put in a couple of hours of work," he offered. "Where's Arleta?"

"She got a ride home with Isaiah. You just missed her."

"But you're just in time to help us repair this wall," one of Hannah's brothers said. "Have a slice of pizza and then grab your toolbox and any roofing materials you have in your buggy."

"Sorry," Jacob mumbled, his mouth full. "This was the last piece. But there's plenty of *kuchen* left. Have some of that." He shot Noah a mischievous look.

"*Jah*, you can have a really big slice. I'll cut it for you," Honor offered, wiping her hands on her apron and walking over to serve him pie.

Deep down, Noah knew his primary intention in coming there wasn't to help—it was to interfere with Arleta and Isaiah becoming too friendly with each other. So when Honor handed him a plate, he thanked her and accepted what was probably an unsavory confection, figuring he was getting exactly what he deserved.

Chapter Six

When Isaiah dropped her off half an hour earlier, Arleta had discovered Sovilla asleep on the sofa. But now, as she passed through the living room with a basket of wet laundry that she hadn't been able to remove from the clothesline until the rain let up a little, the older woman's eyes fluttered open.

"Hi, Sovilla. Are you feeling okay?"

Sovilla adjusted her headscarf and pushed herself into an upright position. "I'm fine. I didn't plan on dozing off, though. *Kumme*, sit down and tell me all about your morning."

"I will, just as soon as I hang these clothes in the basement," Arleta replied.

"*Gut*. I'll fix us a cup of tea."

As Arleta wrung out the clothes and placed the wet dresses on hangers and clipped the socks, shirts and trousers to the rope strung in the basement, two things occurred to her. The first was that when she arrived here, Sovilla didn't have the strength to perform a simple task such as putting a kettle on for tea, like she did now. It was another small but important change. The

Englisch doctor had looked at blood counts and X-rays to determine how well she was recovering, but Arleta was more impressed that she could now navigate around her kitchen unassisted again—an especially significant milestone for an Amish woman. Sovilla might not have been able to prepare meals quite yet, but she seemed well on her way.

The second thing that struck her was how eager Sovilla seemed to chat with her, which made Arleta wonder if she'd only been napping to pass the time while she was alone. *I hope she wasn't too restless*, Arleta thought.

In any case, nothing about her demeanor now indicated that she'd been *glad* to get rid of Arleta for a few hours. Quite the opposite; she seemed glad to have her home again. *I don't know how I could have thought she was tiring of me—at least not to the point of wanting me to leave permanently*, Arleta mused once again. Furthermore, she recognized that even if Sovilla *had* needed a little time to herself, she shouldn't have taken it personally. After all, Arleta felt better for having gotten out of the house, too, just as Noah had implied would be the case. She hurried upstairs to tell Sovilla all about the work frolic, including who was there, what they did and what the restaurant looked like inside.

"So did Honor give you a ride home or did Faith?"

"Actually, neither of them did. Isaiah brought me home, since he had work he needed to do on the farm."

"In the rain?" Sovilla raised an eyebrow.

Nothing gets past her. Arleta had also been leery of Isaiah's claim that he was needed on the farm—or at least, that he had urgent work to do in the fields. She suspected the same thing Sovilla clearly did: that he'd been making up an excuse because he wanted to be alone with Arleta. Ordinarily she would have declined the ride and waited until the skies cleared before she walked home, since she didn't want to give him the impression that she reciprocated his interest. But to be honest, she was eager to get back.

For one thing, she was growing wary of Hannah's distinct unfriendliness toward her. She didn't treat anyone else that way. While Arleta appreciated that Hannah didn't know her nearly as well as she knew the others, she thought that should have been all the more reason for Hannah to be inclusive toward her. If the shoe were on the other foot and Hannah were the newcomer, Arleta would have gone out of her way to make her feel welcome. Instead, every time she spoke to her, Hannah replied curtly. After a while, Arleta gave up making the effort.

The other reason she was eager to get back to the house was because she'd had such a good conversation with Noah earlier that morning, and she figured once it started to rain, he'd have to return home early, too. She was hoping after their Saturday chores were done, he'd want to visit with her and his grandmother. Maybe the trio would play a game, although just having an unhurried conversation together would have been a treat.

"I wonder what's keeping Noah," she remarked, glancing out the window as she thought about him now.

"He probably waited out the storm in his buggy and now that the rain's let up, he's back to work again." Sovilla leaned forward in her chair and wagged a finger at Arleta. "But don't change the subject. You were telling me about Isaiah giving you a ride home..."

Arleta understood what kind of information she was fishing for, so she pointedly stated, "There isn't really anything more to say about that. Isaiah is a nice *mann*—he reminds me of my *brieder*." She must have gotten her point across that she wasn't interested in him romantically because Sovilla relaxed against the cushion and took another sip of tea, a self-satisfied smile on her lips.

"When does the restaurant open?"

"It opens to the public in two weeks from *Muundaag*. But the Millers are hosting a potluck for the entire *kurrich* two weeks from today as a celebration." She told Sovilla that the family intended to have a time of prayer, asking the Lord to bless their business and their customers, followed by supper. Then they'd sing and roast marshmallows in the large outdoor firepit by the pond on the land behind the building.

"*Wunderbaar*. What do you want to make to bring?" Sovilla asked.

Arleta understood why Noah's grandmother wanted to attend—having just been released from near isolation, she undoubtedly was eager to socialize with her community in a festive environment again. But Hannah's chilliness toward Arleta made her wish *she* didn't have to accompany Sovilla to the event. *It will be different with the entire* kurrich *there—even if Hannah doesn't want to talk to me, there will be plenty of other people who will*, she reminded herself. *Besides, Sovilla will be there.*

She wondered if there was any chance Noah would show up at the potluck when he was done with his side projects for the day. Again, she felt a twinge of conscience, because she kind of hoped he wouldn't, since she had lost all her enthusiasm for helping him rekindle his romance with Hannah.

I just don't think she'd be a gut *match for him*, she

reflected. Actually, Arleta couldn't really picture him with Honor, either. Nor with any of the women she'd met at church. *But there's always the possibility someone will have a single female relative his age visiting New Hope, and if that were to happen, Sovilla would jump at the opportunity to push them together*, she speculated.

The idea filled her with melancholy, which in turn filled her with shame. Sovilla dearly wanted her grandson to live a full life, a life that included the joy of having a family of his own. And Arleta cared about Sovilla and Noah, and wanted God's best for both of them. So then, why did she suddenly have such a stingy attitude about him meeting someone at the potluck? It wasn't as if Arleta was *jealous* that Noah could enter into a courtship and she couldn't, was it?

Where is *he, anyway?* she wondered. It was raining harder now and there was lightning, too. It seemed unlikely that Noah would continue working during such inclement weather. Besides, Arleta had been so upset last night that she'd forgotten to pack him a lunch, the way she usually did. If for no other reason, it seemed he would have hurried home to eat.

I know what I'll do—I'll make beef casserole for supper, since that's his favorite and he'll be famished. Even though Sovilla insisted smells no longer bothered her the way they used to, Arleta opened the front door to let the fresh air in as she chopped the onions. She intended to have all of the ingredients ready so she could put the casserole together the minute he got home; because of his work schedule, he'd eaten so many reheated leftovers that for once she wanted him to have a meal straight from the oven. Once she'd prepped everything for the casserole, she decided to make a batch of oatmeal raisin cookies, too, since Noah had once mentioned how much he liked those.

"We're not sticking to a strictly healthy meal plan tonight," she apologetically told Sovilla.

"Am I ever *hallich* to hear that," Sovilla uttered. "I've almost forgotten what dessert tastes like."

Arleta giggled. "It hasn't been *that* long since I've made a treat, has it?"

"*Neh*, I suppose not. But you reminded me to tell you when I got a craving for bumbleberry pie…and I think the time has *kumme*."

"*Jah*, I'll make you one as soon as the berries are in season. For now, these cookies will have to tide you over."

"Just don't let Noah see where you keep them or they'll be gone faster than you can say *schnickelfritz*."

"It's okay. I'll hide the cookie jar in the bottom cupboard. He'll never look there—he's too tall."

But Sovilla needn't have worried; Noah still hadn't arrived after the cookies had cooled and been put away and he didn't show up for supper, either. In fact, he didn't come through the door until his usual time, eight o'clock.

"We were beginning to worry that you'd floated downstream," Sovilla joked, referring to the day's deluge.

"You must be *hungerich*. I've kept your meal warming in the oven. I'll fix a plate for you," Arleta said, eager to surprise him with his favorite foods.

"*Denki*, but I already ate. I'm stuffed." He hung his wet hat on a peg by the door.

"The *Englischers* at Grandview Estates invited you to supper?" Sovilla sounded incredulous, as if the notion of Noah dining with *Englischers* was absurd. Which struck Arleta as strange, considering he ate side by side with Mike Hall every day. He accepted rides in his truck a couple times a week, too. Sometimes it seemed to her that Amish people had double standards regarding their associations with *Englischers*.

"*Neh.* I ate at the Millers' *haus.* Hannah made beef casserole."

"What a coincidence—that's what Arleta made, too," Sovilla said with a chuckle.

But Arleta didn't find it funny; she found it disappointing. Not just that her surprise was ruined, but that Noah had gone to Hannah's house in the first place. She didn't want to appear overly nosy, so she couldn't ask him outright why he'd visited her. Fortunately, however, Sovilla had no compunction about questioning him. "How did you wind up at the Millers'? They don't live anywhere near Grandview Estates."

"I—I—I—" Noah stuttered and his ears turned deep crimson; if he was trying to hide how embarrassed he was, his body language was giving him away. "I had to quit working on the playhouse because of the storm, so I went to the restaurant to pitch in. There was a leak in the roof so I helped the Miller *buwe* repair it. But we kept having to stop and *kumme* back inside because of the lightning and rain. Eventually everyone except for Jonathan Miller and me went home. Since his *brieder* and Hannah left him without a buggy, once we were finished I gave him a ride back to their *haus* and their *mamm* insisted I stay for supper."

Arleta immediately suspected it was Hannah, not her mother, who really wanted Noah to stay for supper. Without thinking, she blurted out, "Hannah told us her *mamm* has been bedridden for the past week. Is she better now?"

What she was challenging was how Hannah's mother could have insisted he stay for supper if she couldn't even get out of bed. But Noah apparently thought Arleta was suggesting he shouldn't have been around her if she was ill, because she might be contagious.

"*Neh*, she's not completely better yet. But I don't think I could have picked up any germs. I wasn't anywhere near her and she only stuck her head into the kitchen for a minute."

Did Hannah's mamm *also suggest her* dochder *serve beef casserole for supper?* Arleta wryly questioned him in her mind.

She found that hard to believe. It was far more probable that Hannah had recalled how much Noah liked beef casserole from when they were courting, so she'd made it especially for him. Arleta should know; she'd done the same thing herself.

But I *did it because I appreciate how hard Noah works and how* hungerich *he'd be when he got home. I think Hannah did it because she* likes *him and she wants him for a suitor again*, she deduced. *That* has *to be the reason she acts so aloof around me—she's annoyed that I'm living here.*

Arleta was sure of it now. And given how ill at ease Noah seemed, she was fairly confident he was keeping something from her and his grandmother. *It must be that he's developing feelings for Hannah again*, she surmised. *What else could cause him to fidget like that?*

Noah momentarily felt as if Arleta could see right through him. But that was ridiculous; there was no way she could have known he'd gone to the frolic specifically to interfere with what he suspected was a blossoming romance between her and Isaiah. So maybe that little frown dragging down her countenance was because she thought it was hypocritical of him to be around Hannah's mother when he'd emphatically told her that she and Sovilla should avoid people who were ill.

Or maybe her expression was a reflection of his own discomfort. For all he knew, she felt embarrassed because she realized that their peers would have told him she'd gotten a ride home with Isaiah. Regardless, there was no way of knowing for sure what was on her mind. He was tired and his stomach hurt—it must have been from eating Honor's *kuchen*. So he excused himself to take a shower and then go upstairs for the night.

Once he was in bed, he reflected on the events of the day. Of all the challenging situations he'd encountered—his conversation with Arleta that morning, the installation setback because of the rainstorm, the leak in the restaurant roof—none was as difficult as eating supper with the Millers.

I never should have stayed, he thought. But when he'd gone inside to see if one of the boys had accidentally exchanged his straight edge for theirs, Eliza Miller had heard him talking and she'd gotten out of bed to personally invite him to supper. She'd been one of his mother's closest friends in New Hope, and she was so grateful for the work he'd done to repair the roof on the restaurant that Noah felt it would have been rude not to accept her invitation.

Surprisingly, eating a meal with the Millers hadn't been painful because being with Hannah reminded him of the night of the fire. It had been painful because being with the boys and their father reminded Noah of being with *his* brothers and dad. He'd gone so long without that kind of rambunctious camaraderie at the supper table that he hadn't realized how much he'd missed it until he had it again, and then his lonesomeness had felt overwhelming.

Noah had always loved being one of four children in his family, and he'd always hoped to have at least that many children of his own… But he knew there was no sense dwelling on what was gone from the past or impossible in the future. He had to refocus on his present goal—earning enough money to take care of his grandmother's medical expenses. *The problem is that I got distracted by all this thinking and talking about socializing. I can't believe that I even tried to prevent Isaiah from becoming Arleta's suitor*, he marveled. So before rolling over and going to sleep, he resolved that from now on he was going to concentrate solely on his customers again, no matter what anyone else—Jacob, his grandmother, Arleta or even Isaiah—said or did.

The following morning the air was muggy and the sun was blazing—an oppressive combination. Seeing Arleta lace up her boots before they set out for church, Noah remarked, "Didn't you bring any sandals? They'd be a lot cooler." In many places, Amish women—especially the older generation—wouldn't dream of coming to church in sandals, but in New Hope, it was a common practice.

"*Neh.* But these shoes are fine," she replied. She wasn't frowning as she'd been last night, but she wasn't smiling, either.

"Your feet are going to get really hot. Some of the younger *meed* go barefoot. I'm sure no one would think twice if you did, too."

"I'm not a *maedel*, I'm a *weibsmensch*. That's how I prefer to act and that's how I prefer to be treated," Arleta replied hotly as Sovilla held a finger to her lips and shook her head at Noah in the background.

I was just trying to be helpful, he thought, wondering what he'd said wrong. To avoid insulting Arleta again, he didn't speak much on the way to church and neither did she, although Sovilla chatted away enough for all three of them.

The preacher's message was based on a passage from Romans 12, touching on themes of not conforming to the world, not thinking better of yourself than of others, using your gifts in service to the Lord and overcoming evil with good. Noah noticed about halfway through the sermon that his grandmother's eyes were closed, but he didn't wake her. It wasn't uncommon for people to fall asleep during the three-hour service, especially during the warm summer months. The preacher wouldn't be offended if he spotted her dozing, because he knew that worshipping with her district was so important to Sovilla that she'd risked her health to come to church time and again. Noah closed his eyes, too, but not to sleep—he was silently thanking the Lord that Sovilla seemed to be doing so much better now.

After the service ended and lunch had been served and eaten, Noah strolled across the lawn and was hitching the horse and buggy when Arleta approached. "Your *groossmammi* wanted me to tell you she left already. She's going to spend the afternoon at the Stolls' *haus*, catching up with Almeda now that she and Iddo have returned to New Hope again. They'll give her a ride home later this afternoon."

Noah chuckled, realizing Sovilla probably hadn't

wanted to tell him herself, because she feared he might have questioned whether it was wise to be out for the entire afternoon. "She's sure making the most of the doctor's *gut* report isn't she? My *groossmammi*'s not letting any moss grow under her feet."

"*Jah*—she seems to be enjoying getting out," Arleta agreed.

While they were talking, Hannah Miller walked up beside her, carrying a round, covered dish in her hands. She greeted them both, before explaining that she was looking for Sovilla. When Noah told her that his grandmother had already left, Hannah extended the plate to him. "I made this last night—it's bumbleberry pie, in celebration of the improvement in Sovilla's health. She'd mentioned the other day that she hasn't been eating desserts lately, so I thought this might satisfy her sweet tooth. Could you bring it home for her?"

"Sure." Noah was relieved to notice that ever since the hike to the gorge, it was becoming a little easier to make small talk with Hannah. Or at least, the sight of her didn't make him feel quite as guilt-ridden as it used to. Remembering his manners, he added, "*Denki.* It is her favorite, you know."

"*Jah.* I remember that was the reason she gave your *schweschder* and me the recipe—so that if Mary didn't make it for a potluck, there'd always be a chance I would." Hannah added wistfully, "I have such a *gut* memory of that day."

When she blinked and gazed out over the field behind him, Noah was struck with a realization: Hannah had been his sister's closest friend. She'd probably cared about Mary even more than she'd cared about Noah. And he'd been so consumed by guilt and grief that he'd never thought to offer her any consolation after she'd lost her best friend. "Mary was so *hallich* when you moved to town," he acknowledged now, as a sort of belated condolence. "She loved baking with you, and she would have wanted to help with your restaurant."

Hannah met his eyes and nodded and for a moment Noah thought she was going to cry. But instead she gave him a tiny smile and then said, "See you later."

As she took off across the lawn, Noah addressed Arleta, who was poking at a stick on the grass with the toe of her boot. "You ready to leave?"

"I need to go to the phone shanty to call my *schwe-schder.* I'm going to walk home." She began backing away.

"I'll give you a ride. It's too hot to walk all the way home from the shanty."

"That's okay. Leanna knows I'm going to call, but there's always the chance someone else will be using the phone before us, so I don't want you to have to wait around."

"I'm not in a hurry. I don't mind."

"*I* do—I'd like my privacy," Arleta said sharply. Then she modified her tone. "Besides, you'd better get that pie into a cool place pretty soon or it will spoil."

Noah didn't know what she was so grouchy about today, but he knew a hint when he heard one. So he swiftly got into the buggy, set the pie on the seat beside him and took off for home.

Arleta felt guilty for behaving so miserably—or maybe it was that she was behaving so miserably *be-cause* she felt guilty. Guilty when Noah had drawn at-tention to her shoes and stockings. Guilty listening to the preacher reading the passage in the Bible about not being conformed to the world. And especially guilty about being so annoyed at Hannah Miller.

Last night she'd lost at least four hours of sleep brooding about why Noah had been asked to stay for supper at the Millers' house yesterday. Arleta had half convinced herself that she'd given the invitation too much significance. She'd reasoned that if Hannah were truly interested in him, she'd be more likely to hide her interest in front of her brothers and parents—not openly invite him to eat supper with them, wouldn't she? Then again, Arleta considered that it was possible Eliza Miller was aware of her daughter's fondness for Noah, so she'd played matchmaker by asking him to dine with them. Back and forth Arleta's thoughts went for half the night and it frustrated her that she couldn't come to any certain conclusion.

Today, however, there was no mistaking Hannah's affection for Noah. *First, she tried to win him over by making beef casserole*, Arleta thought. *Now today she's trying to win his* groossmammi *over with a bumbleberry pie.* A pie she'd made a special effort to bake last night, after having spent the entire day working on the restaurant and then making supper for her family and Noah.

How did she make it anyway? I thought she mentioned she'd used up all of her frozen berries from last season? Arleta grumbled to herself as she cut through a thick stand of pine trees on a shortcut to the shanty. The blackflies were out, and she had to wave her hands around her head to keep them from landing on the exposed skin of her neck—she usually had a severe, although not allergic, reaction to insect bites.

She knew I *wanted to make a bumbleberry pie for Sovilla and she* knew *I haven't been making a lot of sweets lately. So she beat me to the punch. It's as if she was deliberately trying to prove that she's more domestic than I am. And that* she'd *make a better wife for Sovilla's grandson or something.* Which was ridiculous, since they weren't in competition; Arleta certainly had no desire to be courted by Noah or to become his wife.

But if that was true, then why had she felt so upset when she noticed the look he gave Hannah as they were reminiscing about the day Sovilla taught her how to make bumbleberry pie? It was obvious the two of them had shared a strong connection while they were courting. And from the tone of their discussion in the churchyard, it was just as obvious they still had deep feelings for each other.

But I am not *envious of her*, Arleta told herself. *I'm hurt that she's been so cold to me, while being so syrupy toward Noah and Sovilla.*

She lifted a low branch so she could pass beneath it, careful not to disturb a spiderweb. When she stood up straight on the other side, she realized she'd happened upon a little brook. She had been so preoccupied with her ruminations that she hadn't heard the current tinkling over the stones, but as she drew nearer, its music danced in her ears.

Stopping on the embankment, she gazed at the sparkling stream of water. It wasn't more than six or eight inches deep and a couple of feet wide. She easily could have crossed it without getting her feet wet—a flat, dry rock protruded right in the middle and she could have stepped on that. But she didn't think she was headed in the right direction because she didn't recall a stream the last time she'd taken this route. *I'll have to turn around*, she thought. *But first, I'm going to cool off.*

She unlaced her boots and then rolled her socks off and tucked them inside. Her feet were pale and tender, and she inched down the rocky slope toward the water. At first, she just dipped her toes in and the coldness made her nerves tingle straight. Then she boldly plunged both feet into the water. "This is *wunderbaar*!" she shouted.

Holding the skirt of her dress up so she wouldn't get the hem wet, she wiggled her toes. Then she kicked upward, laughing when she sprayed herself with icy droplets. Had she ever felt as refreshed before in her life as she did now? *I regret everything about getting my tattoo except for this one moment*, she thought, aware that if she hadn't worn socks on her feet for almost two years straight, she never would have appreciated just quite how freeing it was to take them off and dunk her feet in a glacial stream.

She took a few steps forward, but the bottom of the stream was comprised of small, sharp-edged rocks and her soles were too delicate to walk on them, so instead she perched on the flat rock in the middle of the stream. Dangling her feet into the water, she closed her eyes and inhaled the pine scent of the air. Five, ten, fifteen minutes passed and with each one, Arleta became more and more aware of how ungodly her thoughts toward Hannah had been.

Reflecting on the preacher's sermon from this morning, she recalled what he'd read in the book of Romans about living at peace with others and being "kindly affectioned" to them. *Oh, Lord, I'm sorry for my attitude toward Hannah*, she prayed. *I am envious of her. I'm envious of Noah, too, because they can court and fall in love and get married and I can't.*

She burst into tears and lay back on the rock's surface, covering her face with her arms for several minutes. Eventually, she dried her eyes on her sleeve and placed her hands at her sides. Looking up through the trees at the sky, she said, "*Gott*, please help me desire and rejoice in what's best for Hannah and Noah. Please help me to be a better friend to both of them." She swished her feet through the water a couple of times before adding, "And *denki*, Lord, for refreshing my body and renewing my mind."

Noah couldn't remember the last time he'd spent a Sunday afternoon alone at home, and he didn't know quite what to do with himself. *This is what it's going to be like after* Groossmammi *dies and I'm all alone.* The thought came out of nowhere, and it made him shiver even though his shirt was sticky with sweat.

He tried taking a nap, but the upper level of the house was so hot he couldn't sleep. So he came downstairs and reclined on the sofa, rereading the passage in Romans that the preacher had read that morning before finally setting the Bible on the end table and nodding off.

It seemed as if no time had passed when he woke with a start and glanced at the battery-operated clock on the mantel-piece: 5:15. The house was completely quiet—hadn't Arleta or Sovilla returned yet? "Anyone home?" he called, but his question went unanswered. Maybe they'd come back and were napping, too?

But when he walked down the hall to the bathroom, he noticed their doors were open and their rooms were empty. Groggy and uncomfortably warm, he splashed water on his face and then went out to the barn for the second milking. *I'm sure* Groossmammi *is fine—she's with Iddo and Almeda and they'll both take* gut *care of her*, he reasoned. *But I wonder what's keeping Arleta? She should have been back a long time ago.*

It occurred to him that maybe she'd come home and left again, so when he went back into the house, he checked the kitchen counters and living room end tables for a note, but there was no indication she'd returned. *I hope she's okay*, he thought as he tromped outside and began pacing on the porch. He considered going out in the buggy to search for her. But even if he left a note telling his grandmother where he went, Noah didn't want Sovilla to return to an empty house. She'd gone all day without a nap—excluding the brief snooze she'd taken in church—and she might be tired and weak and need assistance getting around.

After uttering a prayer for Arleta's safety, Noah decided to go heat up the leftovers so their supper would be ready when they returned. He opened the door to the gas-powered refrigerator, withdrew a large covered dish and peeked inside. Arleta's beef casserole. Even though he'd had it the night before at the Millers' house, his mouth watered; Hannah's casserole was good, but it didn't compare to Arleta's. He just hoped there'd still be enough leftovers so he could take some with him to work tomorrow and eat them cold for lunch.

While the casserole was heating, he pulled out the plates and utensils and set them on the table. Fixing supper temporarily distracted him from worrying about whether something had happened to Arleta. But after he'd placed the water glasses and pitcher on the table and she still hadn't returned, he decided he'd better turn off the oven after all and go look for her.

Right after he twisted the dial, Noah heard a buggy pull up the driveway. He dashed out onto the porch to see Iddo helping Sovilla down from the carriage. Noah hopped down the steps to exchange pleasantries with the deacon and his wife. After the couple's buggy pulled down the lane, he took his grandmother's arm and supported her up the porch stairs.

"I have to sit here to rest a minute before I go any farther," she told him, settling onto the bench. "Could you ask Arleta to bring me a glass of water?"

"She's not home—I'll get it."

Before he reached the door, Sovilla questioned, "Where did she go?"

"I'm not sure. The last I spoke to her she was—"

He was interrupted by the sound of a buggy rounding the bend. It turned up the driveway, pulled by the same horse that Noah had seen hitched at the restaurant yesterday—Isaiah's. *I don't believe this*, he thought. *For the past hour I've been worried about Arleta and she's been out running around with Isaiah?*

He was so irritated he hardly looked at her as she got out of the carriage. Unfortunately, his grandmother waved to Isaiah, calling, "Is that you, Isaiah Wittmer? *Kumme* say hello."

If Arleta had any intention of keeping her courtship with Isaiah a secret, the cat is definitely out of the bag now, Noah thought. But as she bounded up the steps, she didn't seem ruffled in the least; she was practically *glowing*.

"Hi, Sovilla. Hi, Noah," she greeted them. "I hope you weren't too worried about me."

"I just got home—why would I have been worried?" Sovilla said.

By then Isaiah had secured his horse to the fence, and he clomped up the steps and greeted them, too, a complacent grin lighting his eyes.

"Did something happen, Arleta?" Sovilla asked again.

"I got lost in the woods on the way to the phone shanty to call my *schweschder*," she explained. "I came out on the wrong side, over by the Wittmers' farm."

"She was confused because while she was in the woods, she stumbled across a stream and she didn't recall there being one the last time she took that short-cut," Isaiah added.

"*Jah.* Isaiah told me it's too small to have a name and that its bed is dry most of the year, which is why I didn't remember it. It's only running now because of the heavy rains we've had. When I reached it, I tried to backtrack but I got all turned around. Eventually I ended up on the western edge of the Wittmers' property," Arleta said. "Anyway, I'd been wandering around for a couple of hours, so Isaiah gave me a ride home."

"That was kind, Isaiah," Sovilla said. "As long as you're here, you ought to *kumme* in for supper."

Isaiah sniffed the air. "I think I will—it smells *appenditlich.*"

Sovilla and Arleta exchanged quizzical looks, so Noah told them he was heating the leftover casserole.

"Great," Arleta said. "I made oatmeal raisin cookies yesterday, too. We can have them for dessert—unless you want to share your bumbleberry pie, Sovilla."

"What bumbleberry pie?" she asked as she led everyone inside. When Arleta told her Hannah had prepared it for her, she said, "I'd be *hallich* to share. But Isaiah is our guest. He can decide what dessert we should have."

"Well, considering I had *kuchen* yesterday at the frolic, I think I'd like cookies tonight, please."

Arleta was all smiles. "Sounds *gut*, but you and Noah will have to close your eyes while I take the cookie jar out of its hiding place," she said, causing Isaiah to laugh heartily.

For a brief moment, Noah had a peculiar misgiving about Arleta's account of getting lost in the woods. This afternoon she had been so insistent that she walk home on such a hot day that it caused him to wonder, *Did she* really *get lost or had she planned all along to pop in on Isaiah?* The niggling doubt reminded him of how he'd felt after Isaiah had offered to carry Arleta across the stream; something felt amiss but he couldn't put a finger on it.

But then he dismissed his qualm, reminding himself all that was important was that she was home safe. Even if she *had* connived a way to get together with Isaiah, it was none of Noah's business. *My business is earning money so* Groossmammi *can get medical treatments in Mexico if she needs to*, he declared inwardly. *And the sooner we eat supper, the sooner I can go to bed and start a new day of work.*

Chapter Seven

Arleta felt so relieved after she'd confessed her envy of Hannah to the Lord that she decided she was going to do everything she could to encourage Noah to attend the potluck at the Millers' restaurant in two weeks. She didn't have as many opportunities to talk to him about it as she would have liked because he began working even longer hours, and he often showered and went straight to bed when he came home in the evenings. But she dropped as many hints about it as she could without nagging him, and Sovilla added her two cents, too.

Meanwhile, the days flew by. The strawberries and raspberries were ripe, and she spent several mornings picking at a local farm owned by a co-op of Amish families. In the afternoons, Sovilla would wash and slice the berries and then Arleta took over the jam-making and canning processes, since the older woman still didn't quite have enough stamina to be on her feet for that long.

When Arleta called to talk to her mother and sister one afternoon on the way home from purchasing more jar lids, she learned that they'd been making jam and preserving fruit, too. "I miss having your help around here," Leanna complained. "Especially since *Mamm* has been sick."

"*Mamm* is sick?" Arleta repeated, alarmed. "What's wrong with her?"

"It's only a forty-eight-hour bug. I had it last week, too. Everyone around here has been getting it, but it passes quickly. Especially for the *buwe*—I think their stomachs are made of steel."

Arleta chuckled, happy that her mother wasn't seriously ill. "Well, it's *gut* that you're finished with *schul* now, so you're home during the day to help *Mamm*."

"*Jah*, but I may not be home for the entire summer. You'll never guess what I'm going to do."

Arleta figured her sister must have been planning to visit their relatives in upstate New York. "Are you going to *Ant* Betty and *Onkel* Eli's *haus*?"

"*Neh*, nothing quite as exciting as that," her sister answered with a wistful sigh. "I'm going to babysit for an *Englisch familye* who comes to Serenity Ridge for the summer. They have twin *buwe* and one *dochder*."

Her sister's news roiled Arleta's stomach, and she pressed her hand against her abdomen. "Y-you are?"

"*Jah*, if *Mamm* and *Daed* agree to it. But I don't think they'll say *neh*, since it's only for a couple of weeks and the Greens will provide me transportation both ways."

"But why would you do that? Are *Mamm* and *Daed* having money problems? Because I've been saving and—"

"*Neh*, it's not that. It's because Emma's *mamm* has something called a pituitary tumor and she's having surgery. Emma's *schweschder* is going to take a few weeks off her job at the restaurant to care for her and their little *brieder*, first. Then Emma will take a turn staying home in the middle of August. That's when I'm going to fill in for her."

Arleta knew Emma's father had died two years ago and her family had been struggling to make ends meet, even with abundant help from their community. So it made sense that Emma would need to work now that she was finished with school. Because Serenity Ridge, like the other Amish communities in Maine, was a relatively new and small district, jobs for young women were scarce. Arleta understood why Emma needed to work out of their community, for an *Englisch* employer. However, she couldn't comprehend why it was necessary for Leanna to fill in for her.

"Can't the *Englisch familye* hire an *Englischer* while Emma's gone?" she asked.

"*Neh.* They told Emma that they have a very high regard for the way we Amish people raise our *kinner*, so they really don't want anyone else to babysit for them."

"I'm sure if they put their minds to it, they can find a suitable *Englisch* nanny for a couple of weeks," Arleta argued. "I don't think it's wise for you to work for them."

"Why not? *You* worked for an *Englisch familye*, and you loved it."

Exactly, Arleta thought. Somehow, she was going to have to convince her sister—and possibly her parents—that allowing Leanna to work out wasn't a good idea, even if it was beneficial to Emma's family. She gently discouraged her, saying, "I love working for an Amish *familye* so much more. I didn't know it at the time because I had no outside work experience to compare it to. But if I had to do it all over again, I'd never work for an *Englisch* family."

"I'm not too *hallich* about the idea, either," Leanna admitted. "I didn't want to tell you this, but, well, the only reason I'm doing it is so I can give the money to Emma. I know she's really worried about her *mamm*, and their *familye* has already gone through so much. Besides praying, this is the only thing I can do that will really help her."

Arleta squeezed her eyes shut and two hot tears rolled down her cheeks as she contemplated her dear, sweet sister's generosity toward her friend. She sniffed and dropped the subject for now, instead telling Leanna about the upcoming potluck at the Millers' restaurant.

"Will the potato *bauer* be there?" her sister asked.

"*Jah*, probably. But don't worry. As I said, I'm not interested in him and nothing or no one will keep me from returning home at the end of the summer. I promise."

"Oh." There was silence on the other end of the line.

"What's wrong?"

"It's just that you were right… I *have* kind of gotten used to having the entire bedroom to myself."

"Hey!" Arleta exclaimed.

Her sister giggled and quickly reassured her she was just kidding. "I miss you a lot."

"I miss you, too." Arleta knew it was time to get back to Sovilla now, but she could tell there was something else on Leanna's mind. "Are you sure *Mamm*'s getting better?"

"*Jah*, I'm sure."

"Then what's wrong?"

"I… I'm worried about your feet being cold all the time. Emma's *mamm* couldn't stand being cold, either, and they thought it was because of her thyroid but now she has this pituitary tumor," Leanna blurted out. It sounded as if she was on the brink of crying.

Arleta was, too. She choked back a sob and her eyes filled. She assured her sister that she was perfectly healthy but then, after they'd hung up, she allowed her tears to flow freely. As guilty as she'd felt about getting a tattoo, it didn't compare to the guilt she felt about Leanna worrying that Arleta might have been seriously ill. *I haven't been seriously ill—I've been seriously sinful*, she silently cried. *My deception about my tattoo is even worse than the tattoo itself. And my innocent, trusting* schweschder *has absolutely no idea.*

Arleta was tempted to tell her the truth in order to put her mind completely at ease. But if Arleta disclosed the real reason why she always wore socks, it might give Leanna ideas about going astray, too—especially once she faced the kinds of situations that she was bound to encounter while working with *Englischers.*

What am I going to do? she wondered, climbing back into the buggy. As she headed home, she came up with a plan: if she couldn't dissuade her sister from babysitting for the *Englischers*, she'd find out how much money Leanna would earn and *she'd* give that amount to Leanna to give to Emma's family. Which might mean Arleta wouldn't be able to save enough by the end of the summer to have her tattoo removed, but it would be worth it if it spared her sister from being tempted in some of the same ways Arleta had been tempted. She could always earn a little more money here and there with sewing projects or selling baked goods. *As for the* Englischers, *they'll just have to settle for a different babysitter for two weeks*, she thought. *Better that they should compromise their standards than my* schwe-schder *should compromise her beliefs.*

It was Friday afternoon and Noah was bone tired. He had been putting in extra-long hours for the past two weeks. *It's paying off, though,* he thought as he mentally calculated how much money he'd saved so far compared to the amount he still needed to cover the estimated expenses of a trip to Mexico. He was exactly on target for where he needed to be financially at this point. *If I can pick up the pace tomorrow, I'll be able to complete the pool* haus *roof on Walnut Street and move on to installing the shed roof on South Main...*

A boom of thunder broke through his thoughts and he felt the building—a public gym that was scheduled to open in two months—vibrate beneath him. He and his crewmates gathered their supplies and clambered down just in time to take shelter inside, since the owner had given Noah the key so they could store their tools and materials there while they were working on the installation.

"Look at that dark cloud. We might as well go home now," Jacob suggested, standing in front of the ceiling-to-floor windows. "It's already three o'clock."

"*Neh*, I think it's going to pass," Noah objected. "Let's wait a few minutes."

"I'm *hungerich*," the teenager complained. "Does anyone have anything to eat?"

"Yeah, I've got a steak in one pocket and an ice cream cone in the other," Mike said, razzing him.

Since Noah had worked through their lunch break without eating, his stomach was starting to growl, too. However, because the worksite was so far from their homes, Mike had given his Amish coworkers a ride and Noah's cooler was still in his truck. "I've got a big slice of strawberry pie in my cooler. You can have it once the rain stops," he offered Jacob.

"Why wait?" The young man was out the door and back in a flash, but he still got drenched. He removed his hat and shook his head and upper body like a wet dog before opening the cooler. "Look at all this food Arleta packs for him," he said in amazement to David and Mike. "This is three times as much as my *ants* send with me."

"That's because I'm usually not home for supper." Noah reached in to pull out a container of fried chicken and potato salad. Since there was only one fork, he used it for the potato salad and Jacob ate the pie with his hands, which was what the Amish in New Hope often did during after-church lunches, too. "I think she packed a couple of roast beef sandwiches if either of you want one, David and Mike."

They rummaged through the cooler, selected what they wanted and then the four men sat down in a row, leaning against the wall. While they ate, David told them about the horse he was training and Mike described going deep-sea fishing for the first time the previous weekend. As Noah stuck a fork into a potato and lifted it to his lips—Isaiah was right; Arleta made especially delectable potato salad—it occurred to him that he hadn't had time to go fishing or canoeing at all this spring or summer. He hadn't thought twice about it until he'd heard his coworkers talking about their hobbies and interests. *Maybe later in the summer I'll get the chance to go,* he thought. Listening to the other men, Noah rested his head against the wall and his shoulders relaxed as he enjoyed the conversation and company of his crew.

They polished off their food in no time and then passed around the cooler again, until it was completely empty.

"Tell Arleta that pie was *appenditlich*," Jacob said. "Is she making it for the potluck tomorrow night?"

"I'm not sure," Noah replied.

Every time he'd come home, no matter how late it was, Arleta and Sovilla seemed to be having the same discussion about what main dish Arleta should bring to the potluck and what she ought to make for a dessert. At first, Noah was baffled by their ongoing indecision, but then he realized they were probably just talking about the menu as an excuse to bring up the subject of the potluck. He figured Arleta was excited about the event because she'd get to see Isaiah in a social setting again. And that Sovilla kept mentioning it because she didn't want Noah to forget when it was, in case he changed his mind about going. After a while, he tuned them out, so he never did hear what dish and dessert they'd finally decided to bring.

"I guess we'll find out when we get there." Jacob belched and patted his stomach. "You're going to go, aren't you?"

"*Neh*. I've got to work late tomorrow."

"That's okay—the best *schpass* will start after dark anyway. Some of us are staying to clean up and then we're going to set off fireworks over the pond behind the restaurant. You should *kumme* for that."

If by "some of us" Jacob meant the same group of single people who had gone hiking at the gorge several weeks ago, Noah wasn't interested. Even though he felt slightly more comfortable around Hannah now, he didn't want to get distracted by the flirtations going on between various members of that group again. "I'm usually beat by the time I'm done working on Saturday."

"That's exactly why you should *kumme* to the potluck." Surprisingly, it was David, not Jacob, who urged him to reconsider. "You're working yourself too hard."

"He's working *us* too hard, too," Mike griped, but it was clear from his smile that he was kidding.

"Yeah, you can say that again," Jacob chimed in. He pointed out the window. "See that? The rain's coming down in sheets. You should let us go home for the day. We'll *kumme* in early on *Muundaag*."

Somehow, Noah doubted that but Jacob was right about the weather; if anything, it was raining even harder now. "All right," he agreed. "Let's go."

So Mike drove them home, pulling up in front of Noah's house last. "Hey, I know I probably shouldn't say this, but David and Jacob are right—you look like you could use a break."

Noah appreciated his coworker's well-intentioned sentiment. "Don't worry. I'm going to take a break on the Sabbath—the day of rest."

"Getting enough rest is an important part of taking a break, but it's just as important to kick back and have some fun once in a while—especially since fireworks and food are involved," Mike said. "If I were Amish, I'd be the first one in line at that potluck supper."

"If you were Amish, there wouldn't be anything left for the rest of us to eat," Noah replied, laughing as he got out of the truck.

He went into the house where Sovilla was filling a glass at the kitchen sink. She turned toward him and lifted a finger to her lips. "Sarah's here with the *bob-bel.* He's finally fallen asleep."

Noah nodded, slid off his boots and tiptoed into the living room behind his grandmother. He softly greeted Sarah, who was sitting on the sofa, before he noticed Arleta standing on the opposite side of the braided rug. She cradled the baby in her arms, swaying back and forth ever so slightly. Although the weather outside was dreary, her smile seemed to illuminate the dim room when she looked at Noah and mouthed the words, Kumme *see him.*

He crept forward and peered over her shoulder as she tilted the baby so he could see his face. But when he gazed down, what captured his attention was *Arle-ta's* expression as she beheld the baby. In that instant she looked so…so *maternal* that he felt both smitten and repelled. Smitten because he could imagine her as a mother and a wife. And repelled because he couldn't imagine *himself* as a father and a husband.

When she blinked her fair, wispy lashes and then angled her face so her eyes met his, he felt as if his knees were about to buckle. "Isn't he *schnuck*?" she whispered.

Noah's mouth was parched. *"Jah,"* he croaked.

"Do you want to hold him? He's fast asleep now."

"*Neh.* I'd better not. I haven't washed up and I need to…to take care of the livestock." Fortunately, his legs held out long enough for him to put his boots back on and shuffle outside, across the yard to the barn. There he plopped down on a hay bale. Resting his forearms against his thighs, he leaned forward, absently staring down at the dirt floor. Droplets darkened the ground between his legs, and he felt so despondent that they could have been his tears. But it was only rainwater, dripping from the ends of his hair because he'd left the house without donning his hat.

He didn't know how long he perched there, motionless, but when his muscles began to cramp, he rubbed the nape of his neck and prayed, *Please,* Gott, *give me strength to keep going.* He wasn't sure whether he was asking for physical strength to keep going for the day or emotional strength to keep going as a bachelor for the rest of his life. It was probably a little of each.

He slowly shifted into a standing position and began tending to the animals. By the time he returned to the house, Sarah's husband must have picked her and the baby up, because Sovilla and Arleta were alone.

"I'm making pork and asparagus stir-fry," Arleta told him. "I've never made it—I've never even tasted it before—but it's supposed to be a healthy recipe. I hope you like it."

"I—I actually ate my lunch just before I came home." Noah didn't know if that was really why he wasn't hungry, but right now he couldn't imagine swallowing so much as a grain of rice. "I'm going to go shower and then I'm hitting the sack."

"Already? It's only six o'clock," Sovilla protested.

"*Jah*, but you keep telling me I need to get more rest."

Actually, what she'd kept telling him was that he needed to have more *fun*, but instead of pointing that out, she took a different tack, reasoning, "I suppose if you go to bed now, you'll be able to get an earlier start to your day tomorrow. And the sooner you get to work, the sooner you can *kumme* home. You might even be back in time to go to the potluck with us."

Noah could have guaranteed right then that wasn't

going to happen, but instead he gave his grandmother and Arleta a weak smile and said good-night.

On Saturday morning, Arleta rose extra early so she could be up before Noah left for work. She figured he'd be especially hungry after going to bed without any supper. And, although it was probably futile, she thought she'd urge him one last time to come to the potluck that evening. She was pinning on her prayer *kapp* when she heard the kitchen door opening—he'd just returned from milking the cow. Knowing he'd probably pour himself a bowl of cereal if she didn't tell him she planned to make scrambled eggs and sausage, she flew down the hall and into the kitchen, where he was standing near the table. Attempting to come to a quick halt, Arleta slid across the floor in her stocking feet and crashed into him. She would have fallen over backward if he hadn't caught her, one hand encircling her waist, the other around her shoulders in an awkward embrace.

"Oops—I'm sorry," she apologized as he stabilized her upright. "Did I hurt you?"

Still holding on to her, his face so close to hers she could distinguish the variegation of blues within the bright irises of his eyes, he answered, "*Neh.* Did you hurt yourself?"

Arleta felt a number of sensations—breathlessness, dizziness, tingling—but none of them was painful. "*Neh.*"

He loosened his grip a little. "You steady now?"

"*Jah*, I am."

He dropped his arms and stepped backward. "Where are you off to in such a hurry?"

"Nowhere. I was trying to catch up with you before

you left so I could make you a nice hot breakfast. I figured you must be *hungerich* after going to bed without supper."

He looked chagrined. "I, uh, I actually got up around midnight and ate some of that stir-fry."

"Cold?"

He shrugged. "I was afraid if I warmed it on the stove, the smell might wake you and *Groossmammi*."

Arleta appreciated how thoughtful he always was. "Go wash up and I'll put on a pot of *kaffi*. Breakfast will be ready in a few minutes." She half expected him to object, but she was glad when he didn't. She was even gladder he tiptoed down the hall and back again without disturbing Sovilla's slumber. It was a rare treat to get to spend time alone with him. As Arleta prepared breakfast, they chatted about the pool house roof he needed to work on that day and discussed whether Sarah's son looked more like her or her husband. Then Noah told Arleta how much his coworkers enjoyed the feast she'd packed for him the day before.

"That? That was just leftovers," she said modestly. "You must have all been starving—food always tastes better than it really is when you've worked up an appetite."

"*Neh*, it was truly *appenditlich*. Even Jacob said so—and he doesn't usually give compliments or exercise *gut* manners," Noah insisted. "And your roast beef sandwich practically made a convert out of Mike."

"A convert?" Arleta questioned. "Why—is he a vegetarian?"

Noah cracked up. "*Neh*. I meant a convert to the Amish faith—he thinks it would be *wunderbaar* to eat that way all the time. I wouldn't be surprised if he shows up at the potluck wearing a straw hat and suspenders."

Arleta laughed. "Well, if he did he might be sorely disappointed by what I'm bringing."

"You finally decided?"

"Your *groossmammi* decided for me. Four bean salad, peppered deviled eggs and pickled green beans." The dishes were traditional staples at Amish picnics and summer potlucks in New Hope, but they wouldn't necessarily appeal to an *Englischer* like Mike.

"What about dessert?"

"I'm making strawberry-rhubarb coffee cake. I figured a lot of other people would bake pies, so this will be a little different." Arleta recognized this would be the perfect moment to urge Noah to stop by the restaurant after work, but for some reason she felt hesitant to do that. She'd thought that she'd gotten over feeling envious about the possibility that Hannah and Noah might want to rekindle their courtship, and she'd been trying to encourage him to come to the event for the past two weeks. So why was she having a sudden change of heart?

It took all of her willpower to say, "If you intend to come to the restaurant after you get done working, I can make up a plate and put it aside for you. Otherwise, there might not be anything left except for whatever Honor makes."

Noah laughed loudly, but before he could give her a definitive answer, Sovilla padded into the room.

"What's *voll schpass*?" she asked, scratching her head through her scarf. Her hair was beginning to grow back, and she said her scalp itched all the time.

"Private joke." Noah winked at Arleta.

Sovilla's eyes darted back and forth between the two of them. "It must be a really *gut* one," she said, and Arleta quickly turned toward the stove so Sovilla wouldn't notice if her face appeared as red as it felt.

Half an hour later, they'd just finished breakfast when a horn sounded in the driveway. Noah jumped up and went outside. When he returned, he explained that he'd forgotten his toolbox in Mike's truck, so Mike had swung by to drop it off. After swilling down the last of his coffee, Noah said he needed to leave. By then, Sovilla had scurried down the hall to shampoo her itchy scalp, and Arleta was in such a rush to pack Noah's cooler that she never did bring up the subject of the potluck again. Which was a shame, because after Noah left and she stood at the sink washing dishes, she realized how much she really hoped he'd attend—not for Hannah's sake, but for *hers.*

After supper, as she stood near the sink washing dishes again—at the Millers' restaurant this time—she had that same wish. The potluck had been a time of great fellowship, food and fun, and Arleta had enjoyed getting to know many of the district members better. But she'd kept scanning the dining area, hoping Noah had arrived. And even when the sky began to darken and the adults joined the children outside so they could roast marshmallows at the firepit down by the pond, Arleta continued to keep watch for Noah. *It's not too late*, she thought. *He still might* kumme.

Jacob must have noticed her craning her neck as she dangled a marshmallow on a stick over the flames because he asked, "Are you looking for someone?"

Embarrassed, she didn't answer, instead saying, "I

wonder if Sovilla's getting tired. Lovina and Wayne brought us here—they're probably ready to go."

"You're not going to leave, too, are you?" Faith asked. "Some of us are lighting fireworks out over the water after all the *familye* with little *kinner* leave. You should stay."

Arleta was going to say she couldn't because she didn't have a ride home when Jacob echoed, "*Jah*, you should stay. I told Noah about it, too, so he might stop by. If he doesn't, I can drop you off before I take Faith home."

Noah might still be coming! Arleta accepted their invitation and then went back up to the restaurant to make sure Sovilla didn't mind. "If Noah comes, that means you'll be on your own for a few hours. Is that okay?" she asked the older woman.

"Of course it is. I'll be asleep anyway," she replied. "And don't you worry—as soon as I walk *in* the door I'm sending Noah *out* the door. He'll give you a ride home."

Arleta smiled to herself, grateful for Sovilla's persistence in pushing her grandson into a social situation. After walking with her and Lovina to where Wayne was hitching the horse and buggy, Arleta darted back to the pond. Within another hour, the gathering around the firepit had dwindled to Isaiah, Honor, Hannah and her brother Jonathan, Faith, Jacob and Arleta. There was no sign of Noah yet.

As a safety precaution, they were waiting until the fire died out before they brought the fireworks down to the pond anyway, but Isaiah said if Noah didn't arrive in the next fifteen minutes, he was going to have to leave. "I'm beat," he remarked, yawning.

"You sound like an old *mann*," Jacob joked.

"Better an old *mann* than a little *bobbel* like you," Isaiah ribbed him back. Then he pointed at Arleta's feet. Except when she went to church, lately she'd been wearing white cotton socks instead of dark stockings. "Still wearing socks, I see. They're so bright they practically glow in the dark."

Feeling self-conscious that he'd drawn attention to her feet, Arleta joked, "Well, your teeth are so bright that your *smile* practically glows in the dark." Her remark made Isaiah grin even wider.

"I'm *hungerich*," Jacob suddenly announced.

"How could you possibly still be *hungerich*?" Honor questioned him. "I saw you refill your plate five times."

"I'm not *hungerich still*. I'm *hungerich again*. Besides, I ate so much other stuff that I didn't have room in my stomach to try any of the desserts. There has to be a leftover pie or two in the kitchen. Can I go look?" he asked Hannah.

"*I'll* go look. The restaurant opens on *Muundaag* and I don't want you scavenging through the cupboards like a bear," she replied, laughing. "Since everything is spick-and-span in there, I'll bring something out for you to eat it here."

"Meanwhile, you can *kumme* help me get the fireworks, Jacob. I promised my *daed* I'd keep them locked in the storage shed behind the restaurant until all the *kinner* went home," Jonathan told Jacob. "You can give us a hand, too, Isaiah."

"I'll help you get the food, Hannah," Arleta offered.

"Neh," she replied sharply. "I'd like Honor to help me."

Arleta's cheeks stung. She'd hardly spoken to Hannah all evening because they'd both been so busy serving and mingling and cleaning up that they only saw each other in passing. But she'd hoped that if they spent a little one-on-one time together now, Hannah might warm up to her. Arleta hung her head, trying to gather her composure after being slighted yet again.

Once everyone was out of earshot, Faith sidled up to her. "Don't take Hannah's attitude to heart. She's just jealous."

Arleta snapped her head upward, surprised both because Faith had noticed Hannah's curtness and because she had attributed it to jealousy. "Why would she be jealous?"

Just then there was a commotion over in the parking lot—apparently Noah had arrived and the other young men were greeting him. As delighted as Arleta was that he'd finally made it, she urged Faith to answer her question before everyone circled back to the firepit. "Why would she be jealous?" she repeated.

"I shouldn't be telling you this..." Faith whispered. "But you-know-who used to be her suitor and she hoped they'd get married. But he broke it off with her because he didn't feel ready. That was years ago and she was devastated. Then this spring, he started showing signs he was interested in courting her again, but he's the type who needs a lot of...of *encouragement*. He doesn't have as much self-confidence as it seems. But then you showed up and you two get along so well and—"

Faith wasn't able to complete her thought because Noah, Isaiah and Jacob had come within a few yards of them, but Arleta got the picture. It was exactly as she suspected: Hannah had been surly toward her because she thought Arleta was interested in Noah, or vice versa.

It's not my fault that Noah and I get along so well—or that he ended their courtship, she thought defensively.

Almost immediately, she also remembered that she'd prayed the Lord would help her be a better friend to Noah and Hannah. And even though Arleta didn't think it was fair or kind for Hannah to treat her the way she had, it *was* understandable. She *loved* Noah, after all—she'd hoped to marry him. *I wish there was something I could do to show her that Noah and I aren't interested in each other romantically*, she thought. Yes, she had enjoyed having his arms around her that morning, but that was an accident, not an intentional embrace. Besides, even if she was drawn to him, it wasn't as if Arleta and Noah could ever have a future together. But what could she do to alleviate Hannah's envy?

"Hi, Arleta, hi, Faith," Noah greeted them as he stepped up to the firepit. They said hello back. The flames were almost out so Arleta couldn't see his expression, but she could hear the pleasure in his voice as he said, "I'm *hallich* I got here in time. I haven't lit fireworks for about ten years, and I heard that Hannah's bringing dessert out, too. I'm really looking forward to this."

"*Jah*, but unfortunately, Jonathan forgot the key to the storage shed at his *haus*. He just left to get it," Isaiah explained. "Unfortunately, I'm too tired to stick around until he gets back, so I guess I'll say *gut nacht* now."

"You're not going to stay for dessert—or should I say, for *more* dessert?" Hannah asked. She'd come up behind them, carrying what looked like a box or some type of container.

"*Denki*, but my stomach is already sore from everything else I ate." Isaiah bid everyone goodbye and began hiking up the hill to the parking lot.

Arleta seized the opportunity to show Hannah once and for all that she wasn't interested in Noah. "Do you mind dropping me off, Isaiah?" she called.

"Not at all," he answered, waiting for her to catch up with him.

At the same time, Noah questioned, "You want to leave already? I can give you a ride—"

"Neh," she interrupted him. "You just got here and you're looking forward to enjoying the evening with your friends. *Gut nacht*, everyone."

Then she scurried up the hill, as if to prove—contrary to how she actually felt—that she couldn't get away from Noah fast enough.

Chapter Eight

"Arleta and Isaiah seem very fond of each other," Hannah remarked, as if Noah hadn't noticed.

Until now, he had half convinced himself that the time Arleta had gotten a ride home from Isaiah after getting lost in the woods was merely happenstance, but there was nothing coincidental about the way she'd asked Isaiah for a ride home tonight. She'd practically chased him down! Isaiah hadn't seemed to mind her approaching him in front of everyone else like that, but Noah had been taken aback by her boldness. He'd never known an Amish woman to be so blatant about expressing her interest in a man. On occasion—such as in Jacob's case—an Amish man might overtly pursue a young woman romantically, not caring whether his peers witnessed his audacious behavior as he attempted to win her over, but it was never the other way around. If an Amish woman had her eye on someone, she'd be much more subtle about letting him know than Arleta had been.

"Jah." Noah acknowledged Hannah's observation, but he didn't encourage further discussion. His stom-

ach was sour, and the sight and sound of thc fireworks had given him a splitting headache. To make the evening even worse than he could have anticipated, he had been forced to give Hannah a ride after Jonathan confided he wanted to take Honor back to her house without his sister in the buggy. And of course, Jacob and Faith took off together, too. *Everybody is pairing up*, Noah thought. *But what else did I expect?*

Fortunately, the Millers didn't live very far from their restaurant, so it was only a matter of minutes that Noah had to be alone with Hannah in the buggy. After making the remark about Isaiah and Arleta, she clammed up until bidding him good-night when he dropped her off in front of her house. If there was one good thing about having such a bad headache and being so annoyed by Arleta's behavior, it was that it completely distracted Noah from the fact that the last time he'd brought Hannah home was on the night of the fire.

I knew *it was a mistake to hang out with the others after the potluck ended*, Noah thought as he pulled onto the main road. *But I didn't have much of a choice.* When Sovilla had come home and found him eating a late supper of scrambled eggs, she'd insisted he go pick Arleta up. It was just the push he'd needed, as he'd been on the fence about whether or not he ought to try to participate in lighting fireworks, as Jacob had suggested.

Actually, if he were really being honest, Noah would admit that all day he'd been thinking about how he'd caught Arleta in his arms when she'd slipped on the kitchen floor, knocking into him. With the exception of hugging his relatives, that was the first time in his life he'd embraced a woman that closely. Even when he'd kissed Hannah as a teenager, he hadn't put his arms around her—he'd held her hand in his. In a strange way, clutching Arleta so she wouldn't fall felt more meaningful to him than kissing Hannah had felt. Which didn't make any sense. Just as it didn't make any sense for him to believe that Arleta had really wanted his company at the potluck. *She was so intent on running after Isaiah that she hardly even acknowledged me*, he thought.

He'd gone all that way for what? A headache and a raspberry tart he didn't even enjoy because his stomach was doing flips. *That's the last time I'm compromising my better judgment*, he thought. No matter how much his grandmother insisted, cajoled or pleaded, he wasn't going to any more social events with Arleta this summer, not even to pick her up.

In fact, the next morning at the breakfast table when Sovilla asked them if they'd had fun the evening before, he answered bluntly, "*Neh.* I wish I hadn't gone. I wound up with a *baremlich* headache."

"You did? Oh, that's too bad." Arleta clicked her tongue against her teeth. "I thought you were really enjoying yourself and that's why you stayed out late."

"It wasn't that late. But I did have to drop Hannah off at home," Noah started to explain. Then he caught himself, realizing that Jonathan had confided his interest in Honor to him privately, and he wouldn't appreciate it if Noah disclosed his secret to Arleta and Sovilla.

"Hannah?" Sovilla cut in, obviously confused. "If Noah was taking Hannah home, how did you get back here, Arleta?"

"Isaiah gave me a ride."

"I don't understand. Why didn't Noah give you a ride, too?"

Arleta's face turned pink, just like it had on the day

when Sovilla announced at breakfast that the young woman didn't have a suitor. Seeing her discomfort, Noah's annoyance at Arleta melted. He realized that while she might not have cared if her peers knew how infatuated she was with Isaiah, she was clearly bashful about talking to Sovilla about it.

"Isaiah was leaving anyway, so Arleta went with him since I wanted to stay longer than she did," he answered for her. "At that point, I didn't have a headache yet."

"Jah," Arleta agreed, giving him a grateful look. "I was tired but I didn't want to spoil Noah's *schpass*."

Sovilla eyed Arleta and then Noah before shaking her head in apparent disbelief. "I don't understand you two. You're so young and in such *gut* health, yet you act as if you've got anvils tied to your legs, dragging you down. *I'm* supposed to be the one who's old and sickly."

"She sure doesn't *look* sickly, does she?" Arleta asked Noah, eager to change the subject. She knew he wouldn't want to discuss whatever was going on between him and Hannah with Sovilla. And clearly, something *was* going on, since he'd given her a ride home. It was exactly what Arleta hoped would happen, yet now that it had, she didn't particularly want to hear him talk about it, either.

"*Neh.* Her coloring is a lot better now. Her eyes are brighter, too," Noah remarked. "But the real test of how well she's doing and how much energy she has will be whether she can stay awake in *kurrich* this morning."

"Ach! Twenty-three years old and you're still a little *schnickelfritz*!" Sovilla shook her finger at Noah, laughing.

Arleta loved seeing her so energetic. *It must be*

because she has a ray of hope about her grandson courting again, she thought. Imagining that Noah's relationship with Hannah had the potential to bring Sovilla joy made Arleta happy, too.

Or at least, it made her *want* to feel happy. But some small part of her felt lonely—felt left out—knowing she couldn't enter into a courtship like the one she'd helped revive between Hannah and Noah. She tried to shake off her low mood but later, as she sat in church listening to the first preacher deliver a sermon based on 1 Timothy about being a good example to others, Arleta grappled with feelings of regret and shame. Then, after worship and lunch were over, she was helping clean up and she tripped, almost dropping the tray of leftover food she was carrying into the kitchen.

Hannah and Faith were standing nearby and they'd seen her stumble so she poked fun at herself, quipping, "Pride goeth before a fall."

"You said it, not me," Faith retorted, causing Hannah to giggle.

Maybe Arleta was being too sensitive, but it sounded as if Faith's jest had an edge to it—as if she truly believed Arleta was a prideful person. And Hannah seemed to be laughing *at* Arleta, not *with* her. *It seems like she should be nicer to me than that, now that it's clear* she's *the one Noah's interested in*, Arleta thought. Her shoulders drooping, she set the tray of food on the counter for someone else to put away and went upstairs to see if Sovilla was ready to leave.

But the older woman informed her that she was going to spend the afternoon visiting with the deacon and his wife at their house. *Sovilla has a more active social life than I do*, Arleta glumly thought. She headed outside and waited in the shade of a maple tree for Noah to pass by on his way to hitch the horse and buggy. As she was standing there, Isaiah approached and her spirits lifted. *At least there's one person my age in New Hope who's always* hallich *to see me.*

Today, however, Isaiah wasn't smiling. "Hello, Arleta," he said in a low voice. "There's, uh, something I'd like to speak with you about in private..."

Fearing he was about to invite her to go for a ride with him—possibly so he could ask to be her suitor—Arleta felt her upper lip and forehead breaking out in beads of sweat. Given her recent behavior, including trailing after him to ask for a ride home last evening, as well as allowing him to carry her across the stream at the gorge, it was understandable that he would have thought she was interested in a courtship with him. But she didn't want him for a suitor. For a friend, yes, but not for a suitor. Trying to stall until she could think of a tactful way to turn him down, she said she'd be happy to chat with him but she wondered if he needed a glass of water, first. "You look a little pale. Do you feel all right?"

"*Neh*, not really. My stomach hurts and I'm not sure if I have the bug that's been going around or if it's from something else. Something that's been weighing heavily on my mind," he admitted.

Oh, neh, she fretted, *I hope he's not going to tell me he's lovesick!* "Well, a lot of people are getting the stomach flu in New Hope. My *schweschder* told me it's going around Serenity Ridge, too. But the *gut* news is that it only lasts two days, tops," she rambled nervously.

When she stopped to take a breath, Isaiah cut in.

"*Neh.* I think my stomachache might be because I've been troubled by something I'm ashamed of doing."

That wasn't what Arleta expected him to say, and she wasn't quite sure why he'd want to confess something he was ashamed of to *her.* "Oh?" she uttered.

"*Jah.* You see, I'm afraid I… I'm afraid I may have led you to believe that I might be, uh, might be seeking a courtship with you, but I'm not." He tentatively glanced at her from beneath the brim of his hat.

Arleta at once felt like laughing because she was relieved and like crying because she'd been so vain to imagine Isaiah wanted to be her suitor. *Pride* does *goeth before a fall*, she scolded herself. Tongue-tied once again all she could say was, "Oh?"

"*Jah.* I mean, you're a lot of *schpass* and I enjoy your company, but I kind of think of you as being like a kid *schweschder.* I'm really sorry if I've given you the wrong impression, Arleta." He paused and looked at the ground before meeting her eyes again. "I, uh, I know I can trust you not to say anything about this, but I'm actually interested in courting someone else. I just haven't had the courage to express my feelings to her because… well, because I'm afraid of how she'll respond."

Isaiah appeared utterly miserable and Arleta knew she was to blame for the misunderstanding between them. So instead of telling him she didn't want him for a suitor, anyway, she simply said, "I completely understand and I appreciate your honesty."

"Really? You're not angry at me?"

"*Neh*, I'm not. And I hope we can continue to be friends."

"*Jah*, of course." Isaiah smiled but he still appeared

wan, and Arleta regretted that she may have contributed to his distress.

She leaned forward and spoke quietly, as people were beginning to stream past them toward the area where their horses were tied to the long stretch of hitching post. "You know, Isaiah, whatever *weibsmensch* you'd like to court would be fortunate to have you for a suitor. You should take the risk and tell her how you feel."

"I'd like to," he said, "but I'm not as open as you are."

Ha! Arleta laughed contritely to herself. *If he only knew what I'm hiding...*

Noah approached them just then and greeted Isaiah before asking Arleta if she was ready to leave. She was, but after her conversation with Isaiah, she needed time alone to think, so she told Noah she intended to walk, instead. "I might stop at the phone shanty, so don't be surprised if I'm not home for a while."

"I probably won't be there by the time you get back anyway," he replied before striding away as if he were in a hurry.

He must be taking Hannah out for a ride, Arleta deduced, but of course, she didn't ask him if that's what he planned to do after he went home and changed.

"I hope you don't get lost in the woods again. But if you *kumme* out on the wrong side, feel free to stop in at the farm," Isaiah said with a chuckle, and then he walked away, too.

Within five minutes of leaving the church, Arleta's dress clung to her back and her socks were wet with perspiration, too. She couldn't wait to take them off when she got to the stream in the woods, but the water was even shallower than the first time she'd been there and the mosquitoes were out in full force, so she hurried off to call her family. Since she hadn't arranged to speak with them ahead of time, she reached the voice mail recording for the phone nearest their house in Serenity Ridge but she didn't leave a message. What would she have said? "I'm only calling to let you know a *mann* who wasn't my suitor just broke off a courtship I didn't even have with him"?

"I'm sweltering," she whined plaintively when she walked through the front door to Sovilla and Noah's house thirty minutes later. The first thing she did was remove her shoes and socks, and then she went straight into the bathroom. Sitting on the edge of the tub, she turned on the water and stuck her feet beneath the faucet. She didn't feel quite as refreshed as she'd felt the first time she'd visited the stream, but the water cooled her skin considerably.

I might as well make the most of being in the house alone, she thought, and decided not to put on another pair of socks after drying her feet. She retrieved her stationery, poured herself a glass of lemonade and then wandered outside to sit on the double wooden glider on the porch. The sun was hitting her directly in the eyes, but it was still cooler there than it was in the house so she stayed put.

Too drained to even push the chair back and forth, she sipped her drink and contemplated how she'd phrase a letter to her parents, warning them against allowing Leanna to work out at the *Englischers*' home. But when she drew a blank, she tried to mentally compose a letter to her sister, instead.

She wondered if she should be so candid as to caution her, *If you work with* Englischers, *you might be tempted to start acting like one.* Or, worse, *You might want to* become *one.* No, her sister would scoff at the possibility. Arleta remembered when Jaala, the deacon's wife in Serenity Ridge, had inquired whether she was concerned that her *Englisch* employers might have a bigger influence on Arleta than she had on them. In retrospect, she appreciated that Jaala had cared enough to try to protect her, but at the time, she'd felt insulted.

Maybe she should write, *It's Sunday afternoon and everyone else is out socializing and courting but I'm sitting at home by myself, which is something I expect to do a lot in the future. I have no hope of ever getting married or having children and I feel estranged from my family and community—sometimes I even feel estranged from the Lord. I'm pleading with you not to make the same kind of mistakes I made, beginning with working in an* Englischer's *home...*

Arleta wasn't going to tell her sister any of that; she didn't have the courage. She set her tablet aside and closed her eyes. Leaning back, she rested her head against the side of the house, stretched her legs out in front of her and allowed the tears to flow freely down her face.

The next thing she knew, she felt a shift in temperature as a shadow blocked the sun. "Arleta?" Sovilla asked, touching her arm.

She sat up with a jerk and swiftly drew her feet back under the glider, panicked. Had Sovilla seen her ankle? "I must have dozed off. Have you been standing there long?"

"*Neh.* I got home about an hour ago. You were sleeping so soundly you didn't hear me go past. I didn't wake you because you'd said you've been tired, but I shouldn't have let you sleep so long. It looks as if you've gotten sunburned. I'll go get an aloe leaf from the fridge."

Arleta touched her cheeks, which were warm. Her forearms were bright pink and freckling; she'd definitely gotten a burn. But her more pressing concern was how she was going to get inside and put on a pair of socks without Sovilla seeing her tattoo.

A minute later, Sovilla returned with a knife and an aloe leaf, which she cut open so Arleta could spread its cool gel over her skin. "That feels *wunderbaar*," she said as she rubbed a generous blob of it onto her forearm. Although the tops of Arleta's feet were hot and tingling and she knew they were burned, too, she was relieved that Sovilla didn't suggest that she apply aloe to them, as well. She kept her legs bent beneath her and her ankles pressed together, out of sight.

"I've got to go take a shower," Sovilla announced, scratching her head. "This heat is making my scalp itchier than usual today."

"I'll be right in as soon as I gather my things," Arleta said. She waited until she heard the bathroom door close before she darted inside to her room and pulled on a pair of socks. The fabric caused the tender skin on her feet to sting, but she figured it was nowhere near the amount of discomfort she would have experienced if Sovilla had discovered her secret.

"Where have you been all afternoon?" Noah's grandmother questioned him when he arrived home just in time to eat supper. Since cooking big meals on the Sabbath wasn't permitted by the *Ordnung*, on Saturday Arleta had set aside some of the four bean salad, peppered deviled eggs and pickled green beans she'd made for the potluck. She'd also baked an extra strawberry-rhubarb coffee cake just for them to enjoy at home.

"I went to Little Loon Pond," he mumbled, his mouth full. After church, he'd returned home to change and pick up his fishing equipment and then he'd journeyed to the pond, which could be accessed from behind his coworker David Hilty's property. The Amish in New Hope kept two communal canoes there for anyone in their district to use. Although he hadn't gotten a single nibble on his line all afternoon, Noah didn't mind. There was a cool, gentle breeze blowing over the water, and as he paddled close to the shaded shoreline, he became more and more relaxed. He hadn't had such a peaceful outing since his grandmother had been diagnosed with cancer. Any residual exasperation he'd felt about Arleta's behavior the previous evening completely dissipated. Afterward, he decided he'd try to go to the pond at least every other Sunday for the rest of the summer, which he hoped would keep Sovilla from badgering him to get out more often.

"Was anyone else there?"

"A few other people, *jah*." Noah had spotted Honor and Jonathan canoeing, too, but he pretended not to see them in order to give them their privacy. He quickly shifted topics so Sovilla wouldn't question him further. Noticing Arleta was quieter than usual and she was poking at her food instead of eating it, he asked if she was okay.

"I'm a little out of sorts," she mumbled without looking up.

Noah wasn't sure whether she meant she was physically out of sorts or if she was emotionally upset. It occurred to him that she might have had an argument with

Isaiah. They'd seemed to be having a very serious conversation when he'd approached them in the churchyard after lunch. Because Arleta had declined a ride home with Noah, he assumed she was either planning to meet up with Isaiah later or hoping he'd offer her a ride once Noah left. Maybe things didn't go according to plan?

That's not for me to wonder about, he reminded himself. However, so many people had been sick from church lately that he did feel justified in asking, "Do you think you've caught the bug that's going around?"

"*Neh.* I think I caught too much sun today." Frowning, she stood up. "I'm sorry, but I have to excuse myself. I'll *kumme* back to clear the table in a little while."

"That's okay, dear. Noah and I can manage. You go lie down. I'll check on you in a little while," Sovilla instructed. The fact that Arleta didn't insist on doing the dishes or object to the older woman's caregiving indicated how ill she must have felt.

"I hope Arleta's all right. I wouldn't want you to catch anything from her," Noah remarked.

"I hope she's all right for her *own* sake, the poor *maedel.*"

Sovilla had a way of scolding Noah for being insensitive without actually saying he was being insensitive. But he couldn't help worrying about his grandmother's health—if Arleta had the flu, she'd get over it in a couple of days. If Sovilla contracted it, she might end up in the hospital.

Groossmammi's *come too far in her recovery to suffer a big setback like that now*, Noah thought. While protecting his grandmother's health was his top priority and he would spare no expense to keep her well, he didn't want to have to pay for a hospital bill—which would put a big dent in his Mexico trip funds—if hospitalization could be avoided.

"To be on the safe side, I think we should consider asking Arleta to return to Serenity Ridge until she feels better. I seem to remember her telling me her *familye* already had the bug, so they won't catch it. Maybe Lovina would be willing to *kumme* stay with you and cook for a couple of days."

"Don't be *lecherich*! Arleta got too much sun, that's all."

"Maybe, but you can't be too careful, *Groossmammi*. You have a weakened immune system."

His grandmother slowly wiped her lips and set her napkin aside. "Arleta has taken great pains to keep me well. She has kept this *haus* as clean and germ-free as humanly possible, and she's prepared nutritious, *appenditlich* meals. Not to mention, she's put up with all my moods and demands. And now you want to repay her by sending her home when *she's* ill?"

"Her *repayment* is her salary. She earns a lot of money doing all those tasks you just listed!" The words were out of Noah's mouth before he could stop them, and he hardly realized what they sounded like until he noticed his grandmother's disgusted expression.

"I don't care if you're paying her a *million* dollars. Nor do I care whether she's merely sun sick or she has the plague—I am *not* sending her home when she's ill," Sovilla declared. "I trust her to take precautions to keep me from catching any illness she may have, and I trust the Lord to know all of my needs. If you don't, then *you* can ask her to leave. But you'll need to stay home with me until she returns, because I am not imposing on our friends for something I consider an unnecessary measure. So I'd advise you to pray about it and sleep on it before you carry out your plan. Now, if you'll excuse me, I'm going to go reciprocate a tiny bit of the tender care to Arleta that she's shown to me."

After Sovilla tottered down the hall, Noah cleared the table and rinsed the dishes. He didn't know what had gotten into his grandmother. Why did she consider it such an affront to ask Arleta to leave until she was well again? Considering Sovilla's fragile health, it seemed like a reasonable request to make.

Yet a couple of hours later as the suffocating heat in the loft made it difficult for him to breathe, much less to sleep, Noah questioned whether *he* was the one who'd been unreasonable. *I suppose it's possible that Arleta really is suffering from too much sun exposure.* Since he didn't know if she was actually contagious, was sending her away worth upsetting his grandmother and forfeiting three or four days' worth of salary? After praying about it, Noah decided he'd wait until the morning to see if Arleta felt better before he asked her to leave.

He had arranged for Mike to pick everyone up an hour earlier than usual since they'd gone home early on Friday, so the sun hadn't even risen yet when Noah came in from milking the cow. Surprisingly, Arleta was standing at the stove, frying bacon. "*Guder mariye.* You're up early. Does that mean you feel better?" he asked.

"It means I feel *hungerich*," she said, ridding Noah's mind of any worry that she'd had the stomach flu, which typically lasted for two or three days, not for a single evening.

Gut, *that's one issue resolved. I just hope by the time I get home I'm not still in hot water with* Groossmammi, Noah thought. To help mend the rift between them, right before he went out the door, he wrote Sovilla a note that said, *Dear Grandma, I was wrong and I'm sorry. Signed, Your twenty-three-year-old Schnickelfritz.* He folded the paper into a small square and tucked it into her Bible, which she read in the morning daily.

As Mike drove his three coworkers to the site, Jacob informed Noah and David that he'd heard that Isaiah had to go to the ER the previous evening. Apparently he'd caught the stomach bug and had vomited so many times he became severely dehydrated, but he felt a lot better once he received medication and IV fluids.

"That's *baremlich*, but I'm grateful to *Gott* it wasn't something more serious," David replied.

"So am I," Noah emphatically agreed.

Jacob monopolized the conversation the rest of the way to the gym, yammering on about how great the potluck was. "You won't believe it," he said to Mike and David. "But Noah actually showed up—and afterward, he gave a certain *maedel* a ride home."

"You mean Arleta? She's living with his grandmother and him, you know, so that doesn't really count for giving a girl a ride home," Mike said.

"*Neh*, Arleta got a ride from someone else. Noah left with—"

David cut him off midsentence, most likely to spare Noah any embarrassment. "I saw you canoeing on the pond on *Sunndaag*, Noah. Were the fish biting?"

"*Neh.* But I enjoyed paddling around."

"Enough about that. What *I* want to know is if your cooler is filled with potluck leftovers," Mike hinted.

Noah actually had no idea what was in his cooler, since Arleta had packed it while he'd been in the other room writing a note to his grandmother. "You'll just have to wait and see," he replied.

But by the time lunch hour rolled around, Noah didn't feel like eating anything. His head hurt again, and he was so woozy he couldn't stand to watch the other men consume their food—or to work their way through *his* cooler.

After sitting alone in the shade and sipping water for twenty or thirty minutes, his nausea passed and he concluded he'd gotten overheated. *If I didn't know that the sun had affected Arleta the same way, I'd be worried* I *have the stomach flu*, he thought. He still didn't feel hungry, but since the other men had devoured his lunch, it was just as well.

When he arrived home it was nearly six o'clock and Noah expected to smell supper cooking, but instead he found Arleta sitting on the glider on the porch, wringing her hands. "What's wrong?" he immediately asked.

"I'm afraid your *groossmammi* has been ill. She's sleeping right now, but she's had a very rough afternoon." She described Sovilla's symptoms, which were similar to how *he'd* felt at lunch.

His fists clenched at his sides, Noah tried to remain calm. "Was she outside in the sun a lot today?"

"*Neh.* Except to use the bathroom, she's hardly been out of bed. She's too weak," Arleta explained. "She only has a slight fever, so that's a *gut* sign. I was going to go call the *dokder* to ask if she should make an appointment as a precaution, but I didn't want to leave her on her own. And at first, I thought the vomiting would pass quickly, the way it did for me last night."

Noah couldn't believe his ears. "You got sick to your stomach last night and you didn't tell me?"

Arleta's sunburned cheeks turned an even deeper shade of pink. "I—I—I'm sorry, but I—"

"What *gut* does it do to be sorry? You should have been *safe*!" He paced to the opposite end of the porch and stood staring across the yard, his back toward her. "She'd better not end up in the hospital like Isaiah did!"

Arleta gasped. "Isaiah's in the hospital?"

"*Neh*, not anymore." Noah spun around to face her. "But maybe if you had cared as much about my *groossmammi*'s health as you obviously care about your suitor's, she wouldn't be sick right now. In fact, Isaiah is probably the reason she's sick. You caught the stomach virus from him and passed it on to her!"

"*What* are you talking about?"

"I saw you cozying up to him on *Sunndaag* after *kurrich*, Arleta. And *all* our peers saw you chasing him down on *Samschdaag* evening. If you're that brazen toward him in public, I can only imagine what you're like around him in private—"

"Absatz!" Arleta shouted, leaping to her feet. She marched to the door and jerked it open. Before going inside, she paused to say over her shoulder, "Since you don't believe I care about your *groossmammi*'s health, you'll need to find a replacement for me as soon as possible. Meanwhile, I'd appreciate it if you'd keep your opinions about my character to yourself."

Not a problem, Noah thought as she disappeared into the house. *Unless it's absolutely necessary, I don't intend to speak to you at all.*

Chapter Nine

Arleta sobbed into her pillow so Sovilla wouldn't hear her. There was only one time in her life when she'd felt more hurt than she did right now, and that was when Ian broke up with her in a letter. *After all this time, how could Noah suggest I don't care about Sovilla's health?* She considered that to be almost a worse insult than his remark about the way she behaved toward Isaiah, although they were both horrible things for him to say. *I've tried* so *hard to take care of Sovilla. And I've tried to be a* gut *Amish role model ever since I was baptized into the* kurrich. *I haven't done any of it perfectly, but it's just so unfair—so* unkind*—of Noah to suggest I've done the exact opposite*, she lamented.

And why had he assumed Arleta was the one who'd brought the bug home to his grandmother? Sovilla had received visitors at the house, she'd gone to the potluck and she'd gone to church. It was far more likely that she'd gotten sick from being around someone else in the community than from Arleta, who was hypervigilant about washing her hands and covering her mouth when she coughed or sneezed. She was meticulous about food preparation, too. Most important, Arleta's symptoms were too short-lived to be the flu, she was sure of it.

Sniffling, she rolled over and lay still on her back, listening for movement in the next room. She was relieved to hear faint snoring; that must have meant Sovilla's stomach had settled down enough for her to sleep. Earlier in the evening, Noah had gone to the phone shanty and spoken to the doctor on call at the clinic. She'd told him that as long as Sovilla didn't run a high fever or become dehydrated, there was no need to make an appointment, since the virus would run its course without medication. Still, most people who'd had the flu said the stomach and intestinal issues lasted for a full twenty-four hours, at least, followed by lesser bouts of nausea and weakness. Arleta realized she'd told Noah to find a replacement for her immediately, but she hoped to stay in New Hope until she was sure his grandmother had completely recovered from the flu.

She'd been so upset about what Noah had said and about Sovilla being ill that it hadn't occurred to Arleta until just now that by quitting her job, she had also given up her goal of earning enough money to get her tattoo removed. *It's okay*, she tried to convince herself. *I was going to give Emma's* familye *a portion of my savings anyway, so Leanna won't have to babysit for the* Englischers. Besides, as Noah had indicated, everybody already thought she behaved inappropriately, so what did it matter if she had a tattoo or not? *At this point, I'm done caring about what anyone—especially people who are as unfair as Noah and as cold as Hannah—think about me*, she defiantly decided. *And I'm done wearing socks to bed, too!* She reached down, tugged them off and dropped them on the floor beside her bed. Then, utterly drained, she shut her eyes and went to sleep.

She must have dozed for two or three hours before she was woken by the sound of the bathroom door closing. She bounded out of bed and down the hall to see if Sovilla needed help. But Sovilla's door was shut; that meant it was Noah who was in the bathroom. As Arleta turned to go back to her room, she heard the unmistakable sound of retching: he was ill. *Great. Now he's going to blame me for that, too*, she thought and she slid into bed.

But she lay awake, listening for him to walk past her room on his way back upstairs. After ten or fifteen minutes passed with no sound of him going by, she got up, put on her bathrobe and tiptoed down the hall. Rapping lightly on the bathroom door, she quietly asked, "Are you okay, Noah?" Her question was met with a groan. A few seconds later, the door opened and she realized he wasn't standing in front of her—he was sitting on the floor.

"I feel *baremlich*," he moaned, his eyes bloodshot and his face pale.

She extended her hand. "Here, I'll help you up."

"*Neh.* Not yet."

Understanding what he meant, Arleta replied, "I'll go make up the couch, so you can be closer to the bathroom if you need it."

"Denki," he muttered, and abruptly closed the door.

Arleta flew into her room and donned her *kapp* so she could pray for Noah as she brought fresh sheets and a pillow into the living room. No matter how deeply he'd hurt her, it pained Arleta to see him so sick and after turning the couch into a temporary bed, she circled back to the bathroom and knocked on the door again. This time, he took her hand and allowed her to help him into a standing position. He was so unsteady that she had to prop him up all the way into the living room, where he collapsed onto the sofa.

She brought him a glass of cold ginger tea, but he shook his head, apparently too drained to speak. She went back into the kitchen and took ice cubes from the tray. She knew he probably couldn't tolerate more than a few slivers at a time, but she didn't want to wake Sovilla by pounding the ice. So she put the cubes into a plastic bag, grabbed the meat mallet from the drawer and darted outside to crush the ice into chips against the ground. Then she rushed back inside to bring them to Noah in a glass.

But the couch was empty and she spotted him in the hall, crawling toward the bathroom. After he came out, she helped him back to the sofa and sat in the armchair across from him so she could support him down the hall the next time he felt sick to his stomach. They must have made half a dozen trips back and forth before he finally fell asleep. Arleta smoothed back his dark, damp hair to place a hand on his bare forehead; he was still feverish, but not quite as hot as before.

No sooner did she drop into the armchair than she heard Sovilla's door open, so Arleta popped back up and repeated a similar process of assisting her back and forth between her bed and the bathroom. The older woman finally fell back asleep just as the sun was coming up. Arleta returned to the living room to steal a few minutes of rest in the armchair. Only then did it occur to her that her bare ankle was exposed, but before she could get up to put on her socks, she nodded off to sleep.

* * *

Noah opened his eyes and quickly shut them again. Then he reopened them just a crack, squinting as he looked around the living room. The sunlight seemed brighter than usual, and he wasn't sure if he was dreaming or not. He had hazy recollections of sipping water, eating crackers, using the bathroom or talking to Sovilla and Arleta at various times during the night, but he didn't know if any of it had actually happened.

But when Arleta came into his range of vision, he was certain she was real, not a dream, because he felt her cool hand on his forehead and heard her murmur, "I think your fever's gone."

He tried to ask how his grandmother was, but his throat was too scratchy to get the words out. Arleta supported his head and lifted a glass to his lips so he could take a sip of water. "Is *Groossmammi* okay?"

"*Jah*, she's doing very well. She's taking a nap in her room. She fared a lot better than you did. After the second day, she was almost as *gut* as new."

Noah tried to sit up but it made him dizzy so he rested against the pillow again. "The second day? How long have I been sleeping?"

"Off and on since *Muundaag.* It's *Freidaag* now."

"Freidaag? Neh!"

"*Jah*, it is. Feel your chin—you're growing quite the beard."

Noah touched his cheeks and chin; they were prickly with hair. "I don't remember so much time passing. I must have been really sick."

"You were. How do you feel now?"

"Baremlich." Although most of the past week was a blur, one thing he recalled perfectly was what he'd said

to Arleta when he'd found out Sovilla was ill. As terrible as he'd felt physically, he felt even more wretched for accusing her of not caring about his grandmother's health when clearly *he* was the one who'd brought home the flu.

"*Jah*, that makes sense. You'll probably be weak for several days." Arleta adjusted the pillow behind his head and then tucked the sheet around him. "What can I do to make you more comfortable?"

Noah clutched her fingers to get her attention. She stopped fussing with the bedding and tipped her head quizzically at him. "I don't feel *baremlich* because of the flu—well, I do, but I feel more *baremlich* about the things I said to you," he confessed. "I am very, very sorry, Arleta."

She pulled her fingers free of his grasp. "Don't wear yourself out talking about that now."

"*Neh*, this is important. Please listen." So she sat down in the armchair facing him. His voice crackling with dryness and emotion, he continued, "I was completely out of line. What I said was a reflection of my fear, not of your care for *Groossmammi*. I panicked because she's the only *familye* I have, and it's my responsibility to make sure…" Noah didn't usually feel so sentimental. Maybe it was that the virus was affecting his emotions, but his eyes welled and he couldn't complete the thought.

As Arleta leaned forward to help him take another sip of water, she assured him, "She's okay, Noah. She's fine. *Gott* kept her from becoming severely ill."

"*Jah*. But He used *you* to help her—to help both of us—recover. I can't say enough how grateful I am. Or how sorry I am. *I* was the one who brought the flu home to her, not you." Again, he was embarrassed when his vision blurred with tears.

"You don't know that for sure. You don't know where she got it."

"Maybe not, but I know she *didn't* get it from you. Please forgive me for accusing you of making her sick. Of not caring about her health," Noah pleaded.

"I *do* forgive you for that." Arleta set the water glass on the end table and then took a deep breath and said, "But there was something else you were wrong about, Noah. Your implication that I've behaved inappropriately with Isaiah in private was hurtful, untrue and ungentlemanly."

Noah had been so upset when he'd come home to discover Sovilla was ill that he'd said things he couldn't fully remember. But seeing the pain in Arleta's eyes and hearing the indignation in her voice brought the gist of his remarks back to him. "*Neh.* The implication I made was worse than that—it was *ungodly.* I am so ashamed, Arleta—and so sorry."

She bit her lip and nodded, but he could tell she was hesitant to accept his apology and he didn't blame her. Using all of his strength, he pushed himself up on one elbow. Grasping the back of the sofa with the other hand, he pulled himself the rest of the way up, until he was in a sitting position, directly facing her. The effort made him dizzy, and he rested his hands on his knees until they stopped trembling. Ordinarily, he never would have admitted what he was about to disclose—he could hardly admit it to himself—but he had to make Arleta believe he didn't really mean what he'd said.

"I—I made that remark—that horrible remark—because I wanted someone to blame for *groossmammi* being sick. And I blamed you and Isaiah because, well, because I've been envious of your courtship."

"Pah!" Arleta uttered. "Isaiah is *not* my suitor. I have no romantic interest in him whatsoever and I never did."

"Really? But you seem so enam—" He stopped talking before he put his foot in his mouth again.

Fortunately, Arleta giggled. "I seem so enamored of him, is that it? I suppose I can understand why you and our peers may have thought that. I *was* 'chasing him down' for a ride after the potluck. But that was only because I wanted to allow *you* the opportunity to give Hannah a ride home alone."

"Why would I want to do that?"

Arleta's cheeks flushed and she looked down at her lap. "You know, so you could renew your courtship with her."

Aha, that's *why she looks so guilty. Someone must have told her I used to be Hannah's suitor.* "I'm about as interested in a courtship with Hannah as you are with Isaiah."

Arleta lifted her head. "Really?"

"*Jah.* I can't see myself in a courtship with anyone. That's why I was envious of your courtship with Isaiah—because I know that a courtship isn't something I can ever have." Whoa. Noah's fatigue must have dulled his inhibition because he'd come very close—*too* close—to confiding far more than he wanted to confide. He rubbed his forehead, hoping Arleta wouldn't pick up on what he'd just admitted, but it was too late.

"What's stopping you from having a courtship?"

"I don't know why I said that. I might still be feverish," Noah said with a laugh, but Arleta wasn't distracted.

"If it's because of your obligations to Sovilla, there's no reason you can't care for your *groossmammi* and care about a *weibsmensch* at the same time, you know," Arleta said. "And I don't think anything would make Sovilla happier than seeing you in a courtship."

"You don't have to tell *me* that," Noah said with a wry laugh. Dropping the subject, he asked, "Could you please help me up now?"

His legs were so weak that as soon as he got up, even though Arleta was holding on to him, he had to sit back down again. While he was resting before he gave it a second try, Sovilla entered the room.

"Noah, you're awake, my little *schlofkopp*!" She joyfully called him a sleepyhead and then crossed the room to kiss his forehead before sitting down next to him. "How are you feeling?"

He glanced at Arleta, whose smile showed the small opening between her teeth—she'd completely forgiven him. "I feel *wunderbaar* now, relatively speaking. Except I can't wait to shave off this beard."

"Oh, but it gives me a glimpse of what you'll look like when you get married. I think he wears it well, don't you, Arleta?"

"*Jah*, he looks very handsome in it," she said, winking at Sovilla—or maybe at Noah. And he felt so invigorated by her compliment that he rose from the couch all by himself.

Of course, after making up with Noah, Arleta didn't leave New Hope. In fact, wild horses couldn't have dragged her away, especially now that she had *two* patients to attend to. Not that Sovilla was much of a patient; she was a little wobblier than usual, probably because she still wasn't eating enough, even though the nausea and stomach pain had long passed. But Noah was so weak he needed help just crossing the room, and he spent the next several days sleeping more hours than he was awake.

Fortunately, that week was an off-Sunday, so the trio was able to worship at home and after they'd prayed and read the Bible together, Sovilla went to her room to nap and Noah rested on the couch, as he still didn't have the strength to climb the stairs. Arleta sat opposite him, gazing at his face. The angles of his jaw and cheekbones were more pronounced, once he'd shaved off his beard. It occurred to her that she didn't realize he'd been slowly gaining weight since she'd been there until he got sick and lost it again. Still, she thought he looked as masculine as ever, although his physical traits were the least important of the attributes she found attractive about him.

No wonder Hannah wishes she had a second chance to have him as her suitor, she thought. As uncharitable as it was, she felt a small measure of satisfaction to discover Noah wasn't interested in courting her. *I'm sorry that it will hurt her feelings when she finds out, but I just can't see him with her. I never really could...*

"Are you sitting there watching me sleep?" Noah asked, opening one eye.

Caught, she joked, "*Neh*—because you're not actually sleeping. But I'll leave if I'm making you uncomfortable."

"You're not. I can't really sleep anyway." He slowly sat up and swung his feet around to the floor. "You know, when I was sick, I had the strangest dreams. In one of them, you weren't wearing socks."

Arleta's pulse quickened. "Do you remember anything else about that dream?"

"You mean like did you have hooves instead of feet?" He laughed. "Now that I think about it, I do remember something else. It was the oddest thing."

"What was that?" Arleta squeaked.

"You were holding a mallet."

Relieved, she cracked up and told him about going outside to crush the ice into chips for him so she wouldn't wake Sovilla by making such a loud noise in the house. She thought he'd find it amusing to picture her outside in the middle of the night pounding ice with a meat mallet, but instead he shook his head, frowning. "What's wrong?" she asked.

"*Me.* I'm wrong. I mean, I *was* wrong. So wrong. You've taken such *gut* care of *Groossmammi* and me, right down to the smallest detail and—"

"Noah," she interrupted him. "You apologized and I've forgiven you so there's no need to continue to feel sorry or to keep apologizing to me. Otherwise, it's as if you haven't accepted my forgiveness."

"Okay. *Denki*," he said. Then he sighed. "I don't think *Groossmammi* is going to let me go to work tomorrow. Not that she can really stop me, but I'd better prepare for an argument."

"*I'm* not going to let you go to work tomorrow—and I *can* stop you. I'll hitch the horse to the fence at the end of the lane if I have to," Arleta threatened. She was laughing, but she meant it. "You can hardly balance well enough to cross the living room floor. How do you expect to pull yourself up a ladder or walk on a rooftop?"

"*Jah*, I guess I can give it another day of rest."

Another week is what you'll need, Arleta thought,

but she didn't say it aloud. There was no need for her to convince him; his body would show him his limitations.

Sure enough, over the next couple of days, Noah's strength began to return, but at a much slower pace than he wanted it to. By Thursday morning, he was chomping at the bit to return to work, but he still wasn't even capable of caring for the animals; Arleta had to do it. She didn't mind, but it frustrated Noah that she was single-handedly managing the household, livestock and yardwork and he couldn't help her.

"See what happens when you don't get enough rest for weeks on end? Along comes a virus and knocks you completely out of commission," Sovilla chided him. "You lectured me about my weak immune system, but I think yours was even more fragile."

Arleta noticed that after so many days of being housebound together without a break, Sovilla and Noah were getting on each other's nerves. "It's such a pretty day today. Noah, why don't we take a ride to the market together? I need flour because tomorrow Sovilla's going to teach me to make a bumbleberry pie. And maybe we can stop off at the lake you told me about. What's it called again?"

"It's a pond. Little Loon Pond. But I don't think it's a *gut* idea to leave *Groossmammi* alone for that long."

Sovilla harrumphed exaggeratedly. "And *Groossmammi* doesn't think it's a *gut* idea for *you* to *stay with her* for so long."

Arleta tried not to giggle. "We'll leave after lunch and we'll be home before supper. How does that sound?"

"Like just what the doctor ordered," Sovilla said.

Noah seemed less pleased than his grandmother was but once they were underway, his mood lightened considerably. Although Arleta had insisted on hitching the horse and buggy herself, Noah had taken the reins once she'd given him a boost into the buggy. She asked him to stop at the store first, so she could get her errand out of the way before they relaxed at the pond. "I'll only be in there a few minutes," she said, as she climbed down onto the pavement in front of the little market on Main Street. He said he'd circle the block instead of hitching the horse in the back parking lot.

He hadn't returned yet when she came out of the store, so she stood in the shade of the awning. After a few minutes passed, she began to get worried. *Maybe I shouldn't have pushed him to* kumme *out*, she thought. But just then, his buggy rounded the corner and he pulled over by the sidewalk.

Climbing in, she asked, "Are you okay?"

"*Jah.* I wanted to get a treat for us to enjoy at the pond. You get to choose which one you want." He handed her a small paper bag.

Arleta peeked inside. The bag contained two plastic spoons and two small containers of homemade ice cream from the local ice cream parlor farther down Main Street. One was pink-colored and the other was clearly chocolate-flavored. She didn't even have to ask whether the pink was strawberry or peppermint; she wanted the chocolate. "What a sweet thing to do, especially since you had to hitch the horse and get in and out of the buggy by yourself."

"That's how I felt about you running outside to pound ice into chips for me," he said, his eyes fixed on her.

A delicious shiver rattled her shoulders, and Arleta broke eye contact with him and quickly set the bag on the seat between them. "The ice cream is making me cold already," she fibbed.

When they reached the pond, Noah turned down the dirt road that ran parallel with David Hilty's backyard. His coworker had cleared this path on his property specifically so his Amish district members could have easy access to the waterfront without cutting across his lawn and disturbing his family. After hitching the horse to the post David had erected, Noah slowly led Arleta through a short wooded path to a grassy clearing where two canoes lay overturned in front of the glassy water.

"Oh, look how beautiful the pond is—it's crystal clear. And it feels about ten degrees cooler here than in town," she marveled appreciatively.

"*Jah.* I like the gorge, too, but this is actually my favorite spot in all of New Hope."

"I can see why. Do you want to go out in a canoe or eat our ice cream here?"

Feeling a little winded, Noah suggested they should eat their ice cream first and canoe later. He helped Arleta spread the blanket she'd brought and they sat down, stretching their legs out in front of them. For a few minutes, they licked the creamy treat from their spoons, taking in the pristine scenery without talking. Soon, the tranquility of the setting—or maybe it was Arleta's soothing presence—made Noah realize how agitated he'd been earlier.

"I'm sorry if I've seemed cranky lately," he told her. "It's frustrating that I can't return to work yet."

"I understand. It can't be much *schpass* for you to be stuck in the *haus* with two *weibsleit* all day when you're used to being outdoors with your coworkers."

Actually being "stuck" indoors with Arleta had been the best part of his recovery. "*Neh.* That's not it. It's that I keep calculating how far behind I am financially, and there's absolutely nothing I can do about it. My body just isn't strong enough yet."

Arleta squinted at him, a pinched expression on her face. "You're struggling financially?"

Ach, had he actually said that aloud? Noah had only meant to assure Arleta it wasn't her company—it wasn't Sovilla's, either—that was making him cantankerous. But now that it had slipped out, there was no taking it back and he didn't want Arleta to mention his concern to Sovilla, so he clarified his statement. "I'm not struggling presently, *neh*... If I explain, do you promise not to tell my *groossmammi*?" When she nodded, he delved into the details of his plan to save enough money to take Sovilla to Mexico if it became necessary.

"Oh, so *that's* why you've been working so many hours!" she exclaimed.

"*Jah.* Why? Did you think it was because I'm greedy?"

"*Neh.* Not at all. I just figured it was because you were trying to keep up with customer demand," she said. "I should have known it had something to do with Sovilla—you're always so careful to put her needs first."

"It was *dumm* to work such long hours without taking enough breaks, though. *Groossmammi* was right—that's why the flu hit me so hard. Now I'm not sure if I'll ever catch up."

Arleta set her spoon in her empty cup and placed it at her side. "Listen, Noah. I've long felt that you've overcompensated me for staying with—"

"Neh, neh, neh," he cut her off. "I didn't tell you about my concern so you'd offer to—"

Now *she* cut *him* off. "Wait, just hear me out, please. I've felt guilty taking such a big salary for what feels like such a little bit of work. Especially now that Sovilla is doing so much better. I'd be *hallich* to work without pay for the rest of the summer—and I'd *still* feel as if I earned more money than I deserved."

Noah was adamant—it was *his* responsibility to take care of his family, and that included meeting their financial obligations. "I committed to paying you a certain salary, and I'm going to honor that commitment. I'll think of another solution if it becomes necessary to go to Mexico. But *denki* for your offer."

Arleta turned to face him, her eyes as vibrant green as the leafy branches overhead. "I respect your decision, Noah, but if you change your mind, my offer still stands. I'd do anything I could to help Sovilla if her cancer recurs. You know how fond I am of her."

Jah*, but do you know how fond* I *am of* you*?* Noah thought. He was about to reiterate his gratitude for her offer when Arleta swiveled her head and bent her knee to her chest, clutching her ankle.

"Ouch!" she screeched. "Something just bit me!"

Noticing a wasp crawling over her ice cream cup and aware that she often swelled up from insect bites and stings, Noah said, "I think you've been stung. Here, let me look."

"Neh," she yelped, hopping up off the blanket.

"Do you want me to ask the Hiltys if they have antihistamine?"

"*Neh!* I want you to give me some space!" she wailed and limped toward the water, tears streaming down her cheeks.

* * *

Although a burning pain coursed through Arleta's ankle, she wasn't crying because of the wasp sting. She was crying because for the past hour, she been allowing herself to *pretend* she was on a date. Which wasn't difficult to do, considering that Noah had bought her ice cream and confided an intimate secret to her and gazed at her with the same cherishing expression as he'd looked at the pond, his favorite place in all of New Hope. But then the wasp had stung her on the ankle, of all places, cruelly reminding her that she shouldn't be entertaining any notion of a courtship, not even a pretend one. *That's* why she was crying.

That, *and* because she was terrified that Noah would discover her secret. She hadn't meant to speak so harshly to him, but she didn't know how else to make him back off so she could unlace her shoe and examine her ankle. Even before she removed her footwear and peeled off her sock, she could tell how bad the swelling was because of how tight her skin felt. She took off her other shoe and sock and walked into the pond up to her shins. The chilly water alleviated her pain a little, but more importantly, as she stood there gazing toward the opposite shoreline, she was able to regulate her breathing. In turn, her heart rate, which had accelerated wildly from the release of histamine, also slowed.

When she finally turned around again, she spotted Noah standing beside the blanket, watching her. "Is that helping?"

"A little." As she began wading toward him, he moved in her direction, too. She quickly hurried out of the water and slapped mud over her ankle before he reached her. "I've read that when the mud dries, it can draw the wasp venom out. But I don't know if it's actually true."

"I guess it's worth a try."

"I'm sorry, but I don't think I can go canoeing now," she said, reaching to put her sock and shoe on her right foot.

"That's okay. I wouldn't have been able to paddle very far anyway. I'm beat. How about if we *kumme* back, let's say, a week from *Sunndaag* when I'm stronger?"

"I'd really like that," Arleta agreed. Noah picked up the blanket and empty ice cream containers, and Arleta retrieved her other sock and shoe. Then he extended his arm. "Is that so I can lean on you or so you can lean on me?"

He laughed. "A little of each."

So she took his arm and they hobbled down the path toward the buggy. *This might not have been a real date*, Arleta said to herself, *but I can't think of a more romantic way for it to end.*

Chapter Ten

To Arleta's disappointment, Noah returned to work the following Monday. They'd been getting along so well—in between Arleta's chores, they'd play spades with Sovilla or checkers with each other, read the Bible aloud or just chat. In the afternoons when Sovilla was napping, Arleta and Noah would take a stroll around the yard to build up his endurance and tolerance of the heat again. Those were the times Arleta liked best, mostly because she was alone with Noah, but also because he'd begun telling her stories about his family, which he hadn't done since he'd shared the anecdote about him and his brothers "skitching" when they were teenagers.

So after Mike picked him up on Monday morning, Arleta felt sulky and restless. She did the breakfast dishes and hung out the laundry and then went into the living room and plunked into a chair with a huff. "It's unbearably hot already and it's only nine o'clock," she complained to Sovilla. "I hope I sent enough meadow tea with Noah. I don't want him to get dehydrated."

"I'm sure he has plenty."

"*Jah*, but I should have packed more fruit for him. I

should have cut his sandwich into quarters, too, so he could take several breaks instead of eating it all at once. That's not *gut* for his stomach."

"I thought you were supposed to be tending to *me*, not to him," Sovilla said.

"Oh!" Arleta sprang to her feet. "What can I do for you?"

"I was teasing, dear."

"You don't feel ill?"

"*Neh.* And I think when I have my tests done next Thursday, we'll find out I'm as fit as a fiddle."

Arleta had been so wrapped up in helping Noah recover that she'd completely forgotten about Sovilla's important appointment. "*Gott* willing, that's exactly what we'll find out. But maybe you should eat a handful of blueberries daily, just in case. I read an article that said blueberries contain something called antioxidants, which play a role in preventing cancer."

"Was that in the same book that suggested putting mud on a bee sting?" Sovilla asked. She had been incredulous the afternoon Arleta limped into the house with mud caked on her ankle. Fortunately, by the time Arleta was done showering, the swelling had subsided considerably and she'd put on a fresh pair of socks so neither Noah nor his grandmother ever caught a glimpse of her tattoo.

"*Neh.* I read about antioxidants in one of Noah's pamphlets in the kitchen drawer." Because she sensed Sovilla was still skeptical, she said, "But it didn't actually say the blueberries *would* prevent cancer, or how quickly they might work. Just that it's *gut* to include them in your daily diet."

"Do raspberries and strawberries contain these antioxidants, too?"

"*Jah*. Why?"

"Because I need to teach you how to make a bumbleberry pie before you leave New Hope."

Arleta was scheduled to go home about a week after Sovilla's follow-up doctor's appointment, which was when Sarah would be available to come over again, baby in tow, if the older woman still needed care. That meant Arleta had a little less than three weeks left in New Hope. On one hand, she looked forward to returning to Serenity Ridge because she missed her family so much. On the other hand, she knew she was going to miss Sovilla terribly, too. And she couldn't even allow herself to imagine about how sad she'd be when she left Noah.

Pushing the thoughts away, she tried to refocus on their conversation. What was it they'd just been talking about? Oh, yes, Sovilla was going to reveal her special recipe for bumbleberry pie. "I've heard that you have a secret."

She was referring to Sovilla's secret ingredient, but the older woman murmured, "Almost everyone has a secret, dear—which is a pity, since the majority of our secrets are shameful ones."

Clearly, she wasn't talking about ingredients, and Arleta's pulse raced like it had when she'd been stung by the wasp. Had Sovilla seen her tattoo the night Arleta hadn't been wearing socks and she'd helped the older woman back and forth down the hall? "What do you mean?"

"Oh, I suppose I'm just thinking aloud about how the more we try to keep the things we're ashamed of a secret, the more miserable we become. Shame has a way of robbing us of the abundant life—the *joy*—that Christ wants us to have."

Sovilla's words struck a chord with Arleta, and her mouth was so dry she could hardly speak. "But don't you think sometimes it's wiser to keep a secret to yourself than it is to share it...like if telling it could hurt someone else? Or if you know that someone is going to judge you unfairly for whatever it is you don't want them to know?"

"*Jah.* It's wise to exercise discretion depending on the circumstance and the people involved. But there's a big difference between keeping a secret to yourself and holding on to shame. If we've confessed a wrongdoing to the Lord, He's faithful to forgive us."

Recognizing the Bible passage Sovilla was referencing, Arleta interjected, "1 John 1:9 is one of my favorite verses."

"*Jah*, mine, too. I repeat it to myself frequently. The problem is, even though I believe *Gott* forgives me for my transgressions, sometimes I have a difficult time forgiving *myself.* I think a lot of people struggle with that tendency."

I know I *do*, Arleta thought, relieved to know she wasn't the only one.

Sovilla pushed herself up from the chair, exclaiming, "Just listen to me! You asked about my secret ingredient and instead I delivered a sermon. *Kumme*, let's go bake a pie before Noah returns home and I can't tear you away from the checkerboard again."

If it's that obvious to her how much I've been enjoying Noah's company, maybe it's obvious that I'm hiding something, too, Arleta thought as she followed Sovilla into the kitchen. *Maybe that's why she just said all of those things about secrets and shame?*

But even if she did suspect something, Arleta decided she wasn't going to worry about it. She only had a couple more weeks left in New Hope and as Sovilla indicated, it would be a pity if the secret shame of her tattoo robbed her of the joy she experienced in Noah's presence.

Not going to work may have felt frustrating to Noah, but *going* to work felt nearly futile. He'd work for half an hour, and then he'd need to rest for ten minutes. His hands weren't steady enough to set the screws at the proper tightness, and David had to check all of them. But worst of all, his concentration was lagging and he lapped a section of metal paneling the wrong way—a mistake not even Jacob made after his first week of training. Yet his coworkers never complained; in fact, they encouraged him to take more frequent breaks.

"If you try to get back up to speed too soon, you'll relapse," David warned. "We're meeting our deadlines, so no need to worry."

It was true; the crew had worked extra hours during Noah's two-week absence and were right on target to fulfill their contractual obligations. "I don't know how you've managed to do it, but I sure appreciate it."

David gestured toward Jacob, who was helping Mike carry more panels across the lawn. "If you can believe it, Jacob has really stepped up. Apparently, the *maedel* he's been courting hinted that she couldn't marry a *mann* who didn't have a stronger work ethic." He chuckled. "It's almost as if the two of you have switched roles.

He's working till seven or eight at night, and you're out picnicking in the day."

"What? Who told you that?"

David gave him a sheepish look. "My wife saw you and Arleta down by the pond the other day."

"We weren't *picnicking*. My *groossmammi* wanted me to get out of the *haus* and Arleta needed to go to the store. We stopped at the pond and had a dish of ice cream. We weren't there more than an hour," Noah explained, abashed that his coworker may have thought he was being lazy.

But David indicated he thought just the opposite when he grinned and said, "That's too bad—maybe you'll get to stay longer next time." He handed Noah a caulking tube; caulking was one of the least strenuous tasks in installing metal roofing. "Listen, *suh*, you could spend the next month napping in a hammock if you needed to and no one here would utter a word of complaint or question your diligence."

"Denki," Noah replied. He was grateful for his coworkers' industriousness, and he knew David's sentiment was sincere. It was a huge relief not to have to worry about the business, but there was still the matter of his side projects to consider. Noah was skeptical about making it through a full day of work as it was, so he couldn't envision himself putting in additional hours in the early evening, too. At least, not this week.

That meant he'd be three weeks behind in meeting his financial goal; the week he'd been sick, the week he'd recovered and this week, when he was easing back into work. *How will I ever make up for the lost time?* he wondered. Being bedridden for the past couple of weeks had given him even more time to pray about his grandmother's health, and he hoped they'd hear she was cancer-free when she had her bloodwork and scans done the following week. But he still had to be prepared for the possibility they'd need to travel to Mexico. *Maybe by next week, I'll be strong enough to pick up my pace with my side projects*, he thought.

As he caulked the flashing around the roof vent, Noah's mind drifted to Arleta. He wondered what she was doing at home right now. Usually around this time, Sovilla would be napping and he and Arleta would be taking a stroll around the house. During those times, Noah often found himself reminiscing to Arleta about his family—that's how natural it felt to talk to her. Noah could tell her anything. Well, *almost* anything. He'd never tell her what he'd been doing the night of the fire, of course.

From there, his mind leaped to thoughts of Hannah and Isaiah. It was funny how both Noah and Arleta suspected each other of having a romantic interest in their peers. Yes, he'd once courted Hannah, but in retrospect he would describe his feelings for her as infatuation, not *love.* And Arleta had said she had no romantic interest whatsoever in Isaiah. *It just goes to show the* narrish *conclusions people can leap to*, he thought.

Then it struck him that after seeing them together by the pond, David Hilty's wife may have concluded they were courting. Noah trusted David to exercise discretion, but he didn't know his wife well enough to guess if she'd disclose her observation to anyone else or not. *What if* Groossmammi *caught wind of a rumor like that?* he asked himself. He was pretty sure he could anticipate her response: initially, she'd be delighted…and subsequently, she'd be crushed to find out it wasn't true. He'd never hear the end of it. Noah supposed the one way to avoid disappointing her was not to do anything to perpetuate the rumors. In other words, he should tell Arleta he changed his mind about going to the pond again.

He *should.* But that didn't mean he wanted to. *Arleta's only going to be here for a few more weeks*, he thought. *Why should I give up spending time with her—which I really enjoy—just to spare my* Groossmammi *from disappointment? I shouldn't be penalized just because* she *chooses to believe rumors.*

For the rest of the afternoon, Noah wrestled with his conscience, unsure about whether he should cancel his outing with Arleta or not. But when he returned home and ambled up the walkway, he spied a bumbleberry pie cooling on the porch railing. Arleta sat in the glider nearby, flipping through one of her recipe books from the library. When she looked up, she gave him such an affectionate smile it literally put a hop in his step and as he bounced up the stairs, he knew exactly what he was going to do.

Arleta never would have *wished* Noah's weakness on him, but she couldn't deny how happy she was that it kept him home in the evenings instead of out working on extra installation projects. It was agonizing enough to be separated from him during the day. By late afternoon, her eagerness to see him again was so irrepressible that she'd have to wait on the porch, so Sovilla wouldn't notice how many times she glanced at the clock.

I think I'm falling in love with him and he's falling in love with me, too, she imagined writing to Leanna.

She never did, of course. Instead, she sat with a blank tablet on her lap, unable to pick up her pen. She knew what she really ought to write was a letter to her parents, urging them to prohibit her sister from working for an *Englischer* family. But thinking about writing *that* letter reminded her of her tattoo, which in turn made her have to face how unrealistic it was to harbor daydreams about falling in love with Noah. And she cherished that reverie too much to give it up, at least until she had to leave New Hope.

Meanwhile, the only thing she anticipated more than his daily return home was their expedition to the pond on Sunday. So, after they returned home from church and Sovilla said she had an upset stomach and needed to nap, Arleta squeezed her fingers into fists behind her back to keep herself from crying. Noah was in the barn, giving the horse fresh water, but she knew as soon as he learned his grandmother was sick, he'd cancel their trip to the pond so they could stay home and keep an eye on her. Arleta agreed that was the prudent thing to do, but after spending the week imagining canoeing across the picturesque pond with him, staying home and playing spades while Sovilla snored in the next room didn't seem nearly as romantic.

Fortunately, she had underestimated Sovilla's bossiness. "Why would you stay here on a beautiful day like this?" she scoffed. "It's not as if you're going to watch me sleep."

"*Neh*, but we'll be here for you if you need help," Noah said.

"You can help me by taking the last of that bumbleberry pie with you so I won't eat it," Sovilla said. "That's the third one Arleta has made this week, and they've been so tasty that I've made a glutton of myself. Which is the only reason my stomach is upset."

"Okay," Noah agreed. "We won't be gone long, *Groossmammi.*"

"Whether you're gone five minutes or five hours won't make much difference to me—I'm going to settle in for a long nap," she said.

"I hope she's really all right," Noah said as they pulled out onto the main road a few minutes later.

"If you feel uncomfortable leaving her, we can go back. She's probably asleep by now so she won't shoo us away again," Arleta reluctantly suggested.

Noah glanced over at her. "I was actually hoping you'd assure me she'll be fine, not suggest we go back."

Delighted that he still wanted to go to the pond as much as she did, Arleta replied, "I think she *will* be fine. But how about if we pray for her?" Noah nodded so as he guided the horse toward the pond, Arleta prayed that Sovilla's stomach pain would subside, she'd have a refreshing rest and that the Lord would put Noah's mind at ease.

By the time they arrived at the pond, he was smiling broadly and Arleta was practically singing with glee as she commented about what a cool, sunny day it was and how much she hoped at least one of the canoes would be available for their use. When they got to the pond, they were pleased to see both canoes overturned onshore. Flipping one of them over, they found two life vests, but only a single paddle stashed beneath it. Which was fine with Arleta—it meant instead of keeping her back toward Noah as she helped paddle, she'd be able to face Noah during their excursion.

He quickly unlaced his boots, took off his socks and

rolled up his pant legs. Arleta had been so excited about their trip that she'd forgotten to come up with an excuse about why she had to leave her footwear on.

Fortunately, when Noah noticed she wasn't taking her shoes off, he asked, "Are you afraid you'll get stung on your ankles again?"

"*Jah.* It was *lappich* of me to forget to bring an antihistamine."

"I'd better help you in, then," he said. Since half of the canoe was still on dry land, she easily stepped inside without getting her feet wet. Then Noah held her hand for balance as she inched toward the seat at the far end. He set the insulated bag containing their pie and water bottles in the middle of the vessel and then pushed off shore and hopped in. He paddled with such long, determined strokes that she never would have guessed at how ill he'd been the week before.

"I want to take you to the other side to show you something really pretty."

"It's *all* really pretty," she raved. The pond was encircled by gentle hills comprised of tall pines and leafy oaks and maples. Large, rounded rocks protruded in clusters at various spots along the shoreline, which was typical in that part of Maine. The water was so clear and still she could see to the bottom if she peered over the side; up in the distance, the trees were mirror images of themselves on the water's surface. "It's like we're rowing through the hills!" she exclaimed, enchanted.

But Noah was right; the alcove he brought her to was even prettier, like a pond within a pond. Shaded by nearby maple trees, the little circle of water was dappled with sunlight that danced with the breeze. To their right, cobalt blue damselflies darted between pink water lilies with orange centers; to the left, a torrent of water cascaded over a graduated bank of rocks on shore. The sight of the waterfall was rivaled only by its sound and Arleta closed her eyes. “Listen to that,” she murmured.

“If you like how it sounds and looks, you’ll love how it feels. I don’t think we’ll run into any bees over there—you want to go dip your feet in?”

Arleta opened her eyes to see Noah looking expectantly at her. She hated to disappoint him when he was so eager to share an experience that he treasured with her, but there was no way she could remove her socks. “I’d like to, but I’m actually a little chilly.”

“Jah,” he said agreeably, looking toward the sky. “Today feels more like autumn than like summer.”

Reluctant to acknowledge that August was already here—today was August 2—Arleta reminded him, “Summer’s not over yet. We’ll still have plenty more hot days. It would be more refreshing to stick our feet in if the weather’s warmer.” *And maybe by then I could think of an excuse to cover my tattoo with a bandage ahead of time.* It was a foolish idea, but if it meant she could come back here with Noah, Arleta would have risked giving it a try.

“*Jah.* We probably shouldn’t stay too long here today anyway,” Noah said. “But I think we’ve got time to eat some of that pie you packed, don’t you?”

Unfortunately, he’d set the insulated bag in the middle of the canoe, too far out of reach for either of them to retrieve it. So Noah very carefully stood and climbed over the seat until the bag was within his grasp. He gave it to Arleta and then sat down knee-to-knee with her. They had to eat the pie with their hands since Arleta had forgotten to pack forks, but afterward they dipped their fingers in the water to wash them.

Then Arleta unzipped the bag, removed a bottle of water and leaned forward, extending it to him. "You must be thirsty after all that paddling."

Her eyes were glistening, and the sunlight sparkling across the surface of the water illuminated her face from beneath. Once again, just as on the day she arrived in New Hope, Noah had the feeling he knew her from somewhere else.

Then it struck him: he *had* seen her at the house building six years ago after all. *She's the one who brought me a glass of lemonade when I was hiding in* Daed's *workshop.* Noah recalled how he'd felt that day. Even though he'd known his church family and members of the surrounding Amish communities were rebuilding his house as a demonstration of their love and care for Sovilla and him, he had felt so undeserving that he couldn't face them. And he may have been imagining it, but it seemed to him that they averted their eyes whenever they passed him, too, as if they knew how miserably he'd failed his family and couldn't stand the sight of him.

But Arleta, Arleta had broken through his isolation and dejection by seeking him out and bringing him a glass of lemonade. By looking *into* his eyes, instead of away…

A breeze blew her *kapp* string across her cheek and without thinking, Noah lifted his hand to brush it away. "Such a lovely face, how could I ever forget it?" he murmured to himself.

Except he hadn't murmured to himself; apparently

he'd said it *aloud*, because Arleta replied, *"Denki,"* and then sat straight again, holding his gaze.

He supposed he should have felt embarrassed or rushed to explain that he'd been thinking about where he'd met her before. But Arleta didn't seem at all flustered by his remark and he wasn't sorry for saying it, so he couldn't apologize. After a few seconds, she glanced down to unscrew the top of her water bottle and he did the same with his. And as he lifted it to his lips and swallowed, he thought about how the only time any drink ever tasted better was the day she'd brought him the lemonade.

"We should get back now," he said when his bottle was empty.

"Jah," she agreed. "Or else Sovilla will worry about us instead of the other way around, for a change."

He chuckled in agreement but he paddled back slowly and then walked to the buggy even slower, not wanting this feeling, or his time alone with Arleta, to end. *Maybe it doesn't have to*, he reflected as the horse pulled the carriage down the final road leading to his home. *Maybe the Lord has brought her into my life again for a reason. It could be that—*

"Ambulance!" Arleta pointed with one hand and grabbed Noah's arm with the other, jarring him from his thoughts.

He had been so preoccupied he hadn't registered that the emergency vehicle was barreling in his direction. Noah managed to bring the buggy to a halt and keep the horse settled as the vehicle whizzed by, its lights flashing and sirens screaming. There were two other houses on this long, flat country road, both belonging to *Englischers*, and if Sovilla *had* actually had an emergency, she wouldn't have been able to summon an ambulance since she didn't have a phone. But Noah was immediately gripped by fear. *Something's happened to* Groossmammi *and I wasn't here to help her! I was out flirting with a* maedel, *just like on the night of the fire.*

He urged the horse into a quick canter, despite Arleta's protests, only slowing the animal to a trot when they reached the private lane where Noah's house was located. Even so, they took the turn at such a fast clip it seemed the carriage came precariously close to tipping. Instead of veering off toward the barn where the dirt driveway forked, Noah brought the animal to a halt in front of the house. Without a word to Arleta, he jumped down and bolted up the porch steps and into the kitchen. *"Groossmammi!"* he shouted upon finding it empty. *"Groossmammi!"* He rushed into the living room just as Sovilla flew in from the opposite entryway, wide-eyed, her hand on her heart.

"What is it? What's wrong? Did something happen to Arleta?"

"Neh." He embraced his grandmother so tightly against his chest that her headscarf went crooked. "I—I—I saw an ambulance and I—I thought something happened to you," he said, gasping in between words.

Sovilla patted his back. "Hush, now. Hush. I'm okay. Nothing happened." Noah's grandmother stood in the middle of the floor, holding him in her arms and humming, the way she might have comforted a baby, which seemed fitting because Noah was crying like one.

After a few minutes, he quieted but didn't pull away from her embrace until he heard footsteps on the porch; Arleta must have returned from stabling the horse.

"Please don't tell Arleta," he implored quietly, backing toward the hall. Sovilla seemed to understand he meant he didn't want Arleta to know that he'd overreacted, or why.

A minute later, as he stood over the sink in the bathroom, he heard Arleta ask, "Is Noah okay? All of a sudden he rushed home so quickly, I didn't know what was wrong."

"He's not feeling quite himself—he dashed into the bathroom."

"Oh, that's too bad. We'd had such a pleasant afternoon, but maybe he overdid it. Next time, we should go on a shorter outing."

There won't be a next time, Noah thought as he splashed cold water on his face. *Twice was two times too many.*

Arleta didn't understand it. On Sunday at the pond, Noah had told her she had a lovely face. A face he could never forget. But in the three days since then, unless she initiated a conversation, he hardly spoke a word to her. *Maybe it's just that he's exhausted from taking on too much too soon*, she surmised on Wednesday evening. After all, he was back to the same schedule he'd followed before he got sick; working all day, returning home to have a few bites of supper and then heading out to work on additional side projects until dark.

"Do you think Noah's okay?" she asked Sovilla. For the third night in a row, he'd gone straight to bed when he returned from his second job, even though it wasn't yet nine o'clock.

"He's probably just tired—he's still recovering, dear."

"*Jah*, but he seems…downhearted or something."

"Perhaps he's worried about what the doctor will tell me tomorrow."

Of course—that's it. I shouldn't have been so self-centered to think he's been distancing himself from me on purpose, Arleta thought.

As she lay in bed that night, she prayed for Sovilla's healing, just as she'd been praying ever since she came to New Hope, as well as for Noah's peace of mind. The only other thing Arleta could think of doing that might be helpful was to remind him that she was willing to forfeit her salary if it turned out his grandmother needed additional medical care. She decided she'd talk to him before he left for work in the morning. But when she woke, it was Sovilla who was drinking coffee alone in the kitchen.

"Guder mariye," she greeted her. "Is Noah up yet?"

"*Jah*, he left extra early, since he's coming home at noon to accompany me to my appointment."

"What time is the driver arriving?"

"Eleven forty-five."

"Then we won't have time to eat lunch before we go. I'll make sandwiches for us to eat on the way," Arleta offered.

"I'd appreciate that, dear, but I think it's best if Noah and I go alone to this appointment. It's…it's a *familye* thing, you see," Sovilla said, apologetically squeezing Arleta's hand.

"*Jah*, of course. I completely understand." She plastered a smile on her face and kept it there for the rest of the morning. But after Noah came home and the driver picked them up and she stood on the porch waving, Arleta ran into her room and bawled into her pillow. *It serves me right to be so disappointed*, she thought, feeling much the same way she felt after Ian broke up with her. *That's what I get for imagining I'm more special to someone than I actually am.*

Chapter Eleven

Noah paced on the sidewalk in front of the medical center in Portland. A nurse had just told him Sovilla had finished meeting with the doctor and offered him the use of a phone so he could arrange for their ride home. But then his grandmother had been delayed in coming out, so Noah had gone outside to ask the driver to wait a little longer. Apparently, their ride hadn't arrived yet, either.

As he strolled up and down the concrete, alternately scanning the exit for Sovilla and the parking lot for their van, he prayed, *Please,* Gott*, give me the strength to accept it if my* groossmammi *has cancer again. And please provide me a way to help her get additional care.*

He pressed a hand to his abdomen. Ever since he'd spotted the ambulance tearing down the road by his house, he'd had a knot in his stomach. It eased up a little after he'd discovered that no harm had befallen his grandmother, but right now, it was so tight that his discomfort rivaled the pain he'd experienced when he came down with the flu.

At least Arleta's *not here*, he thought, grateful that

Sovilla hadn't invited her to accompany them to this appointment, as he feared she would. Noah wouldn't have wanted Arleta to see him in this state, nor would he have wanted to be alone with her while Sovilla was getting her scans and consulting with her oncologist. It had been awkward enough to be in her company when the three of them ate supper at night. He was counting down the days until she left New Hope, and he wouldn't have a constant reminder that once again, he'd put his own pleasure above his family's safety. The fact that his grandmother *hadn't* actually had an emergency was irrelevant; he still felt ashamed and irresponsible.

"Noah!" Sovilla flagged him down as she emerged from the revolving door, tears in her eyes.

Oh, neh. *Please,* Gott, *give me strength*, he requested again as he strode toward her to take her arm. "What did the *dokder* say?"

"It's gone. The cancer is all gone," she told him.

"That's *wunderbaar, Groossmammi*!" Noah squeezed her hand, trying to be discreet in public. But the expression on his face must have shown his elation, because an elderly *Englisch* couple passing by smiled at them.

"Good news?" the white-haired lady asked.

"The best," he said.

"Praise God for that," the man remarked.

Which was exactly what Noah was already doing, silently praying, Denki, *Lord*, as he helped Sovilla into the silver minivan that had pulled up in front of them.

On the return trip, he and Sovilla sat side by side in the back seat, quietly watching the scenery go by. Noah continued to rejoice inwardly about his grandmother's health, and he assumed she was thinking similar thoughts. It wasn't until they were almost home that she spoke to him, using their *Pennsylfaanisch Deitsch* dialect so the driver couldn't understand them.

"I don't know why the Lord has blessed me with a second chance—with *continued* life," she said. "Especially when your *schweschder* and *brieder* and *eldre*'s lives were so short in comparison."

Noah swallowed. They'd just gotten such joyful news; why was his grandmother reminding them of something so sorrowful now? "*Groossmammi*, please," he pleaded, but she ignored him.

"For the longest time, I wished *I* had been the one who died in that fire, instead of them. I didn't understand why the Lord took young *kinner* home instead of an old *weibsmensch* like me. And I blamed myself for going to Ohio to visit my *schweschder*. I thought if I had been here, I could have prevented the fire since I was always more vigilant about the lamps than anyone else was."

"It wasn't your fault," Noah objected. *It was mine.*

"I know that now. But for some months afterward, I felt guilty and selfish because, quite frankly, I had been so delighted to get away to my *schweschder*'s *haus*. I missed her so much and she doesn't have any *kinskinner* living with her and…it was something pleasant I looked forward to each year," Sovilla confided. She paused, allowing Noah to absorb what she was telling him. "But ultimately, I trusted that my *suh*'s life—your *familye*'s lives—were in *Gott*'s hands, not mine. And that I wasn't at fault for enjoying the time I spent with my sister. But that I *would* be at fault if I didn't appreciate and accept the blessings the Lord gave me in the years following your *familye*'s deaths."

Noah never knew his grandmother had struggled with feelings so similar to his own. When she described how she'd thought it was her fault that his family had died, he recognized how misplaced her guilt was. Was it possible his guilt was misplaced, too? He turned his head to the side, blinking away a single tear.

Sovilla patted his knee. "You've taken excellent care of me, Noah, but when the Lord calls me home, I'm going, regardless." She chuckled. "But for today, I'm going to thank Him for the *gut* news and celebrate by enjoying a slice of bumbleberry pie when I get home. In addition to praising the Lord, what else are you going to celebrate?"

He shrugged. "I don't know."

"I'll make a suggestion," she said bluntly. "Arleta is worried about you, and I think she's hurt by your recent behavior toward her. Take her out for pizza."

Noah could tell by her tone that her suggestion wasn't really a suggestion; it was more or less an order. Besides, he really did want to speak to Arleta. So, after they'd returned home and shared the wonderful news with Arleta, and after she'd burst into tears and embraced Sovilla, Noah invited her to go into town for supper with him. She seemed to hesitate before accepting, which made sense, given how standoffish Noah had behaved toward her recently. But by the time the server brought their pizza to the table, they were talking and laughing as easily as ever.

"You're not eating much," Arleta said as she reached for her third slice and he hadn't even finished his first. "Is your stomach bothering you?"

"*Jah.* But it's not from having the flu. I'm nervous because there's something I need to talk to you about," he admitted, setting his fork aside. Arleta put her pizza down on her plate, too. Noah took a swallow of water before continuing. "I am so grateful for your help during *groossmammi*'s recovery, as well as during mine, after I had the flu. I knew early on that the Lord was blessing us with your presence as a caregiver. And over time, I realized that He was blessing me with your friendship, too. And now I wonder if...if it's possible that He might want to bless me—hopefully, to bless *both* of us—by allowing me to become your suitor. I care about you deeply, Arleta, and it would be my privilege if I could demonstrate my affection and regard for you within the context of a courtship." Noah held his breath.

Arleta's lips parted and she blinked at him in surprise. "I'm very flattered that you'd ask to be my suitor," she said, and his heart plummeted. "But courtship often leads to marriage and I can't even consider that... I—I—I mean, I'm only twenty and..."

"There's no pressure or expectation about marriage. If we get to a point when we're serious about taking a step in that direction, we can talk about that then. But right now, my intention would be for us to get to know each other better, that's all." Noah added earnestly, "Even if we only courted for a couple of weeks, I'd consider it time well spent."

Arleta's mouth widened into a smile. Her eyes shone and she nodded. "In that case, I'd be *hallich* to have you as my suitor, Noah."

Arleta lay in bed, hugging her pillow. She was overjoyed about Sovilla's clean bill of health and thrilled that Noah had asked to be her suitor. Even the knowledge that she'd eventually have to break off their courtship didn't keep her from grinning. *I won't let it get out of hand*, she told herself. *I'll just enjoy having him as my suitor until next Saturday, when I return home. And maybe we'll exchange letters for a month or two after that. Then I'll end it, just like I did with Stephen, by saying it's too difficult to keep up a long-distance courtship.*

After all, this might be the only chance she had to have a suitor. And where was the harm in a little romance, provided she kept it light? Noah already expressed his feelings of affection for her; it would have been too awkward to turn him down and then continue to live in the same house with him. So she'd actually been *sparing* his feelings to accept him as her suitor. Besides, he'd said there was no pressure and he'd be happy to court her for even a few weeks.

On and on her rationalizations went. For every qualm she had about saying yes to Noah, she had two excuses to justify her decision. *I'll only be in New Hope until next Saturday, and I intend to soak up every last minute of my time with Noah*, she thought, as she rolled over and drifted off.

In the morning, she overslept, not rising until she heard Noah's footsteps on the porch as he returned from milking the cow. Arleta dressed quickly and went into the kitchen where he was sitting at the table and Sovilla was pulling a batch of muffins from the oven. "You shouldn't be doing that," Arleta chastised her after saying good morning.

"Why not? Haven't you heard? I'm cured," Sovilla jested wryly. "No more mollycoddling for me. It's time I start pulling my weight around here again."

"But making breakfast is *my* job," Arleta objected. "I wanted to fix breakfast scramble for Noah."

At the same time, Noah exclaimed, "Arleta can't leave yet!"

"My, my." Sovilla smirked, obviously amused by their outbursts. If she hadn't already guessed it, there couldn't have been any doubt in the older woman's mind now that the two of them were courting. "I'm not taking away your job, Arleta, and I'm not sending her home early, Noah. I just had a craving for muffins, that's all."

After that, they could hardly make eye contact with each other. Noah's cheeks stayed pink throughout the meal, and Arleta was so flustered she flipped a serving spoon out of the dish, sending bits of scrambled egg flying everywhere. Now that they were courting, she felt self-conscious interacting with him beneath Sovilla's watchful eye. And she was almost relieved when Noah returned from work that evening and announced that he had to dash out the door almost immediately after supper to work on the installment he'd started earlier in the week.

Before leaving, he sidled up to Arleta as she stood at the sink, washing dishes. "I probably won't complete the project until tomorrow," he whispered into her ear. "But there's no need for me to take on any new jobs next week. And we can go out alone together on *Sunndaag.*"

"To the pond?" If so, Arleta was going to have to think of an excuse to bandage her ankle in case he wanted to get out of the canoe by the waterfall.

"Neh," Noah replied. "Jacob said he and Faith plan to use the canoe. I thought we'd go back to the gorge. There's another trail I want to show you there."

"What will we tell your *groossmammi*?" Arleta whispered. Although they'd never blinked at telling Sovilla where they were going together in the past, now that they were actually courting, it seemed important for them to be more discreet about their outings.

"I don't know. I'll think of something," Noah promised.

But as it turned out, shortly after they'd had their home worship services and finished their lunch on Sunday, Lovina stopped by to pick up Sovilla and take her to the Stolls' house for a visit with Almeda. "Are you going canoeing today, too?" she asked Arleta.

"I'm sorry?"

"Honor said some of the *meed* are going canoeing. Faith and Hannah, I believe. Some of the *buwe* your age, too. I thought you'd be going with them."

"*Neh*, not today," Arleta said. *They didn't invite me. But that's okay—I'd rather go out with Noah, anyway.*

After Lovina and Sovilla left, Noah went to hitch the horse and Arleta put drinks and snacks into a thermal bag. As she stepped onto the porch, she noticed a buggy had pulled up in front of the house. Hannah Miller got out, carrying a container in each hand.

They exchanged greetings as she climbed the steps. "I brought you raspberries I picked from our patch. I thought you might want to use them when you make bumbleberry pie."

"*Denki.* Sovilla will be *hallich* to have fresh fruit," Arleta said, even though the trio had agreed they'd had their fill of bumbleberry pie for a while. She set the fruit inside the doorway and when she turned around, she noticed Hannah had taken a seat in the glider, as if she intended to stay. "Sovilla's not here," she informed her.

"That's okay, I didn't *kumme* to see her." Hannah blushed and glanced down at her feet, as if she were embarrassed. Had she come to see *Noah*? To ask him to go canoeing with the others? Arleta wondered. If she had, it seemed an even bolder gesture than when Arleta asked Isaiah for a ride, but before she could question her, Hannah said, "I came because there's something I need to say to you."

Arleta took a seat, too. She hoped whatever Hannah had to say, she'd say it quickly because she didn't want to waste even a moment of her time alone with Noah. *"Jah?"*

"I—I wanted to apologize for how I've treated you—for being so unfriendly," she said, hugging her arms to her chest as if she were cold. "I was jealous because I thought Isaiah was interested in you. That he wanted to court you. See, he used to be my suitor and we broke up a long time ago…anyway, I won't bother you with the details about that because it looks like you're on your way out. I just wanted you to know how sorry I am for how I acted, and I hope you'll forgive me."

Arleta couldn't contain her mirth—Hannah had never been interested in *Noah*; she was interested in *Isaiah*!—and she giggled. "*Jah.* Of course I forgive you."

Hannah lowered her brow. "Then what's *voll schpass*?"

"I'm laughing because Isaiah thought I was interested in him, too. And I don't blame him—especially not after I asked him for a ride home from the potluck. But I only did that because I was trying to give you and Noah the opportunity to ride home together. I sensed you were…not pleased with me and I figured it was because you thought I was interfering with a potential courtship between you and Noah."

"Noah and me? *Neh.* I couldn't ever see myself with him. Granted, we courted briefly when we were younger, but it was more of a crush than a serious courtship. Besides, he broke up with me and since then, we've hardly spoken."

Noticing the quaver in Hannah's voice, Arleta asked, "But that hurt your feelings, *jah*?"

"*Jah.* Not because I thought we had a future together, but because…well, because I always felt like he always kind of blamed me for his *familye*'s deaths. Or at least, that's what he associated me with."

"You? What did *you* have to do with the fire?"

Hannah met her eyes. "You won't tell anyone?"

"*Neh.* Not a soul," Arleta gravely replied.

"The night it happened we'd gone out on a date and afterward, we came back to my *haus* and were sitting on my porch. Noah should have dropped me off and then left because it was getting late, but we were sharing our first kiss and…anyway, by the time he got home, his family had perished. After that, he immediately broke off our courtship. I understood, because he was grieving at the time. But for years, he wouldn't even look at me. I felt like he blamed me."

"Oh, Hannah, that's *baremlich.*" *It wasn't her fault—it wasn't Noah's fault, either, but I can understand why he may have felt like it was.* That *must be why he never allowed himself to court anyone after that…*

"*Jah.*" Hannah picked at her thumbnail. "Like I've said, ever since then, we've hardly spoken but recently—in fact, it was that day I brought a pie over to your buggy after *kurrich*—something between us changed for the better. Like he'd forgiven me or something. And I wish him all the best. I truly hope one day he meets someone he wants to court, but I'd never consider him for myself as a suitor again." She stood up. "Anyway, I'd better get going. *Denki* for listening to what I had to say and for forgiving me, Arleta. I feel a lot better now."

"You're *wilkom*," she answered, even though *she* felt a lot worse. *Sovilla had said Noah hasn't courted anyone since he'd courted Hannah—which means he must* really *like me. After all he's been through, how can I toy with his feelings, knowing our relationship can never progress?* It was one thing to deceive herself, but to deceive Noah, when he was making himself so vulnerable after years of closing himself off, was absolutely disgraceful. Arleta had been selfish to accept his proposal of courtship, and she cared about him too much to toy with his feelings.

Dear Gott, she prayed. *Please forgive me. And please help Noah forgive me and accept my change of heart, too.*

Noah leaned against the side of the house, stupefied. He had been on his way to hitch the horse when he realized he'd forgotten his hat, so he'd turned around to get it. That's when he overheard Hannah talking to Arleta on the porch. Telling her that he and Hannah had been kissing the night of the fire. That *he*, essentially, was the one to blame for his family's deaths because he hadn't gone home when he should have. "That's *baremlich*," she had replied, but Noah didn't know exactly how to take her remark. Was it uttered in disbelief? Disgust? Or was it an expression of sympathy?

As appalled as Noah was that Hannah had told Arleta his shameful secret, in a way he was also relieved that she knew now, before their courtship progressed and he fell deeper in love with her than he already was. *What she does next will show me what she truly thinks of me*, he realized. *It will show me if it really* is *possible that the Lord wants to bless me with a wife and a* famlye. *Or at least, with a courtship that has the potential to lead to marriage.*

"Noah," Arleta called to him as she came around the corner. "What are you doing there?"

"I forgot my *hut.* I'll be right out. You can get in the buggy." He jogged into the house and returned a few seconds later. They traveled a good three miles in silence until, unable to stand the suspense any longer, he prompted, "You're awfully quiet. Is there something on your mind?"

"*Jah.* Could we pull over up there? I need to get out for a minute."

Noah's hands trembled as he held the reins, guiding the horse off the main road, stopping on a wide dirt shoulder. He followed Arleta when she got down and walked a few yards into the nearby meadow of tall grass and late summer wildflowers. She plucked a black-eyed Susan and twirled its stem between her fingers before turning around and saying, "I'm sorry, Noah, but I don't think I can be in a courtship with you."

He had sensed this was coming, but her decision still made his knees go weak. "Why not?"

"I just… It's like I said, I'm only twenty and I'm not really ready for a courtship."

"That's not the real reason, Arleta, is it?" he challenged. "You don't want to be in a courtship with me because of what Hannah Miller told you about—" He couldn't bring himself to say the words even now. "About me. I heard her talking to you so don't deny it."

Arleta's eyes were brimming. "I don't deny that she told me about the night of the fire, Noah, but that wasn't your fault. And it doesn't change the way I think of you at all, not one bit. I think you're the most thoughtful, responsible, devoted young *mann* I've ever met. And I think you're going to make a *wunderbaar* husband for some woman one day."

"If you really believe all of that, why don't you want me for your suitor?"

Arleta backed away, crying. "I'm sorry, but I can't tell you that. I just can't." Then she spun around and ran across the meadow and down the hill.

Some blessing a relationship with her turned out to be, Noah thought bitterly as he watched her disappear into the woods to take the shortcut home. *I wish she'd keep running all the way back to Serenity Ridge.*

Then, since he didn't want to have to be at the house alone with her, he climbed into the buggy and continued toward the gorge, where he spent the rest of the afternoon hiking. When the sun dropped low in the sky, he figured he had missed supper, which was what he intended, and he headed home.

"Did you have a nice time?" Sovilla asked when he stuck his head in the living room to say hello.

"Mmm. I'm beat—I'm going to go read for a while," he muttered, eager to get upstairs without bumping into Arleta. "Then I'll probably go to sleep. I've got a long week ahead of me—I'm going to be working in the evenings again." He had decided this was the perfect solution for avoiding Arleta.

His grandmother pressed her lips together and shook her head, but instead of scolding him, she said, "I'm *hallich* I'll have Arleta's company for another week—and for this evening. Where is she?"

"She's not here?"

"Neh."

Noah's first thought was that she'd arranged for a ride back to Serenity Ridge. He strode down the hall and rapped on her door. When there was no answer, he pushed it open; her Bible was still on the nightstand and her hairbrush was on the dresser. "She must have gotten lost in the woods again," he told his grandmother, grabbing the flashlight from its hook.

"So she wasn't with you today?"

"We—we got separated." Noah didn't take the time to explain further. As he hurried back toward the meadow where he'd dropped her off, he felt a mix of apprehension and resentment. *She's probably fine. For all I know, she emerged from the wrong side of the woods again and she's eating supper with the Wittmers,* he thought, tromping through the tall grass. Alternately, he worried. *What if she crosses paths with a wild animal?* There had been moose in the area and it was almost dusk, which was when they usually came out into the open.

"Arleta!" he shouted once he'd reached the woods. "Arleta!"

The farther he walked without seeing any sign of her, the harder his heartbeat drummed in his ears. His neck and back broke out in a sweat, and his familiar fears overtook him as he recalled what his grandmother had said after she found out that Isaiah had carried Arleta across the stream. "You ought to be more responsible, Noah. She's our guest."

Since he didn't know what direction she'd taken and had to scan the entire area carefully, Noah had to resist the urge to break into a run. "Arleta!" he yelled frantically. "Arleta, where are you?"

Although the sky was still bright, the woods were dense and dark. Noah turned on his flashlight and swept the beam from tree trunk to rock to tree trunk in front of him. "Arleta!" he shouted.

"Here I am," she wailed. "I'm over here!"

Noah rushed in the direction of her voice, stopping just short of a shallow but steep and rocky ditch. He could tell from her tone she was injured, and he lowered himself down beside her. "Where are you hurt?"

"My ankle. I can't walk," she sobbed. "I think it's broken."

He handed her the flashlight to distract her from the pain. "You shine this on our path, okay? On the count of three, I'm going to pick you up." She moaned and pressed her face against his chest as he lifted her from the ground and then again when he staggered up the rocky incline. After that, he was able to stay on a level path, and her crying subsided although it didn't stop.

"This is going to be jarring, Arleta. I'm sorry," he said, when they reached the buggy. She nodded and clung tighter to him, groaning into his chest as he hoisted her into the carriage. After he'd helped her into a sideways sitting position with her leg resting on the seat, he said, "Before we go to the phone shanty to call for help, I need to make a splint to stabilize your ankle. First I have to remove your shoe—"

"*Neh!* Don't touch it!"

"I promise I'll be careful." He gently cupped the sole of her shoe, but she screamed at him to stop. He lifted his head to look into her eyes, but they were squeezed shut as she sobbed. Her complexion was so pale it seemed aglow. "I'm concerned you'll get a worse injury from the carriage jostling around. Please, Arleta, don't make me do that to you. Haven't I caused you enough harm already?"

"I—I—I have a tattoo." She panted the peculiar sentence more than she actually spoke it, and Noah assumed she was delirious with shock. But then she continued, her words coming out in spurts as she cried, "On my ankle. A ta-tattoo of an *Englischer*'s initials inside a heart. I was on *rumspringa.* I was going to leave the Amish. I was going to marry him and I'm—I'm so ashamed…"

And then she passed out.

Arleta didn't remember any of the buggy ride from the meadow to the phone shanty and little of the ambulance ride from the phone shanty to the hospital. Nor could she recall what the doctor said the name of the second bone was—talus was the first—that she'd broken when she'd slipped into the ditch and landed on the rock. So when the curtains around her gurney in the emergency room parted and Noah peeked inside and gave her a small smile, she wasn't certain whether she was imagining him or not.

But then he came to her side and touched her cheek, just as tenderly as he'd done in the alcove at the pond, and she knew for certain she had to be dreaming, because he never would have looked at her so lovingly in real life—not once she'd told him about her tattoo.

"How do you feel?" he asked, taking his hand away. He wasn't a dream after all.

"A little better. Physically better, anyway. But I'm still so ashamed of…" Now that she wasn't in excruciating pain, Arleta felt too inhibited to repeat that she'd once planned to marry an *Englischer* or that she'd gotten a tattoo. "Of doing those things I told you about."

Noah was quiet a moment before questioning, "Are those things why you don't want to court?"

Lowering her eyes, she nodded.

"Please don't allow something in your past to prevent me from being your suitor now," he implored, his voice quiet but clear as a bell.

Arleta shook her head in disbelief. "How could you want to court me after what I've done?"

"The same way *you* could want to court *me* after what *I've* done."

"It wasn't your fault that your *familye* perished, Noah. *I* sinned deliberately."

He shrugged. "Sin is sin and shame is shame, whether it's big sin or little sin or real shame or false shame... Did you confess your wrongdoings to the Lord?"

"Jah."

"Then He's forgiven you. And as you once told me, you apologized and God has forgiven you so there's no need to continue to feel sorry or to keep apologizing. Otherwise, it's as if you haven't accepted the Lord's forgiveness."

A tear rolled down Arleta's cheek. "But...but how can *you* bear to know I have another *mann*'s—an *Englischer*'s—initials inscribed on my skin?"

"In my mind, those letters don't stand for another *mann*'s name. When I look at them, I see the same thing I see when I look into your eyes. I see that I'm forgiven." Noah repeated slowly, "*I.F.*—I'm. Forgiven. And you're forgiven, too, Arleta. So please, may I be your suitor?"

Arleta fixed her eyes on his. "*Jah*, I'd like that very much," she said.

Epilogue

Noah watched his wife stretch her feet out in front of her. She had eventually confided in her parents about her tattoo and she'd told Sovilla, who'd already had an inkling. And although Arleta knew she was forgiven for her past, Noah had helped pay to have the heart and initials removed, so that it wouldn't become a stumbling block for other people, like Leanna. Now, in late November, Arleta still went barefoot around the house. She said it was to make up for the two years she wore socks every single hour of every single day.

"I can't believe I'm twenty-three, the same age you were when we met," Arleta whispered, rocking their six-month-old daughter to sleep in her arms.

"You're not the same age as I was when I met you—I met you at the *haus* building when I was seventeen."

"*Jah*, that's right," she acknowledged. "What I meant was I can't believe I'm the same age that you were when we started courting. So much has happened in these past three years… Fifteen months of our long-distance courtship. Our wedding. Our *bobbel* being born a year after that. Your *groossmammi...*" She didn't want to finish the thought but Noah finished it for her.

"*Groossmammi* going home to be with the Lord," he said. "You know, she told me once she was ready—but whether *I* was ready or not, her life was in *Gott*'s hands and there was nothing anyone could do to change that."

Arleta chuckled. "That sounds like Sovilla, all right." Just then the baby sighed in her sleep and Noah and Arleta both chuckled.

"*Groossmammi* was so thrilled to see her namesake before she died."

"*Jah.* One day I came into the living room and I caught her telling little Sovilla her secret ingredient for bumbleberry pie. She said it was such a *gut* secret that it was worth sharing, even with a *bobbel.*"

"Do you know what else is worth sharing?"

"What?"

Noah crossed the room and sat on the sofa beside his wife. "This," he said, and gave her sweet, gap-toothed mouth a warm kiss.

* * * * *

A WIDOW'S HOPE

Vannetta Chapman

This book is dedicated to JoAnn King,
who has recently become an avid reader.
JoAnn, you're a constant source of encouragement
and joy. Thank you for your friendship.

Acknowledgments

I would like to thank Melissa Endlich
for inviting me to join the wonderful group
of authors at Harlequin/Love Inspired.
I'd also like to thank my fellow LI authors
who have willingly answered questions,
explained procedures and offered guidance.
Thank you to Steve Laube for overseeing my career.

And a big thanks of gratitude to my husband, Bob,
for getting up at first-bark and taking care of pets,
laundry, grocery shopping, cooking
and the countless other things that I neglect
because I'm squirreled away in my office.

And finally, "Giving thanks always
for all things unto God and the Father in the name
of our Lord Jesus Christ" (*Ephesians* 5:20).

And we know that all things work together
for good to them that love God.
—*Romans* 8:28

The Lord hath heard my supplication;
the Lord will receive my prayer.
—*Psalms* 6:9

Chapter One

Monday mornings were never easy. Though Hannah King heard her four-year-old son calling, she longed to bury her head under the covers and let her mother take care of him. She'd had a dream about David. It had been so real—David kissing her on their wedding day, David standing beside her as she cradled their newborn son, David moving about the room quietly as he prepared for work.

But he wasn't in the room with her, and he never would be again. A late-summer breeze stirred the window shade. In the distance she could hear the clip-clop of horses on the two-lane, a rooster's crow, the low of a cow. Summer would be over soon. Here in northern Indiana, where she'd grown up, September was met with a full schedule of fall festivals and pumpkin trails and harvest celebrations. She dreaded it all—had no desire to walk through the bright leaves, or decorate with pumpkins or bake apple pies. Fall had been David's favorite time of year. Matthew was born in September. The accident? It had occurred the last week of August. That terrible anniversary was one week away.

This year, the thought of autumn overwhelmed her. Her entire life left her feeling tired and unable to cope. She was happy to be home with her parents, but she hadn't realized the extent of their financial troubles until she'd already moved in. Their church in Wisconsin had used money from the benevolence fund to pay for Matthew's surgeries, but her parents had paid for all of his rehab from their savings. Now they were operating month-to-month, and the stress was beginning to show. She needed to find a job, to help them with the bills, but how could she work when her primary responsibility was to care for Matthew?

She should at least make an attempt to find employment, but she wanted and needed to be home with her son. If she were honest with herself, she dreaded the thought of interacting with other people on a daily basis. She hadn't enough energy for that.

Hannah pushed off the bedcovers, slipped her feet into a pair of worn house shoes and hurried to the room next door as her mother stepped into the hall.

"I can take care of him if you like."

"*Nein*. I'm awake."

She should have said more, should have thanked her mother, but the memory of David was too heavy on her heart, her emotions too raw. So instead she quickly glanced away and opened the door to Matthew's room.

Though her son was four years old, soon to be five, he still slept in a bed with rails along the side. This was mainly to keep him from falling out.

The thinnest sliver of morning light shone through the gap between the window and the shade, fell across the room and landed on little Matthew. He was lying on his back, his legs splayed out in front of him. Matthew smiled and raised his arms to her, but instead of picking him up, Hannah lowered the wooden rail that her *dat* had fastened to the bed and sat beside him. Matthew struggled to a sitting position and pulled himself into her lap. For a four-year-old, his arms were incredibly strong, probably to make up for the fact that his legs were useless.

"Gudemariye, Mamm." The Pennsylvania Dutch rolled off his tongue, thick with sleep.

"Good morning to you, Matthew."

He reached up and touched her face, patted her cheek, then snuggled in closer.

She gave him a few minutes. Long ago, she'd learned that Matthew needed time to wake up, to adjust to the world. When he was ready, he said, "Potty?"

"Sure thing, Matt."

But before she could pick him up, her father was standing in the doorway. No doubt he'd been awake for hours, and he carried into the room the familiar smells of the barn—hay, horses and even a little manure. It was an earthy smell that Hannah never tired of.

"I thought I heard young Matthew awake."

"Daddi!" Matthew squirmed out of her lap and launched himself at her father, who caught him with a smile and carried him into the bathroom across the hall. She could hear them there, laughing and talking about the upcoming day.

Hannah slipped back into her room, changed into a plain gray dress, black apron and white *kapp.* Once dressed, she hurried to the kitchen. If she'd thought she could help her mother make breakfast, she was sadly mistaken.

Steam rose from the platter of fresh biscuits on the

table. Another dish held crisp bacon, and her mother was scooping scrambled eggs into a large bowl. Hannah fetched the butter and jam, set them in the middle of the table and then gladly accepted the mug of coffee her mother pushed into her hands.

"Did you sleep well?"

Hannah shrugged, not wanting to talk about it. Then she remembered her bishop's admonition to speak of her feelings more, to resist the urge to let them bottle up inside. Easy enough for him to say. His spouse was still alive and his children did not struggle with a disability. It was an uncharitable thought and added to her guilt.

She sipped the coffee and said, "I fall asleep easily enough, but then I wake after a few hours and can't seem to go back to sleep, no matter how tired I am."

"Normal enough for a woman in mourning."

"It's been nearly a year."

"Grieving takes a different amount of time for different people, Hannah."

"I suppose."

Her mother sat down beside her, reached for her hands.

"Did you have the dream again?"

"Ya." Hannah blinked away hot tears. She would not cry before breakfast. She would not. "How did you know?"

Instead of answering, her mother planted a kiss on her forehead, making her feel six instead of twenty-six. Then she popped up and walked back across the kitchen, checking that she hadn't forgotten anything they might need for breakfast. Holding up the coffeepot, she asked Hannah's father and son, "Coffee for both of you?"

"*Mammi.* I drink milk."

Matthew's laughter lightened the mood. Her father's steadiness calmed her nerves. Her mother's presence was always a balm to her soul.

The first week she was home, her dad had insisted on learning how to care for Matthew, how to help him into his wheelchair. Now Hannah turned to see her father and son, her father standing in the doorway to the kitchen, his hands on the back of Matthew's wheelchair. Both looked quite pleased with themselves and ready to tackle whatever the day might bring.

Jacob Schrock didn't need to hire a driver for the day's job. Though the Beiler home was technically in a different church district, in reality they were only a few miles apart. That's the way things were in Goshen, Indiana. There were so many Amish that his own district had recently divided again because they had too many families to fit into one home or barn for church.

Theirs was a good, healthy community. A growing community.

Which was one of the reasons that Jacob had plenty of work.

The night before, he'd loaded the tools he would need into the cargo box fastened on the back of his buggy. The lumber would be delivered to the job site before lunch.

Bo stood stamping his foot and tossing his head as if to ask what was taking so long. Jacob hitched the black gelding to the buggy, glanced back at his house and workshop and then set off down the road. As he directed the horse down Goshen's busy two-lane road, his mind raked back over the letter he'd received from the IRS. How was he going to deal with the upcoming audit and complete the jobs he had contracted at the same time? The accountant he'd contacted had named a quite high hourly rate. The man had also said he'd need a thousand-dollar retainer in order to start the job. Jacob had given serious thought to hiring the accounting firm in spite of their high fees, but in truth he didn't make enough money to afford that.

Jacob had asked around his church, but no one who was qualified had been interested in accounting work. The one young girl who had expressed an interest had quit the first day, and who could blame her? Jacob's idea of filing consisted of giant plastic bins where he tossed receipts.

Jacob loved working for himself, by himself. He'd rather not have anyone in his small office. The bulk of his income came from residential jobs and a few small business contracts, but his heart and soul were invested in building playhouses for children with disabilities. He needed to juggle both, and now, on top of that, he needed to prepare for the audit.

Twenty minutes later he pulled into the Beilers' drive. It wasn't a home he'd ever been to before; that much he was sure of.

Jacob parked the buggy, patted Bo and assured him, "Back in a minute to put you in the field. Be patient." Bo was a fine buggy horse, if a little spirited. Jacob had purchased him six months before. The horse was strong and good-tempered. Unfortunately he was not patient. He'd been known to chew his lead rope, eat anything in sight and paw holes into the ground. He did not handle boredom well.

Grabbing his tool belt and folder with design plans,

Jacob hesitated before heading to the front door. This was always the hardest part for him—initially meeting someone. His left hand automatically went to his face, traced the web of scar tissue that stretched from his temple to his chin. He wasn't a prideful man, but neither did he wish to scare anyone.

There was nothing he could do about his appearance, though, so he pulled in a deep breath, said a final word to the horse and hurried to the front door. He knocked, waited and then stood there staring when a young, beautiful woman opened the door. She stood about five and a half feet tall. Chestnut-colored hair peeked out from her *kapp*. It matched her warm brown eyes and the sprinkling of freckles on her cheeks.

There was something familiar about her. He nearly smacked himself on the forehead. Of course she looked familiar, though it had been years since he'd seen her.

"Hannah? Hannah Beiler?"

"Hannah King." She quickly scanned him head to toe. Her gaze darted to the left side of his face and then refocused on his eyes. She frowned and said, "I'm Hannah King."

"But…isn't this the Beiler home?"

"*Ya*. Wait. Aren't you Jacob? Jacob Schrock?"

He nearly laughed at the expression of puzzlement on her face.

"The same, and I'm looking for the Beiler place."

"*Ya*, this is my parents' home, but why are you here?"

"To work." He stared down at the work order as if he could make sense of seeing the first girl he'd ever kissed standing on the doorstep of the place he was supposed to be working.

"I don't understand," he said.

"Neither do I. Who are you looking for?"

"Alton Beiler."

"But that's my father. Why—"

At that point Mr. Beiler joined them, telling Hannah he would take care of their visitor and shaking Jacob's hand. Surely he noticed the scar on Jacob's face, but he didn't dwell on it. "You're at the right house, Jacob. Please, come inside."

"Why would he come inside?" Hannah had crossed her arms and was frowning at him now.

He'd never have guessed when he put on his suspenders that morning that he would be seeing Hannah Beiler before the sun was properly up. The same Hannah Beiler he had once kissed behind the playground and several years later asked out for a buggy ride and dinner. It had been a disastrous date for sure, but still he remembered it with fondness. The question was, what was she doing here?

But then he peered more closely at Alton. Yes, it was Hannah's father for sure and certain. Older, grayer and with wrinkles lining his face, but still her father.

"I haven't seen you in years," Jacob said to Alton.

"Do we know each other?"

"Barely." Jacob chuckled, though Hannah continued to glare at him. "Hannah and I went on a date many years ago."

"It was hardly a date," Hannah chimed in.

"I took you in my buggy."

"Which hadn't been properly cleaned, and your horse was lame."

"I should have checked the horse more carefully."

"We never even made it to dinner."

"I'm surprised you remember."

"And I had to walk home."

"I offered to walk with you."

Hannah rolled her eyes, shook her head and headed back into the house.

"She hasn't changed much," Jacob said in a lower voice.

"Oh, but she has." Alton opened the door wider so that Jacob would come in. "I'm sorry I didn't recognize you."

"It has been ten years."

They passed through a living room that appeared to be sparsely but comfortably furnished. Jacob could smell bacon and biscuits. His stomach grumbled and he instantly regretted that he hadn't taken the time to eat a proper breakfast.

"So your dating Hannah must have been when we were at the other place, on the east side of the district."

"Indeed."

"Obviously we've moved since then." Alton stopped before entering the kitchen, seemed about to say something and then rubbed at the back of his neck and ushered Jacob into the room.

"Claire, maybe you remember Jacob Schrock. Apparently he took our Hannah on a buggy ride once."

Jacob heard them, but his attention was on the young boy sitting at the table. He was young—probably not school-age yet. Brown hair flopped into his eyes and he had the same smattering of freckles as his mother. He sat in a regular kitchen chair, which was slightly higher than the wheelchair parked behind him. No doubt moving back and forth was cumbersome. If he had a small ramp, the chair could be rolled up and locked into place.

He should talk to Alton about that. It would be easy enough to create from scrap lumber.

Hannah was helping the child with his breakfast, or perhaps she was merely avoiding Jacob's gaze.

The boy, though, had no problem with staring. He cocked his head to the side, as if trying to puzzle through what he saw of Jacob. Then a smile won out over any questions, and he said, *"Gudemariye."*

"And to you," Jacob replied.

Hannah's mother, Claire, motioned him toward a seat. "Of course I remember you, Jacob. Though you've grown since then."

"*Ya*, I was a bit of a skinny lad." This was the awkward part. He never knew if he should share the cause of his scars or wait for someone to ask. With the child in the room, perhaps it would be better to wait.

Hannah continued to ignore him, but now the boy was watching him closely, curiously.

"You're taller too, if I remember right. You were definitely not as tall as Alton when you were a *youngie*. Now you're a good six feet, I'd guess."

"Six feet and two inches. My *mamm* used to say I had growth spurts up until I turned twenty." Jacob accepted a mug of coffee and sat down across the table from the boy.

"Who are you?" he asked.

"I'm Jacob. What's your name?"

"Matthew. This is *Mamm*, and that's *Mammi* and *Daddi*. We're a family now." Matthew grinned as if he'd said the most clever thing.

Hannah met Jacob's gaze and blushed, but this time she didn't look away.

"It's really nice to meet you, Matthew. I'm going to be working here for a few days."

"Working on what?"

Jacob glanced at Alton, who nodded once. "I'm going to build you a playhouse."

Hannah heard the conversation going on around her, but she felt as if she'd fallen into the creek and her ears were clogged with water. She heard it all from a distance. Then Matthew smiled that smile that changed the shape of his eyes. It caused his cheeks to dimple. It was a simple thing that never failed to reach all the way into her heart.

And suddenly Hannah's hearing worked just fine.

"A playhouse? For me?"

"For sure and certain."

"How come?"

Jacob shrugged and waited for Alton to answer the child.

"Some nice people want you to have one."

"Oh. Cool."

"*Dat*, we can't…"

"We most certainly can, Hannah. The charity foundation contacted me last week to make sure it was all right, and I said yes. I think it would be a fine thing for Matthew to have."

"Will I be able to move around in a playhouse? Like, with my wheelchair?"

"You most certainly will," Jacob assured him.

"You're sure?"

"I'm positive."

"Because it don't always fit good. Not in cars or on

merry-go-rounds. Sometimes not even in buggies and we have to tie it on the back."

"Your chair will fit in your playhouse. I can promise you that."

Matthew laughed and stabbed his biscuit with his fork, dipped it in a puddle of syrup he'd poured on his plate and stuffed the gooey mess into his mouth.

Hannah's head was spinning. Surely it was a good and gracious thing that someone had commissioned a playhouse for Matthew, but would it be safe for him to play in one? What if he fell out of his chair? What if he rolled out of the playhouse?

How could her father agree to such a thing?

And why was it being built by Jacob Schrock? She hadn't thought about him in years, certainly hadn't expected to see him again. Why today of all days, when her heart was sore from dreaming of David? Why this morning?

"Can I help?" Matthew asked.

"Oh, no." Hannah abandoned her future worries and focused on the problems at hand. "You'll leave that to Jacob."

"But *Mamm*..."

"We can't risk your getting hurt."

"I'll be super careful..."

"And you'd only be in Jacob's way."

Matthew stabbed another piece of biscuit and swirled it into the syrup, but he didn't plop it in his mouth. Instead he stared at the food, worried his bottom lip and hunched up his shoulders. Her son's bullheadedness had been quite useful during his initial recovery. When the doctors had said he probably couldn't do a thing, Matthew had buckled down, concentrated and found a way. There were days, though, when she wondered why *Gotte* had given her such a strong-willed child.

Jacob had drunk half his coffee and accepted a plate of eggs and bacon, which he'd consumed rather quickly. Now he sat rubbing his hand up and down his jaw, his clean-shaven jaw. The right side—the unscarred side. Was the injury the reason he'd never married? Was he embarrassed about the scar? Did women avoid him? Not that it was her business, and she'd certainly never ask.

"I just wanted to help," Matthew muttered.

"Now that you mention it, I could use an apprentice."

"I could be a *'rentice*." Matthew nodded his head so hard his hair flopped forward into his eyes, reminding Hannah that she would need to cut it again soon.

"It's hard work," Jacob cautioned.

"I can work hard."

"You sure?"

"Tell him, *Mamm*. Tell him how hard I work at the center."

"You'd have to hand me nails, tools, that sort of thing."

"I can do that!" Matthew was rocking in his chair now, and Hannah was wise enough to know the battle was lost.

"Only if your *mamm* agrees, of course."

She skewered him with a look. Certainly he knew that he'd backed her into an impossible corner. Instead of arguing, she smiled sweetly and said, "If your *daddi* thinks it's okay."

Hannah's father readily agreed and then Jacob was pulling out sheets of drawings that showed a playhouse in the shape of a train, with extra-wide doors—doors wide enough for Matthew's chair, room to pivot the chair, room to play. How could she not want such a thing for her child? The penciled playhouse looked like the stuff of fairy tales.

When she glanced up at Jacob, he smiled and said in a low voice, "We'll be extra careful."

"I should hope so."

And then she stood and began to clear off the dishes. The last thing she needed to do was stand around staring into Jacob Schrock's deep blue eyes. A better use of her time would be to go to town and pick up the Monday paper so she could study the Help Wanted ads. It looked like that wasn't going to happen. There was no way she was leaving Matthew outside, working as an apprentice to a man who had no children of his own. She'd come home to find he'd nailed his thumb to a piece of wood, or cut himself sawing a piece of lumber, or fallen and cracked something open. Secondary infections were no laughing matter for a child who was a paraplegic.

She'd be spending the morning watching Matthew watch Jacob. As soon as he left for the day, she'd head to town because one way or another, she needed to find a job.

Chapter Two

Hannah pushed aside her unsettled feelings and worked her way through the morning. She managed to complete the washing and hang it up on the line, and she helped her mother to put lunch on the table, all the while keeping a close eye on what was happening in the backyard.

When it was time for lunch, Matthew came in proclaiming he was an "official 'rentice now," and Jacob followed behind him with a sheepish look on his face.

Her father joined them for the noon meal. Earlier, he had stayed around long enough to confirm where the playhouse would be built and then he'd headed off to the fields. It worried her sometimes, her father being fifty-two and still working behind a team of horses, but her mother only scoffed at that. "What is he supposed to do? Sit in a rocking chair? Your father is as healthy as the bull in the north pasture, and if it's *Gotte's wille*, he'll stay that way for many more years."

The meal had passed pleasantly enough, though Hannah didn't like how enamored Matthew was with Jacob

Schrock. They laughed and described their morning's work and talked of trains as if they'd been on one.

"There's a place in town called Tender Jim's." Jacob reached for another helping of potato salad. "Have you heard of it, Matthew?"

Matthew stuffed a potato chip into his mouth and shook his head.

"Down on Danbury Drive. Isn't it?" Her father sat back, holding his glass of tea with one hand and pulling on his beard with the other. "Nice *Englisch* fellow."

"And what were you doing in Tender Jim's?" Claire asked.

"Curious, mostly. I'd taken Dolly to the farrier and had to wait a bit longer than I thought I would. Wandered down and talked to the fellow."

"Did he have trains?" Matthew asked.

"Oh, *ya*. Certainly, he did. Small ones and large ones."

"As large as my playhouse?"

"*Nein*. They were toys."

"Perhaps we could go by and see them sometime," Jacob said.

Hannah jumped up as if she'd been stung by a bee. "Matthew has a full week planned with his physical therapy appointments and all, but *danki* for the offer."

This was exactly why she didn't want a man like Jacob around—or any man for that matter. They'd raise her son's hopes, promise him things they wouldn't deliver and then disappear one day when they realized that Matthew was never going to walk, never going to be normal.

She pretended to be occupied with putting things up in the refrigerator as Jacob, her father and Matthew went out to look at the "job site." Her job was to protect Matthew—from strangers who would pretend to be friends, and from upheaval in his life. Which reminded her that she still hadn't been to town to purchase a newspaper.

She needed to stop worrying, which was easier said than done. Jacob would be finished with the playhouse in a day or two and then Matthew wouldn't see him anymore. Didn't Jacob mention that he was part of a different church district? She hadn't been home long enough to sort the districts out, but she did know there were a lot of Amish in the area. It would explain why she hadn't seen him at church.

Hannah and her mother cleared away the lunch dishes and put together a casserole for dinner and then her mother sat at the table. Hannah continued to peer out the window. What were they doing out there? How could Matthew possibly be helping? Why would Jacob want him to?

"Come sit down a minute, Hannah."

"But—"

"Come on, now. You've been on your feet all morning."

Hannah peeked out the window one last time, then walked to the table and sank into one of the chairs. *Mamm* was putting the finishing touches on a baby quilt for a new mother in their congregation.

Hannah had to force her eyes away from the pastel fabric and the Sunbonnet Sue and Overall Sam pattern. Her mother had given her a similar quilt when Matthew was born. When Hannah had first wrapped her son in that quilt, she'd trusted that only good things would happen in their future. She'd hoped that one day she would wrap her daughter in the same quilt. Now such beliefs didn't come so easily.

"I know you wanted today's paper, but last week's is still next to your father's chair in the sitting room."

"How did you know I wanted a paper?"

"Matthew told me you mentioned it."

Had she told Matthew?

Abandoning any attempt to figure out how her mother knew things, Hannah fetched a highlighter from a kitchen drawer and the newspaper from the sitting room, folded it open to the Help Wanted section and sat down with a sigh.

"I wish you wouldn't worry about that."

"But we need the money."

"*Gotte* will provide, Hannah."

"Maybe He's providing through one of these ads."

The next twenty minutes passed in silence as Hannah's mood plummeted even lower. The part-time positions paid too little and the full-time positions would require her to be away from home from sunup to sundown, if she could even get one of the positions, which was doubtful since she had no experience. She could always be a waitress at one of the Amish restaurants, but those positions were usually filled by younger girls—girls who hadn't yet married, who had no children.

"He's nice. Don't you think?"

"Who?"

"You know who."

"I don't know who."

"We sound like the owl in the barn."

Hannah smiled at her mother and slapped the newspaper shut. "Okay. I probably know who."

"I guess you were surprised to see him at the door."

"Indeed I was." Hannah should have kept her mouth shut, but she couldn't resist asking, "Do you know what happened to him? To his face?"

"A fire, no doubt." Her mother rocked the needle back and forth, tracing the outline of a Sunbonnet Sue. "We've had several homes destroyed over the years, and always there are injuries. Once or twice the fire was a result of carelessness. I think there was even one caused by lightning."

"A shame," Hannah whispered.

"That he had to endure such pain—yes. I'll agree with that. It doesn't change who he is, though, or his value as a person."

"I never said—"

"You, more than anyone else, should realize that."

"Of course I do."

"You wouldn't want anyone looking at Matthew and seeing a child with a disability. That's not who he is. That's just evidence of something he's endured."

"There's no need to lecture me, *Mamm*."

"Of course there isn't." She rotated the quilt and continued outlining the appliqué. "I can see that Jacob is self-conscious about his scars, though. I hate to think that anyone has been unkind to him."

"His scars don't seem to be affecting Matthew's opinion. He looks at Jacob as if he had raised a barn single-handedly."

"*Gotte* has a funny way of putting people in our life right when we need them."

"I'm not sure this was *Gotte*'s work."

"I know you don't mean that. I raised you to have more faith, Hannah. The last year has been hard, *ya*, I know, but never doubt that *Gotte* is still guiding your life."

Instead of arguing, Hannah opted to pursue a lighter subject. "So *Gotte* sent Jacob to build my son a playhouse?"

"Maybe."

She nearly laughed. Her mother's optimism grated on her nerves at times, but Hannah appreciated and loved her more than she could ever say. *Mamm* had been her port in the storm. Or perhaps *Gotte* had been, and *Mamm* had simply nudged her in the correct direction.

"You have to admit he's easy on the eyes."

"Is that how you older women describe a handsome man?"

"So you think he's *gut*-looking?"

"That's not what I said, *Mamm*."

Claire tied off her thread, popped it through the back of the quilt and then rethreaded her needle. "Tell me about this first date you two had, because I can hardly remember it."

"Small wonder. I was only sixteen."

"*Ya?* Already out of school, then."

"I was. In fact, I was working at the deli counter in town."

"I remember that job. You always brought home the leftover sandwiches."

"Jacob and I attended the same school, in the old district when we lived on Jackspur Lane. He's two years older than me."

"I'm surprised I don't remember your stepping out with him."

"Our house was quite busy then." Hannah was the youngest of three girls. She'd always expected her life to follow their fairy-tale existence. "Beth had just announced her plans to marry Carl, and Sharon was working with the midwife."

"I do remember that summer. I thought things would get easier when you three were out of school, but suddenly I had trouble keeping up with everyone."

"The date with Jacob, it was only my second or third, and I was still expecting something like I read in the romance books."

Her mother tsked.

"They were Christian romance, *Mamm*."

"I'm guessing your date with Jacob didn't match with what you'd been reading."

"Hardly. First of all, he showed up with mud splattered all over the buggy, and the inside of it was filled with pieces of hay and fast-food wrappers and even a pair of dirty socks."

"Didn't he have older brothers?"

"He had one."

"So I guess they shared the buggy."

Hannah shrugged. "We'd barely made it a quarter mile down the road when we both noticed his horse was limping."

"Oh my."

"It was no big thing. He jumped out of the buggy and began to clean out her hooves with a pick."

"While you waited."

"At first. Then I decided to help, which he told me in no short fashion not to do."

"There are times when it's hard for a man, especially a young man, to accept a woman's help."

"I waited about ten minutes and finally said I was heading home."

"Changed your mind before you were even out of sight of the house."

"Maybe. What I knew for sure was that I didn't want to stand on the side of the road while Jacob Schrock took care of his horse—something he should have done before picking me up."

"Could have been his brother's doing."

"I suppose."

"I hope you didn't judge him harshly because of a dirty buggy and a lame horse."

"Actually, I don't think I judged him at all. I simply realized that I didn't want to spend the evening with him."

"Well, he seems to have turned into a fine young man."

Hannah refolded the newspaper and pointed her highlighter at her mother. "Tell me you are not matchmaking."

"Why would I do such a thing?"

"Exactly."

"Though I did help both of your sisters find their husbands."

"I need a job, *Mamm*. I don't need a husband. I have a son, I have a family and I have a home. I'm fine without Jacob Schrock or any other man." Before her mother could see how rattled she was, Hannah jumped up, stepped over to the window and stared out at Jacob and Matthew.

"At least you parted friends…or so it seems."

Hannah suddenly remembered Jacob kissing her behind the swing set at school. It had been her first kiss, and a bit of a mess. He'd leaned in, a bee had buzzed past her and she'd darted to the right at the last minute.

The result was a kiss on the left side of her *kapp*. She'd been mortified, though Jacob had laughed good-naturedly, then reached for her hand and walked her back into the school building. It was three years later when he'd asked her out on the buggy ride.

Remembering the kiss, Hannah felt the heat crawl up her neck. Before her mother could interrogate her further, she busied herself pulling two glasses from the cabinet and said, "Perhaps I should take both of the workers something to drink."

She filled the glasses with lemonade, snagged half a dozen of her mother's oatmeal cookies, put it all on a tray and carried it outside.

After setting it down on the picnic table under the tall maple tree, she turned to watch Jacob and Matthew. In spite of her resolution to maintain a safe distance from Jacob Schrock, her heart tripped a beat at the sight of him.

Which made no sense, because Jacob Schrock was not her type.

He was eight inches taller than she was, whereas David had been her height exactly.

He was blond. David had been dark haired.

His eyes were blue, and David's had been a lovely brown.

Nothing about the man standing near her son appealed to her, least of all the suggestion that he knew what was good for Matthew.

She couldn't help noticing, though...

The sleeves of his blue shirt were rolled up past the elbow, revealing his muscular, tanned arms.

Sweat gleamed on his forehead and caused his blond hair to curl slightly.

As she watched, he handed one end of a tape measure to Matthew, stepped off what was apparently the length of the project and pushed a stake into the ground.

When he was done, Jacob glanced up, noticed her waiting and smiled. Now, why did his smile cause her heart to race even faster? Perhaps she needed to see a doctor. Maybe the depression that had pressed down on her like a dark cloud for so long had finally taken its toll on her heart. Or maybe she was experiencing a normal reaction to a nice-looking man doing a kind deed.

Of course, he was getting paid for it.

But he didn't have to allow Matthew to tag along.

He certainly didn't have to smile at her every time she was near.

Jacob stored the tape measure they were using in a tool belt and said something to Matthew. When her son twisted in his wheelchair to look at her, she had to press her fingers to her lips. Yes, he still sat in his chair, but he looked like a completely different boy. He had rolled up his sleeves, sweat had plastered his hair to his head and a smear of dirt marked his cheek. When he caught her watching, he beamed at her as if it were Christmas Day.

In short, he looked like a normal child having a great time building a playhouse.

Jacob glanced back at Hannah in time to catch her staring at Matthew, the fingers of her right hand pressed against her lips. Jacob considered himself open to beauty. Maybe because of his own disfigurement, he found contentment in noticing *Gotte*'s handiwork elsewhere.

He'd often stood and watched the sunset, thinking

that *Gotte* had done a wonderful thing by providing them such splendor. He'd helped his brother when it was time for birthing in the spring: goats, horses, cows, and once when a terrible storm came through and they couldn't get to the hospital—a son. Jacob didn't mind that such things brought him to tears, that he often had to pause and catch his breath, that he was sensitive to the joys of this world.

But when he looked up and saw Hannah, an unfamiliar emotion brushed against the inside of his heart. It couldn't be attraction, as he'd never asked a woman out on a date because of how she looked—not before the fire and not since. He hadn't asked a woman out in years, and he wouldn't be starting today. As for her personality, well, if he were to be honest with himself, she was pushy, obviously overprotective of her son and taciturn to the point of being rude.

She was beautiful, though, and more than that, her obvious love for her son was moving. Her vulnerability in that moment reached deep into his soul and affected him in a way he didn't realize he could be touched.

So he stooped down and said to Matthew, "Best take a break. Your *mamm* has brought us a snack."

He walked beside the boy as they made their way toward the picnic table.

"*Mamm*, I'm helping." Matthew reached for a cookie, broke it in half and stuffed the larger piece into his mouth.

"It appears you worked up an appetite."

Matthew nodded, and Jacob said, "We both did."

Hannah motioned for him to help himself. He popped a whole cookie into his mouth and said, "Wow," before he'd finished chewing. Which caused Matthew to dissolve in a fit of laughter.

"What-id I-ooh?" Jacob asked, exaggerating each syllable.

"You have to chew first," Matthew explained. "And swallow!"

Jacob did as instructed, took a big sip of the lemonade and then said, "*Danki*, Hannah. Hit the spot."

"Looks as if actual construction on this playhouse is slow getting started."

"Measure twice, cut once," Matthew explained.

"We've managed to mark off the dimensions and unload my tools."

"You brought all that lumber in your buggy?"

"*Nein.* The store in town delivered it. I guess you didn't hear the truck."

"I guess I didn't."

"It was this big," Matthew said, holding his arms out wide.

"The playhouse will go up quickly," Jacob assured her. "I'll begin the base of the structure today. The walls will go up tomorrow, and the roof and final details the third day."

"Kind of amazing that a child's toy takes so long to build." Hannah held up a hand and shook her head at the same time. "I did not mean that the way it sounded. It's only that when you consider we can build a barn in one day, it seems funny that a playhouse takes three."

"Sure, *ya*. But this isn't a barn, and, as you can see, young Matthew and I are the only workers."

"I'm going to help," Matthew exclaimed, reaching for another cookie.

Hannah's son was rambling on now, explaining that

he could mark the wood before Jacob made the cut and hand him nails as he hammered.

"Wait a minute, Matt. We have therapy tomorrow."

"But—"

"*Nein.* Do not argue with me."

"*Ya*, but this is kind of therapy."

"What time is Matthew's appointment?" Jacob asked, recognizing the escalating disagreement for what it was. Hadn't he argued in the same way when he was a young lad? Maybe not over physical therapy appointments, but there was always something to pull him away from what he'd wanted to do—fishing, searching for frogs, climbing trees.

"Matthew is scheduled for therapy three afternoons a week—Tuesday, Wednesday and Friday."

"That's perfect, because I need help tomorrow morning."

Matthew and Hannah both swiveled to look at him.

"In the afternoon, I'll be doing other stuff that an apprentice isn't allowed to do. But the morning?" Jacob rubbed his hand up and down his jawline as if he needed to carefully consider what he was about to say. Finally he grinned and said, "Mornings will be perfect."

"Yes!" Matthew raised a hand for Jacob to high-five. "I gotta go inside and tell *Mammi*."

Without another word, he reversed the direction of his chair and wheeled toward the house.

"That was kind of you," Hannah said.

"Actually, he is a big help to me."

Instead of arguing, she again pressed her fingers to her lips. Was it so she could keep her emotions inside? Stop her words? Protect her feelings?

"It's only a little thing, Hannah. I'm happy to do it. It's plain to see that Matthew is a special young man."

She picked up the plate of cookies and stared down at it. "He never eats more than one cookie. In fact, he often passes on snacks and desserts. Today he ate two and drank a full glass of lemonade."

"Is that a problem?"

He thought she wouldn't answer. She glanced at him and then her gaze darted out over the area where construction had not yet begun. "The doctors said that the steroids might suppress his appetite, but that it was best to encourage him to eat more."

"And what purpose do the steroids serve?"

"They're supposed to decrease swelling around the spinal cord." She placed the plate on the tray and transferred the empty lemonade glasses to it, as well. "I'm sorry. I didn't mean to bore you with the details."

"Do I look bored?"

She sat on the picnic bench then, staring back toward the house, seemingly lost in her worries over Matthew. "The last thing we needed is him losing weight. Then there are the other complications..."

"Such as?"

"Children with spinal cord injuries often struggle with pneumonia and other breathing disorders. Secondary infections are always a worry—it's why I was afraid for him to help you. If he were to get a cut or take a nasty fall, it could spiral into something worse."

"It must be a lot for you to monitor."

"Matthew needs all his strength, even when it comes in the form of oatmeal cookies."

"I'd like to ask what happened, but I know from personal experience that sometimes you feel like sharing and sometimes you don't."

Hannah jerked her head up. She seemed to study his scars for a moment and then she nodded once. "It's true. Sometimes I want to talk about it, *need* to talk about it, but then other times..."

"I'm listening, if today is one of those days you want to talk."

She pulled in a deep breath and blew it out. "There's not really that much to tell. David and I bought a farm in Wisconsin, after we were married. Life was difficult but *gut*. Matthew came along—a healthy baby boy. My husband was out harvesting, and Matthew was riding up on the bench seat with him. This was a year ago... one year next week."

"What happened?"

"There was a snake coiled in the grass. The work horse nearly stepped on it. He reared up, throwing both David and Matthew. David was killed instantly when the harvester rolled over him. I suppose because he was smaller, Matthew was thrown farther. Otherwise he would have been killed, as well."

"Instead he was injured."

"He suffered a complete spinal cord break."

"I'm so sorry."

Jacob allowed silence to fill the hurting places between them. Finally he asked, "Surgeries?"

"*Ya*—two. The first was for the initial diagnosis, to evaluate and stabilize the fractured backbone. The second was a follow-up to the first."

"And you had to handle it all alone."

"Of course I didn't." Now her chin came up and when she glanced at him, Jacob saw the old stubbornness in her eyes. "My church helped me, my sister came to stay awhile and then…then my parents suggested I move home."

"Family is *gut*."

"*Ya*, it is, except that our being here is a drain on them."

Jacob was unsure how to answer that. He didn't know Claire or Alton Beiler well, but he was certain they didn't consider Hannah and Matthew to be a drain. It was plain from the way they interacted that they wanted their daughter and grandson at home with them.

"I'm happy to have Matthew working with me, Hannah, but only if it's okay with you. I promise to be very careful around him."

She didn't answer. Instead she nodded once, gathered up the tray and followed her son into the house.

Leaving Jacob standing in the afternoon sunshine, wondering what else he could do to lighten the burden she carried, wondering why it suddenly seemed so important for him to do so.

He needed to stay focused on his business, on making enough money to pay an accountant before the audit was due, on the other playhouses he would build after this. But instead, as he went back to work, he found himself thinking of a young boy with dirt smeared across his nose and a beautiful mother who was determined to keep others at arm's length.

Chapter Three

Hannah was grateful that she was busy the next morning. Maybe it would take her mind off of finding a job, which was becoming all she thought about. She'd spent an hour before breakfast going over the Help Wanted ads once again, but nothing new had appeared. There wasn't a single listing that she felt qualified to do, and she doubted seriously that anything new had been listed in the last few days. So instead of obsessing over what she couldn't change, she focused on helping her mother.

Tuesday was baking day. They mixed bread, kneaded dough, baked cookies and prepared two cakes. The kitchen was hot and steamy by the time they were finished. Her mother sank into a chair and said, "You're a big help, Hannah. I wouldn't want to do all of this alone."

Of course, she wouldn't need so much if they weren't there.

And Hannah knew that her mother rarely baked alone. Most weeks her niece Naomi came over to help. Still, the compliment lightened her heart as she called to Matthew. She'd helped him change into clean clothes after lunch, and he had promised not to get dirty. Now he was sitting in his chair, watching out the window as Jacob raised the walls of his playhouse.

"Looks like a real train, huh?" her mother asked.

Hannah cocked her head left and then right. "Can't say as it does."

"To me it's plain as day."

"Which is all that matters." She reached out and mussed her son's hair. "We should get going so we won't be late."

They made it to the PT center in downtown Goshen twenty minutes before their appointment. For the next two hours, Hannah sat in the waiting room and crocheted, or attempted to. Her mind kept wandering and she'd find that she'd dropped a stitch and then she would have to pull out the row and start over. After an hour, she'd made very little progress on the blue shawl, so she decided to put it away and flip through some of the magazines.

The center served both Amish and *Englisch*, so the magazine selection was varied. There were copies of the *Budget*, but there were also copies of *National Geographic*, *Home & Garden* and even *People* magazine.

She reached for *Home & Garden*.

On the cover was a picture of a sprawling country home, with flowers blooming along the brick pavement that bordered the front of the house. Orange, yellow and maroon mums filled containers on the porch. Pink begonias hung from planters on either side of the door.

"It would be nice if life were like those pictures." Sally Lapp sat down beside her with a *harrumph* and a sigh. Sally was plump, gray and kind.

"How's Leroy?"

"*Gut*. I suppose. Ornery, if I were to be honest."

Sally reached into her bag and pulled out a giant ball of purple yarn and two knitting needles. She'd shared the previous week that she was expecting her forty-second grandchild, and they were all sure it would be a girl. If by some strange twist of fate it was a boy, she'd save the blanket for an auction and knit another in an appropriate shade of green or blue.

"Is Leroy able to get around any better?" Hannah asked.

"Old coot tried to move from the living room to the bedroom by himself, without his walker. I was outside harvesting some of the garden vegetables when he fell." She glanced over her cheater glasses at Hannah, but never slowed in her knitting. "Fell, bruised his hip and scared a year of life off of me."

"I'm so sorry."

"Not your fault, child. How's young Matthew?"

"Gut." Hannah flipped through the magazine, too quickly to actually see anything on the pages.

"There's more you're not saying, which is fine. Some things we need to keep private, but take it from me—it's best to share when something is bothering you. Share with someone you can trust not to shout it to the nearest *Budget* scribe."

Hannah considered that for a moment. Maybe it would help to share her worries, especially with someone outside the family, and she could trust Sally to keep anything she said confidential.

"The Sunshine Foundation purchased supplies for a playhouse for Matthew—a special one, you know. It will have handicap rails and all."

"What a *wunderbaar* thing."

"And the National Spinal Cord Injury Association hired someone to build it."

"Even better. I know your father is very busy with his crops."

"Jacob Schrock showed up yesterday—to build the playhouse, which is in the shape of a train. I'm afraid that Matthew is fairly smitten with him."

Sally glanced at her once, but she didn't offer an opinion. She continued knitting, as if she were waiting for Hannah to say more. But Hannah didn't know what else to say. She didn't know why it bothered her so much that Matthew liked Jacob.

"I suppose I'm worried is all. I know Jacob will be done in a few days and then…most likely… Matthew won't see him anymore. I've tried to explain this, but Matthew doesn't listen. He prattles on about how he's Jacob's apprentice."

"It's natural for young boys Matthew's age to look up to their elders—your father, your brothers-in-law, the men in church."

"*Ya.* I know it is. But those are all people who are a constant presence in his life."

"Soon he will be in school," Sally continued. "I'm sure you realize that some teachers stay a long time, but others only last a year."

"I hadn't thought of that."

"Some people are in our lives permanently. Others? *Gotte* brings them to us for a short time."

Instead of answering, Hannah sighed.

Sally turned the baby blanket and began a row of purl stitches. They flowed seamlessly together with the knit stitches. The result was a pattern that looked as if it had been produced in an *Englisch* factory.

"Jacob Schrock, he's a *gut* man."

"Is he in your district?"

"He was, but we had to split recently. So many families. So many *grandkinner*."

"I went to school with him, but that was years ago."

"Before his accident, then."

"Ya." Hannah pulled the shawl she was supposed to be working on back out of her bag, but she didn't bother with hunting for the crochet needle.

"Terrible thing. Both of his parents were killed. The fire chief said the blaze was caused by a lightning strike. Jacob was out in the buggy when it happened. I heard that he saw the blaze from the road, ran into the burning house, and pulled out his *mamm* and his *dat*, but it was too late."

Hannah's hand went to her left cheek. "That's how he got the scars?"

"For sure and certain. He was in the hospital for a long time. The doctors wanted to do more surgeries… graft skin onto his face. They said that he would look as *gut* as new."

"So why didn't they?"

Sally shrugged. "He would still be a man who had lost his parents in a fire, who had endured unfathomable pain. Removing the scars from his face wouldn't have removed the scars from his heart."

"Yes, but—"

"Jacob decided not to have the additional surgeries. Our bishop would have allowed it, but Jacob said no. He said the money that had been donated should go to someone else."

"Kind of him."

"*Ya*, he is a kind man. He was also very depressed

for…" Sally stared across the room, as if she were trying to count the years, to tally them into something that made sense. "For two, maybe three years. Rarely came to church. Kind of hid inside his house."

"What changed?" Hannah asked. "When did he start making playhouses?"

"I suppose the playhouse building started a few years ago. As to what changed, you'd have to ask Jacob."

"He seems happy enough now."

"Trouble finds us all from time to time. Now Jacob is dealing with this tax audit."

"Tax audit?"

"They're not saying he did anything wrong, mind you. Only that he'll have to produce ledgers and receipts."

"Can he?"

Sally grimaced as she again turned the blanket and began a new row of knit stitches. "My granddaughter tried to work for him. She lasted less than a day. Said that he'd apparently been paying his taxes based on some system he kept scribbled on random sheets of paper. Said she couldn't make any sense of it at all."

"Oh my."

"And the receipts? Thrown into bins with the year taped on the outside. A giant mess according to Abigail. Said she'd rather keep waitressing than deal with that. Fortunately, she was able to get her old job back."

"But what about Jacob?"

"He's still looking for someone." Sally's needles stopped suddenly, clicking together as she dropped them in her lap. "Seems I remember you being very *gut* in math."

"That was years ago."

"It's an ability, though, not something you forget."

"I wouldn't—"

"And didn't you mention last week that you were worried about your parents' finances?"

"Well, yes, but… I'm looking for a job that pays well, something in town perhaps."

"Any success?"

"Not yet."

Sally picked up her needles again, and Hannah hoped the subject was dropped. She could not work for Jacob Schrock. He would be out of her life by the end of the week. The last thing she needed was to be in constant contact with him, working with him on a daily basis. The way he looked at her? Such a mixture of pity and compassion. She didn't need to face that every day, and how could she leave Matthew?

Always her mind circled back to that final question. How could she leave her son eight, maybe even nine hours a day? Could she expect her mother to pick up the slack? How was *Mamm* supposed to cope with one more thing on top of all she had to do?

Matthew wheeled through the doorway and into the waiting room, a smiley sticker on the back of his hand, and Hannah began gathering up her things. It was as she turned to go that Sally said, "Think about it, Hannah. It could be that you would be a real blessing to Jacob, and maybe…maybe it would solve your problems in the process."

She'd have to ask Jacob about the job.

Only of course, she wouldn't. It was all none of her business. Soon he'd be done with the playhouse and she wouldn't see him again, which would suit her just fine.

Dolly clip-clopped down the road, more content with the day than Hannah was.

She would be content, if she had a job. If they didn't have financial problems. If she wasn't so worried about Matthew.

It would be crazy to consider working for Jacob.

He might be a kind, talented man, but he was also damaged. He'd suffered a terrible loss, which might explain why he pushed his nose into other people's business. Just the day before, he'd looked at her as if she was crazy when she'd tried to put a sweater on Matthew. True, it was eighty degrees, but Matthew had been known to catch a cold in warmer weather than that.

Nope. Jacob Schrock didn't belong in her life.

Matthew peeled the sticker off his hand and stuck it on to the buggy.

"Your therapists said you did a *gut* job today."

"Uh-huh."

"They also said you did everything fast, that you seemed to be in a rush to be done."

"Are we almost home?"

"A few more miles."

"Faster, please."

"You want me to hurry this old buggy mare?"

"*Daddi*'s horse is faster."

"Indeed." Her father had ordered a second buggy horse when she'd come home to live. Hannah had protested it wasn't necessary, but he'd insisted. Come to think of it, maybe he'd insisted because Dolly was getting older and they'd have to replace her soon, which didn't bear thinking about. Dolly was the first buggy horse that Hannah had learned to drive.

While Matthew stared out the window, he pinched

his bottom lip in between his thumb and forefinger, pulling it out like a pout and then letting it go. It was a habit that she saw only when he was anxious about something.

And she didn't doubt for a minute that the source of his anxiety was right now hammering two-by-fours into the shape of a train.

They were about to pass the parking area for the Pumpkinvine Trail. Hannah pulled on the right rein and called out to Dolly, who docilely turned off the road.

"Why are we stopping?" Matthew frowned out at the trail, a place he usually enjoyed visiting.

"We need to talk."

Now he stared up at her, eyes wide. "Am I in trouble?"

"No, Matt. Not at all."

"Then what?"

Instead of answering, she studied him a minute. Already he had such a unique personality—with his own likes, dislikes and ideas. Admittedly, she felt more protective of him than most mothers might feel of a nearly five-year-old child, but she understood that this concern wasn't only about his disability. It was also about his not having a father, about his missing the presence of a dad in his life.

"You like Jacob a lot. Don't you?"

"Yes!"

"But you remember that he's only at our house because some people paid him to be there."

"Uh-huh."

"He's doing a job."

"And I'm his *'rentice*."

Hannah sighed, closed her eyes, and prayed for patience and wisdom. When she opened her eyes, Matt reached out and patted her hand. "Don't worry, *Mamm*. He's a *gut* guy. Even *Daddi* said so."

"Oh, *ya*, I'm sure he is."

"So what's wrong?"

"Nothing's wrong, really. But you do understand that Jacob is only going to be at our house for a few days, right? Then he'll have another job, building another playhouse for someone else."

Matt frowned and pulled on his bottom lip. "Another kid like me?"

"I don't know."

"Okay."

"Okay?" Hannah reached out and brushed the hair out of his eyes.

"Uh-huh."

"What do you mean, okay?"

"It's okay that Jacob won't be at our house because he'll be at somebody else's house making them happy."

Since she didn't have an answer for that, she called out to Dolly, who backed up and then trotted out of the parking area, back onto the two-lane.

She was willing to admit that possibly her son saw things more clearly than she did. Didn't the Bible tell them they were to become like little children? Hannah wasn't sure she'd be able to do that—her worries weighed too heavily on her heart, but maybe in this situation she could follow Matt's lead. At least for a few more days.

And she would double her efforts looking for a job because she most certainly was not going to ask Jacob about what kind of help he needed.

* * *

Jacob had always enjoyed working on playhouses. He liked building things with an eye for small children. Some people might say it was because his own father had built him a similar type of playhouse. But his father had also taught him to play baseball and he had no urge to coach the *youngies*. His father had taught him how to sow seed and harvest it, but he had no desire to be a farmer.

He was grateful for his father, for both of his parents, and he still missed them terribly. But learning to build wooden playthings for children had been a gift from *Gotte*, a real blessing at the lowest point in his life. Today he was able to share part of that blessing with young Matthew, and he wanted every piece of it to be as good as he could make it.

So he measured everything twice—the main doorway into the train, the back door which ended on a small porch and the entryways between the cars. Wheelchairs required extra room and Matthew would probably require a larger chair as he grew. Though he was nearly five now, children as old as ten or even twelve often played on the structures that Jacob made. As Matthew grew, no doubt his chair would become a bit bigger. Jacob wanted the playhouse to be as accessible to him as his home.

He sanded the floor smoothly so that the wheels of the chair wouldn't hang up on an uneven board.

He added a little extra height so that Matthew's friends who would be standing and walking and running could play along beside him.

And when he heard the clatter of a buggy, he put

down his tools and ambled over to meet Hannah and Matthew.

"Hi, Jacob. I can help now."

"You already helped me this morning. Remember?"

"*Ya*, but—"

"Actually I'm about to call it a day."

"Oh."

"There is one thing I need...won't take but a minute."

"Sure! Anything. What is it?"

"I need you to come and do an early inspection."

"You do?"

"Yup. I need my apprentice's opinion before I move forward."

"Cool!"

Hannah had parked the buggy, set the brake and jogged around to help Matthew out.

Jacob stepped forward as if to help, but a frown from Hannah and a short shake of her head convinced him not to try. She was obviously used to doing things on her own. So instead he stood there, feeling like an idiot because a woman weighing roughly the same as a hundred pound sack of feed struggled with simply helping her son out of a buggy.

As he watched, she removed the straps that secured the wheelchair to the back of the buggy, then set it on the ground, opened it, secured something along the back. Finally she opened the buggy's door wide so that Matthew's legs wouldn't bang against anything.

"Ready?" she asked.

"Ready." He threw his arms around her neck and she stepped back as she took the full weight of him, then settled him into the chair.

How would she do this when he was seven or ten or

twelve? How would Hannah handle the logistics of a fully grown disabled son? Was there any possibility that he would ever regain the use of his legs? Jacob had a dozen questions, and he didn't ask any of them because it wasn't really his business.

He reached into the buggy, snagged Matt's straw hat and placed it on his head. The boy gave him a thumbs-up, and adjusted himself in the chair as easily as Jacob straightened his suspenders in the morning.

"Let's go," Matthew said.

"Whoa. Hang on a minute. We need to see to your *mamm*'s horse first."

"I can take care of Dolly," Hannah insisted.

"Nonsense." He stepped closer to Hannah and lowered his voice. "What kind of neighbor would I be if I let you do that?"

"You're our neighbor now?"

"In a sense."

"So you want to take care of my horse?"

"*Ya.* I do."

"Fine. I'll just go inside and have a cup of tea."

"But I thought you might go with us and..." His words slid away as she walked toward the house, waving without turning around.

"Come on, Jacob. Let's do this."

Matthew wheeled alongside him as he led the mare into the barn.

"Her name's Dolly," Matthew said when they stopped inside the barn.

The horse lowered her head so that she was even with the boy. Matthew sat in front of her and stroked from her forehead to her muzzle.

"Good Dolly," Matthew said.

Jacob unhitched the buggy, took off the harness and placed it on the peg on the wall, and then led Dolly through the barn to the pasture.

"Now?" Matt asked.

"Now."

Matt had to move slowly over the parts of uneven ground that led to where the playhouse was being constructed. It was definitely the best place for the structure, as Alton had noted. But the going was a little rough, and it occurred to Jacob that a wooden walk would make things much easier. He had enough lumber scraps at home to do it. An extra day, maybe two, and he could have a nice smooth path from the driveway to the playhouse.

"That is way cool," Matt exclaimed, sounding exactly like an *Englisch* boy Jacob had built a playhouse for the week before. Kids were kids, and *cool* was a pretty standard response to something they liked.

"Let's show you the inside."

Jacob let Matthew go first and watched as he maneuvered his way up the small ramp and into the main cabin of the train. The engine room was to his left and the passenger car was to his right. Beyond that was a small back porch. On an actual train, this would be the end of the observation car, and the area would resemble a roofed porch. Now that he thought about it, a roof wasn't a bad idea. He could add it easily enough.

Matthew made his way to the front of the train. Jacob had created a space where he could pull up his wheelchair and pretend he was in the conductor's seat. To his right Jacob had fastened a wooden bench and in front of him there were knobs and such for him to pull and pretend to direct the train.

"Wow," he said.

"We're not finished yet, buddy. We still need to put on the roof, and…other stuff."

"Can I help?"

"I'm counting on it. I'll be here early tomorrow morning."

They were standing right next to each other, or rather, Jacob was standing next to Matthew. Before Jacob realized what was happening, Matt had pivoted in his seat and thrown his arms around his legs.

"Danki," the boy said in a low voice.

"Ger gschehne." Jacob found that his voice was tight, but the words of their ancestors passed between them as easily as water down a riverbed.

Jacob pushed Matthew's chair the length of the car. They moved slowly, studying every detail, until Hannah's *mamm* came outside and rang the dinner bell.

Jacob did not intend to stay and eat, but it seemed that Claire expected it. She'd already set an extra place at the table. It would have been rude to refuse, or so he told himself.

The meal was satisfying and the conversation interesting. He realized that too often he ate alone, that he actually missed the back-and-forth between family members. There was no reason for it either. His brother lived next door, and he had a standing offer to eat with them.

Why had he pulled away?

Had it been so painful to see what he would never have?

There was no such awkwardness with Hannah's family. Claire spoke of the painted bunting she'd spied on the birdbath. Alton updated them on the crops. Hannah described how well Matthew had done at physical therapy.

As for Matthew, he was practically nodding off in his seat by the time they'd finished eating.

Hannah excused herself, transferred him from the dinner chair to the wheelchair and pushed him down the hall.

"She's pretty amazing, your daughter." He hadn't meant to say the words. They'd slipped from his heart to his lips without consulting his brain.

If Alton and Claire were surprised, they hid it well. Claire stood and began clearing the table. Alton offered to see him out. They'd stepped outside when Jacob shared his ideas for a wooden walk to the playhouse as well as a small platform for the dinner table.

"Must be hard on Hannah, on her back I mean—moving him from one chair to the other so often."

"And I have to be fast to beat her to it. Your ideas sound *gut*, but I'm afraid the grant doesn't cover that, and I don't have any extra money at the moment."

Jacob waved away his concerns. "I have leftover lumber. It won't cost me anything but time."

"Which is precious for every man."

"It's okay. I don't have to start the next job until Monday." He didn't mention the orders he had at his shop. He could put in a few hours each night and stay ahead on that.

"Then I accept, and I thank you."

"You can tell me it's none of my business, but Hannah seemed particularly preoccupied tonight. Is something wrong? Something else?"

Alton stuck his thumbs under his suspenders. "Money is a bit tight."

"How tight?"

"Missed a few payments on the place."

"What did your banker say about that?"

"Said they could extend me another thirty days, but then they'll have to start the foreclosure process."

"I'm sorry, Alton. I had no idea. Have you spoken to your bishop?"

Alton waved that idea away. "My family has received plenty of help from the benevolence fund in the last year. We'll find a way through this on our own."

"And Hannah?"

"Hannah is determined to find a job."

The entire drive home he thought of Alton's words, of the family's financial problems and of the help he needed in order to prepare him for the IRS audit. He could ask Hannah. It wasn't a completely crazy idea. He remembered that she was good at sums, and it wasn't as if she needed to understand algebra. It only required someone more organized than he was.

She was stubborn and willful and curt at times, but he wasn't going to be dating her. He was going to hire her.

Or was he?

It wasn't until he was home and cleaning up for bed that he realized the error of his thinking. He caught sight of his reflection in the small bathroom mirror and stared for a moment at his scars. His fingers traced the tissue that was puckered and discolored. He'd been so fortunate that his eye wasn't permanently damaged, and in truth he'd become used to the sight of his charred, disfigured flesh.

Others, though, they often found his face harder to

look at. They would turn away, or blush bright red and hurry off. Sometimes children cried when they first saw him.

Had he forgotten about those reactions?

Did he really think that his appearance wouldn't matter to a woman, to an employee? Hannah had been polite, sure, but that didn't mean that she wasn't horrified by the sight of his scars.

As for the thought of her working with him, she probably wouldn't want to spend her days in the company of a disfigured man. Possibly he even reminded her of the accident that had killed her husband. He would be a constant reminder of her misfortune.

He'd been around her for two days, and he was already creating sandcastles in the sky. Probably because he'd felt an instant connection to her and that was okay and proper. As a friend. As a brother. But what about as an employer?

He hadn't spent much time around women in the last few years. It was simply easier not to. Sure, he knew what he was missing out on, but it wasn't as if he had a chance with any of the single girls in their district. Even the widows could do better than him. He might have grown comfortable with his disfigurement, but he wouldn't ask that of a woman.

But he wasn't thinking about courting. He was thinking about a business arrangement, which was crazy. He'd seen the look of relief pass over her features when he'd promised her he would be done this week. She was already looking forward to having him out of their lives. Why would he offer her a job?

On top of which, she'd had enough tragedy in her life. He wouldn't be adding to that burden with his own problems. No, she'd be better off working in town, working for an *Englisch* shop owner. He'd do best to keep his distance. As for the audit, perhaps he could scrape up enough money for the accounting firm. He'd need to do something and do it quick, because the clock was ticking down to his deadline. Not that he remembered it exactly, but it was within the next month. That much he knew for certain.

Four weeks, maybe a little less.

By then, he needed to have found a solution.

Chapter Four

Hannah had scoured the paper on both Wednesday and Thursday looking for a job. What she found was discouraging. The Amish restaurant in town wanted her to work the four-to-nine shift. She wouldn't be home to share the evening meal or put Matthew to bed. The thought caused her stomach to twist into a knot.

Amish Acres in Nappanee needed someone in the gift shop, and they understood that Amish employees didn't work on Sundays. They even provided a bus that picked up workers in downtown Goshen for the twenty-minute ride. But she would be required to work on Saturday. In an Amish household, Saturday was a day spent preparing for Sunday—cooking meals, cleaning the house, making sure clothes were cleaned and pressed. She wouldn't be able to do any of that if she worked at Amish Acres.

And with any of the jobs she considered, the same questions lingered in the back of her mind. Who would take Matthew to his physical therapy appointments during the week? Could she really expect her mother to add one more thing to her already full schedule? Could her mother handle the physical demands of lifting Matthew in and out of the buggy?

She studied the local paper once more Friday morning, in between helping her mother with the meals and taking care of Matthew. After lunch, she again donned a fresh apron and set off to take Matthew to his appointment. She had an interview for a job late that afternoon, and her father had offered to meet them in town.

"You didn't have to do this," she said as she helped Matthew into the other buggy.

"I like riding with *Daddi*," Matthew piped up. "He drives faster than you do."

"I could have..."

"What? Taken him with you? *Nein*. It's not a problem. My order had come in at the feed store, and young Matthew can help check off items as they load them in the back of my buggy. Besides, I know this interview is important to you."

"Yes, but it's not for another hour. I could have brought him home."

"Go and order yourself a nice cup of tea at that bakery." Her father had clumsily patted her arm and then turned his attention to Matthew.

"Ready, Matt?"

"More than ready. Is Jacob done with the playhouse yet? Is he still there? Because I made him a drawing. I need to give it to him."

Hannah didn't hear the rest of the conversation as they pulled away. She didn't have to hear it to know what Matthew was saying. He'd been talking about the playhouse and Jacob all week.

She, on the other hand, had specifically avoided Jacob that morning. The more she thought about the job opening he had, the more irritated she grew. He definitely knew that her family was in a tough financial situation. She'd heard her father talking to him about it. Why hadn't he offered her the job?

Did he think she wasn't smart enough to handle a column of numbers?

Did he worry that she wouldn't be a good employee?

Or maybe—and this was the thing that pricked her heart—maybe he would be happy to be free of her and Matthew. Building a playhouse for a week was one thing. Involving yourself in someone's life, especially when that someone had special needs, was another thing completely.

Hannah's interview was at the new craft store in town. The ad said they were looking for an experienced quilter. That was one thing Hannah was quite good at, but then wasn't every Amish woman? Still, if it was the job she was meant to have, *Gotte* would provide a way.

She arrived early and carefully filled out the employment questionnaire, balancing the piece of paper on her lap with only a magazine under it for support. When she had finished, the cashier had taken it from her and told her to wait. The young girl had returned twenty minutes later and led her into a back office.

The owner of the shop was in her forties, stylishly dressed, sporting short black hair, dangly earrings and bright red fingernails.

She stared at the questionnaire for a moment and then she asked, "Do you wear your bonnet every day?"

"Excuse me?"

"Your…" The woman touched the top of her head.

"It's a prayer *kapp*, and *ya* we always wear it when we are out in public."

"Oh, good. I think the customers will like that, and your clothing—it's so quaint, so authentic. Wouldn't want you showing up in jeans and a T-shirt."

"I don't own any jeans."

"It would also be helpful if you'd park your buggy out front so that tourists can see it."

"There's no shade out front, and I wouldn't want Dolly to stand on the concrete pavement all day."

"I see." The woman pursed her too-red lips and steepled her fingers. "I'm sure we can work something out. Also, we'd like you to speak as much German..."

"Pennsylvania Dutch," Hannah corrected her softly.

"Excuse me?"

"We speak Pennsylvania Dutch and *Englisch*, of course."

"Yes, but that's the thing. I'd rather you speak your language." The woman sat back and rocked slightly in her leather office chair. "I know you people aren't particularly business savvy, but this is a big venture for my executive board. We have stores in Ohio and Pennsylvania, but this is our first in Indiana. I intend for it to be the best."

"Which means what, exactly?"

"Tourists come here to catch a glimpse into a different life, to experience in some small way what it means to be different."

"I'm different?"

"We don't want to minimize that—we want to showcase it. We'll be selling the experience of meeting an Amish person as much as we're selling fabric."

"Selling?"

"And didn't you mention on your form that your son..."

"Matthew."

"Isn't he disabled? If you could bring him in with you, just now and then when he'd be in town anyway, I think that would be a real plus."

"Bring Matthew in for *Englischers* to gawk at?"

But the woman wasn't listening. She'd already opened a file and was flipping through sheets of paper. "How would you feel about appearing on the flyers that we're going to place around town? You're young enough, and if we added just a touch of makeup I think you'd photograph well."

The muscles in Hannah's right arm began to quiver and a terrible heat flushed through her body. She hadn't been this angry since…well, ever. Knowing she was about to say something unkind, Hannah gathered up her purse, politely thanked the woman and rushed from the store.

Once she made it back outside, she stood beside Dolly, running her hand down the horse's neck and breathing in the scent of her. Slowly the tide of anger receded, and she was left shaking her head in amazement. How could a person be so insensitive? How could she think that such tactics were acceptable? Hannah would not allow herself or her son to be put on display. What was the woman thinking? Only of her business, of making a profit, of selling the Amish experience.

Hannah understood that tourism was a big part of the Goshen economy. It benefited both *Englisch* and Amish, and there were many places that treated Plain folks with respect. Meeting people from other states was fun for both parties, and the added income was often a big help to families. But she would not be wearing makeup or putting her son and horse on display for anyone.

She would not be working for the new craft shop in town.

Jacob looked up as Hannah pulled into the drive. He'd been watching for her. He'd actually finished the job a few hours ago, and now he was looking for things to do until she came home. Since they didn't attend the same church, it would be his last time to see her unless they happened to run into one another in town or at a wedding or funeral.

Hannah practically jumped out of the buggy and didn't so much as glance his way.

Was it possible that she was unhappy with what he'd done?

Jacob turned and surveyed the play area. The train playhouse was complete, and if he allowed himself to think about it, the finished structure looked better than he'd imagined. The boardwalk leading to it was smooth and wide enough for Matthew's wheelchair.

But the crowning jewel of the project wasn't the structure itself but the boy he'd built it for. Matthew was sitting in the front engine room, a train conductor's hat perched jauntily on his head as he tooted the horn and spoke to his imaginary passengers and crew. The young boy had quite an imagination, and he was enthusiastically happy with the new playhouse. Jacob closed his eyes, prayed that *Gotte* would bless young Matthew, and his family—his grandparents, his aunts and uncles, and of course his mother.

He'd no sooner thought of Hannah than she appeared before him, clutching an envelope in her hand.

"Hire me to work in your office."

"Excuse me?"

"Sally Lapp says you're looking for someone."

"*Ya*, I am."

"So why haven't you offered the job to me?" She took a step closer and Jacob took a step back.

"I didn't think—"

"Didn't think I could handle it?"

"Of course you can, but—"

"I beat your class at math drills even though you were two years older."

"I remember."

"And I have experience in accounting. I did some before Matthew was born."

"That's *gut*, but—"

She waved the envelope in front of his face so that he had to step back again or risk being swiped by it.

"Do you know what this is? A notice from the bank. *Dat* has less than a month to come up with his back payments. If he doesn't, they'll begin the foreclosure process."

"I'm sorry to hear that."

"While you were out here building a playhouse my parents stand to lose their farm."

"The playhouse didn't—"

"Didn't cost them anything? *Ya*, I know. But we do. Matthew and I do. There's the extra food and the clothing and Matthew's medical expenses…" Her eyes shone brightly with tears, and she quickly pivoted away.

He gave her a moment—counted to three and then did so again. Finally he stepped forward and said, "I'd be pleased to have you work in my office. I didn't ask because I wasn't sure you'd want such a challenge."

He couldn't bring himself to admit that he didn't think she'd want to be around him, that his scars might repulse her or even remind her of Matthew's accident.

"You don't think I'm up to it, do you?" The fire was back—softer, simmering this time.

"I don't doubt your bookkeeping skills, Hannah. However, I'm not sure you realize how terrible I am at filing and record keeping."

Hannah waved that away. "I know all about that. I even know you had one girl quit after only a day."

"And I didn't blame her."

"So what did you plan to do?"

"About?"

"About the IRS audit." Hannah squinted up at him quizzically, waiting to hear what his plan was. Only Jacob didn't have a plan.

"I still have almost three weeks. I figured…well, I figured it would work itself out somehow."

"That's not a plan."

"You've got me there."

"Is this a permanent position?"

"I haven't really thought about it."

"Why am I not surprised?"

"It could be, I guess. Don't know how much work there would be once the records are straightened out. I guess we could get past the audit and then decide."

Hannah crossed her arms and studied the playhouse, really saw it for maybe the first time since he'd begun construction. "It's a *gut* playhouse."

"*Ya*, it is."

"Matthew loves it."

"He's a great kid."

"Danki."

"Ger gschehne." And there it was, a tangible bond between them—the ways of their parents and grandparents, the river of their past that set them apart and also drew them together.

"I'll start Monday," she said and then she named what she expected to make per hour.

Jacob almost laughed. He would readily pay more if she was able to get him out of the paperwork jam he'd created, but instead of offering more he simply nodded. Perhaps he could give her a bonus once the audit was complete.

Hannah's eyebrows rose in surprise that he'd agreed, but she was holding something back. She was chewing on her thumbnail, a habit they'd all teased her about in school. The memory blossomed in Jacob's mind with the force of a winter wind—Hannah standing at the board, worrying her thumbnail as she worked out some impossibly difficult math problem. At least it had seemed impossible to him.

"What is it?" he asked, the question coming out more gruffly than he'd intended. "What's worrying you?"

She stood straighter, glanced at her son and then looked back at Jacob. "I'll need to take off during Matthew's appointments."

"Of course."

"So you wouldn't…you wouldn't mind?"

"*Nein.* Your son's therapy is important. I would be a fool not to understand that."

She nodded once, and then she stuck the offending envelope from the bank in her apron pocket and went to her son. She climbed the steps and sat beside him in the engine room, leaving Jacob to enjoy the sight of them and the sound of their laughter as Matthew set his conductor cap on her head.

"We were hoping Jacob would stay for dinner."

Hannah's mother set the large pot of chicken and dumplings in the middle of the table. Beside it was a loaf of fresh bread, butter and a large bowl with a salad that Hannah had managed to throw together.

"He told me he has a mess at home to clean up." Matthew slathered butter on top of his piece of bread and took a large bite. When he caught Hannah staring at him, he smiled broadly.

Her father spoke of the rain forecast for the next week. Her mother had been to visit a neighbor and her infant girl. She described how the baby cooed, how rosy her cheeks were, even how she smelled.

Finally Hannah broke into the conversation. "I have a job."

Everyone stopped eating and stared at her.

"With Jacob. I have a job with Jacob." She felt the blush creep up her neck. "I'm going to be helping him with his accounting. It might not be permanent."

"That's *gut*," her father said, reaching for another helping of dumplings. "You always excelled with numbers."

Her mother nodded in agreement. "And you have a real knack for organizing things. Since you've been here you've straightened up every closet and cabinet, even my spices."

"They were a mess."

"Well, now they're in alphabetical order."

"Which makes them easier to find."

"I think it's *wunderbaar*, dear."

It was Matthew who was the most excited about her news. He'd begun tapping his spoon against his plate. "So I will get to see him. You told me that I might not see him anymore, that he'd be helping other kids. But if you're working for him, I'll get to see him. Right? He even said he'd teach me to whistle."

And that was when Hannah knew she'd made a big mistake. Possibly she'd found a way to help her parents, but in the process she had delayed the inevitable. She could tell by the sparkle in her son's eyes that he didn't realize Jacob was not a part of their family, not even really their friend except in the most broad sense of the word.

The elation she'd felt at landing the job slipped away. She would need to be very careful, not with her own emotions—which weren't an issue at all since she was not attracted to Jacob Schrock—but with Matthew's.

She would protect her son.

Whether from financial hardship that might push him out of his home or emotional attachments that couldn't possibly last.

Chapter Five

Jacob spent Saturday catching up on projects that he'd let slide in order to complete Matthew's boardwalk. There was a dresser that he'd promised to redo for Evelyn Yutzy. Her granddaughter had recently arrived in town, moved from Maine back to Indiana, and they'd converted the back porch into a bedroom. It was insulated, so the girl wouldn't freeze, but she needed somewhere to put her clothes.

He had only half-finished the crib for Grace Miller, and her baby was due in two weeks. He couldn't put it off any longer. Then there was the workbench that he'd agreed to make for Paul Fisher. It was good that business was…well, busy. But Jacob's heart was with the playhouses, something that he charged as little as possible for. In order to make a living he had to take care of the individual work orders as well as the business projects that he had lined up.

Speaking of which, he was supposed to begin a cabinetry project on a new house the following week. He'd written the details down somewhere, but where? He wasted the next hour looking for the small sheet of paper, which he eventually found in his lunch pail.

Normally once he started a project he had no problem focusing on it, but he found himself lagging further and further behind as the day progressed. He stopped for lunch and went into his house, but even there he couldn't help looking around him and seeing the place through Hannah's eyes. It was pitiful really, and he didn't know how it had happened.

Dishes were stacked in the sink, where he usually ate standing and staring out the window. Copies of the *Budget* covered every surface in the sitting room, along with woodworking magazines that the library gave him when they were too far out-of-date to display. That seemed ridiculous to Jacob—woodworking wasn't something that changed from one season to the next. Still, he enjoyed receiving the old copies and looking through the magazines. He occasionally found new ideas to try.

When his childhood home had burned down, he'd purchased a prefab house and had it delivered to the property. The building was small, around six hundred square feet, but more than what he needed. The workshop had been left intact. As for the fields, his brother Micah farmed them in addition to his own, which was adjacent to the old homestead.

The workshop was larger than his home. The vast majority of it was filled with supplies, workbenches and projects in various stages of completion. The office was a cornered-off ten-by-ten space. On one side of the room, windows looked out over the fields. On the other, windows allowed him to see into the workshop. As far as mess, it was in worse shape than the house. Jacob's heart was in the projects, not the filing systems, or lack thereof, and that showed. He was attempting to move around stacks of paperwork in the office when his brother Micah tapped on the open door.

"Am I interrupting?"

"*Ya.* Can't you see? I'm making progress on my backed-up carpentry orders."

"Huh. Looks to me like you're tossing papers from one shelf to another." Micah crossed the room, stopped in front of one of the plastic bins and raised the lid. "What is all this stuff?"

"Receipts, I guess."

"What's your system?" Micah pulled out a Subway sandwich receipt, stared at it and then turned it over and stared at the writing on the back.

Jacob snatched it out of his hand and tossed it back into the bin. "If it was something that I felt like I needed to keep, I threw it in a bin. The next year I'd buy another from the discount store and begin tossing things in it. There's one for the past…six years."

Micah let out a long whistle. "No wonder the IRS is interested in you, *bruder.* They must have heard about your filing system."

"The last thing I want to talk about is the IRS."

"*Gut.* Because it's not why I came by."

Jacob grunted as he picked up a bin from the floor and dropped it on the desk. Deciding it looked worse, looked even more disorganized there, he put it back where it was.

"Why did you come by?"

"To invite you to dinner, and don't tell me you have plans."

"I do have plans. I should be out there working." He shifted his gaze and stared through the window into the workshop. He could just make out the corner of Grace Miller's crib. It would probably take him another two hours to finish it.

"Then why aren't you?"

"Why aren't I what?"

"Out there working."

"Because Hannah's coming on Monday, and if she sees this place like it is, she'll probably turn tail and run."

When his brother grinned and dropped into a chair, Jacob realized that the news was already out about his new bookkeeper. No doubt Micah was here to tease him, and the dinner invitation was just a handy excuse.

"Heard young Matthew likes his caboose train."

"*Ya*, he does. Young kids like him, kids who don't lead normal lives, the little things seem to make a big difference."

"And what about Hannah?"

"What about her?"

"Still as pretty as when she was in school?"

"Seriously? That's what we're going to talk about?"

"Why not? It's the first woman you've shown interest in since your accident."

"I'm not interested in her." Jacob reached up and scratched at his scar. "I'm hiring her to bring some order to this chaos."

"So you don't find her attractive?"

"I didn't say that."

"You do find her attractive, then."

"This is the problem with you."

"Problem with me?"

His brother smiled as if he'd just told the funniest

joke. It made Jacob want to chuck the bin of papers he was holding right at his head.

"You always think you know what's best for me, but you don't."

"And you always think that your scars preclude you from dating, but they don't."

"What would you know about scars?"

Micah stood, raised his hands, palms out, and shook his head. "I don't know why we do this every time."

"I know why. You insist on sticking your nose in my business."

"We worry about you. Emily and I both do."

"Would you please stop? Would you just trust me to live my own life the way it's meant to be lived?"

"Alone? Moping over what happened?"

"You weren't there, Micah. Don't pretend that you know what happened. Don't pretend you can understand. I'm the one who pulled their bodies from the fire. I'm the one who didn't get there fast enough."

Micah strode to the door, but he stopped dead in his tracks, the afternoon sunlight that was streaming through the open workshop door spilling over his shoulders. Because his back was to Jacob, his words were muffled, softer, but they hit him just as hard as if they'd been standing face-to-face. "You say that you trust *Gotte*, and yet you won't let anyone into your life. You say that you pray, but you don't believe."

And with that, he trudged back outside, across the field and to his own home—leaving Jacob to wonder why everyone thought they had to fix him. They didn't live in his skin. They didn't look at his scars every morning, and they knew nothing of his guilt and loneliness.

Jacob understood his scars for what they were—the penance that he deserved for not saving his parents from the fire that took their lives.

Hannah had been living back in Goshen long enough that Matthew no longer drew obvious stares when they met for church. She was grateful for that, thankful that their neighbors were learning to accept him.

She looked forward to their church services. Loved the familiar faces she'd grown up seeing and the sound of her bishop's voice—the same man who had baptized her. Other than the loneliness that occasionally plagued her and the constant worry over Matthew's health, she was happy, living again with her family.

Church was held every other Sunday and always at a member's home. This week they were at the Yutzy place, which was on the northwest side of town. A portion of their property bordered the Elkhart River. It was a beautiful, peaceful spot, and Hannah could feel its calming power even as she made her way into the barn where they would have church. The large main room had been cleaned out, the doors and windows flung open, and benches arranged on two sides of a makeshift aisle.

At the back of the benches a few tables had been set up with cups of water and plates of cookies for the youngest children. It was sometimes difficult for them to make it all the way through a three-to four-hour meeting without a small snack.

The service was exactly what she needed to quiet her soul. She'd spent too much time since Friday worrying about the job at Jacob's. She knew she could do the work, but would Matthew be okay without her? Was she doing the right thing? Could the small amount of money she was making help her parents' financial situation?

The questions had spun round and round in her head, but that all stopped when they stood to sing the *Loblied.* The words of the hymn reminded her of the good things in her life, the things that *Gotte* had given her. She forgot for a moment the tragedy of losing her husband and the trials of having a special needs son.

Once the service was over and she'd finished helping in the serving line, she went to find her sisters. Both Beth and Sharon were in the last trimester of their pregnancies. In fact, their babies were due only a few weeks apart. They'd tried to help in the serving line and had been shooed away.

"Finally we get you to ourselves," Sharon said. The oldest of the three girls, it had taken her some time to become pregnant after marrying. The twins were two lovely girls full of energy and laughter and a tiny bit of mischief. Another six years had passed before Sharon had finally become pregnant again. She and her husband were hoping for a boy, just to balance things out a bit.

Beth had one daughter, ten-year-old Naomi. She'd had Naomi when she was very young, only seventeen. There had been some problems, and she thought that she couldn't have any more children, but her protruding stomach was testament to the fact that *Gotte* had other plans.

Being around them, watching them rest a hand on their baby bumps or sigh as they tried to push up out of a chair caused an ache deep in Hannah's heart. She'd imagined herself pregnant again, had thought she'd have a house full of children like most Amish women. She had been certain that she would remain married to the same man all of her life. She'd never imagined herself as a young widow.

She searched the crowd of children for her son and finally spied Matthew in his chair, pulled up to a checkerboard that had been placed over a tree stump. One of the older boys who had a foot in a cast was playing with him. As she watched, Matthew glanced occasionally at the children who were playing ball, and it seemed to Hannah that an expression of longing crossed his face.

"Tell us about your new job." Beth was the middle child and the negotiator of the family. It was Beth who had convinced Hannah to move home. Hannah hadn't wanted to be a burden to her parents, but Beth had convinced her that home was where she needed to be and that family could never truly be a burden.

"Tell us about Jacob." Sharon's eyes sparkled. She'd always been one to tease. Perhaps because of her work as a midwife, she believed in enjoying life. She saw moments of great joy every day and the occasional tragedy, as well.

"There's nothing to tell about Jacob, and as far as the job...well, I'm fortunate to find work at all." She described her attempts at finding employment in town. She even mimicked the craft shop owner's voice when she asked if Hannah could bring Matt in occasionally so the tourists could gawk at him.

"Maybe she meant well," Beth said.

Sharon rolled her eyes. "And maybe she has no filter, no sense of what is proper and what is improper. Some business owners—and I've seen it in Amish as well as *Englisch*—they become too enamored with how much money they can make. They forget their employees are people."

"Anyway. I suppose I was upset because of the interview, and I had no other ideas of where to apply." Hannah glanced around to be sure no one else was within earshot. Fortunately most of the women had moved to a circle of chairs under the trees, and the men were congregated on the porch or near the ball field. "I confronted Jacob. I walked right up to him and asked him why he hadn't offered me the job."

"Oh my." Beth placed both hands on her belly. "How did he take it?"

"He was surprised, of course. Amish women are supposed to be quiet and meek."

Both Beth and Sharon laughed at that. Sometimes the reputation that Amish women had earned was frustrating, other times it was simply ludicrous. While they did believe that the man was the spiritual head of the house, the women Hannah knew had no trouble voicing their opinion or standing up for themselves.

"What happened then?" Sharon asked.

"He agreed. It's a temporary position until his audit is over. Then we'll see if there's enough work for me to continue."

"Oh, I'm sure there's enough work. He's probably just afraid you wouldn't want a permanent position. I still see his sister-in-law Emily because our homes are fairly close together. The dividing line for our districts is between us. Anyway, she tells me that Jacob's a real wonder with the woodworking..."

"Have you seen the playhouse he made?" Beth interrupted. "It's amazing. I stopped by yesterday and even Naomi spent an hour out in it, and she's ten. I haven't seen her in a playhouse since the summer she was six and her *dat* knocked together something from old barn lumber. Wasn't even really a lean-to, but she would drag every little friend that came over out to play there."

"What are you worried about, Hannah?" Sharon studied her sister. "You might as well share with us. Is it Matthew? Is he feeling all right?"

"Matthew's fine, I guess."

"You guess?" Now Beth was on alert. "Tell us. What's happened?"

"Nothing has happened." Hannah blew out a sigh of exasperation. "I'm starting a new job that I know nothing about."

"Which you asked for—" Beth reminded her.

"I'm leaving Matthew with *Mamm*, and she has enough to do."

"I've already spoken to her about that. She's welcome to bring Matthew by anytime—"

"You're seven months pregnant, Sharon, and you're still delivering babies. The last thing you need is—"

"My nephew? Actually I do need to spend time with him and so do my girls. He's family, Hannah. We want him around."

"Naomi asks me every day if Matthew can come over." Beth rubbed the side of her stomach. "We'll help *Mamm*. Don't worry about that."

Which effectively shut down her doubts about leaving Matthew during the day.

"I'm not sure it will be enough money," she admitted. "The amount they owe? I was surprised. I knew they'd helped me and Matt, but I didn't know… I didn't know they'd sacrificed so much."

"It's what families do, Hannah." Sharon took on her

older sister tone. "You've forgotten because you moved away. You and David moved, what was it..."

"Three months. We moved three months after we were wed."

"Right, and I understand how you'd want to try the community in Wisconsin, but while you were there maybe you learned to be independent, maybe too independent."

"Now you're with family, and we take care of one another," Beth chimed in.

Hannah didn't need a lecture about family. Yes, she appreciated her parents and sisters and brothers-in-law, but they didn't understand just how much of a burden Matthew's disability could be. They hadn't experienced an emergency run to the hospital because of a minor cold that had quickly morphed into pneumonia.

"Back to the money..." she said.

"Simon has some saved, which he has offered to *Dat*." Sharon's husband worked at the RV factory in Shipshewana two days a week. The rest of the time he farmed their land.

"Carl does too." Beth raised her foot and stared at her swollen ankle. "*Dat* told me he doesn't want to take it unless he's sure it will cover the balance. He doesn't want to drain our savings for a place he might lose anyway."

And there it was—the real fear of losing their childhood home. It was common for Amish to up and move for a variety of reasons—a disagreement with the way the church district was being run, a rumor that land was more plentiful and less expensive in another state, even a vague restlessness to see somewhere different.

But this wasn't that.

This was being forced from your home, and to Hannah that made it a much graver thing.

"How much will you make?" Sharon asked.

Hannah told them the hourly wage she'd asked for and how many hours she thought she could work. "Not a full forty," she explained. "I told him that I still want to take Matthew to his appointments."

"We could do that for you."

"I know you could, Sharon. I know you both would, and *danki* for offering." She smoothed her apron out over her lap, then ran her hand across it again before looking up to meet her sisters' gazes. "This is something I'd like to continue to do, if I can."

Both sisters nodded as if they understood, and maybe they did.

Sharon scrounged around in her purse for a receipt and a pen. On the back of the receipt she added up what Simon had saved, what Carl had pulled together and what Hannah would make in the next month minus any taxes she would have to pay.

"You saw the letter." Sharon chewed on the end of the pen. "How much did it say they owed?"

When Hannah quoted the amount, Beth leaned closer to the paper. "We're a little short."

"But we still have thirty days."

"Twenty-eight." Hannah glanced over at her mother, who was sitting with the other women and watching the *youngies* play ball. "Twenty-eight days. Between now and then, we need to find a way to come up with the difference."

Chapter Six

Hannah tried on all three of her dresses Monday morning. The gray one made her look like a grandmother. The green was a bit snug. Had she actually gained weight since moving home? She could thank her mother's cooking for that. The dark blue was her oldest, but it was all that was left other than what she wore to Sunday services, and she wouldn't dare wear that to Jacob's workshop.

Frustrated that she cared about how she looked, she donned the dark blue dress, a fresh apron and her *kapp*. One last shrug at her reflection in the window, and she walked down the hall to Matthew's room. She didn't enter, though. Instead she paused at the door. She heard her son moving around, and yet he hadn't called out to her. That was a good sign. It meant he'd slept well.

She turned the knob and walked into the room.

The sky had barely begun to lighten outside, but she pulled up the shades and then sat on his bed. He smiled up at her, curling over on his side.

"You look *gut*—pretty."

"Danki."

"Are you excited?"

"About my job?"

"Ya." He reached out for her apron strings, ran them through his fingers. "I would be excited, if I was going to spend all day with Jacob. Why can't I go? Please…"

He drew out the last word, and Hannah almost laughed. It sounded so normal, so everyday, that she actually didn't mind the whining.

"We've been over this. I will be working with numbers all day—"

"I can write my numbers."

"Yes, but I'm afraid it's a bit more complicated than that."

"And Jacob will be working."

"He will."

"On a playhouse?"

"I don't know."

Matthew considered that for a moment, and then he said what must have been on his mind all along. "I'd like to see some of his playhouses. They're not all trains—I know that because he described a few. I'd like to see what the others look like."

"Would you now?"

"Do you think that maybe…maybe we could?"

Hannah hesitated. She didn't want to encourage this infatuation that her son had for her boss. At the same time, as Sally had pointed out, it was natural for Matthew to look up to men in their community. "If they're in the area, and he tells me where they are…well, I don't see why we couldn't drive by when we're out on errands."

Matthew's smile was all the answer she needed. How could such a small thing bring him such joy? How was it that he managed to accept his condition so easily without bitterness? He pushed himself into an upright position and raised his arms for Hannah's father to pick him up.

"I didn't hear you come in," Hannah said.

"Because I'm as quiet as a cat and as quick as a panther." Her father winked at her as he carried Matthew out of the room.

"Have you ever seen a panther, *Daddi*?"

Matthew had slept well, woke up with no signs of a cold or infection and was showing a real interest in the things going on around him. It was a good day for certain, so why was a part of Hannah still worried?

She walked back into the room to fetch Matthew's clothes for the day.

"He'll be fine." Her father paused to kiss the top of her head, which made her feel like a small child again. It also made her feel loved and cared for. "And I appreciate your taking the job. I hope you know you don't have to."

"I know, *Dat*, but I want to help."

"Your *mamm* and I appreciate that."

"It's important—to be able to stay in this place, to raise Matthew surrounded by familiar things and people."

"Familiar to you, but not so much to Matt." Her father glanced across the hall into the bathroom to be sure that Matthew was fine without him. With a nod to indicate that the boy was all right, he sat down beside her on the bed. "You know, Hannah, it could be that *Gotte* has other plans for us, that we're not meant to stay in this house or even in this community."

"But you would want to…if you could. Right?"

"Things turn out best for the people who make the best of the way things turns out."

"Really, *Dat*? Your answer is a proverb?"

His smile eased the anxiousness in her heart and reminded her of Matthew. The two were more alike than she had realized.

"If you enjoy the job and if you can help Jacob, then you have my blessing. Listen to me closely though, Hannah. If you find it's too much pressure, I want you to remember that your priority is your son, not how much money you can make."

"*Ya, Dat*, but it's something I want to do."

He nodded as if he understood, and maybe he did.

Hannah barely ate any breakfast, though she did help to clean up the kitchen. After going over the morning instructions one last time with her mother, the entire family shooed her out of the house.

She hurried toward Dolly, who her father had already hitched to the buggy, turning back to call out, "I left Jacob's phone number on the sheet."

"We have it, but we won't need it."

"And I'm sorry I can't go to the store for you."

"Stop worrying. Matt and I will take care of it."

"I'll try. See you around four thirty."

Her mother had actually packed her a lunch. She should have done that herself.

Clucking to Dolly, she set off down the road.

When was the last time that she'd gone somewhere without her son? When was the last time she'd been alone? She found herself enjoying the drive, smiling at the other drivers on the road—both Amish and *Englisch*—and noting how well the flower gardens had bloomed. Every home she passed had some spot of color brightening their lawn, or bordering their vegetable rows or in pots on the front porch. Goshen was a tourist destination, nearly as popular as Shipshewana, and the houses and businesses made every effort to present a clean, colorful picture.

It took her less than twenty minutes to reach Jacob's place, and she was embarrassed to find herself there a full thirty minutes early.

"He'll think I'm overeager." She shook her head as she pulled down the lane. So what if she was? What did it matter? She was impatient to finally be of some help instead of a burden, and if she were honest, a little bit of her was looking forward to the quiet and challenge of a column of numbers.

Jacob was sitting on the front porch of the workshop when Hannah pulled down the lane. He shouldn't have been surprised that she was early. She seemed like the kind of person that would be.

By the time she set the brake on the buggy, he was standing there beside her. He took the reins and slipped them around the waist-high tie bar situated a few feet from the front of the shop.

"I can't believe that I've never been here."

She seemed a bit out of breath and flushed and beautiful. He shook the thought out of his mind and tried to pay attention to what she was saying.

"Not even when we were kids?"

"Maybe for church. I can't remember."

"The place looked different then."

He pointed to the area where his parents' home had been. "Micah and I cleared off the site after the fire and extended my mother's garden to cover the old homestead. We thought it would be a nice way to remember them."

"It's lovely, and I'm so very sorry about your parents."

"Every life is complete." He said the words without thinking about them. It was what they believed, what they always said during such times. It was only during those terrible nights when he relived the destruction of the fire in his nightmares that he struggled with the concept. In the light of day, with Hannah smiling at him, it was easy enough to believe that *Gotte* had a plan and purpose for each of their lives and that sometimes that plan was beyond their understanding.

"And you live over there?"

He glanced back at the twenty-foot prefab. It looked rather pitiful and shabby in the morning light. He'd done nothing to spruce it up—no porch or rocking chairs or flowers. It wasn't really a home, and he knew that. "*Ya.* It's temporary."

"How long have you lived there?"

"Six years."

Hannah looked directly at him for the first time since arriving, a look of surprise coloring her features. When he started laughing, she did too. He didn't mind her seeing the humor in the situation, mainly because she was laughing with him instead of at him.

Finally Hannah said, "I suppose it's enough for a bachelor."

"It is. Let me show you the workshop."

He took her through the main room, explaining the various stages that each project went through from commission to design, cutting, assembling, sanding and finishing.

"There's a lot to it," Hannah said.

"Ya." He was proud of his workshop. Every tool had a place. He cleaned each item after he used it and placed it on a peg on the wall. Sawdust was swept up each evening. Small projects were kept in large cubbies under one window that ran almost the entire length of the room. Bigger projects were lined up along the other wall. Design plans for playhouses were rolled and stored in smaller bins behind his worktable. A potbelly stove, rocking chair, hand-hooked rug made by his sister-in-law and small refrigerator adorned one corner.

The room looked better than where he lived.

"Bathroom's back in that corner."

"Place smells nice—like a lumberyard."

"The office is over here." He pointed to the room in the opposite corner.

Hannah raised an eyebrow and motioned for him to lead the way.

When they walked into the room, Jacob experienced a flash of panic. Who would want to work in this cramped little space all day? He'd made a feeble attempt to clean it up, but there was no hiding the fact that it had been neglected for years.

"This was my father's office. As you can see, I haven't used it much." He walked to the shelves and glanced at the items that had been there since the day his father had died. He hadn't wanted to move a thing, hadn't felt like he should. Fortunately, Hannah wouldn't need shelves, as there was a large desk.

Hannah stood there, frozen, letting her gaze drift from left to right and then back again. He waited for her to say something, but for once she seemed speechless.

"These tubs are full of receipts, and as you can see, each is labeled with the year."

"Ya?"

"I also put in the deposit slips each year, so you should be able to figure out what I earned versus what I spent. I tried to keep up with what people paid me by noting it on slips of paper, and you'll find a few of those."

"Slips of paper…"

"I'm afraid that after I figured my taxes each year, I probably tossed the worksheets, though I did keep a copy of the returns and they're in the box, as well."

Hannah raised the lid off one of the tubs, stared inside for a moment and then quickly closed the lid. "Well. I see I have my work cut out for me."

"I cleared off the desk."

"Danki."

"And there's a ledger, which I've never used."

"Obviously."

Jacob wondered if she would tell him that it was too big a job, that he was crazy to have been so lax with his record keeping, that he deserved whatever penalties the IRS threw at him. Instead she set her purse and lunch bag on the desk.

"You can write down your hours on that pad, and I'll pay you on Monday for the previous week's work if that's okay."

"That will be fine." Hannah touched the desk chair, which looked as if it might fall over.

How long had he had that thing? His dad had purchased it in some garage sale years and years ago.

"I'll go and look after Dolly."

"Oh, I can do that. I just wanted to make sure you hadn't changed your mind first."

He gave her an odd look, shook his head and said, "I'll be back in a minute."

And then he turned and left, because if he stood looking at Hannah King one more minute, wearing her pretty blue dress with the morning light shining through on her freshly laundered *kapp* and lightly freckled face…he'd start daydreaming again, and that was the very last thing that he needed to do.

Once Jacob left the office, Hannah glanced over at the bins in horror.

She stepped closer to the window and stared out at the fall day, watching as Jacob moved Dolly into the shade and fetched her a bucket of water. A man who cared properly for animals was a good man. Why hadn't Jacob ever married? Why did he live in a tiny trailer on this large piece of land? Surely he could afford better.

At least it looked as if business was booming.

She was good at math, and she had helped her husband with his business records in Wisconsin, but she'd never seen a mess like this before.

She stepped closer to one of the bins, opened the lid and peered inside. She pawed through the stack of paper—all sizes of paper, from a receipt from a cash register, to a bill that looked as if it had been scribbled on across the back, to a Publishers Clearing House flyer.

Looking closer, she sent up a silent thanks that at least she could read his handwriting.

Jacob walked back into the room, and she slammed the lid shut again.

"Problem?"

"Why would you say that?"

"I don't know. You look as if you've seen a runaway buggy."

She tried to smile. "Nope. No buggies. Just lots of receipts."

Jacob's smile vanished. "I know it's a lot of work, Hannah, but at least I kept the receipts separated by year."

"*Ya*, I see that."

"Six years. Six bins. That helps. Right?"

"I'm sure it will."

He stepped closer and reached out to put his hand on her arm.

"Hannah, I need to tell you something."

She didn't move, didn't breathe.

"I appreciate what you're doing, more than you could know."

She tried to listen to his words, but her heart had taken off at a galloping pulse, and she was staring at his hand on her arm. His fingers against her skin stirred something inside of Hannah, something she didn't realize she still possessed. Mixed with hope, and sprinkled with a dash of optimism—all things she hadn't felt in quite some time.

Jacob seemed to notice her discomfort. He dropped his hand to his side, then fiddled with the sleeve he'd rolled up to his elbows. "You're a real godsend."

"I haven't done anything yet." She laughed nervously and moved around the desk, running her fingers across the wood.

"I guess I'm headed out for the day. Just…make a list of any questions, and we'll go over them this afternoon or first thing tomorrow morning."

"Jacob—"

He seemed to brace himself against what she was about to say.

"I should thank you—for the job."

"Thank me?"

"The way I asked, *nein*, demanded, you to give it to me—that wasn't proper."

"You were right, though."

"I was?"

"This place is a mess. Even I can see it."

"There's a lot here for one person to take care of. You probably should have hired help earlier. I hope I can rise to the challenge."

"I remember how you were with numbers in school."

"That was a long time ago."

He'd stuck his thumbs under his suspenders and walked to the door, but now he turned back toward her. "I did know about your father's difficulties. I just wasn't sure you'd want to leave Matthew."

"And I don't, but my parents and my sisters…everyone is going to pitch in and help. That's what family does, *ya*?"

Instead of answering, Jacob fetched his hat from a hook on the wall and rammed it on his head. "If anyone calls, please write down a message."

"Oh, you're leaving?"

"*Ya.* I just said I was headed out."

"I thought you meant…to the fields or something."

"My *bruder* works the fields on this place. I work here in the workshop or out on jobs."

"So that's where you're going? To a job?"

"One of the local builders has me putting in cabinets this week, in the new homes on the north side of town."

"Oh..."

"Some weeks I work here in the workshop."

"I see."

"I prefer to work on the playhouses whenever it's possible, but the cabinetry work—"

"It pays the bills."

"*Ya.* That it does." He looked out the office window.

Hannah wondered if he was stalling, though she couldn't imagine why. He seemed quite uncomfortable with her there and no doubt couldn't wait to be gone.

"I'll just get to work on these receipts, then. Most current year first?"

"I suppose."

"Okay..."

"I guess I'll see you this afternoon."

Hannah pushed her *kapp* strings back. "I planned to leave around four thirty."

"Weren't you taking Matthew to therapy today?"

"*Nein*, that's tomorrow and, well... I thought we'd wait and see how much work there actually is for me to do, and whether it's going to be a problem getting everything in order before your audit."

She wanted to say something more, to somehow put him at ease, but she had no idea how. Then she remembered the reason she was there.

"The IRS letter, you still have it?"

"Oh, *ya.* It's in the top right drawer. I guess you need to look it over."

"And you're sure you wouldn't rather take this all to an accountant?"

"I did go and see one, but the price they quoted was quite high."

"I'll try, Jacob."

"Which is all I can ask. The letter seems pretty straightforward as far as what they want to see, which is why I need you."

"They don't take boxes full of receipts?"

"Apparently not." He pulled his hat off, turned it round and round in his hands. "If there are any other supplies you need, there's petty cash in the bottom drawer."

Jacob left so abruptly that Hannah stood staring after him for a moment. She'd spent much of the night worrying about how she'd be able to work with him in such close proximity. Apparently that wouldn't be a problem. He wouldn't even be on the property. Hannah waited until she saw his buggy drive past the workshop and down the lane before returning inside to the small office.

Though he'd apparently made an effort to clean the mess off the top of the desk, dust lay thick across its surface.

A clean desktop is the sign of a cluttered desk drawer. The proverb popped into her mind unbidden. Walking around to the other side of the desk, she spied what she'd known was somewhere close by…a box stuffed with everything that had been on top of it.

The window was smeared with dirt, and the floor hadn't been swept in ages.

He wasn't paying her to clean the office. On the other hand, who could work in these conditions? Would the IRS agent want to receive books covered in dust and grime? Not to mention what this room would do to her clean apron.

She tsked as she walked back through the main room

in search of cleaning supplies. Finally she found them in a corner on the far side of the building—a broom, mop bucket, rags and even furniture polish. She carted it all back to the office and set to work.

Two hours later the place was sparkling. Opening the window had allowed a fresh, clean breeze to blow through. The desk was made from a beautiful dark cherry wood, and it shone from the furniture polish she'd used. She ran her palm across the surface and wondered if Jacob had built it. The chair was a real hazard, so she walked back into the main room and found a stool that was at least sturdy.

The box beside the desk held a tape dispenser, some pens, a stapler and rubber bands that had long ago aged to the point that they snapped when she tried to put one around a bundle of receipts. She dug through the supplies and found a box of pencils (though there was no sharpener that she could see), and a pad of paper.

As she ate her lunch, she began making a list of supplies, then found the petty cash box and placed both next to her purse. She'd stop by the general store while Matthew was at therapy the next day.

Finally she pulled the most recent bin over to the desk.

An hour later she had a list of questions for Jacob.

She couldn't begin entering things in the ledger until she spoke with him, and apparently that wouldn't be until the next morning. She could tape up receipts, but even the tape was yellowed and old, which left her quite a few hours to kill before she had to leave. Glancing around the small office, she decided one thing she could do was clear a bigger workspace.

She walked into the main room of the workshop and

snooped around until she found two empty boxes. Taking them back into the office, she cleared off the items on the shelves. Dusty canning jars filled with an odd variety of nails and screws and even buttons. A broken pipe. A spool of thread. Some very old *Farmers' Almanac* editions dating back forty years.

She couldn't fathom why he was keeping most of the items, and she was tempted to scrape all of it into the trash bin. The basket by her desk wasn't large enough. Plus, it wasn't her place to decide what was and wasn't trash.

It was her place to put his financial records in order, and to do that she needed more space.

It took a little pushing and grunting, but she'd managed to move the desk closer to the shelves.

Now she'd be able to easily move between both, and she could also look out the window instead of having it at her back. She poured another mug of coffee from her thermos, snagged a cookie from the lunch her mother had packed and moved to the front porch. Sitting there she looked out over Jacob's land.

It was *gut* land. She could tell that, though she was only a farmer's daughter, not a farmer herself. It looked well cared for, so Jacob's brother must spend a fair amount of time working there. But the place that Jacob lived? She stared at it a minute before shaking her head in disbelief and going back into the office. There was no understanding the ways of men, especially confirmed bachelors.

Having no way to put off the inevitable, she once again pulled over the most recent bin containing the previous year's receipts and began pulling out scraps of paper. Perhaps she could stack them together by what appeared to be type—supplies, income notations, even hours spent on a job that were scribbled on a flyer about their annual school auction.

The rest of the afternoon flew by and the list of questions grew and grew until they filled up two sheets of paper. She was surprised to look up and see the hands on the clock had passed four. She was thinking of gathering her things to leave when she heard the clatter of a buggy. She wasn't too surprised when she glanced out the window and saw it was Jacob. Perhaps he had finished his day's work early.

She was standing in the doorway looking around in satisfaction when he walked up behind her.

Jacob had been a little afraid he'd arrive home to find that Hannah had left. The last girl had put a note on the desk and told him he didn't owe her for the morning's work. She'd also suggested he hire an accountant. It seemed that Hannah was made of tougher stuff. Perhaps if she'd survived the first day, it meant that she'd see the project through to the end. It wasn't so much that he wanted her around, but he was a man who could admit that he needed help. As far as accounting and the IRS went, Jacob needed all the help he could possibly find.

He walked up behind Hannah. Her tiny frame blocked the doorway, but he could see over her head into the office. Something looked different, but he couldn't put his finger on what it was.

"Did you have a *gut* day?"

"Ya." She smiled back at him and stepped aside so he could see. "I think I accomplished a lot."

He stared at the office, or at least he thought it was his office, but it looked nothing like the room he'd left earlier that morning. He reached out for the door frame to keep from stumbling backward.

"What did you do?"

"What did I do?"

"What..." He walked into the office, strode across to the shelves that had held the precious mementos from his father. "Where did you put my father's things?"

"Do you mean the broken pipe and the jar full of mismatched doodads?"

Jacob bit back the first retort that came to mind. He closed his eyes—determined to count to ten—and made it to three. "*Ya*, those things. Where are they?"

"I didn't throw them away, Jacob. I put them in boxes and stored them in the utility closet."

"Why would you do such a thing?"

"Because I needed more space than the top of that desk."

"I could have built you a workbench."

"But the shelves were right there, and you weren't here to build me a workbench. What was I supposed to do all day?"

"Who moved the desk?"

"I did."

"By yourself?"

"Yes, by myself. It wasn't that hard. I got behind it and—"

"Pushed. You pushed it across the floor."

He squatted, ran his hand over a scratch in the wooden floor.

"Did I do that? I'm... I'm sorry, but this is a barn. Am I right? It's not like it's your living room."

No, his living room was part of a prefab house that held no meaning at all in his life, no memories of his parents. All he had that remained of his childhood was this old barn, the office, the garden that his mother had loved.

He clenched his jaw, determined not to speak harsh words. What was the old proverb? Think before you speak, but don't speak all you think.

Walking to the window, he stared out at his mother's garden. At least Hannah hadn't pulled up any of the plants in her compulsion to reorganize things. Suddenly he noticed how clean the windows were, and the floor, even the walls looked as if they'd been dusted.

"Did you do any of the work you were supposed to do today?"

"Excuse me?"

"I'm not paying you to clean windows or dust shelves."

"As I think I explained, I need those shelves, and I also need more light in this room if I'm to stare at your receipts all day."

"So you did at least look at them."

"Which was all I could do since I have no idea what your scribbling means."

"My scribbling?"

"When you actually took the time to label what you'd written onto some scrap of paper."

Hannah stomped toward the desk and yanked the bottom drawer open.

"You cleaned out the drawers too?"

For her answer she pulled out her purse and slammed the drawer shut. "I'll be going now."

"Going?"

"And if you expect me to work in this small, stuffy,

poorly lit office, then I suggest you get used to the changes."

"Oh, is that so?"

"And don't bother offering to hitch up Dolly. I'm quite capable of doing it myself."

Chapter Seven

Hannah was so angry her ears felt hot.

No doubt they had been bright red as she stormed out of the office. What did she care if Jacob Schrock knew how aggravated she was?

Hitching up Dolly helped to burn up some of her anger. By the time she'd pulled out onto the two-lane road, she was composing her resignation letter in her head.

But as she drove the short distance to her parents' farm, she realized that she couldn't quit, not yet. She needed a job, and she was good at accounting. She could even bring order out of Jacob's chaos, if he'd let her.

Glancing out at the countryside, it struck her what day it was—the anniversary of the accident. Had her emotions recognized that all along? Was that why she was so emotional?

It wasn't until she was pulling into the lane, arching her neck forward to look for Matthew, that she realized the other source of her anxiety. It was true that Jacob's office had been a mess, and she had needed a better workspace, but it was also true that she was nervous about being away from Matthew all day. She was his mother. She should be there.

Her father met her at the door to the barn. "I'll take care of Dolly. How was your first day?"

"Fine," she lied. "Matthew?"

"In his playhouse. He's had a *gut* day."

Those words eased the worry that threatened to choke the breath out of her.

Had she become a helicopter parent? She knew practically nothing about helicopters. She'd seen one a few times, but she'd never ridden in one. She didn't know how that term could relate to her parenting abilities, but she'd seen the article in a magazine's headlines. Helicopter Parents' Horrendous Kids.

She'd actually paged through it as she waited for the woman in front of her to check out at the supermarket.

According to the article there were ten ways that she'd managed to mess up Matthew's life, and he wasn't even five years old. Among other things, she needed to start letting him work out his social issues, involve herself less in his day-to-day life and in general stop fussing over him. She'd shaken her head in mock despair and placed the magazine back on the rack.

But it wasn't mock despair she was feeling now.

Maybe she really had messed up his life.

She'd been gone less than eight hours, but it felt like she hadn't seen him in a week. The truth was that she couldn't stand to have him out of her sight.

He might need her.

And she was afraid to let him fail.

Hadn't he had enough disappointment in life?

She envisioned outlandish things happening to him. Just that morning she'd worried that he might fall out of the buggy if her mother didn't make sure the door was shut. Her mother had been driving a buggy longer than Hannah had been alive.

Was it so wrong to worry though? Matthew was disabled. He was special, and he had special needs.

She pulled in a deep breath, put the parenting article out of her mind and headed for the train.

The next thirty minutes she spent listening to Matthew tell her about his day, as he pretended they were passengers headed to Alaska, and trying not to laugh as he wheeled himself back and forth across the train with the conductor hat on his head.

Her mood had improved dramatically by the time they went inside to help with dinner.

After they'd eaten and were clearing the dishes from the table, her temper had cooled enough that she'd begun to feel ashamed of herself. Her father had taken Matthew to the barn to help settle the horses for the evening. She peeked out the window, didn't see them and refocused on the plate she was drying.

"Problem, dear?"

"Why do you say that?"

"Because you just put a clean plate in the oven."

"I did?"

"Why don't you sit at the table and start shelling the purple hull peas? You can tell me about your day."

So she did. She told her mother about being overwhelmed by the task of preparing Jacob's files for a tax audit, of cleaning up his office with complete disregard to his preferences and of worrying Matthew might fall out of the buggy.

To her surprise, her mother started laughing and then couldn't stop.

"I don't see what's so funny."

Pulling off her reader glasses, her mother swiped at her eyes.

"I can't even tell if you're laughing or crying."

"I'm laughing."

"But why?"

Instead of answering, her mother put the kettle on to boil and dropped two bags of decaf raspberry tea into two mugs. She set a plate of oatmeal cookies between them and smiled at Hannah.

"You've always been an organizer."

"I have?"

"One day when you were little, I found you sorting through your father's socks, lining them up from most stained to least stained."

"I don't remember that."

The kettle on the stove whistled, and soon Hannah found herself holding a steaming cup of raspberry tea. She inhaled deeply and smiled over the rim at her mother.

"I remember organizing your button jar. It was one of my favorite things to do."

"One time I found them by color."

"And one time by size."

The memory touched a tender spot in Hannah's heart. It reminded her of a time before life had become so complicated. She reached for an oatmeal cookie. It was sweet, crunchy around the edges and full of raisins. It was bliss after a long, trying day.

"I suppose I might have been a bit hasty in scooping everything into the box."

"Perhaps those items had some sentimental meaning to Jacob."

"I don't see how."

"What were they?"

"An old pipe, some glass jars, old copies of *Farmers' Almanac*..."

"Sounds like things that could have belonged to his father."

"But there was nothing valuable there."

"The office used to be his father's?"

"I suppose. That would also explain why he was upset that I moved the desk."

"You moved it?"

Hannah waved away her concern. "Wasn't so heavy when I pushed. I needed to move it to have better light, but perhaps I should have asked first."

"Perhaps..." Her mother reached for a cookie, chewed it thoughtfully and finally said, "You and Jacob are alike."

"No, we're not."

"Hear me out."

Hannah rolled her eyes and immediately felt twelve instead of twenty-six.

"You've both been dealt quite a blow."

"I suppose."

"You've both learned to live with that, and to keep going regardless of the strange and terrible turns that life can take."

Hannah shrugged.

"And you've both kept yourself apart from others."

"We're supposed to do that. We're Amish." She drew out the last word, as if her mother were hard of hearing.

"*Ya*, I'm aware, but you know very well that's not what I mean."

Hannah motioned for her to go on. Somehow it was

easier to accept her mother's advice, her insights, when she was eating one of her favorite desserts.

"Neither of you are used to dealing with other people on a regular basis."

"We both have family."

"True."

"We go to the store."

"Ya."

"See people at church."

"You know what I mean, Hannah King, so don't act like you don't."

Hannah popped the remainder of the second cookie in her mouth. She'd regret eating all of it later, but for now it made her feel marginally better.

"You're saying that because we don't date. Well, I don't. As far as I know, Jacob takes a different girl out in his buggy every night."

"Doubtful."

"I suppose."

"I'm only saying that you're both used to doing things your own way and not asking others their opinion."

"So I've lost my social skills?"

"Pretty much."

"Great."

"But the good news is you have another chance to improve those skills tomorrow."

Hannah groaned and pushed herself up from the table. "Any suggestions for how I should do that?"

"You could start with an apology."

Apologizing was the last thing that she wanted to do. She patted her mother on the shoulder and went in search of her son. After she'd helped Matthew with his bath, tucked him in, read a bedtime story and listened to his prayers, she knew what she needed to do. So she went to her room, spent a few minutes in prayer and finally opened her well-worn Bible. It didn't take long to find the verse that was weighing on her heart. She thumbed through the pages until she found the book of Matthew, the fifth chapter, beginning in the twenty-third verse.

Therefore if thou bring thy gift to the altar, and there rememberest that thy brother hath ought against thee; leave thy gift before the altar, and go thy way; first be reconciled to thy brother, and then come and offer thy gift.

There didn't seem to be much wiggle room in Christ's words. Obviously she had offended Jacob. After speaking with her mother, she understood that clearly. Now all she had to do was work up the courage to admit that she'd been wrong, she'd acted hastily, and she was sorry to have raised her voice and left so abruptly. It shouldn't be that hard of a thing to get through, and even if it was, she was pretty sure apologizing would be the first item on her list at work the next day.

Relief washed over Jacob when he heard Hannah's buggy approaching. He'd convinced himself that he'd blown it and that she wasn't coming back.

He pretended to be busy working on a coffee table when she walked inside.

"I thought you'd be at your job site already."

"I thought you might not come."

Their eyes locked for what seemed like a lifetime, and finally Hannah smiled ruefully, walked toward him and sat down across from his workbench.

"I did consider resigning…"

"You wouldn't be the first."

"But then I realized that I need this job."

"Hannah, we both know you can find a better job—one that pays more and doesn't require you to mop the floor." He glanced up at her and then stared back down at the coffee table. Had he been sanding or staining it?

"Maybe I could find another job, but I didn't like what was out there."

"Apparently you didn't like what was in here, either."

"Jacob, I am sorry for raising my voice at you yesterday and for disregarding your father's things."

Jacob's head snapped up, and he found Hannah staring at him, a look of regret on her face.

"I should have asked first."

He smiled for the first time that day as the knot in his stomach slowly unwound. "*Dat* would have told me to clean the office long ago. He always said he was going to, but then he'd get distracted by something else."

"Still, those items were special to you, and if you want them on the shelves I'll put them back."

"No need to do that."

"I'm not sorry for cleaning or moving the furniture, but if you don't want to pay me for those hours, I understand."

"You're so *gut* at cleaning, maybe you could tackle my house." When she straightened up in alarm, he said, "I'm kidding. What I mean is that I've probably grown used to things being a bit messy."

Hannah ran a finger across the top of his workbench and held it up. "Your workshop is clean enough. See? No dust."

No dust. That meant he had been staining the piece

he was working on, not sanding it, which also explained the rag in his hand. Honestly, what was wrong with his train of thought these days?

"*Ya*, having a clean workspace is important when I'm staining wood, and it helps to keep my tools in good condition." He sighed and grimaced, knowing what he needed to say next. "I'm sure having a clean and functional work area is important for your work too. I'm sorry I overreacted."

"So we're *gut*?"

"We are."

"Great." She hopped off the bench. "Oh, one more thing, though. I would like to leave early on days that Matt has therapy appointments. So today I'll work through lunch and leave at one."

"That isn't a problem."

"You're sure?"

"I thought we had already agreed on that. You'll be taking off early on therapy days—Tuesday, Wednesday and Friday. Right?"

"Right. It's possible I could take some of the work with me and do it in the office waiting room."

"Only if you want to."

She walked across to the office and then pivoted to face him. "Why aren't you at the job site today?"

"The builder didn't get all the supplies in on time, but he was expecting a shipment later today. I guess I'll head back over tomorrow."

"Okay. Do you have time to answer some questions?"

"I can try."

"You might want to bring a mug of coffee."

"For myself or both of us?"

Her smile broadened, and Jacob realized she was one

of the prettiest women he knew. The fact that she had called him on the wreck of an office he'd wanted her to work in? He could see now that he'd deserved that.

"Bring a cup for both of us. I have a lot of questions."

Hannah told herself she needed to get over her nerves if she was going to work in close proximity with Jacob every day. She felt like a schoolgirl with a crush. What was she thinking? She did not have romantic feelings for Jacob Schrock. She was a grown woman with a young child and a job. She was way beyond crushes.

Jacob pulled the old office chair back into the office. "Don't look at me that way. It's not for you to sit on. I brought it for myself."

"*Gut.* What I mean is, I was afraid it would collapse under me."

Jacob's grin widened as he handed her a mug of coffee. "Sorry I don't have anything sweet to go with this. I'm not actually a baker."

Hannah popped up, retrieved her quilted lunch bag and pulled out a Tupperware container filled with snickerdoodle squares. "Apparently my *mamm* thinks this job is going to require massive amounts of sugar."

The food and coffee helped to ease what tension remained between them.

Hannah pulled out the notes she'd made the day before and began firing questions at him.

"What does the notation *R* mean?"

"Money I received for a job."

"And *P* means…"

"Something I paid for."

"Okay. I'd sort of figured those out, but what in the world is *Q*?"

"Means I had a question. Wasn't sure if the receipt was important or not."

"Give me an example."

"Buggy repairs."

"Excuse me?"

"*Englischers* take off car repairs…"

"*Nein.* They take off mileage, and they're allowed so much per mile for traveling to and from locations that are job related."

"So can I take off mileage?"

She tapped her pen against the pad of paper and made a notation.

"What did you write down?"

"A note to call your accountant and ask him or her."

"I don't have an accountant. That's why I'm in this mess."

"You're in this mess because you are ignorant…"

Jacob choked on his coffee.

"By that I mean you're uneducated in the ways of *Englisch* laws. There are going to be questions I can't answer, Jacob. We need to ask a professional."

"*Gut* point."

"I'll make a list and you can call whomever you trust."

Jacob pulled the pad toward him and wrote the name of a Goshen accounting firm across the top of the page, then added the name of the person she should contact.

"You call them. I'm making accountant questions officially a part of your job."

"I imagine they'll bill you for the time."

"It'll still be much less than having them tape up receipts." He leaned back in his chair, causing it to let out an alarming groan, and laced his fingers behind his head. "Do you know how to use the phone?"

"*Ya.* I've used one a few times." She tried not to stare at the muscles bulging in his arms. Who would have thought that a woodworker would be in such good shape?

"So no phone lessons are required."

"I'm a little surprised you have one here in the shop."

"The bishop allows it, and truthfully my mother wanted one. She was always worried one of us would injure ourselves with a table saw. The woman had quite an imagination. Anyway, when the bishop started allowing them for businesses, she ordered one."

"So she could call 911?"

"Ya."

"Did she ever have to?"

"Only when my *dat* was bit by a snake. He wanted to drive himself to the hospital, but she had an ambulance on the way before he could hobble to the horse stall."

"Was it poisonous?"

"Probably not. The critter crawled away, and he didn't have a chance to identify it. The doctors treated him all the same, and *Mamm* was forever saying that she'd saved his life by having the phone installed."

"They sound like very special people."

"They were." Jacob swallowed hard, but he didn't look away from her. "I suppose that sometimes I forget the good memories…you know, trying not to dwell on the bad."

"I can understand that." Hannah thought of what her mother had said, that they'd both been dealt a blow.

Jacob cleared his throat and sat forward, arms

crossed on the desk. "How do you know so much about accounting and IRS reports?"

"I first worked doing some accounting here in town, down at the furniture factory when I was a *youngie*."

"I didn't know that."

"You and I didn't stay in touch after our failed attempt at dating, not really."

"Maybe we should have."

"Why?"

She half hoped that he would answer, but he seemed suddenly interested in the snickerdoodle in his hand, so she let it slide.

"Okay, let's see what else I have here."

They went down her list of questions until she felt like she had a fair understanding of his system—which wasn't much of a system, but at least it was consistent.

Finally she said, "This isn't going to be as complicated as I feared. You only have a few categories that your deductions will fall under. I am curious, though—how did you even pay your taxes without knowing exactly what you'd made and what you'd spent?"

"I tried to fill out the IRS worksheets, but mostly that was a guessing game. Mainly I looked at my balance in my bank account and paid based on that."

"But you must have spent money that wasn't business related."

"Look around, Hannah. Does it look like I've spent much on the place?"

"I see your point."

"No big vacations, no major purchases, it seemed pretty straightforward to me."

"Everyone has to file taxes—even Amish."

"Not if we make under a certain amount, and believe me, if I made over that amount, it wasn't by much."

"That's true for individuals, but businesses must file whether they have a profit or loss."

"Which I did."

"And yet you're being audited. Perhaps you didn't include all the forms you were required to include."

When he looked at her skeptically, she explained, "After I married, I did my husband's taxes for the farm. We even had a nice Mennonite woman come to the local library and help us."

"*Wunderbaar.* Then you know what you're doing."

"Let's hope so." She tapped her pen against the pad.

"What?"

"You might have some money coming back to you. There are a lot of deductions that wouldn't have shown up as an extra expense. Like, say, the use of this part of the barn."

Jacob glanced left and right and then leaned forward. "You mean this room? I've heard it's small and stuffy and poorly lit."

She crossed her arms in defense, but she couldn't help smiling. "*Ya.* I think you're right. Still, it's deductible because it's the place you do business, as is the part out there where you work on your projects."

"You're *gut* at this, Hannah."

"Better wait until we're through the audit to decide that. Speaking of the audit..."

This time it was Jacob that groaned instead of the chair.

"We only have ten days, Jacob."

"Are you sure?"

"According to the letter they sent, an agent will be here to examine your files on September 10."

"Oh."

"Today is August 28."

"Can we ask for an extension?"

"We can, but…the Mennonite woman in Wisconsin, she had a college degree in accounting and worked for a local accountant. She said that the IRS will grant an extension, but they'll look at things more closely because of it. Also, any penalties you have would be greater because more time will have passed since you owed the taxes."

"I just want to build playhouses."

"*Ya,* most business owners love what they do, but they're not prepared for the amount of paperwork that comes with it."

"Can you have it ready? By the tenth?"

"Maybe, if I take it home with me, work on it a little each night and put in as many hours here as possible." Even as she uttered those words, Hannah wondered what in the world she was doing. She wanted to spend time with Matthew. She wanted to work in the garden. She didn't want to spend every free minute taping up Jacob's receipts.

"You would do that?"

"I guess, but is there anyone else who could help? Anyone who could at least tape these receipts onto sheets of paper for me? That would save a lot of time."

"I have five nephews who live next door. They're always bugging me to come see them."

"You don't go next door to see your nephews?"

"I've been busy is all." Jacob began gathering up their cups and putting the lid back on the empty Tupperware.

"How old are they?"

"Oldest is eleven, no…twelve."

"That's certainly old enough to help with this project, and my niece Naomi was looking for a way to earn a little Christmas money."

"Let's tell the *kinder* that I'll pay them two bucks an hour. Wait, will I be in trouble with the child labor laws?"

"I don't think taping receipts for an hour each night falls into that category."

"Gut." He stood, holding the cups in his left hand and tapping on the table with his right. "I'll load up one of the bins later today in your buggy for you to take to your niece."

"Load two. I'll work on one and Naomi can work on the other."

"And I'll take two over to my nephews."

"We need to get the past five years in order. Can you do the last one?"

Jacob shook his head in disbelief. "You're pushy, you know that?"

But the way he smiled at Hannah sent a river of good feelings through her.

Jacob turned to go back into the main room. As she worked she could hear him in there—humming and sanding, and occasionally using some sort of battery-powered tool. She felt a new optimism that maybe they could be ready in time. It would take a tremendous effort, but she'd never minded hard work.

And with the extra overtime hours, she might just be able to help save her parents' farm.

As for Jacob, it wasn't as if they were friends, but it felt good to have an employer she could talk to. It helped to know that he'd forgiven her for her behavior the day before.

Despite the silly schoolgirl feelings she sometimes had around Jacob, she also understood that she was a mother and her sole focus was her child. She wasn't interested in dating or expanding her social circle. Still, they could learn to enjoy working with one another—as long as they kept things on a professional basis, she saw no harm in it.

To be professional one needed to extend certain courtesies, so perhaps her mother was right. Maybe they both needed to work on their social skills.

Chapter Eight

Jacob had fallen into a comfortable routine by Thursday afternoon. On days that Hannah left early to take Matthew to therapy, he would putter around in his workshop until she arrived. Then they'd spend thirty minutes talking about what progress they'd made on the accounting reconstruction, whether she had any questions and if he'd thought of any other items she needed to know about his business.

His excuses for being there were relatively lame—needing to put a final coat of sealant on a birdhouse, giving his gelding Bo time in the pasture, not wanting to get caught in early-morning traffic.

On the days when she didn't leave early, he was gone before she arrived. He did this so he could be at the job site early, finish his work well before four and come home in time to spend the last hour or so with Hannah. They didn't work together. He was usually in the workshop, and she was in the tiny office. But just knowing someone else was there seemed to give the old barn new life.

His schedule was set, and he was pretty happy with it.

He left for work late on therapy days—Tuesday, Wednesday, and Friday. He left for home early on Monday and Thursday. He always had an answer ready in case anyone asked, as if he needed to justify his irregular hours.

He didn't share his excuses with Hannah. Instead he recited them to himself over and over in his mind.

He should be there in case she had questions.

He needed to catch up on his small jobs.

She might need something moved in the office.

But with each day that passed, he understood that those were just excuses. *You might be able to fool someone else part of the time, but you can rarely fool yourself.* The memory of his father's words brought a smile as he made his way home early Thursday afternoon.

Deep inside, beneath all the layers of why it wouldn't work and how foolish he was being, Jacob understood that he was falling for Hannah.

It was hard to believe that she had been working in his office for less than a week. It seemed like she belonged there.

Thursday he arrived home around two o'clock. His days on the job site were getting shorter and shorter, but the boss was happy with what he'd been able to accomplish, and that was what mattered.

He'd opened the large doors of the barn to let in the fall air and was working on a front entry bench for one of his *Englisch* neighbors when Hannah plopped into a chair next to his workbench.

"Problem with the receipts? Let me guess, you can't tell my threes from my eights."

"*Nein.* It's not about the numbers."

"What is it? Is Matthew okay?" He clutched the piece

of sandpaper he'd been using in both hands. Surely she would have told him if Matthew wasn't well.

"He's fine. It's only that he's turning five in a couple of weeks."

"When is his birthday?"

"September 25."

"We should have a party."

Hannah crossed her arms, as if to ward off more unwelcome ideas. "Matthew prefers to have small, private celebrations."

Matthew did? Or Hannah? He was about to ask when common sense saved him and he closed his mouth. It wasn't his business how she raised her child, or at least it shouldn't be. Should it?

"But that's not what I came to tell you. I'm going to need to leave early today, even though it's not a therapy day."

Jacob pushed away the disappointment that welled up inside him. "That's not a problem."

"You're sure?"

"*Ya.* I know you're doing extra work at home. From the stack of pages on your desk it would seem the great taping project of the year is nearly done."

"Speaking of taping...how's your bin coming along?"

Instead of admitting that he hadn't actually started, he asked, "Why do they have to be taped up anyway? A receipt is a receipt."

Hannah's eyes widened and she looked at him as if he were wearing two pairs of suspenders. "Because the IRS doesn't deal in scraps of paper, and when I enter them in the ledger, I do so by date."

"You have to sort them by date?"

Hannah shook her head in mock despair, or maybe

it was real despair. "Stick to your woodwork, Jacob Schrock. Leave the office work to me."

He liked the sound of that. He liked the idea that she planned to stick around longer than the next two weeks.

Hannah went back into the office, ignoring the way that Jacob was looking at her. Maybe she was imagining it, but he seemed happy when she was around, almost as happy as he had been when he was working on Matthew's playhouse.

She plopped down in front of the desk. She was helping him out of a jam. Of course he was happy. Why wouldn't he be happy? Things weren't that clear-cut, though. She understood all too well that he was helping her out of a jam at the same time.

She'd taken the most recent year of receipts herself, and she'd stayed up well past her normal bedtime—sitting at the kitchen table, taping receipts and sorting them by month. Now, back in Jacob's office, she opened the journal and began entering them under the proper category headings. She immersed herself in the work, and thirty minutes later was surprised to hear the clatter of buggy wheels outside.

Looking up, she saw that it was her brother-in-law and began tidying up the desk. She'd brought a quilted bag from home, and she carefully placed the next two months of receipts in it, along with the ledger, a few extra pencils and the battery-operated sharpener she'd purchased at the store.

By the time she'd made it out into the larger room, Jacob was wiping his hands off on a cloth and frowning at the buggy that had parked in front of the workshop.

"Your ride?" he asked.

"*Ya*."

He nodded once, curtly, and turned back toward his workbench.

"I'm taking some work with me, to make up for the time I'm missing." When he didn't answer she added, "Thanks again, Jacob."

He bobbed his head but was suddenly completely focused on cleaning some of his tools. It all seemed like rather odd behavior. Usually Jacob was the friendly, outgoing sort.

Shrugging, she said, "See you tomorrow, I guess."

Still no answer, so she gave up on making conversation and walked outside.

Her brother-in-law had just pulled up to the hitching post and jumped out of the buggy.

"Carl, *danki* for picking me up."

"No problem."

"When *Dat* dropped me off, he thought he'd be able to come back and get me."

"*Ya*, he told me as much, but his errands in town took longer than he thought. It's really no problem, Hannah."

He put his arm around her shoulders and gave her a clumsy hug. Carl was the big brother she'd never had. He'd been in the family over a dozen years, and Hannah thought the world of him. It helped that he was so good with Matthew, who happened to be sitting in the back seat practically bouncing up and down, if a boy with a spinal cord injury could bounce.

Hannah stuck her head inside. "What are you doing here?"

"Carl said I could come."

"And why would you want to do that?"

"I told you, *Mamm*. I want to see where you work. Is Jacob here? Can I come inside?"

"Oh, I don't think we have time for that."

"Sure we do," Carl said. "I even brought his chair."

Hannah resisted the urge to ask why in the world he would do that. Carl was just trying to help, and Matthew's fascination with Jacob hadn't lessened one bit in the last few days. She didn't think this was a good idea, but Carl was already removing Matthew's wheelchair from where it was strapped on the back of the buggy.

"All right," she said with a sigh. "Let's get this over with."

Jacob had immediately gone to the window when Hannah walked out of the room. He knew he shouldn't be aggravated with her. He couldn't expect her to work all of the time, and of course she had a social life. Why wouldn't she? Hannah was a smart, beautiful, young woman. She'd been a widow for over a year now. Of course she was lonely and ready to step out again. He was surprised she didn't have beaus dropping her off and picking her up every day.

When the man jumped out of the buggy and gave her a hug, Jacob understood the full depth of his misery. Not only had he fallen for a woman who could never possibly care for an ogre like himself, but she was already being courted. He could have asked around. He could have saved himself the embarrassment.

He thought to sneak out the back and over to his house or the garden or anywhere that he wouldn't have to watch the two of them when the man walked around to the back of the buggy. He reappeared with Matthew's wheelchair. She had trusted Matthew with this fellow? They must be even closer than he feared.

Now he was torn, but that feeling didn't last long because the man had plopped Matthew into the chair as if he weighed no more than a sack of potatoes. Matthew was grinning up at his mother, and Hannah was pointing at the workshop. There was no way he was going to sneak out of this. He wasn't beneath slipping away and being borderline rude to an Amish man, but he couldn't find it in his heart to ignore young Matthew.

So he pulled in a deep breath, straightened his suspenders and walked out into the fall afternoon.

Matthew let out a squeal the minute he saw him.

"Jacob! Carl brought me over to see where you work."

Hannah reached forward and straightened Matthew's shirt. "I thought he came to pick me up."

"That too." Carl stepped forward and offered his hand to Jacob. "It's been a while."

A while?

"We were in the same church district, before we grew too big and had to split."

He did look familiar.

The man laughed good-naturedly. "Carl Yoder. I'm married to Hannah's sister, Beth."

The flood of relief that swept through Jacob confirmed what he had already figured out—he'd developed feelings for Hannah King, and he was in much too far to back out now.

He spent the next twenty minutes walking Carl and Matthew through the workshop, showing them the types of things he made and answering Matthew's endless supply of questions.

"I want to see your playhouses, Jacob."

"You have one of my playhouses, buddy."

"But I want to see the other ones. The ones that you made for other people. Are they all for disabled kids like me?"

"Yes, they are, but different kids have different special needs."

"I don't know what that means."

"Some disabilities you can see on the outside, but others, they're inside—so those playhouses might not have grab bars. Maybe the person can't see well, so the playhouse is flat on the ground—no steps and no ramps."

"How's that a playhouse, then?"

Jacob laughed and ruffled the hair on the top of Matthew's head.

"Say, isn't there one over by me?" Carl asked. "Built like a ship. That has to be your work."

"*Ya.* Made it last year for a young boy with cancer."

"Can I see it?" Matthew began tugging on his hand. "Can we go there? Would he let me play with him?"

"I'm not sure how Jasper is doing now. We'd need to check with his parents."

"Will you? Will you call them?"

"That's enough, Matthew." Hannah had moved behind Matthew's chair and had pivoted it toward the barn door. "Jacob has lots to do. He can't be ferrying you around to playgrounds because you're curious."

"I could take you both on Saturday."

Matthew squealed in delight and raised his hand for a fist bump. Jacob obliged and then he noticed the frown on Hannah's face.

"Oh. Unless you had something else you needed to do on Saturday."

"I had planned on working on your receipts."

"We could go without you. I don't mind taking him."

"You need to work on receipts too."

"Well, we could do that in the morning and go to see the playhouse in the afternoon."

"Come on, *Mamm*. Please..." Matthew drew the word out in a well-practiced whine, but he added a smile, which caused his mother to sigh heavily.

"Okay, but only for an hour."

"Jacob could come for lunch and then we could—"

"Let's not strain your *mamm*'s patience. She has things planned for her Saturday."

Carl had been studying a row of birdhouses. He picked one up and asked, "How much?"

"Ten."

"Costs you more than that to build it."

"*Nein.* I use old barn wood. Costs practically nothing to build it."

Carl grinned. "I'll take two, then. Beth will love them."

Matthew offered to hold the birdhouses, and Carl once again shook Jacob's hand. "This has been great, but I need to get back before Beth thinks I've taken off for the auction in Shipshe without her."

"I didn't know you were going," Hannah said.

"She wants goats, if you can believe that. As if she doesn't have enough to take care of, and the new baby on the way..." Carl shook his head as if he couldn't fathom the ways of women and offered to wheel Matthew back to the buggy.

Hannah hung back, and Jacob had the feeling that it wasn't to say *thank you.*

"I'm sorry he pressured you into that."

"It's not a problem."

"A four-year-old can be quite persistent once they've made up their mind, and Matthew doubly so. He's been pestering me about coming to see you since I started on Monday."

"I really don't mind."

"The thing is..." Hannah hesitated and then pushed on. "Matthew gets attached to people and then they move on to other...phases of their lives. He doesn't handle that very well."

"Where would I move on to?"

"He gets too attached, if you know what I mean."

"I don't." He waited, wondering what she did mean and trying not to be stung by her suggestion that he was going to somehow let Matthew down.

"It's up to me to protect him."

"From what? *Freinden?*"

"You're not his *freind*, Jacob."

"Of course I am."

"*Nein.* You're my boss."

He stared out the window for a moment, watched Carl lift Matthew out of his wheelchair and place him in the buggy. He wondered how hard it was for Hannah to depend on other people, especially after losing her husband. "Let me take you both out on Saturday, show him a couple of playhouses. We'll keep it to an hour so it doesn't disrupt your whole day."

"Okay, fine. I guess."

"I know the owners, and they wouldn't mind Matthew playing on them. Most are for children his age."

"Playdates don't always go well with Matthew."

"What do you mean?"

"Other children can't possibly understand his limitations, why he needs to be careful…"

"I've worked with several disabled kids. They seem pretty intuitive about such things."

"And I've seen children point and ask cruel questions, or, worse yet, ignore him completely."

"Is that what you're worried about? Or is it that you're afraid I'll somehow let Matthew down? Because I can assure you right now that isn't going to happen."

"He's too taken with you."

"Excuse me?"

"He doesn't understand that you were simply hired to do a job, and that now I'm hired to do a job. He thinks… well, he thinks that there's something more to it."

"Hannah, what you're saying is true, or was true. I was hired for a job, and now I've hired you for a job." He wondered if he should just shut up, but ignored that idea. "I think, though, that Matthew is also right. We're part of a community. We belong to the same church."

"Different districts."

"We are neighbors and *freinden*."

She nodded once, curtly, and turned. He walked beside her as she made her way back outside. Carl had climbed into the buggy and was waiting.

He'd noticed that when she was embarrassed or nervous, she liked to keep her hands busy. At the moment, she was twisting the strings to her prayer *kapp* round and round. He'd also learned that if he waited, she would eventually work through her emotions and pick up the conversation again.

"*Ya*, of course you're right. It's only that I don't want him to get the wrong idea."

"What wrong idea? That I like you? Because I do."

She cocked her had to the side, glancing up at him and allowing her gaze to linger there before flitting away. "We'll see you Saturday, two o'clock."

And then, she scurried back off to the buggy. There was simply no other word for it. She reminded him of a squirrel running back toward its safe spot in the woods.

The question was, how he was ever going to convince her that being with him was safe and that they were more than friends. Were they? Or was his imagination running wild again? He reached up to scratch at the scars on his face.

Scars.

Everyone had them, but his were hideous. He'd thought that keeping them, that refusing the cosmetic surgery, would help pay the debt he owed for not saving his parents. He'd never considered that they might push away someone that he cared about. What if Hannah simply couldn't abide looking at him from one day to the next? She'd never hinted at that, but people could hide their feelings. If she was repulsed by him, it wouldn't mean that she was shallow, only that she was human.

He walked back into his workshop and began sanding again, more aggressively this time.

He didn't know if Hannah was worried about protecting Matthew's feelings or her own, but he did know that she needed to stop shielding the boy from all of life's ups and downs. Matthew needed friends the same as everyone else, and if it meant that someone occasionally let him down…that was part of growing up.

One other thing he knew for certain. He wouldn't be

the one to disappoint Matthew. Now all he had to do was find a way to convince Hannah of that.

It was risky. Putting his feelings out there would mean that he might be hurt, and he'd had his fair share of that already. But not letting her know how he felt? Not taking a chance to get to know her on a personal level? That felt like a bigger risk than he was willing to take.

Chapter Nine

Friday dawned beautiful, cool and crisp. If she'd lived closer, Hannah would have walked to work. As it was, she said goodbye to her family and drove Dolly the few miles to Jacob's place. She was still uncomfortable with the way things had ended between them the day before. Had he actually said he liked her? What did that mean?

Fortunately he wasn't there when she arrived, so she didn't have to worry about being embarrassed about the way they'd left things. She went straight to the office and was soon immersed in receipts and columns of figures and IRS categories. The morning passed quickly and her stomach began to grumble. She was about to pull over yet another box of receipts when she heard a whistle from out in the yard. She hurried to the door and saw Emily Schrock making her way toward the workshop, a basket over her arm and a smile on her face. Hannah hadn't seen Jacob's sister-in-law in years. In fact, the last time she'd seen her they'd been in grade school together.

"Tell me you have some cold tea or hot coffee in there."

"I have both, and scones too—fresh blueberry."

Emily was nearly as round as she was tall, and she always had been as far back as Hannah could remember. She was the traditional Amish woman, and probably could have starred in one of the local Amish plays. Quick with a smile, an excellent cook and, if Hannah remembered right, she had a whole passel of children. As Emily stepped closer, Hannah realized she was also expecting another child, though her baby bump wasn't yet too obvious. It seemed Hannah's lot in life to be surrounded by pregnant women.

"Come in the office. I finally finished cleaning."

Emily let out a long whistle as she walked into the room. "Wow. You did all of this…this week?"

Hannah allowed the woman to enfold her in a hug.

"We're so glad you're here."

"We?"

"Micah and I. We worry about Jacob, and the IRS audit… Micah was ready to hire one of the *Englisch* accountants in town."

"He may still need to. I haven't actually worked through all of his receipts yet."

"And his books?"

"He doesn't have any."

"I suppose that's part of the problem. I'm sure you'll be able to fix it, though. I remember how you were in school. Math was your favorite subject."

"Still is," Hannah admitted. "It's what I enjoy about quilting, the measuring and calculating."

"And what I always make mistakes on. How about we go outside? The rocking chairs looked more comfortable than the stool you have behind your desk."

Hannah readily agreed. As they walked back out

into the fall sunshine, she asked, "How are you? I see you're expecting again."

"I am, and I dearly hope it's a girl, though of course we'll love whatever *Gotte* blesses us with." She opened the thermos and poured two cups of coffee.

It was much better than what Jacob made in the workshop, and Hannah sipped it with pleasure, closing her eyes and enjoying the rich taste.

"You have several boys already, right?"

"Five. Samuel is twelve. He's our oldest. The twins—Timothy and Thomas—are ten. Eli's nine, and Joseph is six."

"I'll never remember all those names." Hannah laughed and plucked one of the scones from the basket.

"You know how it is with Amish families—big and loud and messy." As if suddenly remembering Hannah's situation, she set down the scone she'd been eating and brushed off her fingertips on her apron. "I was so sorry to hear about Matthew's accident, and your husband... a real tragedy."

"Danki." The word was barely a whisper.

"I should have come to see you."

"*Nein.* Why would you? You have your hands full with your own children and husband to care for, your home to maintain and—"

"Why would I?" Emily looked truly shocked at the question. "Because we're *freinden.* Because we take care of each other, like family."

Nearly the same words that Jacob had said to Hannah earlier.

Emily picked up her scone and finished it off with the last of her coffee. "I know we're not technically in the same district, but that doesn't matter. We're still one community. Maybe you could bring Matthew to meet my boys."

"Oh, I don't know—"

"They're rambunctious but they're *gut* boys."

"Where are they at this morning?"

"With my parents, who live on the other side of us. They'll all be in school this year. My youngest is only a year older than Matthew. He's four, right?"

"Nearly five."

"And Joseph is barely six. They could be *gut frienden.*"

Hannah didn't answer that. She thought it unlikely that a healthy six-year-old would want to be friends with a disabled five-year-old. The thought stung her, stirred the old ache, and she pushed it away.

"Tell me about Jacob," she said, more to change the subject than anything else.

"Oh, *ya*, sure. There's not a lot to tell. You know about the fire."

"My mother told me about it."

"Happened six years ago, but he still hasn't healed from that night, in my opinion."

"He was here when it happened?"

"*Nein.* He was downtown, courting a young girl from the next district. He came back late and the home was already ablaze."

"Lightning is what *Mamm* said."

"So the firefighters told us. Jacob blames himself, I think."

"For a lightning strike?"

"More because he wasn't here. He didn't get to them in time, or he might have saved them—at least that's what he said when they were transporting him to the hospital. Maybe he blames Micah too. Our place is next door but over the hill. We didn't realize what had happened until we heard the fire trucks."

"Jacob ran into it...into the fire?"

"He did." Emily began tidying up, offered Hannah another scone, then repacked the picnic basket. "His scars—the ones on the inside—they are far worse than the ones on his face."

"It must be hard—being disfigured."

Emily shook her head so hard that her *kapp* strings swung back and forth. "No one even notices anymore. What they see is what he is—a *gut* man who is hurting."

Hannah realized Emily was right; she hadn't really thought of his scars in a long time. She certainly didn't notice them anymore. "And yet it's hard to be different."

"Not if we're humble, it isn't."

Hannah bit back the retort that came too quickly to her lips. *What would you know of being different?* It was often easy for those not suffering from a thing to tell you how to handle it. She didn't utter either of those thoughts aloud, however. Emily obviously cared for Jacob and only wanted what was best for him.

Hannah set her chair to rocking, determined not to butt into the other family's affairs. Emily, however, wasn't done yet, perhaps because she had no other woman in her household to share her worries and concerns with.

"I know several *gut* women who would be happy to court Jacob, but he can't see past his own scars. It worries me, for sure and certain it does."

"You care about him."

"All I know to do is keep trying, because if you ask

me, Jacob needs a family. He needs to get his attention off himself and onto someone else. He needs to learn to love again."

Friday didn't work out the way Jacob had hoped. He had to be at the job early, before sunrise, so that he could finish the cabinetry work in time for the job superintendent to approve what he'd done. He could have pushed some of the work off until Saturday, but he had plans with Hannah and Matthew the next day. That thought had him whistling through his breakfast of oatmeal and coffee.

He finished the cabinetry job well before lunch. He told himself that he didn't work quickly so that he could at least say hello to Hannah before she left for Matthew's appointment, but in truth he wanted a glimpse of her. Somehow seeing her each day improved his mood, even if it was only to have her shove a scrap of paper into his hands and say, "Can you explain this one to me?"

The job site manager grinned as he checked off the boxes on his approval form. "Hot date, Jacob? I've never seen you work so fast."

"Some orders are backed up in my shop is all."

Which was a true statement, if not completely honest. Or was it completely honest? There was no real reason to be at the shop with Hannah. She seemed to be doing fine on her own.

"Uh-huh, well, as usual you've done an excellent job. Sign here." The man thrust a clipboard toward him. "Your payment should be processed early next week."

"Danki."

"Thank you, and I'll be needing you for that job in

Shipshewana mid-September, if that still sounds good to you."

"Sounds great."

But the thought of riding the construction firm's bus to Shipshewana each day didn't appeal to him as it once had. The truth was that he'd rather be home.

Still, the cabinetry work allowed him to spend time on the playhouses, and he'd received another order for one the day before. He was itching to get to his workshop and work on a design plan. The little girl had cerebral palsy. Her form said that she loved anything pink, sparkly or related to Princess Belle. He'd had to ask a coworker what that last onc meant.

"*Beauty and the Beast?* Surely you've seen it."

When Jacob shook his head, the man had said, "Come to my house. My littlest watches it at least once a day."

So instead of going straight home at noon on Friday, he stopped by the library and used the computers to find a short description of the movie. Pulling out a scrap of paper from his pocket he'd written:

bright, beautiful, young woman.

beast lives in castle.

he has a good heart and she loves to read.

Not a lot to go on, but those three lines were enough. Suddenly he knew what he wanted to build. A castle with bookcases and one of those giggle mirrors that was both safe and fun. He'd seen them on a school playground he'd helped build. In fact, if he remembered correctly, the construction manager had ordered it from the local hardware store.

He walked from the library to the store, ordered the mirror and set off toward home. It was only a little after noon, so he should get there before Hannah left for the day. He'd hardly spent any time with her, but he had peeked into the office each evening. It smelled and looked better, and he had to admit that her changes to the room made a lot of sense. She seemed to be making progress, based on the stacks of taped receipts and notations in the spiral notebook she'd bought. She'd even begun to write in the accounting book he'd purchased.

He arrived a few minutes after noon to find Hannah and Emily sitting in the rockers underneath the porch of the workshop.

"Any scones left for me?" he asked, dropping down onto the porch floor.

Emily peered into the basket. "Looks empty."

"I know you are teasing me, Emily." Jacob pulled the basket out of her hands, dug around inside the dish towels and came away with a giant oatmeal cookie. "This will do."

"You're in an awfully *gut* mood."

"Why wouldn't I be? Finished my job early. The check is in the mail, and I get to work on a new playhouse this afternoon."

"Who is this one for?" Hannah asked.

"Young girl here in town actually. She has cerebral palsy. It's a disease that—"

"I know what it is," Hannah said softly. "CP affects muscle tone, posture, even eyesight."

"The poor thing." Emily poured Jacob a mug of coffee from her thermos and handed it to him. "Any idea what kind of playhouse you're going to build?"

"Apparently she likes some *Englisch* movie called *Beauty and the Beast*, so I'm thinking it should be in the shape of a castle, complete with turrets, bookcases and a funny mirror. That's my initial plan, anyway."

"It will be *wunderbaar*, Jacob." Emily began storing items back into her basket. "I better get home. The boys went to town with Micah, but they'll be back soon."

"I hope my *bruder* and my nephews appreciate you and your cooking abilities." Jacob finished the cookie and snagged the thermos of coffee before she tucked it away. "Sure there aren't more cookies in there? I'm still hungry."

"Because you need to eat real food, not just sweets. Speaking of hungry…don't forget brunch on Sunday."

"Oh, I…"

"Jacob Schrock, you will not be working on Sunday, and since there's no church, I expect you to be at our house by ten thirty in the morning."

Jacob glanced at Hannah, a smile tugging at his lips. "My sister-in-law can be quite bossy, if you haven't noticed."

"You should listen to her."

"I should?"

"Sure. She's a *gut* cook and your nephews apparently don't see you very much."

"Now, that makes me think you two have been talking about me."

Emily stopped what she was doing and studied Hannah, her head cocked. "You should come too."

"Me?"

"Bring Matthew. He can meet the boys."

"Oh, I don't think—"

"And your parents. I haven't seen Claire and Alton in ages."

"I'm sure they have other plans."

Emily ran a hand over her stomach, then placed the basket over her arm and smiled at Hannah. "Just ask them. We'd love to have you."

With a small wave, she set off across the property to her house.

"You two do this every day?"

"I've only been here a week. This is actually the first time Emily has stopped by."

"It's *gut* she did. Emily doesn't get enough girl time according to Micah. I suppose living with a house full of males could try anyone's patience."

But Hannah wasn't listening. She'd dumped the contents of her coffee mug onto a nearby plant, repositioned the rocking chairs and headed back inside without another word.

Jacob followed her, suspecting something was wrong but clueless as to what it might be.

"It would be great if you and Matthew could come Sunday…and your parents too, of course. Emily usually has a small-sized group—enough to get up a game of ball, but not so many that the buggies are crowded together."

Hannah definitely wasn't listening. She'd practically run into the office, and now she was perched on her stool pulling yet another stack of receipts toward her.

"Hannah? What's wrong?"

"We won't be coming on Sunday."

"Oh. I just thought Matthew might enjoy—"

"You don't know anything about what Matthew might or might not enjoy." Two bright red spots appeared on her cheeks, but her gaze remained on the receipts, which she was now pulling out haphazardly. "Meeting new people is very hard for him."

"For him...or for you?"

"That's not fair."

"Oh, really?"

"Yes, really." She jumped off the stool, nearly toppling it over in the process. Hands on her hips, she said, "It's easy enough for you to boss me around, but when was the last time you were at your *bruder*'s house?"

"That's not the point."

"Isn't it? You're telling me that it's *gut* to be together, but apparently you stay here in your workshop whenever possible, hiding away."

"I'm not hiding." His temper was rising, and he fought to keep his voice down. "It's true I've been busy, but I don't avoid seeing them, and you shouldn't avoid introducing Matthew to new people."

"Why would you say that?" All color had drained from her face. "Why would you pretend to know what I should or shouldn't do?"

"I worked with Matthew on the playhouse. I know he's lonely."

"You know nothing! You haven't seen him on Sundays, longing to do what the other children do, but confined to his chair."

"I'm sure that must be difficult for you."

"You don't hear him cry when he has a terrible dream or when he's wet his bed because he can't get up by himself."

"I wasn't saying—"

"You know nothing of our life, Jacob Schrock, and I'd thank you to stay out of it."

With those words, she pushed past him, hurried across the main room of the workshop and dashed into the bathroom, slamming the door shut behind her.

* * *

Hannah managed to avoid Jacob for the next hour. When it was time for her to leave, she would have walked through the main workroom without speaking, but Jacob called out to her before she reached the door.

"If you'd like to cancel tomorrow, if you'd rather not take Matthew to see the playhouses, I understand."

She was mortified that she'd actually hollered at him. He'd been nothing but kind to both her and Jacob, and she'd responded with accusations and bitter words. So instead of jumping on his offer, she murmured, "*Nein.* We'll see you at two o'clock."

She was feeling so miserable about the entire situation that she found herself confessing to Sally Lapp as she waited for Matthew to finish his PT appointment.

"I shouldn't have said those things, but he made me so angry."

"Which is understandable, dear."

"What does he know of raising a child like Matthew?"

"Some people are like buttons, popping off at the wrong time!"

"Now I don't know if you mean me or Jacob."

"Perhaps both."

"Plus we're spending an hour tomorrow with him. Did I tell you about our plan to go and see his playhouses?"

"*Ya.* Sounds like a nice afternoon out."

"But seeing him both days of the weekend? It seems a little much…"

Hannah had brought a stack of the receipts with her and was beginning to enter them in the ledger. She looked down at what she'd done. Her handwriting was a tight, precise cursive and her numbers lined up perfectly, but seeing the progress she'd made on Jacob's accounts didn't ease the guilt she felt.

"I'll need to apologize to him."

"We often feel better after we do."

"And I will, even though he's wrong. Matthew does not need to be thrown into new situations."

"Mothers often know best."

"He's barely had time to settle in from the move, get to know his cousins and *aentis* and *onkels*, not to mention his new church family…"

"And yet children are ever so much more resilient than adults." Sally had finished the blanket she'd been working on the week before. Her yarn was now variegated autumn colors.

It reminded Hannah of cool nights and shorter days.

"So you think we should go to Emily's on Sunday?"

"Oh, it's not important what *I* think. What is your heart telling you to do?"

Hannah stared down at the column of numbers, embarrassed that tears had sprung to her eyes. Why was she so emotional? Why did she feel the need to run from Jacob Schrock? And what was she so intent on protecting her son from when he was thriving?

"Sometimes I'm not sure," she admitted.

"Pray on it. Make a decision when you're rested, not in the middle or at the end of a long, hard day. Maybe talk to your parents."

The door to the waiting room opened, and a nurse pushed Matthew's wheelchair through.

"*Gut* day?" Hannah asked.

"Awesome day."

He pestered her about Jacob all the way home—

wanting to know if she'd seen him, what he was working on, what he'd said about their plans to visit a couple of his playhouses the next day. Hannah realized as they pulled into the short lane leading to her parents' home that it wasn't only Matthew she was trying to protect. She was also trying to protect herself.

Raising any child was difficult, but raising a special needs child presented issues she'd never imagined. She constantly felt on guard for his feelings as well as his personal safety. She didn't think she could handle Matthew's look of disappointment when the other children ran off to play, or the whispered comments when no one thought she was listening or the looks of pity as she pulled his wheelchair from the buggy.

Life was difficult.

The one thing that made it easier was being home, alone, where the eyes of the world couldn't pry. She only guessed that it made things easier for Matthew, but she was certain that it made things easier for herself.

Hannah needn't have worried about making a decision as to whether they should join Jacob's family for Sunday dinner. Emily had spoken with Hannah's mother when they saw each other at the grocer in town. Plans had already been set in motion.

She had no valid objections, so she didn't bother to argue, but the entire thing made her tired and cranky. She had hardly slept Friday night after her argument with Jacob, and Saturday she worked twice as hard around the house—trying to make up for being gone all week. By the time they'd set lunch out on the table, she was tempted to beg off, say she had a headache, stay home and take a nap.

One look at Matthew told her that wouldn't be possible. He was wiggling in his chair and tapping his fingers against the table.

During the meal Matthew peppered her with questions about the playhouses, and when she'd said *I don't know* to over a dozen questions, he moved on to asking her about Jacob's family.

"Do they have animals?"

"I'm sure they do."

"Sheep?"

"Why would they have sheep?"

"Camels?"

Hannah began to laugh in exasperation, but her father combed his fingers through his beard as if he were in deep thought. Finally he leaned toward Matthew and lowered his voice as if to share a secret. "Only Amish man I know in this area with camels is Simon Eberly over in Middlebury. I'm sure I would have heard if Jacob's family had any—so no, probably not."

Which only slowed Matthew down for a moment. He proceeded to fire off questions about camels and declare that he'd love to have one. When Hannah thought her patience was going to snap, her father took Matthew outside to see to the horses.

"He'll be fine, you know." Her mother started washing the dishes, which meant it was Hannah's turn to dry.

"Why do you say that?"

"It's plain as day you worry about him."

"Of course I worry."

"He'll be in school this time next year."

"Unless I hold him back a year. With his birthday being in September, we could decide to wait..."

"He's such a bright young boy. Already he's better

with his letters and numbers than you girls were at that age. Why would you want to hold him back?"

"I don't know, *Mamm.*" Hannah was tired, and she wasn't yet halfway through the day.

The time inched closer to two o'clock, and finally her mother suggested she might want to freshen up a bit.

Hannah waited until she'd left the room to roll her eyes. Freshen up? It wasn't a date. They were driving around to look at playhouses. She'd switch out of her cleaning dress, but she was not donning a fresh *kapp.* She certainly didn't want Jacob to get the wrong idea.

Then she remembered her conversation with Sally Lapp about the way she had treated Jacob. She'd made up her mind then, and she wasn't going to change it now. She needed to apologize to Jacob, and the sooner the better. Suddenly what she wore seemed much less important.

Jacob made sure he arrived exactly at two o'clock.

He'd apparently pushed a little too hard the day before. He hadn't even known that he was pushing, but the way Hannah had melted down told him that he'd touched on a very sensitive subject. He wanted today to be fun and relaxing, not stressful. So he was careful not to arrive early or late.

Which meant that he had to pull over on the side of the road and wait a few minutes before turning down the dirt lane that led to her father's house.

He needn't have worried about being early. Matthew and Hannah were waiting on the front porch. The sight of them—her standing behind his wheelchair, and Matthew shading his eyes as he watched down the lane—caused Jacob's thoughts to scatter, and for a moment he couldn't remember why he was there. Then he glanced over and saw Matthew's playhouse. "You're getting old, Jacob. Or daft. You could be growing daft."

Ten minutes later they were off.

The first stop was Jasper's house. The boy wasn't Amish, but he was sick. For three years now he had been valiantly fighting the cancer that threatened to consume his small body. Though nearly nine years old, he was approximately the same size as Matthew.

"Wanna see my boat?"

"*Ya.* I have a train."

"Did Jacob make it?"

"He did."

"He's *gut* at building things."

Jasper's mom explained that she needed to stay inside with the baby, who was sleeping. "But make yourself at home. I was so glad to hear from you, Jacob, and Hannah, thank you for bringing Matthew. Jasper doesn't have a lot of visitors."

After walking her around the playhouse, which was built in the shape of a sailboat, Jacob pointed to a bench a few feet away. "Care to sit?"

"*Ya.* We cleaned all morning, so I'm tired."

"I heard you're working on a big accounting job during the week."

She laughed, then pressed her fingers to her lips.

"It's okay to laugh, Hannah. You're allowed."

"Oh, am I, now?" She tucked her chin and gave him a pointed look. He raised his hands in mock surrender, and she shook her head, then sighed.

"Do I exasperate you?" he asked.

"*Nein.* It's only that I need to do something I don't enjoy doing."

"Now?"

"Ya."

"I'm intrigued."

"I need to apologize, Jacob." She glanced up at him and then away—toward the sailboat, where Jasper was showing Matthew how to hoist a miniature sail. "I was rude to you yesterday, and I'm very sorry. I know better than to speak harshly to someone, let alone someone who is being kind to us."

"It's my fault. I stuck my nose where it didn't belong."

Now she laughed outright, causing the boys to look over at them and wave.

"Perhaps you did, but it was probably something I needed to hear."

"Apology accepted."

"Danki."

"Gem gschene."

The moment felt curiously intimate, shared there on the bench with the sun slanting through golden trees. Jacob cleared his throat and tried to think of something else to say, but for the second time that day, his mind was completely blank.

"It's a fine line," Hannah said. "Giving him the extra attention and care his condition requires, but not being overly protective. I'm afraid I'm still learning."

"You're doing a *wunderbaar* job. Don't let any fool neighbor or cranky boss tell you different."

Which caused her to smile again, and suddenly the tension that had been between them was gone. He was tempted to reach for her hand or touch her shoulder, but he realized that what Hannah was offering with her apology was a precious thing—her friendship. For now, he needed to be satisfied with that.

Hannah felt herself softening toward Jacob. How could she resist? He was patient with Matthew, kind toward her and it was plain that he was a good man. They stopped at three different playhouses—Jasper's sailboat, a precious miniature cottage built for a young blind girl named Veronica, and a tiny-sized barn made for an Amish boy named John.

"I spoke with John's parents. They said we could come by and look, but that they wouldn't be here."

"Is he sick too?" Matthew asked.

"Not really sick, no, but he needed a special playground nonetheless."

"What's wrong with him?"

"John was born with only one leg. His left leg stops at the knee. It's a bit hard for him to get around at times."

"He uses crutches?"

"He does, and he wears a prosthetic."

"Prophetic?"

"*Nein.* A..." He glanced at Hannah, obviously hoping for help.

"It's a plastic leg, Matthew. Remember the older gentleman you see at physical therapy sometimes? He has one."

"But his is metal. I know because he let me touch it. Looks like a robot. He laughed when I told him so."

"John's is plastic, but I've seen the metal ones." Jacob resettled his hat on his head. "It bothers him sometimes, and he likes to take it off when he gets home. The challenge for me was to make him a playhouse where it was safe to do that."

"This was a fun trip, Jacob. You're a *gut* builder."

"Thanks, Matt."

Jacob's use of a nickname that only her father and her husband had used melted another piece of Hannah's heart.

After they'd visited the small barn, Jacob drove them to town, bought ice cream for everyone and laughed with Matthew as they chased swirls of pink down their cones. It was all Hannah could do to remind herself as they drove home that this was an outing for Matthew, that it had nothing to do with her and Jacob, and that he was not interested in dating her.

Who would want a widow with a disabled child?

She knew how precious Matthew was, but she also understood firsthand the trials, the terrible nights, the emergency hospital visits, the mountain of bills. No, it would be wrong to consider letting anyone share such a burden. A preposterous thought, anyway. Jacob had been nothing but friendly toward her. Yes, he had said *I like you*, but that could be said of the neighbor's buggy.

Raising Matthew was a road that she was meant to travel alone.

When they reached the house, she went to transfer Matthew from the buggy to the chair, but Jacob was there to do it for her. His hand brushed against hers and then his brown eyes were staring into hers, searching her face, causing her hands to sweat and her heart to race.

As they thanked Jacob for the afternoon and she pushed a very tired young boy into the house, she paused to glance back over her shoulder. Jacob Schrock was a good man, and there was no doubt in her mind that *Gotte* had a plan for him, a plan that more than likely included a wife and family.

A whole family.

One that wasn't carrying the weight of her baggage.

Chapter Ten

Sunday morning dawned crisper and cooler than the day before. Jacob owned two Sunday shirts—they were identical in size, color and fabric. So why did he try on the first, discard it, try on the second and then switch back to the first?

He studied his face in the mirror. If he turned right the reflection was of a normal man—not particularly good-looking, strong jawline, dark brown eyes, eyebrows that tended toward being bushy. If he turned right, he saw his father staring back at him.

But if he turned left, he saw in his scars the detour his life had taken—the pain and the anger and the regret. He saw what might have been.

It had taken him some time to learn to shave over the scars. Their Plain custom was for unmarried men to be clean shaven, so he worked the razor carefully over the damaged tissue, using his fingers more than his eyes to guide the blade.

Finishing, he tugged the towel from the rack and patted his face dry. He could lie to himself while he was sanding a piece of oak or shellacking a section of maple wood, but for those few moments each day when he faced his own reflection in the mirror, he saw and recognized the truth.

He was lonely.

He longed to have a wife.

He dreamed of a family and a real home.

There was a small kernel of hope buried deep in his heart that those things were possible.

The moment passed as it always did, and he finished preparing for the visit next door to see his brother's family.

He chose to walk and wasn't too surprised when the only one to meet him was his brother's dog, Skipper. No one had been able to figure out exactly what kind of mutt Skipper was, though there was definitely some Beagle, Labrador and Boxer mixed in his background somewhere. Jacob bent down to scratch the old dog behind the ears and then together they climbed the steps to the front porch. Skipper curled up in a slat of sunlight, and Jacob let himself in.

His brother's voice let him know the family was still having their devotional in the sitting room.

"'Therefore I am troubled at his presence; when I consider I am afraid of Him. For God maketh my heart soft, and the Almighty troubleth me.'"

"That doesn't make any sense." Samuel, the oldest of his nephews, sat on the far end of the sofa. Next to him were the twins, Tim and Thomas, then Eli, who was younger by eleven months, and finally Joseph, the baby of the group at six. All five nephews were lined up like stair steps.

"Why do you say that?" Micah asked, nodding at

Jacob, who pulled a chair from the kitchen and took a seat.

"*Gotte* loves us." Samuel craned his neck and stared up at the corner of the ceiling as if he might find answers there. "The Bible says so. Remember? We read it just last week."

"*Ya*, that's true," Emily said.

"But Job is…what did you read?"

"He's afraid of *Gotte*," Eli piped up.

"Maybe Job did something wrong," Tim said.

"*Ya*, like when we get in trouble, and we know what we did was wrong and we're afraid of you finding out." Thomas pulled at the collar of his dress shirt. "Like last week when I put that big worm in the teacher's desk. It was awfully funny, but I knew even when I did it that I'd pay for it later."

"Sometimes we're afraid because we know we've sinned," Micah agreed. "But think back to the beginning of our reading this morning."

Micah thumbed through the pages of the old Bible—one of the few things they'd been able to recover from the fire. The cover was cracked and singed in places. The pages retained a slightly smoky odor, but it still held the wisdom they needed. Perhaps that Bible was like Jacob. It had been through a lot, but *Gotte* was still able to use it. *Gotte* was still able to use him.

"'There was a man in the land of Uz, whose name was Job,'" Micah read. "'And that man was perfect and upright, and one that feared *Gotte*.'"

Samuel shook his head. "Still doesn't make sense."

"Maybe your *onkel* Jacob can explain it better than I can."

Jacob met his brother's gaze, then turned his attention to the boys lined up on the couch. The five of them were so young to be learning the hard truths of life, and yet it was his and Micah's and Emily's jobs as adults, as elders in the faith and as the boys' family, to prepare them for such things.

Jacob understood what his brother was asking.

He thought of that morning, of the reflection in the mirror of two different men—only there weren't two different men. His scarred self didn't exist in isolation from the whole. He was one person, and if he believed the truth in the Good Book his brother was holding, then he needed to accept the person *Gotte* had created him to be.

Clearing his throat he sat forward, elbows propped on his knees, fingers interlaced. "Job loved *Gotte*, as we do, *ya*?"

All five boys nodded in unison.

"But his experiences had taught him that *Gotte*'s plan for his life might be painful, might be hard to understand at times. Those plans had him scarred and hurting, and so he was afraid."

No one spoke, and Jacob knew that they were waiting, that his family had been waiting for him to reach this point a long time—for six years, to be exact.

"It's a hard thing to know that bad things can happen to us, like the fire that took *Daddi* and *Mammi*."

"They're in heaven now." Joseph swung his foot back and forth, bumping the bottom of the couch.

"*Ya*, they are."

"But you're still scarred." Eli touched the left side of Jacob's face.

"I am scarred," he admitted. "And I have to accept that somehow *Gotte* still has a plan for me, that what happened—that it wasn't a mistake. After all, *Gotte* could have sent a rainstorm and put out that fire… right?"

"Ya." Thomas, the practical one, crossed his arms. "I don't get it."

Jacob's laughter surprised everyone, including himself. "I'm not sure that we have to *get it*, but we do need to keep the faith, whether we understand or not."

They joined hands then, heads bowed in silent prayer, until Micah spoke aloud and asked the Lord to bless their day. The moment he said *amen*, the twins were headed out the door, Eli pulled a book out of his pocket and began to read it, and Micah asked for Samuel's help with setting things up for the luncheon. Joseph muttered something about a pet frog and hurried toward the mudroom.

It was Emily who held back. Standing on tiptoe, she planted a kiss on the left side of Jacob's face. Her stomach was rounded with her sixth child, and she had to lean forward to kiss his cheek. For a moment, Jacob thought he felt the life inside of her press up against him.

"What's that for?" Though he was embarrassed, he couldn't stop the smile that was spreading across his face.

"Just glad to see you is all." But the tears shining in her eyes told him it was more.

He patted her on the shoulder. Even he knew that pregnant women were emotional. He didn't want to be the cause of starting the waterworks before everyone arrived.

He needn't have worried, though. She was humming a tune as she waddled into the kitchen. It was only as he was left standing in the sitting room alone that he realized the song she was humming was "Amazing Grace."

By the time Hannah and Claire were done with the breakfast dishes, Hannah's father and Matthew were in the sitting room, waiting. Their devotional was from Christ's Sermon on the Mount.

Her father patiently answered Matthew's questions and then they all prayed for a few minutes. The devotional time reminded Hannah of her childhood, of sitting with her sisters, squirming on the couch much as Matthew was now squirming in his chair.

It took another hour to pack up the dishes they were taking for the luncheon, along with any special items Matthew might need. The weather was warm for the first weekend of September, and there was no chance of rain, which made it a perfect day for a Sunday social. They had to drive past Jacob's place to reach Emily's.

Matthew pointed out the workshop to his grandparents. "That's where *Mamm* works. I saw it, and Jacob took me around to look at his projects."

He rode in the back seat with Hannah and had his nose pressed to the buggy window. "Why can't we go there?"

"Because lunch is at Emily's," Hannah explained for the third time.

"And Emily is Jacob's *schweschder*."

"*Ya.* She married Jacob's brother, Micah. That makes them *bruder* and *schweschder*."

Matthew had more questions, but they were pulling into Emily and Micah's drive, and their buggy was suddenly surrounded by boys as well as an old gray dog.

Before Hannah had a chance to protest, her father

had loaded Matthew into his wheelchair and Emily's boys had taken off with him across the yard.

"Maybe I should go..."

"He'll be fine," Emily assured her. "Come and have a glass of lemonade. It's warm out today, *ya*?"

She introduced Hannah to her parents and two more couples who were neighbors. They spent the next twenty minutes drinking lemonade and talking about crops and school and the general state of things in Goshen. Hannah was pretending to pay attention, but trying to catch sight of Matthew. Emily's boys had whisked him away, and she hadn't even had a chance to explain how to set the brake on the chair or what to do if he stopped breathing.

That last thought was ridiculous.

Why would he stop breathing?

But he might, and she hadn't explained what to do.

She excused herself from the group of adults and made her way over to the trampoline where Emily's twins were practicing flips. No sign of Matthew there. Hurrying toward the barn she spied the two oldest boys throwing horseshoes. Matthew wasn't watching that either. Which left the youngest boy—Joseph. Her son's life was in the hands of a six-year-old.

Her heart thumped and her palms began to sweat as she hurried toward the barn. Two thin lines in the dirt assured her that Matthew's chair had been pushed in this direction. She practically ran into the barn and slammed straight into Jacob.

"Whoa, there. Something wrong?"

"It's Matthew..." She glanced up at him, remembered his fingers brushing her arm the day before and glanced away. "I've been looking for him. I was worried that—"

"Just breathe, Hannah. Matthew is fine."

"Are you sure?"

"*Ya.* Come with me. I'll show you."

Jacob led her through the main room of the barn and toward the area where Micah kept his horses.

He reached the last stall and stopped, motioning for her to tiptoe toward him. They both peered around the corner.

Joseph was picking up a newborn kitten and setting it in Matthew's lap.

"I can hold him?"

"Sure."

"But what if I—"

"You won't."

"Are you sure I won't hurt him?"

"Look, he likes you."

The cat's cries subsided as Matthew bent over the small furry bundle in his lap.

"He's purring," Matthew said.

"*Ya.* He's happy."

"And the momma cat doesn't mind?"

"Probably not, for a minute or so at least."

They proceeded to discuss the merits of the different kittens—stripes over solids, large over small, loud over quiet. Jacob tugged on Hannah's arm and pulled her away from the stall. They walked out the side door of the barn into a day that was more summer than fall. Perhaps because he'd been in the barn the colors seemed brighter, the breeze sweeter. Or maybe that was due to the woman standing beside him.

He stepped to her left so that the right side of his face would be facing her. Then he realized what he'd done and felt like an idiot, as if he could impress her with half of his face. He hadn't been particularly good-looking before the fire.

They walked away from the barn, and he steered Hannah toward Emily's garden. The vegetables had all been harvested, but the flowers were a sight to behold.

"When Emily first married Micah, she couldn't keep a tomato plant alive. She'd spend time with *Mamm* in the garden every afternoon, and I guess some of *Mamm*'s gardening skills rubbed off on her."

"This is beautiful."

They walked up and down the rows and finally stopped at a bench.

"Danki," Hannah said.

"For?"

"For taking me to him."

"You were worried."

"For inviting us here."

"That was really Emily's doing."

"For being our friend."

"Of course I'm your friend, Hannah."

Instead of answering, she became preoccupied with her *kapp* strings, running them through her fingers again and again.

Finally he said, "Tell me about David."

Her eyebrows arched up in surprise. "My husband?"

"Ya."

"You mean how he died."

"I heard about that, and I'm sorry."

She glanced away, but she seemed more surprised than offended so he pushed on.

"I meant more what was he like? I know he was from

the Shipshe district, but I only met him once or twice, both times at the auction."

"He was a *gut* man."

"I'm sure he was."

"I miss him."

"Of course you do."

Hannah smiled and chuckled softly. "He wasn't perfect, though. He thought Wisconsin was the promised land. We moved there only a few months after we married."

"And was it? The promised land?"

"In truth it was remote, and the Plain community there was different. I won't say it was worse, but it took some getting used to. One half allowed for gas appliances, even solar energy. The other? They were more Old Order, at least in practice."

"I've heard about the ice fishing there."

"*Ach.* The winters were incredibly difficult. We had more than forty inches of snow each of the winters I was there."

"That much?"

"*Ya.* It was very different from here."

"Were you happy—living in this promised land?"

"We were."

"That's *gut.*"

"I haven't spoken of him, for a while. You know how it is in a Plain community."

"We believe his life was complete."

"Yes." Her voice grew softer so that he had to lean toward her more to make out her words. "I want Matthew to know about his father. He might not be old enough to have his own memories, but I want to share mine."

"You're a *gut mamm.*"

She shrugged her shoulders. "Some days I wonder about that."

There was a racket across from them and then Matthew and Joseph tumbled out of the barn, Joseph pushing as fast as he could and then jumping on the back of the wheelchair as if it were a bicycle. Matthew's laughter carried across to them.

"I should go and see if he needs anything."

"Does it look like he needs anything?"

She laughed then. "I suppose you're right."

"I want to show you something."

He led her down the path to the other end of the garden.

"Why have you never married?" Her hand flew to her mouth and her eyes widened. "That was rude of me. I shouldn't have asked."

"It's nothing my family doesn't ask me every chance they get."

"They worry about you."

"I suppose. Emily and Micah, they think because they're happy that everyone should be married with a houseful of *kinder*."

"And you don't want that?"

"I don't know. It would take a special person to be able to put up with me."

"Because of your scars?"

"Partly."

"But they're only…scars."

Jacob glanced at her and then away. "I don't really see them anymore. Sometimes I forget and look in the mirror and I'm surprised. Or a child sees me, say an *Englischer* in town or a new family in our community, and they point or ask questions…"

"Curious, I suppose."

"Yes, but it reminds me that my face is frightening to some people."

"Surely it's not as bad as all that."

Jacob didn't argue the point. She couldn't know what it was like to live his life, to see the looks of revulsion on people's faces.

"This is what I wanted to show you." He led her under an arbor with a thick vine covering it. A path wound through clumps of butterfly weeds with bright orange flowers sitting atop three-foot stems. Back among the taller blooms on a piece of board taken from an old barn, someone had painted the names of his parents and placed it into the ground like a street sign.

"It's how we remember them."

"You have a garden at your house too."

"*Ya.* Not as well tended as Emily's, but we both make an effort to spend time in them. It's our way of being sure my parents' memory stays with the children."

"It's nice here. I like it."

"*Mamm* loved her garden. She sometimes needed time away from two rambunctious boys. *Dat* would tell us to clean up the dishes, and he'd head out to the garden with a cup of hot tea for her. I'd find them there sometimes, holding hands, their heads together like two *youngies*."

"That's a special memory, Jacob."

"It is."

"Thank you for sharing it with me—for showing me this."

"You're welcome. I'm glad you and Matthew were able to come today."

And then he did something he wouldn't have believed that he had the courage to do. He stepped forward, touched Hannah's face until she looked up at him and softly kissed her lips.

She froze, like a deer caught in a buggy's headlights.

Blushing a bright red, she stepped away, stared at the ground, looked back at him and finally said, "I really should see if he needs me."

Jacob nodded as if he understood, but as she was hurrying back over to the picnic tables, it seemed to him that she wasn't actually running toward Matthew. It was more as if she was running away from him, and could he really blame her? What had possessed him to think that she would enjoy a stroll through the garden with him?

What had prompted him to kiss her? Perhaps that had been a mistake. It wasn't something he could take back, though, so he straightened his suspenders and headed over to where the boys were playing horseshoes.

Hannah didn't breathe freely until she was sitting among the women, listening to them discuss the best fall recipes. She wasn't thinking about pumpkin-spice bread or butternut squash casserole, though. She was thinking about her son holding a kitten, about the fact that he had a new friend, about the garden and about Jacob.

She was thinking about that kiss.

When he'd spoken about his scars, she'd had an urge to reach out and touch them, to assure him that they all had scars.

She'd wanted to tell him that she had scars too.

Her heart probably looked worse than his face...it was only that people couldn't see those scars. She kept them hidden. She smiled and pretended everything was fine.

She pretended through the meal as she made sure that Matthew ate.

She pretended as she watched Matthew go off again, this time with Emily's entire clan of boys.

She pretended while the women circled up and spoke of the upcoming school auction.

"I'm growing old and forgetful," her mother said. "I meant to clean out my casserole dish before the leftover potatoes become as hard as concrete."

"I'll get it, *Mamm*."

"Oh, I didn't mean for you to do that."

"It's not a problem." She was actually relieved to be away from the group of women, though she'd run toward them before the meal. Still, an hour spent in their presence and her cheeks hurt from trying to smile. She was happy for an excuse to spend a few minutes alone.

She retrieved the dish from the table, took it into Emily's kitchen and rinsed it out.

As she scrubbed away at the residual cheese, her thoughts returned to Jacob—to doubts and questions and scars and hurts.

She was thinking of that, of how some hurts showed physically while others remained concealed when she stepped outside and practically collided with Elizabeth Byler.

"Hannah. Could you help me with this?"

Hannah made a practice of avoiding Elizabeth, who she remembered from her youth. Elizabeth was a negative person with a nasty habit of gossiping, but the woman was holding a large tray filled with used coffee mugs.

It would be rude to run away.

"Of course. Let me hold the door."

"Emily was going to leave this out in the sun, covered with flies. Best to get them in and cleaned."

"Oh…"

"If you'll wash, I'll dry."

Hannah smiled her answer, since there seemed to be no way to avoid spending twenty minutes in the kitchen with the woman.

She'd barely run soapy water into the sink when Elizabeth started in on what was obviously her agenda.

"Saw you walking off with Jacob."

"*Ya*, he wanted to show me the garden."

"You're not the first."

"First?"

"Probably won't be the last."

"The last to what?"

"Set your *kapp* on Jacob Schrock, which is why I thought it my job to warn you."

"Warn me?" Hannah stared at the woman in disbelief.

"That road goes nowhere. You're wasting your time with that one."

Hannah felt her temper rise. She tried to focus on the mug she was filling with soapy water, but the buzzing in her ears was a sure sign that she was about to say something she'd regret.

"Give it a month, at the most two, and you'll be crying on someone's shoulder about how your heart is broken. Best to listen to sense. No disrespect to Micah, but his *bruder* Jacob is spoiled goods."

Hannah's hands froze on the mug she was washing. "Surely you don't mean that."

"Don't look at me that way, Hannah. You know better than anyone what it's like to live with a person who has been damaged. Would you want Matthew married to someone?"

"Excuse me?" Hannah dropped the mug into the water, causing suds to splash up and onto her sleeves.

"Don't get me wrong. *Gotte* has a plan for every life."

"Nice of you to admit that."

"Jacob's tried dating a few times, but it didn't work out. He has quite the chip on his shoulder. I will admit that financially he's certainly a catch since he inherited that farm from his parents."

"So now he's a catch?"

"Some women think so."

"Elizabeth, I don't know what to say."

"You could thank me for speaking the truth. I'm only trying to help you see straight."

"That's very kind of you."

"Wisdom, Hannah. It comes with age. You'll see. Think about it. What woman would want to wake up to a disfigured husband every morning?"

"That's uncharitable, Elizabeth."

"Not to mention that Jacob feels sorry for himself, as if he's the only one who has troubles."

Hannah gave up on washing the mug, dropped it into the sudsy water and carefully dried her hands on a dishrag. She attempted to count to ten but only made it to three.

"I think I'm needed outside."

"It won't be the first time I'm left to do dishes by myself."

"Maybe that's because you're a bitter, unpleasant person."

Beth's mouth opened into a perfect *O*, but no sound came out.

"I'm sorry. I know your life has been hard too, with Jared's drinking problem and all…"

"I do not want to talk about Jared."

"But your personal trials don't give you a reason to speak ill of Jacob—"

"I did not."

"Also, I'd appreciate it if you'd refrain from determining the course of my son's life when he is but four years old." And with that, Hannah turned and walked back out into the afternoon sunshine, feeling better than she had in a very long time.

It wasn't until she was on her way home in the buggy that she allowed her mind to comb back over Elizabeth's harsh words. Her parents were speaking quietly in the front, and Matthew had fallen asleep with his head in her lap. She was brushing the hair out of his eyes, thinking of what a beautiful and kind child he was, when Elizabeth's words came back to her as clearly as if the woman were sitting beside her in the buggy.

You're not the first.

Probably won't be the last.

Financially he's certainly a catch.

There were women in their district interested in Jacob? Well, of course there were. That shouldn't surprise her one bit, and it certainly wasn't any of her business.

She had no plans of dating the man, despite the kiss. That had been an impulsive thing for him to do. Somewhere deep inside she'd known he was going to. She should have kept her distance. What had she been thinking?

She worked for him. She wanted to help her parents and to provide for Matthew. She didn't need to step out with anyone. She had no intention of doing such a thing. If Elizabeth thought so, that was her misunderstanding.

Jacob was a friend, a neighbor of sorts and her employer. He was nothing more, and though she might defend him to nosy interfering women, she had no intention of falling in love with the man. Her heart had suffered enough damage, or so she told herself as the sun began to set across the Indiana fields.

Chapter Eleven

The next week passed quickly. Jacob managed to finish the bin of receipts that he'd been assigned, as had his nephews and Hannah's niece. If he managed to survive this audit, it would be because they'd worked together.

He peeked into the office as often as he dared, and slowly Hannah managed to create order out of his chaos. She'd asked him to find a filing cabinet, and earlier in the week he'd spied one that had been set out in the trash by a local Realtor. After checking to be sure it was free, he strapped it to the back of his buggy, brought it home, cleaned it inside and out, and oiled the tracks the drawers ran on.

"Could use a new paint job, but I suppose it will do."

"It's perfect." Hannah had already purchased a box of folders and the next day she transferred the taped-up receipts to the file drawers—chronological, three years per drawer, orderly and neat.

He hoped the IRS agent would be impressed. He certainly was. The bins were stacked in the corner of the room and when they were all empty, he carried them to the stall he used as a storage place.

Hannah beamed as if she'd baked the perfect apple pie. She was proud of her work, as she should be. He thought again of the bonus he meant to give her, almost said something, but decided to wait. If he owed money to the government, he would need to meet that obligation first. It would be wrong to suggest she might receive extra money for her labor and then disappoint her.

But he wanted to raise her hopes, to ease the worry he saw in her eyes. How much money had her sisters and parents been able to raise? He spoke to her again about approaching her bishop and asking for help, but she only shook her head and said something about *humility* and *Gotte's wille* and *stubborn men*.

Every time he saw her, he thought of the kiss they'd shared.

Hannah, on the other hand, seemed completely focused on the audit. It was after lunch on Friday when she finally admitted, "I think we're ready."

The office barely resembled the place it had been before Hannah came to work there. A bright yellow basket of mums sat next to a pot of aloe vera. The afternoon light splashed through the sparkling panes of glass. Hannah's sweater was draped across the back of the new office chair he'd purchased and the shelf held her quilted lunch bag. She opened the bottom drawer of the desk and pulled out her purse.

"So you're headed home?"

"*Ya.* Matthew has therapy today."

"Of course. How's he doing?"

"*Gut.* Getting stronger, I think. It helps that he's able to have the same therapist every time he goes."

She stood there, waiting, as Jacob's mind jumped back and forth looking for something else to say. He wasn't ready for her to leave, but he realized he looked like a fool, standing there silently and twirling his hat in his hands. He crammed it back on his head and said perhaps too gruffly, "*Danki* for your help."

"Of course. It's what you hired me for."

"*Ya*, but we both know you've gone above and beyond. I don't know if we'll pass the audit or not, but if we do, it's because of you."

"And your nephews and my niece."

"Ya." The same thought he'd had earlier. It was almost as if she understood his thoughts.

She blushed prettily then, and he nearly asked her out to eat or to go for a buggy ride or perhaps hire a driver to take them to Shipshe. But she was already gathering her things together, talking about a cousin from Pennsylvania who was coming into town and how she needed to help her *mamm* prepare.

It seemed her weekend was full of plans, so he wished her a good afternoon and pretended there was a rocker he needed to finish working on.

There was a rocker he needed to work on—and a dresser, a coffee table, as well as plans for a playhouse later in the month. He tried working on each one, but he couldn't seem to find the right sandpaper, or varnish or idea. Finally he gave up, harnessed Bo to the buggy and headed toward town.

Jacob was standing in line at the library and thought the woman in line ahead of him was Hannah. He made a fool of himself calling out to her only to have the stranger look at him oddly and hurry off.

His gelding, Bo, seemed full of energy, so Jacob decided to head north of town and scout the area where he'd be building a playhouse for a child with Down syndrome. He thought he passed Hannah on the road and his heart rate accelerated and he waved his hand out the window, but it wasn't Hannah. Of course it wasn't. Matthew's therapy appointment was in the middle of town, not on a country road headed north, plus the horse he'd just waved at was a nice roan and Hannah's horse was chestnut.

He even convinced himself that it was her buggy parked in front of his brother's house. When he pulled in, with the excuse that he'd promised his nephews he'd come by and pick up one of the kittens, he found it was one of the older women from the next district who'd stopped by to drop off two bags of clothes for the boys. Too late—he either had to admit he'd made up the excuse or go to the barn and pick out a kitten.

The boys gave him the black one with white patches around its eyes.

"Don't forget to feed it." Tim looked concerned.

"Of course I'll feed it."

"Do you even have cat food?" Thomas asked.

"No. I don't have a cat."

"You do now." Samuel reached forward and scratched the kitten between the ears. "We'll loan you some until you get to the store."

Joseph ran off to fetch a container.

Jacob tried to stifle the groan, but without much success.

"Didn't know you were in the market for a cat, *bruder*." Micah stood grinning at him, as if he too could read his mind.

"I've been wrestled into this."

"*Ya*, my *kinder* are quite convincing."

"And don't leave him in the barn alone, Jacob." Eli

looked at him with the seriousness only a nine-year-old could muster. "Are you sure you don't want two?"

"I'm not sure I want one."

"Then put him in your mudroom. He needs to be able to hear you so he won't be scared."

His trailer didn't have a mudroom, but Jacob decided not to point that out. Perhaps he could make a place for the kitten next to his washing machine, or in the office. Wouldn't that be a nice surprise for Hannah? The IRS agent might not appreciate it, so perhaps he'd wait until the end of the audit. In the meantime, he'd try to find out whether she even liked animals.

He whistled as he drove back toward his house, realizing that he'd made it through Friday. Two more days to stumble through and then Hannah would be back at her desk.

"It's *gut* when family comes to visit, *ya*?" Hannah's mom slipped a cup of coffee in front of her.

Matthew was in bed.

Her father was checking things in the barn.

And the weekend was finally over.

"*Ya*, it is."

"Only…?"

"I wasn't about to add anything else."

Her mother sipped her coffee, studying her over the rim of the cup.

"I suppose I was thinking about the audit tomorrow," Hannah said.

"Are you ready?"

"I've done my best."

"Then you're ready." Her mother reached forward and patted the back of her hand.

When Hannah looked down and saw that, her mother's hand on top of hers, something stirred in her chest. Too often she took her parents for granted, took her life for granted. What would Jacob give for just one more hour of sipping coffee with his parents?

"And now I've upset you."

"*Nein.* It's only, I was thinking of Jacob and how awful it would be to lose your parents."

Her *mamm* sat back, reached for a peanut butter bar, broke it in half and pushed a portion of it toward Hannah. "No one lives forever."

"I know that."

"Not that I'm in a hurry to die."

"I should hope not."

"You're thinking of this all wrong."

"I am?"

"It's true that Jacob is lonely, and that he's looking for his way in life."

"He's lonely?"

"But as for his parents? Don't mourn them, Hannah. They are resting in the arms of *Gotte*, dancing around his throne. What we see dimly they see clearly now."

Hannah couldn't help laughing. "I guess when you put it that way..."

"Now tell me about Jacob."

"About him?"

"Has he kissed you yet?"

"Mamm!"

"You don't have to share if you don't want to."

Hannah changed the subject. They sat there for another half hour, speaking of relatives, the coming fall and Matthew's birthday. What they didn't discuss sat between them. Though Hannah wanted to ask about the amount they owed the bank and how they were progressing toward meeting that debt, she didn't want to ruin this moment on a Sunday night, sitting in the house she'd grown up in. She didn't want to think about where they might be in a month or a year. She wanted to close her eyes and pretend, just for a moment, that everything would be fine.

Hannah and Jacob stood shoulder to shoulder, staring out the window as the small green car pulled down the lane. It stopped well shy of the parking area.

"What's she doing?" Hannah stepped closer, practically rubbing her nose against the glass.

If anything, she seemed more keyed up than Jacob felt.

He attempted to ease her nerves by putting a hand on her shoulder, but she jumped as if he'd stuck her with a hot poker.

"It's going to be fine," he said.

"*Ya*, but what's she doing? Who stops in the middle of a lane?"

"Looks like she's on her phone."

"Maybe she thinks she can't use it in here."

"Or maybe she has an important call. Maybe there's an emergency audit that she needs to leave for."

Hannah bumped her shoulder against his. "Don't joke that way. We need this to be over."

"She's moving again."

The car stopped next to the hitching post.

"How can an *Englisch* vehicle be that quiet?"

"My guess would be that it's electric and expensive."

"Electric? So she has to…plug it in?"

"*Ya*, they have a large battery that holds a significant charge. You have to plug them in at night."

"What if you run out of…" Hannah twirled her finger round and round.

"Juice? There's a backup fuel supply like other *Englisch* cars use."

"How do you know all this?"

Jacob shrugged. They might be Amish, but they didn't live on the moon. Most men, Amish or *Englisch*, were interested when a new type of vehicle came out. He'd read a few articles on electric cars. He considered explaining that to Hannah, but she was already moving toward the door of the barn, so he squared his shoulders and followed her.

The *Englisch* woman looked to be in her early twenties. She had pale skin, spiky black hair and multiple piercings in both ears. Roughly Hannah's height, she looked more like a girl than a woman. She was dressed in a sweater-type dress that settled two inches above her knees and high-heeled leather boots. Jacob wouldn't have guessed her weight to be more than a hundred pounds.

She'd made it out of the car, but now she stood halfway between it and them, staring down at her phone, her thumbs flying over the mobile device. There was a swish sound and then she dropped it into her leather handbag and looked up at them.

"I'm Piper Jenkins, your IRS auditor. You must be Jacob."

"*Ya*, Jacob Schrock. Good to meet you."

She turned to Hannah, but then a buzz came from her purse. She reached into it and scooped out her phone. Rolling her eyes, she dropped it back into the bag.

"I'm Hannah King. I've been helping Jacob with his accounts." Hannah clasped her hands in front of her. She'd admitted earlier that morning that she was worried the auditor would question her credentials.

Jacob almost laughed at the look of relief on her face when Piper said, "Oh, good. I'm glad to hear that he has help. Many of the Amish men I've audited try to take care of accounting on their own, and that doesn't usually end well."

"It's certainly not something I excel at," Jacob said. "If you'd like to come inside, we've set up a place for you to work in the office."

Hannah had arrived a half hour early that morning, all in a frenzy because they hadn't thought to set up a work area for the woman. In short order, Jacob had dragged in a desk that he was working on for a client, Hannah had popped her chair next to the desk and he'd retrieved the stool that she had originally used.

"Are you sure you wouldn't rather have your old office chair?" He'd put it in the corner of his workroom and used it to stack items on. The new kitten, Blackie, had taken it over and turned it into her daytime napping spot.

"That old thing? I'm surprised it holds the cat. No thank you. I'll take the stool."

They'd pushed the desks so that the two women would be facing each other. It was crowded, but it worked.

Now Piper walked into the room, paused a moment and then nodded in approval. "Let's see what you've got for me."

It occurred to Jacob that he should be tense, but honestly he believed that he'd done right by the US Treasury

Department. Perhaps he hadn't filed the correct forms, but he'd paid his fair share of taxes. He wasn't worried about the outcome, especially with Hannah at the helm.

She had saved him, in more ways than one.

He no longer rose each morning wondering what the point was, or went to sleep worried that the days stretched out endlessly in front of him. She'd done more than straighten up his accounting—she'd added hope and optimism to his life.

That thought was foremost on his mind as the two women began pulling out files and pencils and calculators and highlighters and rulers. He'd never been so happy to walk into the other room and pick up a piece of sandpaper in his life. He did not want to be anywhere near what was going on between those two, but he'd stay close just in case they needed him.

His fervent prayer was that they wouldn't.

"It's you and me, Blackie." The cat wound around his legs, purring and leaving a trail of black hair. Arching her back, she stretched, then flopped in a ray of sunlight.

"Uh-huh. Well, the rest of us have work to do."

Three days later, the audit was over.

"We're not allowed to recommend businesses to help with audits." Piper stole one last glance at her cell phone, typed something in with a flurry of her thumbs, then dropped it into her purse. She finished putting her pens, highlighters, computer and notepad into her matching designer backpack. Finally she glanced up at Hannah and seemed surprised to find her still there. "I'm sorry, what was I saying?"

"That you're not allowed to recommend businesses."

"Right. But there is a place on the Goshen Chamber of Commerce website to list your services, and I recommend that you do so. I see a lot of businesses, especially Amish businesses, that could use your organizational skills."

Hannah glanced up at Jacob, who was trying to hide a smile.

"Danki," she said. She didn't add that she wouldn't be listing her services. She had a job with Jacob, and she liked the work. Plus, he needed her. Left to his own devices he'd be stacking up bins of receipts again in no time.

A small buzz permeated the silence. Piper snatched the phone back out of her bag, typed again, smiled to herself,and dropped it back in before turning her attention to Jacob. "I hope you appreciate her."

"Oh, I do." He glanced at Hannah and wiggled his eyebrows.

She gave him her most stern look.

How could he play around with an IRS auditor standing in the office?

"You'll receive a letter within ten days stating that the audit has been closed." She glanced at Hannah, smiled and leveled a piercing gaze at Jacob. "You passed with flying colors, and the refund that you're owed will be applied to this year's bill, per your instructions."

She headed toward the door, then stopped and turned back toward them. "I want to thank you both for the work you do for children with disabilities. It's a very good thing, and I'm sure it brings much joy into their lives."

And then she was gone.

Hannah finally let out the breath that it seemed she'd

been holding since Monday morning. "I wonder what she does on that phone."

"Same as writing a letter—at least that's what the *youngies* say."

"Who has that many letters to write?"

"Indeed."

"Makes me glad we don't have them."

"Oh? You don't want an *Englisch* cell phone?"

"I do not." She knew he was teasing and realized she shouldn't rise to the bait, but she couldn't help herself. "I'm the one who spent the last few days with Piper Jenkins."

"I was hiding in the workshop."

"I noticed."

"Can you blame me?"

"The woman couldn't finish a sentence without checking the screen of her cell phone at least once. Seems a complete waste of time to me." She sounded old, sounded like one of their elders who insisted that all change was dangerous. She didn't believe that, but she didn't know how to explain to Jacob what she was feeling and why.

So instead she turned her attention to pulling out her work for the day—the receipts Jacob had given her from the previous week. She knew he was still standing there, still watching her and it made her heart beat wildly and her palms sweat. Finally she looked up, met his gaze and tried not to return the smile.

She pretended to glance back down at her work. She was finding it harder and harder to maintain the distance she had sworn that she would put between her and Jacob. He'd somehow found a way to worm into her heart, slide beneath her defenses and scale the wall she'd built with such determination.

He reached into his jacket and pulled out an envelope. "This is the missing check you couldn't find."

"Oh."

"I wrote it a week ago."

"You did?"

"And I've been holding it for the right moment."

She glanced up now, and when she looked at Jacob she felt like she was leaping into a giant pool of water. Though she'd been terrified when he'd kissed her, today it seemed like the fear that had permeated her decisions and her emotions since the accident was gone. "Now is the right moment?"

"It is."

She took the envelope and stared down at her name in his familiar handwriting.

"It's for me?"

"*Ya*, it's for you, Hannah, because of how much help you've been."

"But you pay me a salary to be helpful."

"You've gone above and beyond. Believe me, I know that I couldn't have passed that audit without you. I'd have needed to hire one of the *Englisch* accountants, and that would have cost me much more than the amount of the check you're holding."

"Jacob…"

"Open it."

She turned it over, slipped her nail beneath the flap and opened the envelope. When she pulled out the check, when she saw the amount written there, she tried to thrust it back into his hands.

"I can't take this."

"Of course you can."

"It's too much."

"*Nein.* It's the right amount, and it was the right amount whether we passed the audit or not." He walked around, took the envelope and check from her, and set them on the desk. Then he reached for her hands. "I know you've been taking work home, working longer hours than you've been reporting."

"I wanted to be ready." She tried to still the trembling in her arms and resist the urge to look up into his eyes. She knew if she did, if she allowed herself to see the goodness and kindness there, that there would be no turning back.

Jacob's voice was soft, and he rubbed his thumbs over the backs of her hands. "And I appreciate that. The amount of the check, even with what I've been paying you, it's nowhere near what the accountant in town was going to charge me."

"But—"

"I want you to have it, Hannah. I want you to use it to help your father."

And those were the magic words that convinced her to pull her hands away from his, pick up the check and tuck it into her purse.

Her heart was hammering, and she was trying to remember what she was about to do before he'd offered her the envelope.

Jacob walked back to the door and had stepped into the main room, but he pivoted back toward her, still smiling. "I forgot to tell you that your *dat* called. He's going to be later than he thought and asked if I could take you home."

"You don't have to do that."

"It's a long way to walk."

He laughed and she realized what a handsome man Jacob was. She'd not really thought about it. Oh, she'd spent many hours thinking about how she felt around him, but not about his appearance. She understood as she studied him with the afternoon sun slanting across the floor that when she looked at Jacob she didn't see his scars anymore. They weren't who he was, they were simply a reminder of something that had happened to him and of how precious life really was.

"I need to go by the Troyer home. It's on the way to your place. Do you mind?"

"Nein."

"Leave in an hour?"

"*Ya.* An hour will be fine." She couldn't look at him any longer, couldn't meet those eyes that made her feel like she was falling. Instead she stared down at the receipts in her hand until she heard him walk away.

Then she collapsed into her chair and covered her face with her hands.

The audit was over.

They'd passed.

And hopefully she'd made enough money to help save her father's farm.

Chapter Twelve

Jacob tried to focus on the bedside table he was working on finishing. It was a simple piece made from walnut wood, and he should have been done with it already. He opened the drawer, confirming that it slid smoothly along the grooves. Then he stood it up on his workbench and began cleaning it one final time. Some furniture makers used fancy cleansers, but Jacob preferred doing things the old way—a little dish soap in warm water worked fine.

Using a soft cloth, he went over the table's surface three times. He wanted to remove all dust particles before putting on the final coat. Thirty minutes passed, and he found he was still cleaning the piece. In fact, he'd been rubbing the cloth over the same side for several minutes.

Once he was sure it was completely dry, he would apply a final coat of beeswax on the piece, but what was he to do with the next twenty minutes while Hannah finished up in the office? The memory of how she'd smiled at him, of the look of gratitude on her face when she'd accepted the check, made his thoughts scurry in a dozen directions—directions his thoughts had no business going.

Because it wasn't possible that Hannah King was interested in him romantically.

But what if she was?

She hadn't exactly run away when he'd kissed her at his brother's. Okay, she *had* run away, but maybe because she was embarrassed or confused. It didn't necessarily mean she didn't like it.

He dropped the rag in disgust and walked outside.

Maybe fresh air would help to clear his head.

But the problem wasn't the stuffiness in the workshop or the table he'd been working on. The problem was admitting what he felt for Hannah.

He walked across to the garden, wandered down the path and stopped at a bench. Sitting down, he glanced around him, then hopped right back up. He needed to keep moving. He needed to settle the restless feeling that made his heart gallop like Bo running across a field. That was normal behavior for a horse, but he was a man and he should have better control of his thoughts and his feelings.

A butterfly landed on a white aster bush in full bloom and then a red bird hopped onto the path in front of him. He stood there, frozen, watching it. Red birds were his mother's favorite bird. Her voice came back to him in that moment—gentle, full of wisdom, full of love.

A cardinal can be a special sign from your loved one in heaven.

When he closed his eyes he saw both his mother and father sitting on the front porch, talking and shelling peas between them, when the cardinal alighted on the porch rail. He had walked up and laughed at them, told them they looked like two old folks sitting around rocking and gossiping. His father had smiled knowingly, but his mother had pointed out the red bird.

Jacob missed them more than he would have thought possible, even after all these years. They'd been good people and what had happened to them, it didn't make any sense to him.

It wasn't that he doubted *Gotte's wille* for their lives; it was only that he didn't understand why it had to cause such pain…why their lives had to be complete at that moment, why they couldn't have stayed and grown old together and met all of their grandchildren.

Walking on through the garden, he circled back toward the workshop and saw the silhouette of Hannah working in the office. What would his mother think of her? Of Matthew? He knew the answer to both questions, and the knowledge of that caused him to laugh out loud. He'd turned twenty when his mother had begun to tease him about settling down and marrying.

A plump wife and a big barn never did any man harm.

An industrious wife is the best savings account.

Marriage may be made in heaven, but man is responsible for the upkeep.

They had never doubted that he would one day marry, that having a family was the life *Gotte* had chosen for him just as it was for his brother.

Yes, his mother would like Hannah and Matthew.

She would approve of the feelings that Jacob was struggling with.

Both his mother and his father would want him to continue on with his life, and in that moment he knew that it was all right for him to want a family, to want Hannah and Matthew. It was all right for him to move on from mourning his parents, and to finally let go of the guilt that he carried. He might not understand the path his life had taken, the scars and battles and fears that had consumed the last few years, but he understood where he was at this moment.

And he understood that it was time to step out in faith.

Hannah was quiet as they made their way down the road. She knew she should make conversation, but she didn't know what to say, and her mind kept going back to the bonus check.

Had she thanked him properly?

Should she try to do so now?

But Jacob was talking about the weather and seeing a red bird, and the school auction and picnic coming up on Saturday.

"Well?" he asked.

"Well, what?"

"Your thoughts were drifting."

"*Ya*, I suppose they were."

"I was asking if I could take you to the picnic…you and Matthew."

There were a dozen reasons she should say no, but she heard herself say, "*Ya*, Jacob. That would be nice."

He looked as surprised as she felt.

Grinning he resettled his hat on his head. "*Gut.* I'll be by at eleven on Saturday."

Had she just agreed to go on a date with Jacob? What would she wear? What was she thinking? Was it a date if Matthew was going along? How would she explain to her son that they were just friends? How was she ever going to make it through the workday tomorrow without dying of embarrassment each time he walked into the office?

She couldn't date her boss!

He directed the mare to turn down a lane, toward a house that Hannah had never been to before. It was technically in Jacob's district, and it was newer so it hadn't been there when they were children, when the two districts were one.

"Judith and Tom moved here a few years ago. Their daughter's name is Rachel."

"She's the little girl with cerebral palsy?"

"Right. She's eight, loves to read and is fascinated with any story about princesses."

They found Judith Troyer in the garden behind the house, pulling the last of the produce from her garden. She wore a drab gray dress and a black apron. Her hair was pulled back so tightly that it puckered the skin at the edge of her *kapp*.

Jacob introduced her to Hannah and then said, "The giggle mirror arrived. I was hoping I could install it, if you don't mind."

"Of course I don't mind. *Danki* for bringing it over."

Which was when Hannah noticed the small figure in a wheelchair sitting in what looked like a castle's turret, though it was actually only a couple of feet off the ground. Hannah longed to go and look at the playhouse, to see what Jacob had done, but she felt rude leaving Judith, who had returned to harvesting the few remaining carrots, snap peas and tomatoes.

"May I help?"

Judith looked her up and down and finally shrugged. "Suit yourself."

The house wasn't poor exactly. Hannah picked up a basket from the gardening supplies and moved up and down the rows of vegetables. She kept glancing at the single-story home, the garden, the yard. She tried to put her finger on what was missing.

She pulled off a large bell pepper, a lovely deep red with a rich green stem, and glanced back at the house. That was it. There was no color. No flowers in pots or beds or the garden.

Everything was utilitarian.

No toys scattered around the yard. In fact, the only color came from the playhouse. Jacob had somehow found pink and purple roof tiles which he'd fastened to the top of the turret along with a small flag that waved and crackled in the slight breeze.

"Jacob told me about your son," Judith said.

"Oh. Matthew. *Ya*, Jacob built him a playhouse too. It's how we met—how we met again. We attended school together many years ago, but now my family lives in the next district."

"If you ask me, the playhouses are foolishness."

"Excuse me?"

"A waste of *Englisch* money. I would have told the foundation no, but Tom…" She waved a hand toward the barn. "Tom thinks it will help her, as if a playhouse could do such a thing."

"I'm sorry…about Rachel's condition."

"Not your fault." Judith dropped to her knees and began digging up potatoes. Each time she'd find one, she'd shake it vigorously, as if the dirt clinging to its roots offended her, and then place it in her basket with a *tsk* of disapproval.

"Matthew has enjoyed his playhouse. He can spend hours out there, pretending and reading and enjoying the sunshine." She hadn't realized what a blessing the playhouse was until that moment, until she felt a need to defend it to this woman.

"And what good does that do?"

"Pretending?"

"That and playing…"

"Surely children need to play."

"Acting as if all is well when it isn't and it never will be again."

"So our children shouldn't enjoy life? Because their futures are…" She almost said *bleak*, but she didn't believe that. She thought of Matthew's smile, his quick wit, his loving personality. She thought of his legs, withered and useless. Like Jacob's scars, they weren't who he was; they were only representative of what he had been through.

"They have no future." Judith yanked especially hard on a potato, again spraying dirt over her apron. "No real future at all."

"Of course they do. It might be limited. I know that Matthew will never work in a field or build a barn, but that doesn't mean his life is useless. *Gotte* still has a purpose for his being born, for his being among us."

"Your child is what…four?"

"Nearly five."

"My Rachel is eight. Come back in three years and let's see if you're still so optimistic."

Hannah would have offered a hand of comfort to the woman, because her words seemed to come from a place of deep pain, but Judith was back on her feet moving toward the okra plants at the end of the row. "You can leave the basket by the tools when you're done."

Jacob pushed Rachel's wheelchair as they gave Hannah a tour of the playhouse.

Hannah seemed quite taken with the child. She would repeatedly squat by the chair and ask Rachel questions about what books she liked, who her favorite princess was, whether she enjoyed school.

"I don't always go," the young girl admitted.

Her speech was distorted by the disease, but it was easy enough to make out what she was saying if you listened. Her wheelchair had a special head pad, because she sometimes jerked back and forth. Based on what Tom, the child's father, had explained to Jacob, Rachel was better off than many of the children with CP. She could speak, could feed herself, although it required a special spoon strapped to her hand, and her intelligence was on the normal scale.

Jacob thought she was a beautiful child with a very special smile.

"School prepares people to work," Rachel continued. It was obvious she was repeating what she'd been told by someone, probably her mother. "I won't ever hold a job, so I don't have to go if I don't want to."

"I'm sure you go when you can," Hannah said.

"*Ya*, but *Mamm* says that it doesn't matter much and that if I'd rather stay home..." Rachel's right hand jerked to the side, hitting the padded rail that covered every part of the playhouse. "She says that I don't have to go. I like school, though, and *Dat* says that the teacher misses me when I'm not there."

"I'm sure she does."

Rachel grinned up at both Hannah and Jacob.

"I woke up feeling *narrisch*, but after I lay around all morning *Mamm* finally said I could come out here. I always feel better when I'm in my castle."

"Let's see this funny mirror that Jacob installed."

"It's the best."

They spent the next five minutes giggling and making silly faces in the mirror which pulled and distorted their images like taffy. Finally they wheeled Rachel back to the front porch, and Judith came out and retrieved her without a word. Rachel waved as they walked away, and Jacob assured her he'd be back the following week to see if any updates needed to be made to the playhouse.

Once they were back in the buggy, he noticed that Hannah was uncharacteristically quiet.

"Something wrong?"

"Nein."

"Hmmm...because you were laughing with Rachel, but now you seem quite serious."

Hannah stared down at her hands. "It's only that I spoke with her *mamm*, and it left me feeling...uncertain of things."

Jacob sighed. "I should have warned you about Judith. She has *gut* days and bad ones. I take it today was a bad one."

"She's so bitter and angry."

"Tom thinks it's depression. He finally talked her into a seeing a doctor who did prescribe some medication, but many days she doesn't take it...or so Tom says."

"Can't she see how beautiful Rachel is? What a blessing she is? She's that little girl's mother. She should be able to look past the child's disability."

"I agree with you. All we can do is pray that she'll have a change of heart, that the medicine will work. We'll support them however we can."

"It makes me angry," Hannah admitted.

"Because you have a big heart. You care about children."

"I'm sure Judith cares about Rachel. It's only that..." Tears clogged her voice.

"Don't cry..."

They were nearly to her house. He reached over and squeezed her hand, directed the gelding down the lane, and parked the buggy a discreet distance from the front porch. "What's this about? Why the tears?"

"Because...because..." She swallowed, scrubbed both palms against her cheeks and finally spoke the words that tore at her heart. "Because I was like that."

"You weren't."

"I was, Jacob. You don't know...my thoughts, my anger at *Gotte*, even at other people...people with normal families."

"You're being too hard on yourself." He put a hand on each of her shoulders and turned her toward him. "Listen to me, Hannah. You're a kind, *gut* person, and you're a *wunderbaar* mother. But you're not perfect. No one expects you to be. I'm sure you have spent plenty of nights consumed by anger...same as me."

He waited until she met his gaze. "Same as me, same as probably everyone who has endured a tragedy."

He caressed her arms, clasped her hands in his, reached forward and kissed her softly. "But you came out the other side of that anger. Your faith and your family and your friends saw you through. Judith will find her way too. It's only taking a little longer."

Hannah nodded her head as if what he said made sense, but she quickly gathered her purse and lunch box from the floor of the buggy, whispered, "*Danki* for the ride," and fled into the house.

Hannah waited until Jacob had driven away, then she pulled in a deep breath, scrubbed at her cheeks again and squared her shoulders. She honestly didn't know why meeting Judith had affected her so. The woman was bitter and angry and hurting, but Judith's life wasn't her life.

She walked into the kitchen, surprised no one was there. Pulling the envelope with the bonus check out of her bag, she set it in the middle of the table.

Where was everyone?

She peered out the window at the backyard, garden and playhouse, but no one was there either.

Where was her mother?

Where was Matthew?

Then she heard the sound that she spent nights waiting for, the sound that she often heard in her nightmares—a wet, deep, shuddering cough that meant her son was in trouble.

She ran to his room.

Matthew was in his bed, curled on his side, facing toward her with his eyes shut.

Her mother sat beside him in a chair, and on the nightstand next to her was a basin and a cloth that she was wringing out.

"Hannah, it's *gut* you're home. Matthew isn't feeling so well."

She hurried to the bed, dropped beside it and reached to feel her son's brow. He had at least a low-grade fever, maybe more, but what sent a river of fear tumbling through her heart was the cough. He began hacking again, seemed to lose his breath and finally recovered. Opening his eyes, he smiled briefly at her and reached for her hand.

"My chest hurts," he said in a gravelly voice.

His breath came in short, shallow gasps.

"I know it does, sweetie. We're going to get you some help. You'll feel better soon. Deep breaths, okay?"

Matthew nodded and closed his eyes.

He'd fallen asleep early the night before. She should have noticed. She should have paid closer attention, but her mind had been on the audit.

"We need to get him to the hospital," Hannah said.

"It's only a cough..."

"If you'll go and get the buggy, I'll pull together his things."

She'd left early with her father that morning, left before breakfast. She'd checked on Matthew, but only for a moment and even then she'd been distracted.

Her mother still hadn't moved, though she'd set the cloth down by the basin. "It started this morning, and by this afternoon he seemed a little worse so I put him to bed. The fever is only ninety-nine."

"*Mamm*, listen to me." She turned to look at her mother and saw the fear and confusion there, so she knelt down in front of her and clasped her hands. "You did nothing wrong, but we need to take him to the hospital. We need to go now."

Her mother nodded, though she still seemed confused, dazed almost.

Hannah jumped up and began digging through Matthew's dresser for a change of clothes, the favorite blanket that he kept near him when he was sick and the book they'd been reading.

Her mother moved to her side and said, "Tell me what's happening." She reached out and covered Hannah's hands with her own. "Hannah, look at me and explain to me what is happening."

Hannah took a deep breath, tried to push down the anger and fear. "Because of the injury, Matthew's lungs don't work the same. A small cold can change into pneumonia very quickly."

"Since this morning?"

"*Ya*, since this morning."

Her mother pressed her fingers to her lips and then nodded once, decisively. "Are you sure I should hitch the buggy? Wouldn't it be quicker to call for an ambulance?"

"*Ya*, you're right. That's a better idea."

"I'll go to the phone shack right now."

She heard her mother running through the house, heard the front screen door open and then slam shut.

Hannah stopped digging through the bureau drawer and sank to the floor next to Matthew's bed. "It'll be okay, Matthew. It'll be okay, darling."

He tried to smile at her, but fell into a fit of coughing again, and then he began to shake. "I'm so c…co… cold."

"You'll feel better soon. I promise." She pulled the covers up to his chin and pushed the favorite blanket into his hands.

It seemed only a moment before her mother returned and went into Hannah's room to pull together an overnight bag. "Stay with him. I'll get you a change of clothes. Will we ride with the ambulance?"

"I will, but you'll need to bring the buggy."

Hannah was watching out the window, praying the ambulance would hurry, when her mother walked up beside her and pulled her into her embrace. "I called the bishop too. He's praying, Hannah. Soon our whole congregation will be praying for Matthew. He's going to be all right."

Hannah blinked back hot tears and tried to smile. She needed to be strong now—needed to be strong for Matthew and for her family. They hadn't experienced this type of emergency before, and it could be upsetting—the ambulance and the doctors and the hospital. *Englisch* ways could sometimes be overwhelming and disorienting, and she couldn't begin to guess what the financial cost would be. Her mind darted away from that. There would be time enough to worry over money once Matthew was well, and he would get well.

Her father arrived as the paramedics were loading Matthew into the ambulance. He left the horse untied, still hitched to the buggy and ran toward them.

"*Mamm* will explain. I have to go." Hannah kissed him on the cheek and hopped up into the back of the ambulance.

The siren began to blare as the paramedic slammed the doors shut and then they were speeding down the road.

Chapter Thirteen

Jacob stopped by his brother's place around dinnertime. He wanted to tell his brother about the good news with the IRS audit, and it might have been in the back of his mind that a home-cooked meal would be nice for a change. Emily could work wonders in the kitchen, especially given the fact that she did so with five boys wandering in and out of the room.

But he knew the moment that he arrived that something was wrong.

"Jacob, I was about to send Samuel over."

Samuel stood at the back door, his straw hat pushed down on his head so far that it almost touched his eyes—which would have been comical except for the somber look on his face.

"What's wrong?"

"It's Matthew."

"Hannah's Matthew?"

"He's in the hospital."

"That's not possible." He plopped down onto a kitchen chair. "I was just there, only...only an hour ago."

"It happened fast according to Sally Lapp, who heard it from the bishop."

"But—"

"Sally said it's probably pneumonia." Emily placed a glass of water in front of him and sat down in the adjacent chair. "He's at the hospital. Hannah's parents are there with her. So is our bishop and hers. Sally was planning on going up as soon as she could get there. Apparently she and Hannah have become quite close."

"I need to go. I need to be with her."

"*Ya*, you do." Emily reached out and covered his hand with hers, and that simple touch almost unnerved him.

He'd taken his family for granted for too long.

He could see that now.

"I'll… I'll go straightaway."

"I want to go too." Joseph had been sitting at the end of the table reading a book from school. When Jacob looked over at him, he put a homemade bookmark in the book, shut the cover and stood up. "He's my friend. I should be there."

Samuel tried to talk his younger brother into going outside with him, but Joseph would have none of it. He crossed his arms and declared, "I'm going."

Even Emily couldn't dissuade him.

Finally Jacob said, "I'll take him and send him home with someone else if I decide to stay."

"Of course you'll stay, Jacob. Hannah needs you. Bishop Amos can bring him back. He won't mind."

"*Gut* idea."

"I would go, but…"

"Stay here, with your family. Hannah will understand."

His nephew peppered him with questions all the way to the hospital.

"How did Matthew get sick so quickly? We were just playing together last week. Was it because of something we did?" Joseph took a breath, then kept on going.

"I pushed him fast in the chair, *Onkle* Jacob. Did that cause it?"

And the most pressing question, the one that Jacob couldn't answer.

"When will he come home?"

They'd traveled for a few moments in silence when Joseph said, still staring out the window, "Matthew is like David."

"What's that?"

"Like David…in the Bible." He made the motion of winding up and letting go a slingshot. "He's a warrior just like David, only he battles what's wrong with his body."

The hospital's lights broke through the night like a beacon, spilling out into the darkness.

Being situated in the middle of Goshen, where roughly half the population was Amish, there was plenty of buggy parking. Jacob tied Bo to the rail, assured the gelding he'd be back soon. Then he and Joseph practically sprinted into the building, through the automatic doors to the visitor information desk, then down a hall, up an elevator and down another hall.

He heard the murmur of voices before they turned the corner, and he really shouldn't have been surprised, and yet he was. The room was filled with Amish. Hannah's parents, the bishop from both her district and Jacob's, both of Hannah's sisters and their husbands and their children. Sally Lapp and her husband—Sally seemed to be knitting. Leroy was discussing crops with Tobias Hochstetler, who was Claire and Alton's neighbor. So many people, waiting on word of a very special boy.

He thought Joseph would join the other boys playing checkers, but instead he slipped his hand into Jacob's and walked with him over to Hannah's parents.

"Any word?"

"No, Jacob. Sit down. We're all still waiting to hear from the doctor." Hannah's father tossed a newspaper onto the coffee table. "Sit. You look as if you've been rushing around."

"*Ya*, I suppose I have."

It was Joseph who stepped in front of Hannah's *mamm*, eyes wide, his small hat in his hands. "Is Matthew going to be okay?"

"Yes, Joseph. I believe he is going to be fine."

"But right now he's sick."

"Yes, he is."

"So, I can't see him."

"*Nein*. Only his *mamm* can be with him now, but I think Matthew would be very happy to know that you're here."

Joseph pulled in his bottom lip, blinking rapidly. Finally he said, "Okay. I'll just wait—over there," and he walked slowly to where the other boys were. Jacob noticed that he sat beside them, watching the game of checkers, but he didn't join in. Instead his eyes kept going to the hall, the clock, Jacob and then back to the board, as if he was afraid he might miss something.

Someone had brought a basket of baked goods, and there was coffee in the vending machines. After an hour of waiting, Jacob wandered down the hall to purchase a cup. He must have stood there for five or ten minutes, staring at the options of black, cream, cream and sugar, vanilla cream and sugar. The possibilities seemed endless, but it made no difference how he had his coffee, only that the caffeine worked to push back the fatigue. He needed to be awake and alert when Hannah called for him, and he knew that she would.

"Pretty nasty stuff," Hannah's father said, coming up beside him and staring at the machine.

"*Ya*, I remember."

"They let you drink it when you were in the hospital?"

"Not really, but occasionally I'd sneak out of my room and purchase a cup. The nurses, they don't like patients drinking caffeine after dinner. They insisted it wasn't good for us. Probably they were right, but I also think they didn't want us restless when things should be quieting down."

"How long were you in the hospital?"

"The first time…four weeks. I went back for three other procedures. Those other stays were shorter—three to five days most of the time."

"Must have been difficult."

"*Ya.* Being here, under the fluorescent lights with the constant whir and beeping of *Englisch* machines, it grated on me after a while. I think the worst part was being away from everything that was a part of my life—the farm and workshop and family." He blinked away the tears and punched the button for black coffee.

"I meant the surgeries must have been hard, the pain of the injuries."

"*Ya*, that too."

"I'm sorry we weren't there for you, son."

Jacob jerked at the use of the word *son*, or perhaps

it was the touch of Alton's hand on his shoulder that surprised him.

"I barely knew you then, Alton."

"And yet you were a part of our community."

"It was after we'd divided into two districts."

"Still, we are connected through our history, through being one community before. We aren't so big that we can't still care for one another." Alton cleared his throat and chose a coffee with cream and sugar. When he turned to study Jacob, a smile pulled at the corners of his mouth. "Claire and I believe that *Gotte* brought you into Hannah's life for a reason…into all our lives. You've been a *gut* friend to her and maybe something more, *ya*?"

"I have feelings for your *doschder*, if that's what you're asking, but I'm not sure…that is, I don't know if Hannah…"

"Have you asked her?"

"About how she felt? *Nein.* It took all of my courage to ask her to Saturday's picnic."

Hannah's father laughed and steered them back toward the waiting room. "Young love presents its own challenges. You and Hannah, you will find your way."

Is that what he felt for Hannah?

Love?

Something pushed against his ribs, and he thought of the cardinal in the garden he'd seen just that afternoon, of Hannah smiling as she agreed to go to the picnic with him, of the way that Judith had brought such sadness to her, of Matthew smiling as he donned his conductor's hat and asked to be pushed out to the playhouse.

Ya, he did love her. He loved them both, and as soon as he had a chance he planned to make sure she knew.

* * *

Hannah had only moved from Matthew's side to use the restroom. She was aware that her parents were in the waiting room, but she didn't want to go to them until she had some answers. Matthew was still sleeping fitfully, waking every few minutes to attempt to cough the congestion up from his lungs.

A woman in a white coat walked into the room carrying a computer tablet and wearing a stethoscope. "I'm Dr. Hardin. You must be Matthew's mother." She looked awfully young to be a doctor. Her hair was cut in a short red shag, and she wore large owlish glasses.

"*Ya*, I'm Matthew's *mamm*. Is he all right? Did we get here in time?"

"You did the right thing bringing him in so quickly. Often parents wait, hoping the situation will improve on its own. In this case, your quick decisiveness probably saved Matthew a potentially long stay in the hospital."

Hannah had to sit then. Actually she fell into the chair behind her. She hadn't realized how heavy the weight of her guilt was until it was lifted from her. She felt so light that she might simply fly away.

"They explained to me when Matthew was first hurt that it was something we must watch for..." Tears clogged her voice, and she found she couldn't finish the sentence.

Dr. Hardin patted her shoulder, then moved to Matthew's side. She listened to his chest, checked his pulse, placed a hand against his forehead. Hannah knew well enough that the nurse had already done these things, and she appreciated the doctor's attention all the more for it.

She also was comforted by the fact that Dr. Hardin

spoke softly to Matthew the entire time she was examining him. She seemed to understand that he was more than just a patient in a bed.

He was a young boy who was scared and hurting.

He was a young boy with a family that loved him very much.

Hannah liked this doctor and trusted her immediately.

"The chest X-rays do show pneumonia, and the CBC confirms that."

"His blood count..."

"Exactly. Since it's the bacterial form, we'll start him on some IV antibiotics, give him some breathing treatments and he should be feeling better soon." She entered data on her tablet as she spoke. Finally she glanced up and looked directly at Hannah. "I won't sugarcoat it. Children with a spinal cord injury have a harder time recovering from these events. We could be looking at a rough forty-eight hours, but if he responds to the antibiotics, Matthew will be much better within a few days."

"Danki."

"You're welcome. Do you have any questions?"

"Only, did I do something wrong? Where did he... catch this?"

Dr. Hardin was shaking her head before Hannah finished her question. "You can't keep him in a bubble. Matthew could have picked it up anywhere—the store, the library, even at a church service. The important thing is that you recognized the symptoms immediately."

"Only I didn't. I wasn't home today, and my mother didn't know..."

"You got him here in plenty of time, and it helps that

he's a healthy young guy. Apparently he's eating well and getting plenty of exercise."

"*Ya*, both of those things."

Dr. Hardin squeezed Matthew's hand and then walked back around the bed. She stopped beside Hannah and placed a hand on her shoulder. "If you have any questions, ask the nurses or ask them to call me. I'm here most of the time, and I'll be happy to come down and talk to you."

"What happens next?"

"A nurse will come in and start the antibiotics. He needs rest to fight the infection, so expect him to sleep a lot. We'll also continue breathing treatments, and when he's strong enough we'll get him up and around—that's very important with pneumonia patients. We'll do X-rays again tomorrow to be sure that he's improving."

Dr. Hardin had made it to the door when she turned and said, "By the way, Matthew's grandparents have been asking how he's doing. They're in the waiting room down the hall. You might want to give them a status update."

Hannah nodded, but she was suddenly completely exhausted. She wasn't sure she could drag herself down there. Still, her parents deserved to know.

A nurse, an older black man who had introduced himself as Trevor, changed out the bag attached to Matthew's IV. He hummed softly as he worked, and Hannah thought that maybe he was humming a hymn… one of the old ones that both Amish and *Englisch* sang.

I am weak, but thou art strong,
Jesus keep me from all wrong.

He glanced up at her and smiled.

"That's the antibiotics that you're adding to his IV?"

"Yes, it is. Our little man didn't even wake up, which is good. He's resting. If you'd like to step out of the room, I'm sure he will be fine."

"Okay. Perhaps for just a minute..."

"Go. Matthew's fan club is quite worried."

Hannah didn't know what he meant by fan club, but she did need to speak to her parents. She took one last look at her son, pushed through the door and trudged down the hall.

Jacob happened to look up at the exact moment Hannah appeared in the waiting room. She looked so tired, so vulnerable, that he jumped up and went to her.

She raised her eyes to his. "He's going to be okay. They think...they think we made it here in time."

The words were softly spoken, but everyone heard, perhaps because everyone had stopped what they were doing at the sight of her.

As her words sank in, there was much slapping on the back, calls of "praise *Gotte*" and nodding heads—almost as if everyone knew that would be the answer. They'd believed that *Gotte* wasn't done with young Matthew yet. His life wasn't complete.

Jacob led Hannah over to her parents, who were standing now, smiling and obviously relieved.

"Hannah, I'm so sorry that I didn't realize how sick he was. I should have...should have called you earlier. Should have rung the emergency bell or..."

Hannah pulled her mother into a hug. "You did fine. You put him into bed and were caring for him. What more could I ask?"

"So he's going to be all right?" her father asked.

"The doctor said the next forty-eight hours will be critical, but she thinks that we made it here in time."

"That's *gut.* That's such a relief," her mother said.

Her father nodded. "It is *gut*, and we'll stay with you as long as you need us. You're not alone in this."

"I know I'm not, and I appreciate the offer, but you should all go home." Hannah turned toward the group. "*Danki, danki* all of you for coming and for praying for me and for Matthew. I appreciate it more than you know. Don't feel…don't feel that you need to stay."

But no one was willing to go home just yet.

The boys were now laughing as they played checkers.

Hannah's sisters had rushed over to hear the news and now they were hugging her and asking what things they could bring up for her the next day.

Her mom shooed everyone away and insisted that she sit and eat one of the muffins. "You have to keep your strength up, dear."

Bishop Jethro fetched her a cup of coffee.

Bishop Amos tapped his Bible and proclaimed that *Gotte* was *gut.*

Sally handed her a lap blanket that she'd finished knitting. "Hospital rooms can be quite cold. Please, take it. I didn't know who it was for when I started it, only that someone would need it. As I finished, though, these last few hours, I prayed for both you and Matthew."

It seemed that everyone wanted to offer her a word of encouragement, a touch, something to let her know that she had friends and families with her as she traveled this difficult path. But it was Jacob who stayed at her side the entire time. He didn't even consider leaving. Her pain was his pain, and her exhaustion he would try to bolster with his strength. After only a few minutes, she was ready to go back to Matthew's room.

"Can I walk you?"

"Of course."

They padded quietly down the hall, shoulder to shoulder, her hand in his.

When they finally reached Matthew's room, Hannah said, "You can come in if you like."

"Are you sure?"

"*Ya.* Matthew will ask if you've been here. He thinks of you as quite the hero."

"I'm no hero," Jacob protested.

"To that four-year-old boy lying in the bed, you are."

And what am I to you? The question was on his lips, but he bit it back. Hannah's attention was on her son, and she was no doubt exhausted, plus the next few days would be arduous. The last thing she needed was questions from him about their relationship.

He satisfied himself with saying, "You know, you didn't have to make a trip to the hospital to get out of your date with me."

Hannah smiled, and stared down at her hands and then looked back up at him. Rising on her tiptoes, she kissed him on the cheek. "Oh, you think I want out of it, do you?"

"Crossed my mind."

"I could just say I have to wash my hair."

"You could."

"I wouldn't."

"That's *gut* to know." He reached out and placed his palm against her cheek.

She closed her eyes for a moment and he wondered if she missed that...the physical touch of another. She'd been married before. She knew of the intimacies between a man and a woman. Her life had to be lonelier for the loss of it.

They walked into the room hand in hand, and when Jacob saw Matthew in the bed, his heart flipped like a fish that had landed on the bank of a river. The boy looked so impossibly small and vulnerable, and yet he had the heart of a warrior. Who had said that? His nephew, on the ride over.

And it was true.

Jacob pulled up a chair and sat there, holding Matthew's hand and praying silently for the young boy. Hannah used the time he was there to go into the restroom, freshen up and go to the nursing station. When she returned with a pillow and blanket, he jumped up to take them from her and place them in the chair.

"You're going to sleep here?"

"I doubt I will sleep, but *ya*."

"You want to be with him."

"In case he wakes up. Before…sometimes he would wake up in the hospital and not recognize where he was and be frightened."

"You'll let us know if you need anything? You can call my phone in the shop. I can sleep there in case—"

"I need you to convince those people out there to go home."

"Our *freinden*?"

Hannah smiled again, the weariness momentarily erased. "*Ya*, our *freinden*. Especially the children. They have school tomorrow."

"I'll tell them you said so."

He kissed the top of her head before he left. It seemed hardly adequate to show how he felt. He would find a better way. He would show her that he loved her and then he would tell her. He would make sure that both Matthew and Hannah knew.

Chapter Fourteen

Matthew's stay in the hospital lasted longer than anyone could have guessed. His birthday came and went. The days on the calendar slipped by, one after another, until October loomed in front of them. Matthew would improve one day only to slide back for three more. Dr. Hardin assured Hannah that this was normal, that he was fighting a particularly virulent form of bacterial pneumonia and that they were doing all of the right things.

Hannah's parents brought fresh clothes for her and would sit with Matthew to give her a few moments out of the room.

The nurses brought plates of food, even though Matthew was rarely awake enough to eat. "Then it's for you," they assured her. "You need to stay strong too."

Both bishops visited Hannah often, counseled with her and assured her that many people were praying for Matthew.

Her sisters, brothers-in-law and nieces visited every few days. They joked that someone should install a bus line to the hospital, "We'd keep it busy with folks visiting Matthew. He's a very popular guy." Sharon and Beth both had less than two months until their babies were due, and Hannah worried that the traveling back and forth wasn't healthy for them or the babies.

"I want to get out of the house," Sharon admitted. "My girls are turning seven soon, but they think they're turning thirteen. I caught one with lipstick. Now, where did she get that?"

Beth nodded in sympathy. "Naomi went through that phase too, and I suspect she'll go through it again."

She loved having her sisters and her parents and her church family there. For the first time in a long time, she realized that she wasn't alone, that others were willing and eager to lend a hand.

But it was Jacob that she longed to see each day.

He always appeared, though the time varied. If he had a job in the area, he would stop by at lunch. If he was working at home, he'd wait until the end of the day and bring her something fresh to eat from Emily for dinner.

They didn't speak of the date that had never happened or of the kiss in the buggy, but she thought of both often—especially in the middle of the night when she woke and couldn't go back to sleep.

Each time Jacob visited, he brought something for Matthew, and those items lined the windowsill—a wooden train, a book, a piece of candy for when he was well. The string of items was a testament to how long they'd been in this holding pattern, how long Matthew had been battling his illness, how faithful Jacob was.

He always stayed for at least an hour and allowed Hannah to vent her worries, to cry occasionally, to admit when she was discouraged or afraid or depressed.

He never judged her and never questioned her faith, but instead he simply held her hand and assured her that he was there.

On the days when Matthew was better, was actually awake and talkative, they laughed at Jacob's stories of playhouses that he'd built, of getting stuck inside one that was supposed to resemble a baseball dugout, of forgetting to build a door in one that he'd designed to resemble a hobbit's home.

"What's a hobbit?" Matthew asked. He had to pull in a deep breath after he spoke, but his color was better and the doctor was talking about sending him home if his improvement continued.

"You haven't read him Tolkien?" Jacob's eyes widened in mock disbelief.

"We've been a little busy."

"Then perhaps I will pick it up from the library."

But instead of doing that, he'd purchased a copy at the local bookstore. After that, he'd read to Matthew for at least thirty minutes each day. Hannah had trouble understanding why that meant so much to her, why it touched her heart, but it did.

She admitted as much to her mother one day as she was walking her to the elevator.

"Why shouldn't it?" Her mother pulled Hannah away from the elevator. "Your heart is tender, Hannah. You've been through a lot in the last few years."

"That's an understatement."

"And for a time you closed off your feelings."

Hannah crossed her arms. She knew that her mother was correct, that it was an observation, not a criticism, but it was still difficult for her to think of the months following David's death and Matthew's accident.

"It's one thing to bring a gift to someone." Her mother reached out and pulled one of Hannah's *kapp* strings forward. "It's another thing entirely to spend time beside a bed, reading, simply bringing a small amount of joy into a person's life."

"I know it is." She sounded petulant to her own ears, sounded like a child.

"Jacob cares about Matthew. The quickest way to any mother's heart is to truly love her child." With those insightful words, she kissed Hannah on the cheek and pushed the button for the elevator.

After Matthew had fallen asleep that evening, Hannah turned on the small book light Jacob had given her and scanned back through the pages of *The Hobbit*. She'd read it in school, probably the same year that Jacob had. Always they'd had their reading after lunch, when the teacher or one of the older students would read aloud a chapter—sometimes two if they pleaded long enough and hard enough.

Matthew was a bit young for such a big tale, and yet he seemed to enjoy Bilbo's adventures, as well as the groups of dwarves and elves and goblins and trolls. As Hannah looked back over what Jacob had read to him a few hours earlier, she didn't hear the tale in the voice of Bilbo Baggins, though. Instead she heard Jacob's voice—clear and steady and strong.

She could admit to herself that she wanted that. She wanted Jacob in her life, but what she couldn't admit, what she couldn't begin to fathom, was why he would be interested in taking on her and Matthew.

And there it was—in the deepest part of her heart, beneath the fatigue and fear. In the place where her dreams resided, she was certain that Jacob would one day come to his senses and realize that he didn't want the challenge of a disabled son and a mother who was emotionally scarred.

Hannah woke Friday morning with the same questions circling through her mind.

How much was the hospital bill?

How could she possibly pay it?

Was her father's farm secure now?

Had they been able to raise enough money?

Where would they live if they were forced to move?

How would she break the news to Matthew?

Even as her heart rejoiced over the fact that Matthew was well enough to be discharged, Hannah's mind couldn't help rushing ahead to what was next.

"You're exhausted is all." Sharon had stopped by with fresh breakfast muffins. Now she sat in the chair by the window, knitting a baby blanket that was optimistically blue.

"Still hoping for a boy?"

"*Ya*, but if it's a girl, I'll give the blanket to Beth."

"And if she has a girl?"

"Someone in our church will have a boy." She pointed her knitting needle at Hannah. "And stop trying to change the subject."

"Which was?"

"Your exhaustion."

"Pretty lame subject."

"Tell me what's really bothering you."

Hannah bit her bottom lip, walked to the window and stared out at the beautiful fall day. It seemed as if she'd been in this hospital for months instead of weeks. "This incident with Matthew wasn't a solitary event."

"Meaning?"

Hannah glanced at her son, curled on his side, soft snores coming from him. "Meaning it's my life. This could happen again next month or next year. Or it could be something else entirely."

"You're saying that you're not a safe bet."

"Excuse me?"

"We're talking about Jacob, right? Because I know that you wouldn't change your life, your time with Matthew…even if it meant that you could have a perfect child, a healthy husband and a life without financial problems."

"*Nein*, I wouldn't."

"So you're worried about Jacob."

"I suppose." Hannah moved over and sat on the stool next to Sharon's chair. "Maybe you've hit the heart of the matter. This is my life. I am grateful to have Matthew, and somehow I will find a way to be strong for him."

"But Jacob?"

"I can't possibly ask him to shoulder the burdens of my life."

"Isn't that Jacob's decision?"

"He might care for me…"

"*Ya*, that kiss in the buggy seems to suggest he does."

"I wish I'd never told you about that."

"And stopping by every day…bringing Matthew and you small gifts. The man is smitten."

"Caring for someone is one thing."

"Indeed it is."

"Sacrificing the life you have for them, that's another thing entirely."

Sharon dropped her knitting into her bag, reached

forward and put a hand under Hannah's chin. "Look at me, *schweschder.*"

When Hannah finally raised her eyes, Sharon was smiling in her I-know-a-secret, older-sister way. "Perhaps for Jacob, you and Matthew aren't a sacrifice. Perhaps you're a blessing."

Jacob puttered around his workshop all of Friday morning. By lunch he'd finished all of his projects and stored them neatly on the shelf, cleaned off his workbench, stored his tools and even swept the floor. With nothing left to do, he walked into his office, Hannah's office, sat in her chair and asked himself for the thousandth time why she would want to marry someone like him.

He looked up when he heard a long whistle. His brother's boots clomped across the workshop floor. He stopped in the doorway of the office. "Someone has been cleaning house."

"How are you, Micah?"

"Gut." He plopped down into the chair across from him. "Is today the day?"

"That Matthew comes home? *Ya.* Hannah thought they would release him after lunch."

Instead of answering, Micah's right eyebrow shot up.

"Don't give me that look."

"I'm just wondering—"

"I know what you're wondering. Her parents wanted to pick them up, and…well, I thought this was a time for family."

Micah's smile grew.

"Are you laughing at me, *bruder*?"

"You remind me of a lovesick pup is all. You remind me of myself a few years ago."

"Ya?" Jacob didn't bother denying his observation. He felt lovesick—excited, worried, a little nauseous.

"Will she come back to work?"

"She wants to. She even asked me to bring over the box of receipts for her to work on at home until she's sure Matthew's strong enough to leave with her mother." Jacob pushed the box on the floor with the toe of his work boot.

"When are you going to ask her?"

"Ask her?"

"To marry you."

"What makes you think I am?"

"So you're not?"

"I didn't say that."

"So you are."

"*Ya*, only… I want to wait for the right time."

Micah sat forward, crossed his arms on the desk and studied his brother. "You're a *gut* man, Jacob. *Mamm* and *Dat*, they would be proud of who you've become."

Jacob had to look away then, because they were the words he'd needed to hear for quite some time. When had he become so emotional? He felt like he walked through each day without enough skin, as if his every feeling was displayed on the surface. Maybe that was because he'd spent so long hiding behind his scars. He wasn't sure if knowing Hannah had changed him or if time had, and he didn't want to go back, but he hadn't learned how to deal with the deluge of emotions.

He cleared his throat and said, "I thought I'd give her a few weeks to settle in. I don't want to rush her and she has to be exhausted, plus…"

"You're thinking about this all wrong."

"I am?"

Micah tapped the desk. "She wants to be here, working with you."

"You can't know that."

"She wants you in her life, Jacob."

"If I was certain—"

"Waiting will only cause her to worry that you don't want the same thing."

Jacob stared out the window and thought of his brother's words. Hannah did seem worried, preoccupied even. She also seemed so happy to see him. Was she concerned that one day he'd simply stop coming by? Was she worried that he'd realize the awesome responsibility it would be to father Matthew? Did she think that one day he might turn tail and run?

"When did you become so wise?"

"I've been working on it."

"What if she says no?"

"She won't."

"But what if she does?"

"Better to know now. Then you can move on."

"I don't know how to do that."

"You're getting your buggy in front of your horse."

Jacob jumped up. "You're right."

"It's *wunderbaar* to hear you say that."

"I'm going over there right now, and I'm going to ask her."

"Maybe you should shave first."

"*Gut* idea."

"A haircut wouldn't hurt, either."

"I don't have time for a haircut."

"You only ask a woman to marry you once. Why not look your best?"

"Should I wash my buggy too?"

"Wouldn't hurt."

"I was kidding."

"So was I."

Jacob stopped in the doorway. "Shouldn't I take her flowers or something?"

Micah ran his fingers through his beard, tilted his head to the left and then the right. Finally he said, "*Gut* idea. In fact, Emily already thought of it."

"She did?"

"There's a basket of fresh-cut wildflowers by the door."

"For me?"

"For Hannah."

"That's what I meant."

"But you can say they're from you. Emily asked me to bring them over so you'd have something to take with you."

"How did she know I was going to see Hannah?"

Micah shrugged. "Don't bother trying to understand women, Jacob. Just be grateful that *Gotte* created them."

Hannah's mother and father arrived at the hospital before noon.

"I get to go home," Matthew declared.

"So we heard." Alton stuck both of his thumbs under his suspenders. "Didn't realize you had so much to take with you. We might need another buggy."

"Jacob made all of those things for me."

"Did he, now?"

"Were you kidding?" Matthew pulled in a big breath.

He was better, but still weak from the ordeal of the past two weeks. "Do we have enough room?"

"He was kidding," Hannah's mother assured him. "I even brought a backpack to put them in."

She set the bag made from blue denim on Matthew's bed.

"I can't believe you still have that thing," Hannah said. "I haven't seen it in years."

"Why would I throw it away? I knew Matthew would need it soon."

"Was it yours, *Mamm*?"

"It was." She ran her thumb over the shoulder strap. Thinking of her school days, when she was young and innocent and naive, reminded her of how much had happened since then. The surprising thing was that she didn't feel angry like she did before. She would always miss David, and she wished that Matthew hadn't been involved in the accident, but this was the life she'd been given, and she was grateful for it.

Despite what she'd shared with her sister earlier that morning, she was grateful.

"I need to go downstairs for a few minutes. Can you two help Matthew pack up?"

"Sure thing," her mother said.

But her dad stepped out into the hall with her. "I know you've been worried about the farm."

"*Ya*, I have."

"I appreciate all you've done, Hannah. You and your *schweschders*."

"You wouldn't have needed our help if it wasn't for—"

Hannah stopped talking when her father stepped directly in front of her. He placed a hand on both sides of her face like he'd done when she was a child. His touch stopped the whirlwind of thoughts rattling through her mind.

Once he was sure that she was focused on him, he smiled and said, "We're *gut*."

"You…you had enough money?"

"We had enough. You don't have to worry about the bank loan. I stopped by the bank on the way here, and I paid all the back payments. We even had a little extra. If you don't want to keep working for Jacob, you can stay home. If that's what you want to do."

"I enjoy the work," she admitted. "There is less to do now, though. Perhaps Jacob would let me work only two days a week, the days Matthew doesn't have physical therapy."

"That's a *gut* idea."

She stood on her tiptoes and kissed him on the cheek. "I love you, *Dat*."

"And your mother and I love you."

Those words echoed in her ears as she made her way down to the business office. She hadn't wanted to bring up Matthew's hospital bill. Her parents didn't need another thing to worry about. They had enough on their plates. Still, her heart was heavy as she checked in with the receptionist and sat waiting for her name to be called. It seemed every time she solved one problem another popped up. She knew from past experience that the hospital bill would be in the thousands, maybe tens of thousands.

She'd sunk into quite a depression when they finally escorted her back to a small, neat office. The woman's name tag said Betty, and she offered Hannah coffee or water.

"*Nein.* Matthew is waiting to go home, so I should hurry."

"I understand. Have a seat and we'll go over this quickly."

Betty was matronly, probably in her sixties, and she wore her gray hair in a bun. She paused and looked at Hannah when she spoke, and her smile seemed to go all the way to her eyes.

"I'm so glad to hear that Matthew's doing well."

"*Ya, Gotte* is *gut*."

"All the time." Betty smiled broadly and then she opened the file.

"I have a copy for you of the printout listing the charges for Matthew's care." The stack she picked up was at least an inch thick and held together with a large binder clip. She slid the papers across the desk.

Hannah paged quickly through the printout to the last page and nearly gasped at the final amount. She'd known it would be high, but she hadn't expected…

"There must be a mistake," she said.

"I assure you, I went through the billing line by line. It's all correct."

"*Nein.* That's not what I meant. The…the total is wrong."

Betty put on her reading glasses hanging from a chain and turned to the last page of her copy of the bill.

"It says we owe nothing, but I haven't… I haven't paid anything yet. So this must be wrong."

Betty pulled off her glasses and sat back. "No one told you?"

"Told me what?"

"Kosair Charities paid for Matthew's bill."

"Why would they do that?"

Betty shrugged. "It's what they do. It's part of their mission. They understand that having a child with an SCI can be a heavy financial burden, and they try to help those who need it."

"So I don't owe anything?"

"Not a penny."

Hannah brushed at the tears streaming down her face, and Betty jumped up and fetched a box of tissues.

Five minutes later, Hannah made her way back to Matthew's room, carrying the envelope in her purse that stated their bill was paid in full.

Hannah should have taken a nap like her mother suggested, but she was too tired to sleep, which made no sense.

It felt so good to be home, to see familiar things around her, to be back in the Amish world. She kept walking through the house—looking out the window, appreciating the light breeze, relishing the lack of flickering fluorescent light, drinking her *mamm*'s fresh coffee.

Matthew was asleep.

Her mother was in the kitchen, putting together a casserole for dinner.

Her father was in the barn.

Hannah walked out on the front porch, watching for...what was she watching for?

Then a buggy turned down their lane, and she realized it was Jacob and she knew that what she'd been watching for was coming toward her.

When he handed her the basket of flowers, she laughed. "Jacob Schrock, did you pick these?"

"*Nein*. Emily did."

"Well, it was very sweet of her and you."

"How's Matthew?"

"He's *gut*—asleep right now."

"Would you like to take a walk?"

The day was mild enough that she wore a light sweater, but the sun was shining, and the leaves had fallen in a riotous display of reds, greens and gold.

"I'd love that."

As they walked, their shoulders practically touching, the leaves crunching beneath their feet, Hannah felt the last of the tension inside of her unwind. She was home, and that was good. Home and family and friends were what she needed.

But what of the man walking next to her?

Was their future to be as friends, or more?

And dare she ask him now?

They stopped when they reached the pasture fence. Dolly cropped at the grass, and a red bird lighted on a nearby tree limb. Jacob saw it, glanced at Hannah and then started laughing.

"Did I miss something?"

"I think my *mamm* is telling me to get on with it."

"Your *mamm*?"

"It's a long story."

"I've always loved a *gut* story."

Hannah was aware that her heart beat faster when she was around Jacob. She didn't know what to do with her hands—her arms felt awkward whether she crossed them or let them swing by her side. She felt like a teenager who hadn't quite grown into her limbs, and she blushed at the slightest look from him. Were those things love? Or was love the simple fact that she couldn't imagine her life without Jacob in it?

He told her about his mother and how she loved red birds and how she said they were a sort of messenger from *Gotte*.

"Did she believe that?"

"I'm not sure. She could have been teasing. On the other hand…maybe she was serious. I only know that I've been seeing red birds when I needed a nudge in the right direction lately."

"And you needed to see one now?"

They were leaning against the pasture fence, their arms crossed on the wooden beam, watching the mare. Jacob glanced sideways at her, a crooked smile pulling at his mouth. "*Ya*, I did."

Jacob knew now was the time.

He'd known it in the workshop when Micah had told him to go and see Hannah, to ask her, to face his future.

He'd known it when he'd seen Hannah waiting on the porch.

And he'd known it when the red bird had alighted on the fence beside them.

Still, it took courage to ask a girl to marry you, to spend her life with you.

His heart was hammering against his chest, and every time he glanced at Hannah his palms began to sweat. He was acting like a *youngie*, like the lovesick pup that Micah had mentioned. That image brought him to his senses. He wasn't either of those things. He was a man in love, and it was past time to find out if Hannah felt the same way.

He turned to her, clasped her hands in his own and said, "I need to ask you something."

"You do?"

"I care about you, Hannah."

"And I care about you."

"I care about you and Matthew."

"He adores you." Her voice was lower, huskier, and he thought he saw tears sparkling in her eyes. He prayed they were happy tears.

He'd lived in the past for so long that he felt as if his feet were encased in cement, his tongue was tied and his brain had stopped working completely. Somehow he needed to break free from that past.

Taking a deep breath, he squeezed Hannah's hands and plunged into his future. "Will you marry me?"

"Wow."

"Wow yes or wow no?"

"I… I wasn't expecting that."

A pretty blush worked its way up her neck. Jacob had the absurd idea that he might be dreaming this entire thing, that he might wake up and find the lovely woman standing beside him, looking up at him with those beautiful brown eyes, was a figment of his imagination.

"I'm surprised is all."

"Good surprised or bad surprised?" Before she could answer, he rushed on. "I know that I'm not a perfect man, and I would understand if you said *no* because living with me, with a man like me—"

"Do you love me?"

He'd been staring at their hands but now he jerked his head up, reached out and touched her cheek. "Yes, Hannah. I love you, and I love Matthew, and it would be an honor to be your husband and his father."

"We love you too."

"You do?"

"*Ya.* Didn't you know?"

"I'd hoped."

He pulled her to him then, relief flooding through his soul. "You love me, Hannah?"

"Yes." She laughed and pulled back, gazed up into his eyes. "You're a *gut* man, Jacob, and a *gut* friend. I wasn't sure…wasn't sure that you'd want your life to be complicated so."

"Everyone's life is complicated, even Plain folks'."

"Matthew's crisis has passed, for now, but there will be others."

"True of any family."

"It won't be easy."

"I don't expect it to be."

"But you're sure?"

"*Ya.* Are you sure, Hannah?" He took her hand and raised it to his cheek, to his scars, held it there. "These won't bother you?"

"We all have scars. Yours are simply on the outside."

He stepped closer, kissed her softly once and then again, pulled her into his arms. They stood there, with the fall breeze dropping even more leaves around them and Jacob thought that he could feel Hannah's heart beating against his.

When she finally stepped back, still smiling, he asked, "Who do you want to tell first?"

"Matthew. Let's go and tell Matthew."

* * * * *

SPECIAL EXCERPT FROM

LOVE INSPIRED

INSPIRATIONAL ROMANCE

When a wounded veteran and his service dog seek work at the Bright Tomorrows school for troubled boys, can the principal—who happens to be the widow of his late brother—hire the man who knows the past secrets she'd rather forget?

Read on for a sneak peek at
The Veteran's Holiday Home
by Lee Tobin McClain!

Jason stared at the woman in the doorway of the principal's office. "*You're* A. Green?"

Just looking at her sent shock waves through him. What had happened to his late brother's wife?

She was still gorgeous, no doubt. But she was much thinner than she'd been when he'd last seen her, her strong cheekbones standing out above full lips, still pretty although now without benefit of lipstick. She wore a business suit, the blouse underneath buttoned up to her chin.

Her eyes still had that vulnerable look in them, though, the one that had sucked him into making a mistake, doing what he shouldn't have done. Making a phone call with disastrous results.

She recovered before he did. "Come in. You'll want to sit down," she said. "I'm sorry about Ricky running into you and your dog."

He followed her into her office.

He waited for her to sit behind her desk before easing himself into a chair. He wasn't supposed to lift anything above fifty pounds and he wasn't supposed to twist, and the way his back felt right now, after doing both, proved his orthopedic doctor was right.

Beside him, Titan whined and moved closer, and Jason put a hand on the big dog. "Lie down," he ordered, but gently. Titan had saved him from a bad fall.

LIEXP0822

"I didn't realize the two of you knew each other," the secretary said. "Can I get you both some coffee?"

"We're fine," Ashley said, and even though Jason had been about to decline the offer, he looked a question at her. Was she too hostile to even give a man a beverage?

The older woman backed out of the office. The door clicked shut.

Leaving Ashley and Jason alone.

"The website didn't have a picture—" he began.

"You always went by Jason in the family—" she said at the same time.

They both laughed awkwardly.

"You really didn't know it was me who'd be interviewing you?" she asked, her voice skeptical.

"No. Your website's kind of…limited."

If he'd known the job would involve working with his late half brother's wife, he'd never have applied. Too many bad memories, and while he'd been fortunate to come out of the combat zone with fewer mental health issues than some vets, he had to watch his frame of mind, take care about the kind of environment he lived in. That was one reason he'd liked the looks of this job, high in the Colorado Rocky Mountains. He needed to get out of the risky neighborhood where he was living.

Ashley presented a different kind of risk.

Being constantly reminded of his brilliant, successful younger brother, so much more suave and popular and talented than Jason was, at least on the outside…being reminded of the difficulties of his home life after his mom had married Christopher's dad…no. He'd escaped all that, and no way was he going back.

His own feelings for his brother's wife notwithstanding. He'd felt sorry for her, had tried to help, but she'd spurned his help and pushed him away.

Getting involved with her was a mistake he wouldn't make again.